Elpis

Aaron McGowan

ELPIS

AARON   MCGOWAN
Elpis Project ©2011 Aaron McGowan
All rights reserved. No part of this publication may be
reproduced, distributed, or transmitted in any form or by
any means, or stored in a database or retrieval system,
without the prior written permission of the publisher.

Summary: To avenge the death of his parents and
the destruction of his village, Terico seeks to obtain the
four fragments of the Elpis—a source of power that will
allow his enemy Delkol to conquer the world.

ISBN: 978-0-9945522-2-8

5th Edition

Published by Hellfun Publishing Pty. Limited

Table of Contents:

Dear Reader,

Imagination rules the world. Everything we see and create starts from one point, the idea, and the idea is born from our imagination. Where do you see your ideas going?

I want to give my sincerest appreciation for purchasing my novel. To know that you will embark on this wonderful journey of adventure, mystery and pure creativity. I hope you enjoy the detail and depth put into every personality. The world was molded from inspiration, life and ideals we can strive for.

Keep up with my manga-style comics and other books by connecting with me on social media. You can find my growing work on facebook:

www.facebook.com/AuthorAaronMcgowan,

If you love the story, please share it with others! To the start of our long journey together in imagination, thank you for your support.

- Aaron

Elpis

Aaron McGowan

6

1

THE WORLD CHANGES

Terico's father had always told him that creatures capable of saving lives were generally just as capable of taking them. Humans were the prime example of this, but at this moment, three levels down an underground cave, Terico felt that the carnivorous pitcher plant worked just as nicely. The monster's roots were needed to heal some patients in the village's clinic—but one wrong move, and Terico would be lying on a hospital bed himself. Or worse—in a coffin.
Father tapped the Nexi stone at the end of his staff a couple times to cause the smooth, transparent red rock to shine brighter. The light exposed the pitcher plant near the end of the tunnel in its full grotesque corruption. Looming at least ten meters tall, the plant filled the entirety of the rocky nook it rested in. Thorny vines ran up and down the walls and ceiling, all leading back to a giant bulbous vessel that constantly overflowed with noxious black and yellow liquids. It stank of vinegar and decaying animals.

The stench was overwhelming, and made Terico a little lightheaded. He gripped his longsword tighter and took a couple nauseous steps back, bumping into his friend, Turan.

"Watch it, mate." Turan slapped Terico's leg with the flat end of his sword.

Terico shoved the back of his sword's hilt into Turan's stomach, which was well protected by leather armor. Turan let out an exaggerated groan, fell to his knees, and leaned against his sword as he exhaled a slow, dying gasp of breath.

"Pay attention, both of you," Father said. "The moment it feels threatened, the creature will lash out at all of us." He slipped out a green Nexi stone and clipped it into a slot in the center of his sword's hilt. "Best you both stay back a minute."

"You'll need help with this, Dad," Terico said. "I've fought off cavern monsters before."

Father planted his glowing staff in a tight crevice in the floor. "None this big. Not even half this big, unless Turan's... *embellished* stories of the fifteen-meter flying shark bush is to be believed."

"It was *twenty* meters," Turan said, still on his knees.

Terico kept from sighing, choosing to maintain focus on the burbling pitcher plant. Some of the creature's vines were sliding up and down the cave walls a bit, and Terico wondered if this was a sign the monster was awake. It was difficult to discern much when fighting against something without a face.

"I can do this," Terico said. "Use your Nexi stone to hold back the vines, and I'll rush in to stab the heart of the pitcher."

"It doesn't have a heart," Father said. "It will take quite a bit of hacking to kill this thing. How do you plan to avoid its pool of acid?"

Terico pulled a light blue Nexi stone from one of his trouser's pockets and held it up for his father to see.

"Where did you get that?" Father asked.

Terico smiled, not wanting to admit he had snuck off on another overnight adventure. The stone was a reward for his efforts, and he was smart enough to save it for such a time as this.

His father glanced to the side and smirked. "You take after me a little too well sometimes... Very well then. Your mother will kill me though if you lose an arm or something."

"Or scar that pretty face of yours," Turan added.

Father turned to Turan. "You watch Terico's back. And mine too, while you're at it."

Turan jumped to his feet and stood up straight, his sword raised in front of him. "Yes, sir, Mr. Obisious!"

Terico clenched his teeth and stared the poisonous, jagged creature down. *Have to take it down quick*, he thought. *Dad and Turan are counting on me... and so is Mother.* As the village herbalist, Terico's mother was the only one who could create this particular concoction from the pitcher plant's roots. And really, the ones who were counting on him most were the three sick villagers who needed this medicine. Terico had visited them with Mother a few days ago—an elderly man, a young woman, and a four year-old boy. They each had deep red boils beneath their eyes, and were too weak to speak or even move much. Terico wanted to help everyone in town, just as his father had always done. Through his skills with alchemy, the Nexi stones, and the sword, Terico's father had likely helped out almost every single villager at some point. It was thanks to him that the town took any measures at all to prepare for the possibility of attack from the Shires Kingdom, and Terico wished to be prepared for such an event.

Terico readied his sword in his right hand, and gripped his blue Nexi stone in his left. "Let's go."

He charged down the cavern tunnel. Each of his footsteps echoed increasingly faster and louder. Father and Turan followed behind him, their steps almost harmonizing in the reverberations.

Tens of vines leaped off the walls and lunged for Terico. The monster couldn't hear them, but it could feel the threat in the approaching footsteps across the limestone floor. Father swung his sword forward, forcing a dozen Nexi-powered vines to spring out from his blade. With remarkable speed and dexterity, Father directed each of his sword's thin leafy vines to wrap around the incoming thorn-decked tentacles of the pitcher plant. Terico kept running for the monster as his father held its attacks at bay.

The pallid, fleshy vessel of the plant lurched forward. It leaned down, spilling buckets of black and yellow acids. From within the deep pitcher, the monster erupted a large, messy burst of the liquid toward Terico.

Terico skidded to a stop and raised his Nexi stone in front of him. He connected his mind to the stone and felt his blood chill. The air in front of the Nexi stone turned cold in an instant, freezing the acid spray into tiny ice specks that bounced off Terico's cloak harmlessly. He aimed the stone toward the ground ahead of him, freezing the deep puddles of poisonous liquid spread across the floor.

Two set of vines rushed for Terico from either side of him. "Go left, Turan!" Terico turned to his right and hacked at the vines before they could drive their long, jagged thorns into his neck. At the same time, Turan leaped forward and hewed down the vines lunging for Terico's back.

Terico ran for the pitcher plant, careful to keep his footing on the icy floor. More vines were emerging from the monster, but Terico used his opening to transfer what energy he could to his Nexi stone. Before the creature could release another burst of poisonous liquid, Terico chucked the stone into the giant pitcher, freezing all of its acid instantly. The creature rolled forward a bit, then slumped down to its side. Its many vines slowly drooped to the floor around it, and Terico breathed a sigh of relief.

He smiled. *I did it*, he thought. *I did it!*

A sound like scraping glass emanated from the plant. An oozing slit formed down its side, then burst apart into large globules. Dozens of thin, crimson vines rushed out of the creature, and from the end of each sprouted flytraps—huge needle-toothed maws that shrieked like a flock of bats.

Terico beat his sword against them, but there were far too many to keep up with. They ducked and swerved around his swings, then jabbed their needles against him. Terico evaded their attacks as best he could, but he was quickly overwhelmed. The flytraps dug deep gashes into his right arm, down his left shin, across his chest, and into his back before he could slip away from them.

Turan rushed into the herd, screaming. With fast, broad swings he lobbed off several of the flytraps at a time—only for the vines to immediately sprout new ones from their ends.

Terico stumbled back but managed to keep his feet, despite the stinging pain of his injuries. Another set of thin vines launched for him, but it was difficult to fend them off with his right arm badly wounded. His father leaped into the fray, swinging away faster than Terico had ever seen of a swordsman before. Father frantically sliced the vines to bits, but new flytraps continued to emerge from the creature.

"Get back!" Turan yelled. He leaped back from a swarm of flytraps encircling him, then lifted a red Nexi stone directly in front of them. A sea of flames exploded in front of the stone, wiping out the mass of flytraps. Instead of fading into the air, the flames rushed down the vines and into what was left of the half-frozen pitcher plant. Turan aimed the stone for the flytraps attacking Father, then forced his flames to rush down the entirety of those vines as well. Turan bent down to one knee, breathing heavily. The crackling fires quickly dissipated into fleeting embers, leaving nothing but a charred, ash-speckled husk of the plant creature.

Father walked toward what was left of the monster, approaching with an air of caution. There were no vines left to attack him, but he readied his sword to hack away at the thick, mutilated pitcher.

Another tear formed on the plant. A long, bloody spinal cord thrust itself out from the side of the vessel. Terico stared in disbelief as the set of bones floated into the air, then aimed its long, pointed end toward Father—it looked far sharper than any spear.

Father squinted his eyes and smirked.

The spinal cord flew for his head. He turned in place. Terico saw a blur of red and white whoosh past Father. A wave of dust, pebbles, and small rocks flew against Father from behind a moment later. Terico expected the spinal cord to lunge back for Father again, but all was silent. Once the dust cleared, Terico saw Father with his sword raised, blood dripping down its blade. The entire sword was glowing a light orange, and Terico realized Father had switched his hilt's green Nexi stone for an orange one, giving his weapon greater strength. In a split-second Father had positioned his sword at just the right spot for the spinal cord to plow straight through the reinforced blade. Sure enough, Terico found the spinal cord sprawled across the floor, split into two perfect halves down its entire length.

"What was that?" Terico asked, his voice strained from the pain of his gashes.

"Some foul parasite," Father said. "Are you all right, though?"

"Yes, I'll be fine."

"Good," Father said. "A quick lesson then, Terico. If your goal is to kill something, you have to take extra measures to ensure it's truly dead."

Terico realized he should have done more after freezing all the acid. Monsters were often unpredictable, and you could never be too careful with them—

especially when they were this big.

"Sorry. I shouldn't have let my guard down."

"I didn't think it was still alive either," Turan said. "It was just a really weird monster."

Father turned to Turan. "You must be ready for anything in the heat of a battle. Your enemy, be it a monster or a soldier, may always have an ability you are not aware of. I imagine that one day you will learn this the hard way... Regardless, you did quite well here, Turan. I didn't realize you had learned to wield the red Nexi so capably. It's a surprise, but I am impressed. Fire is very difficult to control."

Turan looked to the side and sheathed his sword. "Well... I have been practicing."

Terico was surprised Father was giving Turan so much credit. Admittedly, Turan did a very good job—he had a knack for Nexi stones in general—but Father wasn't one who was quick to give compliments like this. He certainly had never praised Terico much, though in this instance it was understandable, given how badly he got beat up.

"Let's cut the roots from the pitcher, Turan," Father said. "We'll want

to get Terico home so he has time to get his wounds dressed before your classes starts."

Father and Turan were quick to slice off all the thin, wispy roots of pitcher plant. They were scraggly and hued a sickly light blue, and smelled like rotten cabbages. Once they finished removing all the roots, Turan gathered them all in a big pile and carried them with both arms, careful to not lose any of them.

"Need any help walking, Terico?" he asked.

Terico struggled not to wince when he stepped with his left leg. "I'll be fine."

"I'll be sure to let Suran know you got beaten up by a plant," Turan said. "Or when she asks about those cuts at school, you can tell her yourself! She'll be all over you then."

"Yes, and then I can let all the girls at school know about your little collision with the fluff ball bunnies last week."

"They attacked me *in my sleep!*"

When Father started to laugh, Turan was quick to give a detailed explanation of that day's events, in some vain effort to save his pride.

Terico's thoughts meanwhile drifted to Suran, an elvish classmate he had liked for some time now. A part of him wanted to do a good job this morning for her, too. He was glad to help the village get these roots for the medicine, but he had hoped to... perhaps impress Suran a bit as well.

He followed Father and Turan out of the cave, his mind filled with concerns for what he would tell Suran at school. It was pointless to worry, but it helped distract him from the pain of his injuries.

•

The walk back home felt a lot longer than the walk to the cave, but Terico managed to keep up with Father and Turan well enough. The sun had risen while they were underground, and cast the fields of turnips and onions in a warm golden glow. It didn't take long for travelers to pass through the small town of Edellerston, but the fertile landscape was always a sight to behold. As was typically the case, the air felt misty against Terico's skin— even when the heavens were clear, there was almost always a bit of precipitation.

In all his sixteen years of life, Terico had never grown tired of gazing across these farmlands. The modest thatched hovels and simple log structures of Edellerston's populace certainly didn't elicit any sense of adventure, but Terico was grateful for the quiet stability the town offered.

He soon came in sight of the central square, where the small, but bright limestone cathedral rested. It stood as a testament of the villagers' faith in the gods, but also acted as the site for public discourse and special events— including the Long Shadow Festival coming in a few days.

Just a few minutes past the central square was Terico's home, which also served as a shop for Mother's herbs and Father's stones and potions. Herbalism and alchemy often worked hand in hand, and they usually got a couple travelers a day looking to buy some of their wares. Otherwise they spent most of their time and energy developing new concoctions, most of which went over Terico's head.

Father opened the door and led Turan to the dining table, which more often than not was covered with lab materials, rather than food. Turan set the pile of light blue roots down on a clear section of the table, between a few glasses of orange liquid and a set of loosely rolled-up scrolls.

Mother sat at the other end of the table, jotting down a few notes in a hand-sized leather notebook. She set it down and stood up to give Father a hug. Father kissed her on the forehead and draped his forearms across her shoulders.

"Welcome home, dear," Mother said. "I see you all found plenty of berial."

"Should be enough for at least twenty doses, dearest," Father said. "You never fail to impress, dearest forever."

"You're the one who inspires me, dearest of all times, all places." Turan cast an exasperated look in Terico's direction. "I can see where you get your flair for romance."

This sort of dialogue was fairly typical of Terico's parents. It was all sickly sweet, but their smiles were always pure and warm when they tried to outdo each other's praises. Terico had never heard his mother and father argue with each other—they weren't the type to yell at anyone, and it was rare for people to get upset with them in return.

Mother let go of Father and walked over to Terico. "Oh no... you look hurt."

"Giant pitcher plant monster," Terico explained. "It got a few hits in before it died."

Mother pushed back Terico's right sleeve and looked over the gash one of the flytraps gave him. "Oh... let's get that bandaged up, Sea Scrub." It was a name that always amused Turan, though it only referred to the color of Terico's dark blue hair. It was a bit of a stark contrast

with Mother's light brown hair and Father's golden blond—Mother said her father's hair was blue, so it was assumed Terico got it from his late grandfather.

A clanging of pots or pans came from the kitchen. Terico took a few steps to see who it could possibly be, and almost jumped back when he saw Suran standing at the counter, cutting up some turnips. She was wearing a light yellow blouse and green skirt—like the sun shining on a meadow. "Oh, hi, Terico." She gave her knife a little wave, then closed her eyes a bit and gave an adorable smile.

Why Suran was here was beyond Terico, and why she was cooking what smelled like bread and omelets was anybody's guess. All manner of utensils were strewn across the counter, including a dark blue Nexi stone for water, and a red one for fire.

Father chuckled. "As expected of my wife, no visitor leaves without getting put to work!" Mother nudged him in the side.

"Oh, it's not like that," Suran said, blushing a little. "I volunteered to help with the breakfast while she finished with some of her calculations for the medicine."

"That's very nice of you," Terico said. "You don't have to come all the way here to go to this much trouble, though."

"Oh! I came to drop off some herbs." She gave a tiny laugh. "My brother Lanek had a medicine cabinet full of them—some rare elvish herbs—and we thought they'd be more useful here. I just want to do what I can for our sick neighbors... Everyone's pulling together to help them, and it wouldn't be right for me to not do what little I can. Especially when you and Turan are risking your lives, fighting these cavern monsters."

This more than anything else was what Terico liked about Suran. There wasn't a single ingenuine iota in her heart, and she always put the needs and wants of others before her own. Even since they were children, Terico had wanted to become better friends with her. Perhaps at first it was that air of mystery about her that attracted him—the elves had such a deep, magical lore and culture, after all. And he thought Suran was cute too, with bright hazel eyes and long, silky red hair. It was definitely the way she conducted her life, though, that endeared Terico to her.

He just needed to find a good way to share his feelings for her. "No, it was fine," Terico said. "Thanks, Suran. For... everything. This is really nice of you... Thanks!"

"A weak performance," Turan said under his breath.

"Thanks!" Suran said. "It may not be your mother's cooking, but I'll try my best. Everything should be ready in a few minutes."

"Okay, Sea Scrub," Mother said. "Go to the other room and I'll get you some bandages."

Terico sat on the creaky chair in front of the dormant fireplace, while Father and Turan stepped out with their swords to spar for a few minutes. Through the front window Terico watched them have at it, and wondered what Father was saying to Turan. Perhaps instructing him on his footwork— or perhaps complimenting him on his skill with the blade. Turan was very talented for his age, and perhaps the best in their class.

Suran's brother Lanek was arguably just as good of a fighter though, and Terico considered himself rather competent as well. Like everyone else, Terico would take Nexi Power Ranking exams—or NPRs—every few months. It seemed he would always end up with some rotten luck during the tests though, keeping him from advancing to a higher level.
Mother came back with some bandages, a damp cloth, and some healing ointment. "Go ahead and clean your wounds and apply the medicine. I can help you wrap everything up."

Terico rolled up his left trouser leg and soaked up the blood caked on it. Once it was cleaned off he dripped some of the glass bottle's medication onto his fingertips and rubbed them onto the wound. It stung like a hundred needles, but Terico kept from crying out.

"Sorry, it'll hurt," Mother said. "I'm sorry this happened to you, Terico. I never wanted you to get hurt so badly."

"I'll be fine. It's really not a big deal," Terico said. And really, it could have been much worse. A few bad scrapes wasn't anything to worry about, though telling his mother that would be kind of pointless.

She kept a concerned look on her face, but didn't comment further on Terico's injuries.

He glanced out the window again and saw his father patting Turan on the shoulder.

"You look like something's troubling you," Mother said. "Other than your wounds, I mean."

Terico wondered if his worries were that apparent. "It's nothing." Mother tilted her head a bit and gave this straight-lipped frown that meant Terico's response simply wasn't going to cut it.

"I wish I could make Father proud," Terico whispered. "I was hoping to do a good job fighting that plant monster, but... things didn't work out as nicely as I hoped."

Mother nodded a couple times and smiled. "Terico, you've always been the hardest worker I've known. And that includes your father, believe it or not. Just keep fighting, and you will definitely keep improving. That's more than enough to make your father and I very, very proud of you."

Terico turned his head and shut his eyes a few moments. "It doesn't feel like enough. Hard work doesn't mean anything if it doesn't bring results." Mother shook her head and gave a light little sigh. "Men tend to think that way. I think you'll learn for yourself that's not true though, Sea Scrub." She didn't say any more on the matter, so Terico didn't either.

While Mother wrapped up his leg, Terico took off his cloak and long-sleeved shirt so he could tend to the rest of his wounds. The cut across his chest wasn't too deep, fortunately, but it stung like crazy when he spread some of the ointment across it.

"I've finished the breakfast," Suran said as she walked into the room. "I'll keep it warm while..."

Terico looked up and found Suran frozen in mid-stride.

Her eyes gazed down at Terico's chest, and her entire face reddened. She quickly shut her eyes and scurried back to the kitchen. "S-sorry, Terico! I didn't mean..."

Terico couldn't help but smile at her modesty. "No need to apologize, Suran...

You took part whenever our class went swimming. This isn't so different."
"Th-that was a few years ago," Suran said in a quiet voice. "You've grown since then."

Mother tried to hide her amusement, though she made a poor effort of it. "Ah, you've caught her interest now," she whispered. "Your father used similar tactics, now that I think about it."

Once Terico finished tending his wounds, he went to his room to change into clothes that weren't bloodied up, and then joined everyone at the table for breakfast. Everyone simply pushed the lab materials toward the center of the table to make room for their plates, and Turan ate kneeling at the end of the table, since there were only four chairs. Terico sat by Suran, but couldn't think of anything very good to say to her, other than thanking her for the meal. Turan kept up a loud conversation with Terico's parents, so it was simpler to just eat.

"I hope your injuries will get better quickly," Suran said quietly. Her thin eyebrows were arched upward, her face wearing such a worried expression.

"I'm feeling better already." Terico smiled.

"I'm glad," Suran said.

She finished breakfast about the same time as Terico, and stood up to give Terico's parents a slight bow. "Thank you for letting me visit."

"No, thank you," Mother said. "You cooked the meal and brought those elvish herbs. They will be a great help for the patients."

"Oh, thanks," Suran said. Even when thanked, she instinctively thanked people for their thanks.

"I'll help see you out," Terico said, getting up.

He followed her out the door and closed it behind them.

"You shouldn't exert yourself," Suran said. "Can you walk all right?"

"Yes, it doesn't hurt so much anymore," Terico said. *Er, I mean, it never hurt much...* he thought. It was too late to change his words though.

"Well, I need to go help my brother with a couple things before school starts," Suran said. "See you in class." She waved good-bye and started to turn away.

"Wait, there's something else," Terico said. Suran stopped and tilted her head to the side. It was an adorable little gesture, and Terico stumbled for the words to say.

"There's... the festival. The Long Shadow Festival is coming up."

"Oh, yes," Suran said. "That's always fun, with the shadow tracings, and shadow puppet shows."

"Yeah," Terico said. "I was wondering... you're going, right?" "Mmhmm," Suran hummed.

"That's great!" Terico said. "I'll... see you there then?"

"Probably," Suran said. "It's a small town, so even with everyone gathered together, it's not too hard to see everyone."

No, this wasn't quite what I meant to say, Terico thought.

Suran smiled and waved again. "Though if we don't meet up there, I'll see you at school, at least. See you later, Terico!"

She was in a hurry for something, but had been nice enough to finish this conversation with Terico.

It didn't go the way he wanted it to, though. He sighed and headed back inside, wondering when he'd get another good chance to talk with Suran privately. Perhaps at the festival? It was probably his next best opportunity, he decided.

•

Terico waited for Turan to finish breakfast, then gave his goodbyes to his parents before heading off to class. The long wooden school building was situated just outside of town, as there wasn't a good spot for it in the central square. It was one of the more recent structures in Edellerston, built just a few years after Terico was born. Beforehand groups of children were taught at teachers' homes, and typically moved on to apprenticeships at an earlier age than was expected today. Today there were more guidelines for what everyone in the country should learn, and the last couple days had given Terico a lot of old poetry to memorize. Terico much preferred learning more about ways to utilize Nexi stones, and other of the more magical subjects.

Terico and Turan crossed a series of radish fields, and continued on down a trail that ran down an expansive turnip farm. Turan still had his leather armor and sword on him, so he'd probably get an earful from the teacher again about bringing a weapon to class. When Terico brought it up, Turan just gave one of his many carefree "don't worry about it" responses. Their idle chat turned to the inevitable within a few minutes, though.

"So you set up a date with Suran, at long last?" Turan asked.

"Well... not quite," Terico said. He knew this was coming, as Turan had been pestering him to set something up with Suran for some time now. "What?" Turan cried. He gripped his blond hair and gave an exaggerated frown, though he only held this expression for a moment. "Come on,
Terico. I'll give you a deadline if I must. If you don't ask her out by Friday, I'll make a move myself." He closed his eyes and rubbed his chin with the back of his hand a few times. "Turan and Suran. Has a nice ring to it, don't you think? I bet I can win her heart in three days flat."

"Right, right," Terico said. "Just like you've won the heart of every other girl in class. Oh, wait. When *was* the last time you had a date?"

Turan waved his hand toward Terico's face. "Don't sweat the details. I'm just waiting for all the girls to finish fighting over me, and then I can just take the one left standing when the dust settles."

Terico stifled a laugh. "You might need to rethink that strategy of yours."

"Yes, but seriously, Terico." Turan's face turned serious. "You've got to make a move some time with Suran. I mean, you've liked her since you were—what, two?"

"Not that early," Terico said, "but all right, I get your point. I'll see if I can find her at the festival, and maybe take her to a hill to watch the fireworks with me."

"Yes, girls love fireworks," Turan said. "But then again, I love them too."

"Most everyone does, I imagine," Terico said. "I think everyone looks forward to the Long Shadow fireworks."

"Hey, speaking of fire..." Turan pointed to a rising cloud of dark smoke in the distance. There were a number of houses and a couple shops past this end of this field, not far from the school.

Terico instinctively took out a dark blue Nexi stone from his pocket.
"Come on! We might be able to help put out whatever's caught on fire." He ran as fast as he could manage, though it sent painful jolts up and down his left leg with every step. As they approached the town outskirts, Terico saw there were several buildings on fire—perhaps all of them. He glanced back to the central square in the far distance behind him, and found smoke starting to rise there as well. The air filled with screams, cries for help, and weeping.

It's an attack! Terico realized. He wished he had a sword on hand like Turan, but he would have to make do with his Nexi stones.

He reached the nearest burning homes and found three dead bodies, each stabbed several times. A mother. A father. A child. All murdered beside their blazing home. Terico was not familiar with this family, but he still recognized them. He gripped his Nexi stone tight and searched furiously for the perpetrators. There was nobody around, though. The assailants were simply rushing through, killing everyone they could find.

Turan ran off toward the burning shops down the road, and Terico followed him—only to find more dead bodies. Terico looked on ahead to find the school building, also drenched in fire.

Suran!
Terico bolted toward the school, running as hard as he could. He payed no mind to the pain of his injuries—he had to find Suran immediately. There were screams coming from inside. What if Suran was trapped amongst the flames? He had to get her out of there. He had to get all his classmates out of there. Everyone was counting on him.

"Terico!" Turan screamed. "A little help!"

Terico glanced back and stopped, surprised to find two armed men advancing on

Turan from either side of him. Men in white uniforms and silver armor. Their defining element was the flat, featureless white mask each of them wore, which was entirely blank save for an inverted black cross etched across the right eye.

The Brotherhood. The most feared warriors of the Shire Kingdom.

"Use your Nexi stones!" Terico yelled back. "I'll be back as soon as I can!" Terico was confident Turan could fend off these two warriors for a minute, while Terico dealt with the fire in the school. There was no time to question his decision—not if Suran's life was on the line.

Terico bolted to the school building, which pulsated with hazy, painful waves of heat. He lifted up his dark blue Nexi stone and forced it to activate with all the power he could muster. A great burst of water rushed forth from the stone, sweeping across the south wall and onto the roof. With the back entry doused, Terico ran in and continued releasing as much water as he could from his Nexi stone. The flames were powerful, and the fire was vast and overwhelming. It was going to be too difficult to put all of it out.

I have to find her... I have to reach her right now!
He ran into the main hallway, where flaming planks of wood fell from the ceiling and crumbled atop blackened floorboards. Terico put out some of the fire to make room for him to continue further into the building. His heart began to race faster when he realized that all the screams he had heard earlier had stopped. After drenching the door to the nearest classroom, Terico kicked it down, only to find a burning inferno. He saw figures lying on the ground and aimed his Nexi stone in their direction. The fires cleared, and Terico found bodies littering the floor in terrible, bloody piles. Students of all ages lay with gaping holes in their chests and stomachs. Incredulously, some were sliced clean in half.

Terico bent down and puked.

It was all so impossible to believe. Terico knew these people. They were his classmates. His fellow villagers. Kids he was planning to play with at the festival.

He coughed up smoke and nearly fell to his knees. *Have to get out of here*, he thought. *Have to find Suran... Have to get out...*

The continual use of the Nexi stone was draining him of energy—there was no way he'd be able to keep using it much longer. But he didn't see Suran amongst any of the bodies on the ground.

He remembered she had said she needed to help her brother with something. She didn't say what, though.

Terico called out her name, but there was no answer. He yelled again and again, only to have his voice drowned out by the building's raging fires and crumbling structure. After beating down the door to another classroom, Terico was nearly blown away by the heat that rushed through the entryway. He screamed from the sudden blast of searing heat, and had to use the Nexi stone on himself for a moment to keep from burning up. There was nothing to see inside the classroom—it was an utter hell that had already enveloped everything in its path.

"Suran..." Terico cried. He turned back to the hallway and yelled as hard as his smoke-filled lungs could handle. "Suran! Are you there?" She wasn't anywhere.

Terico wanted to just keep using his Nexi stone, to keep putting out as much fire as he could—but he was too weak to keep wielding so much water. And yet he couldn't let himself just leave. What if Suran was in the next room? What if she could still be saved?

The sound of screaming from outside jolted Terico back to his senses. It was Turan.

Terico struggled to run down the hall, but was overwhelmed by the thick blankets of smoke developing in the building. He pushed himself to make it through, until at last he stumbled out the building and fell to his hands and knees. For perhaps half a minute Terico fell into a painful coughing fit, helpless to assist his friend.

He looked up and found Turan in combat with one of the Brotherhood warriors, fighting only a few meters ahead of Terico. Farther ahead lay the body of the other warrior, whose masked face drooped in a puddle of blood leaking from his slit neck. Turan had managed to kill one warrior, but then tried to escape to the school building—but was unable to shake the second fighter.

The enemy was a fast swordsman, but Turan was barely managing to keep up with the man's attacks. It was clear Turan was terribly worn out, however.

Terico pushed himself to stand on his feet, but felt his head go dizzy for a couple seconds. He ignored the feeling and took out a white Nexi stone. If he could blind the enemy with light for a moment, Turan would be able to slit the man's neck just as he had the first warrior.

The sound of movement came from the far end of the school building. Terico glanced back and found a third Brotherhood member, this one wielding a long, jagged-edged sword in one hand, and a fiery red Nexi stone in the other. This had to be the man who burned down the building—and perhaps slaughtered everyone within it.

The man ran toward Terico, raising his bloody, jagged sword

forward. The enemy readied his swing, and Terico leaped forward, thrusting his Nexi stone toward the man's face. While keeping his eyes on the man's sword, Terico activated both his dark blue stone and the white one, simultaneously releasing a wave of water while blasting a sheet of blinding white light. At the same time, the enemy swung his sword and released a burst of fire from his Nexi stone.

Terico shut his eyes, but knew precisely where the man's sword was. As Terico's water devoured the enemy's fire, Terico turned in place and ducked, letting the man's attack pass over him. Terico immediately rose back up and jabbed his elbow into the man's stomach. As the brief flash of light faded away, Terico wrenched the jagged sword from the man's grasp, spun in place, and stabbed him in the back with his own blade.

The sound that emanated from the man's throat—something of shock and horror, crying from the suddenness of the pain, filling with blood—it was an utterly terrifying sound, lasting at least a full five seconds. Terico shoved the man to the ground with a loud, jaw-cracking thump, then pulled the sword from the corpse's back. It was the first time Terico had ever killed someone—but there was no time to dwell on it now. Not when the entire village was in danger.

He turned back to Turan, who continued to fight against the same Brotherhood swordsman—a tall, imposing figure, though nameless behind the mask of the Shire organization.

Terico dropped his Nexi stones, no longer able to keep a grip on them. He had exhausted himself with the fight against the plant monster that morning, and then drained himself even more when trying to put out the fire at the school. Gasping for air, Terico fell to his knees once again, his entire body weak and trembling.

He watched as Turan slipped out a brown Nexi stone from his sleeve and aimed it for the enemy's feet. A dark, swamp like substance flew from the stone, but the enemy had leaped back the moment Turan took out the rock. Turan swung for the man, who dodged and pulled an orange Nexi stone out from a small belt pouch and clipped it to a slot in his sword's hilt.

The man ran around the large, sticky marsh trap and charged for Turan, who lifted his Nexi stone and aimed again. The man's sword glowed a bright orange— even if Turan blocked the enemy's swing, the blade would cleave Turan's sword in two.

Turan released more swamp material at the last moment, shooting the sticky substance all over the enemy's sword. It didn't stop the man from swinging, however. Turan turned and raised his sword to defend the man's still-glowing blade. The man sliced Turan's blade clean in half—but was unable to continue the swing on to Turan's head.

The swamp material connected the enemy's blade to the top of what was left of Turan's blade, and Turan held strong against the momentum of the man's swing. With the Brotherhood swordsman taken aback, Turan pulled his severed sword away, taking his enemy's sword with him. Turan immediately slipped out his red Nexi stone with his left hand and shot fire into the enemy's face. The man leaped back screaming, and jumped straight onto the marsh trap Turan created earlier. Holding his sword with his right hand, Turan spun it so the enemy's sword at the end of Turan's blade pointed back to the enemy. Turan swung like a lumberjack, and slammed the glowing blade straight through the enemy's body, slicing him down from his right shoulder to his left hip.

With the man finally dead, Turan set the weapon and stones down, and took slow, deep breaths. He recovered after just a few breaths, just as a man with long black hair approached him. Terico tried to get up to help Turan in case this man was with the Brotherhood, but it was too difficult to stand. The use of his Nexi stones had curiously increased the pain of his wounds from the plant monster, and he fell into another terrible coughing fit, as if he were still deep in the school full of smoke.

The man walking toward Turan wore a small black vest, leaving his muscular arms and torso exposed. He wore a bandana and the kind of pants and leg guards found in the Shire Kingdom. But most startling were the bright green Nexi stones implanted up and down his arms, plus the light blue stone embedded in his right hand. There looked to be at least a dozen stones in total, and all of them glowed, ready to be utilized at a moment's notice.

"You have talent," the man said, his voice quiet and monotone. "You will make a useful subject."

Turan picked up his red Nexi stone and aimed it for this new enemy. Vines rushed out from all of the man's green Nexi stones simultaneously. Faster than Terico could blink, the man held Turan in the air by ten vines wrapped haphazardly all around Turan's body. Turan's red Nexi stone and sword was in the grasp of another of the man's vines, a safe distance away from Turan's grasp. Turan struggled against the vines for only a moment—the vines reacted instantly to his effort, binding him even tighter.

The vines pressed so hard against Turan's skin, Terico could see his friend visibly in agony—and even bleeding at places.

"You have some skill with Nexi stones," the man went on, calm and placid. He almost sounded disinterested, even. Before Turan could yell a retort, the man caused vines to wrap around Turan's head, forcing a gag to form across his mouth.

Terico wanted to run down to Turan. To pick up a sword and free him from those vines. But Terico could hardly move, let alone fight a man who could wield a dozen Nexi stones at once. He tried to yell Turan's name, but couldn't even manage that. His dry throat kept him from projecting his voice above the cracking and roaring of the village fires.

A couple masked Brotherhood members ran up to the man with the arms decked in Nexi stones.

"There are more town guards than expected at the central square, Commander Augurc," one of them said.

The name was familiar to Terico. Augurc Shire was one of the two brothers who led the Shire Kingdom. A heartless man who conducted all manner of inhuman experiments. There were many stories of his conquests and subsequent Nexi testing on his helpless victims. And if even a fraction of them were to be believed, Augurc was a man deserving of the utmost dread and fear..

"We're finished here," Augurc said. "If my brother's men need help, we will assist them."

Terico watched as the two masked men ran off into the fields, followed by Augurc, who simply walked at a brisk, steady pace. Strangely he seemed to be keeping up with the masked Brotherhood members just fine, however. Turan floated along behind him and to the side, held in the air by Augurc's strong, sturdy vines.

No, not Turan, Terico thought. *I can't let you take Turan. I can't let you take him away for your sadistic experiments!* He got himself to stand up, but felt the whole world start spinning beneath his feet. Terico had never been so afflicted by the Nexi, though he recognized this was the most he had ever used the stones in such a brief period of time. His vision turned blurry for a few seconds, and he had to blink a few times before he could figure out which way he was facing.

Terico found the fields he had walked through to get to the school— but Augurc and Turan were nowhere in sight anymore.

But even if he did find Turan, there were at least three Brotherhood fighters to deal with. Even if Terico had energy to fight with, he'd be no match for three well-trained warriors. But he couldn't just do nothing, either. Turan needed him. How could Terico call himself Turan's friend if he just let Turan be taken away? Terico gathered his Nexi stones and picked up the jagged sword he had won.

He looked back at the school, still burning bright and miserable.
I'm sorry, Suran. I wasn't able to protect you.
He trudged toward the fields, agony pulsating through his body every step of the way.

Turan, don't worry. I'll find you. And if you're still out there, I'll keep you safe too, Suran. And I'll help you as well, Mother and Father. The village will be all right.
I will do everything I can. I will make everything right.

Terico's home was already burning by the time he came in sight of it, most of the wooden structure now a black, smoldering heap. There were no bodies lying outside the house, and Terico knew his parents wouldn't be inside. He continued his way to the central square—his father would surely be at the cathedral, the site he and the town guards always planned to use for a base of resistance in the event of a full-scale attack. Mother was likely with him, perhaps directing villagers to safety.

How many members of the Brotherhood came? Terico wondered. As he trudged down the dirt road to the central square, he found nothing but bloodied corpses, scattered wares, and burning shops and homes. Fortunately the cathedral had not caught on fire, giving Terico some hope that the Brotherhood were being fended off.

And why did they come here? There's nothing for them here... Most of the villagers had never worried too much about the Shire Kingdom's threats on the Fiefs Kingdom, considering how insignificant Edellerston was in the grand scheme of things. This town was within the boundaries of the Fiefs Kingdom, but that technicality had very little impact on everyone's day-today lives.

Terico returned his thoughts to the matter at hand. It didn't matter why the Brotherhood had come. They just had to be dealt with.

Nearing the cathedral, Terico found a number of town guards fighting off a few masked members of the Brotherhood. The enemies were strong and had access to powerful Nexi stones, negating any advantage the guards may have had in terms of numbers. One by one, they were being killed off by the Brotherhood's superior tactics and better training.

The guards needed help, but Terico was too weakened to do much more.
He needed to find his parents—and Turan—and Suran.

Terico quickened his pace, using all his will-power to fight against the stinging agony of his injuries. The pain seemed to be getting worse with every step, to the point where he began to feel dizzy again. He shut his eyes and forced himself up the white stone stairway to the open cathedral entrance. The sound of shattering windows echoed from within, followed by cries of panic. Terico could hear a booming voice amongst the screams, but couldn't make out the words. He pushed himself up the steps faster.

Once at the entry, Terico found dozens of villagers scattering about the building. Terico turned toward a stream of light pouring into the tall, dark cathedral, shining through the shattered hole that had housed the grand, circular stained-glass window. The light obscured the figure of a tall, imposing man wearing dark armor, a cape, and a hood. Standing atop the holy altar, the man raised a sword nearly as tall as he was, and pointed it down toward the aisle between the cathedral pews.

"So that's your decision?" the man asked, his voice loud and booming.

Terico looked down and saw his father standing a few meters in front of the man. Father raised his sword and caused it to glow with orange Nexi energy.

"I know how you would use its power, Delkol," Father said. "I am not so spineless as to just hand it over to you, and let the blood of thousands rest on my hands in the process."

Delkol... Delkol Shire? Terico thought. It was incredulous that Augurc had come here—but Delkol too? Why would *both* leaders of Shire Kingdom come to Edellerston? And what was Father talking about? Terico turned and found Mother standing a couple meters behind Father, gripping a couple Nexi stones in her hands.

   What are they doing?
"Blood will rest on your hands regardless," Delkol yelled. "You know what you have chosen? You have chosen to have every single person in this village die!" Delkol leaped off the altar, his sword in one hand, a glowing silver Nexi stone in the other.

"Now!" Father yelled. Mother raised her Nexi stones toward Father, a clear one in her left hand, and then two stones in her right—a yellow one and a white one. The clear one would enable her to transfer the powers of the other stones to Father and his sword. Terico lifted the sword he had stolen and hurried down the long, echoing hall, refusing to just stand still while his parents were in danger.

Father's sword glowed bright from the orange stone in his hilt, then charged the blade with white, blinding sparks of light. With his blade strengthened and with the power of Mother's white Nexi stone, Father could wield the power of lightning.

He swung his sword toward Delkol, striking a deafening snap of lightning at the hooded figure. Delkol already had his Nexi stone raised, however, and a floating barrier of metallic silver feathers blocked the attack. The lightning and shield both lasted only an instant, and Delkol was quick to reach Father a moment later.

They clashed swords, and a blinding burst of light enveloped the entire cathedral. Terico stumbled to the ground, his whole body numb from the wave of energy. The light cleared, but Terico found it difficult to stand back up. His wounds seared with sheer torment, and his head pounded with a sudden migraine. He looked up at Father and Delkol, struggling against one another with their blades. Delkol's blade glowed silver, covered in etchings of feathers that shifted constantly.

"I will admit your strength," Delkol said. "You and that woman truly grasp the power of Nexi."

A spray of white sparked against Delkol's sword, as Father exerted himself to push against the silver blade. Father's body glowed a light yellow as Mother transferred a protective barrier of energy over his body. Delkol's hood flipped back from the slight gust of wind that emanated from the yellow glow. The man had short, light brown hair, eyes the color of gleaming blue ice, and some beard stubble—but what stood out most blatantly was the thick black scar across his right eye, in the shape of an inverted cross. He cast a long, amused smile. "That won't be enough.

My sword is already against yours."

A Nexi stone on Delkol's hilt glowed a bright, violent red. His sword burst into flames, blasting fire across Father's arms. Father yelled and stumbled back as the fire instantly covered the rest of his body.

"No!" Mother screamed. All the energies of Father's and Mother's Nexi stones faded away.

Delkol chuckled, then lifted his sword and swung, taking a few steps forward in the process.

Terico's father and mother both dropped to the ground. In one long swoop of his fiery silver blade, Delkol beheaded them.

In one simple motion, Father and Mother were dead.

They were *dead*.

And Terico did nothing.

He stared. Wide-eyed. Motionless. His mind went blank. What his eyes were seeing—it didn't make sense. What he saw didn't happen. It couldn't have.

It couldn't have.

Delkol chuckled again as he turned to a group of villagers standing in shock a few meters away. "Is this the best this town offers? Or will the fun of the slaughter turn into the drudgery of the massacre?"

A number of villagers ran for Delkol, armed with only makeshift weapons—whatever knives they happened to have on them, or in some instances a farming tool. The silver feathers and crackling fire of Delkol's blade faded away. He pocketed his silver Nexi stone and took out a dark purple one, which he slid down the length of the blade. The sword began to vibrate violently with glowing purple energy, but Delkol held it so tight that the weapon had no effect on his body.

Three men charged for Delkol from different directions. Delkol swung his sword against the nearest man, slamming the flat side of the blade against the man's chest. The villager flew backward from the impact, careening backward several meters. At the same time, Delkol caused his purple Nexi stone to power his kick against the next man's stomach. This man also went flying backward, arcing several meters into the air. Then in one brief instant, Delkol turned his blade to point for the third man—an elderly man with a fishing knife. The villager ran straight into Delkol's blade. Delkol laughed as he caused his sword to vibrate faster, tearing the old man apart from the inside.

A group of villagers swarmed for Delkol, screaming with sheer rage. Delkol simply swung away with the broad side of his sword, letting the power of his Nexi stone fling everyone through the air. He knocked a young boy against an altar, then turned and slammed his blade against a woman's head, snapping her neck. In long, swift movements, he beat his blade against a green-haired boy Terico's age, then against a man with one leg trying to slip away, then against a girl perhaps four or five years old. Everyone within Delkol's range died a swift, bloody death, screaming and crying.

Terico saw it all happen, but it somehow didn't *mean* anything. These were just things that were happening. Delkol killed everyone, and noboy could even lay a finger on him.

In fact, this was just a game to him. A very easy game. One that he always won, and always enjoyed winning.

Masked Brotherhood members rushed into the cathedral, easily taking down any villagers who tried to escape. The church echoed with a cacophony of grisly horror.

And Terico did nothing. He lay there—unthinking, unmoving. Bodies and body parts were strewn all across the floor, or draped over the pews. A couple corpses and a severed arm landed around Terico over the course of the slaughter, and once it was all over Delkol apparently didn't notice Terico lying there, still alive.

"Your brother is waiting outside," a Brotherhood member told Delkol.

"Begin a thorough search of the entire village," Delkol said. "Sift through the ashes of every single hovel. If the Elpis is here, I intend to find it."
Terico listened to the footsteps of Delkol and his men marching down the stairway. Terico remained where he lay.

Motionless.
Silent.

•

Hours passed, and still Terico lay on the cold stone floor of the cathedral, hardly able to breathe amidst the stench of the dead. He shut his eyes and gripped his hands into fists. Though he lay soundless, Terico cursed himself.
He cursed Delkol, and he cursed himself.

He killed my parents. He murdered them. He laughed. He killed them, and he loved killing them.
And I did nothing.
I did nothing.

I did nothing!

Hour after hour passed, and Terico cursed himself for lacking the power to do anything. Terico's entire world was destroyed, and he failed to do absolutely anything about it.

My parents are dead. Turan is captured... and will probably die. Suran is missing... but is probably dead.

Terico knew that each of these thoughts should have been enough to move him to tears. But he didn't want tears. He wanted to be moved to action.
He wanted to do something about this.

He cursed himself until his whole body trembled.

"Delkol! Delkol! *Delkol!*" he screamed at the top of his lungs.

Though utterly exhausted, Terico willed himself to push aside the corpse draped across him and stood up. He nearly fell back down from lightheadedness, and it took a few seconds for his blackened vision to clear.
The entire village is destroyed. Perhaps everyone I know is dead.
I will avenge you all. Father. Mother. Turan. Suran. I will make things right.
Terico bent down and wearily picked up the jagged sword he earned from the man he killed. It was frigid in his bloody hands, but it filled him with energy.
With a will to hew down Delkol and every single one of his followers.

I swear... I will kill you, Delkol. I will kill you, and I will destroy your Brotherhood.
And I will relish every single second of it.

•

2

FIRST STEPS ON A BLOODY PATH

Terico dug into the soft, moist earth with the only intact shovel he could find. It was stained black and smelled of burnt wood, but it held strong as Terico forced more dirt aside for another mass grave. He had already created one outside the cathedral, where he lay his mother and father, along with everyone else Delkol and his Brotherhood had killed. Terico also finished a large grave at the other end of the central square, and then another one near the homes just outside the west side of town. There were still bodies to bury near the school and shops to the south, as well as the corpses scattered amongst the surrounding farmlands.

Terico had searched the entire village for any other survivors. Checked for a pulse. Watched for movement. Shook the bodies to get any kind of reaction at all. The Shire Brothers and their followers had done a thorough job, often stabbing each victim multiple times to ensure a quick, complete death. The sight of a town guard stabbed five times reminded Terico of his father's advice against the pitcher plant monster. *If your goal is to kill something, you have to take measures to ensure it's truly dead.* Something Delkol's followers understood all too well.

The sun was beginning to set, but there were still many people to bury.

There was nobody else to do it—as far as he could tell, Terico was Edellerston's only survivor. There were a few people Terico knew that he hadn't found yet, but there were also a number of bodies that were burnt beyond recognition.

One body Terico hadn't found though was Suran's. He had checked every square centimeter of the school and the area around Suran's house, but there was no sign of her or her brother Lanek. On one hand it made Terico hopeful—perhaps Suran escaped somehow amidst the calamity. On the other hand, it was just as likely she and her brother were captured by the Brotherhood, just as Turan had been.

A fate worse than death, Terico imagined, especially when considering the nature of Augurc's experiments.

With each push of his shovel, Terico thought of the people he buried, and the time he spent with each of them. He shoveled dirt atop of Suran's parents, and thought of the elvish flatbread they often shared with him. He could almost smell its sweet yet burning spices, despite the overwhelming stench of death and smoke around him.

Beside their bodies were the corpses of a farmer couple and their children. Terico remembered showing the parents some of Father's potions, and explaining how the concoctions would help with some of that year's struggling crops. He also recalled playing rope games with the children from time to time—boys aged twelve, ten, and four, and girls aged fourteen and seven. Each of them were stabbed by the sword, though the older girl was stabbed twice and beheaded. There was a meat cleaver near where she lay, so Terico assumed she had tried defending her younger siblings as best she could.

Terico poured more dirt atop the bodies, moving on to those of the three patients at the clinic Mother was working to help save. The elderly man and young woman were both burnt to death, their bodies barely recognizable. They were too ill to escape from their beds as the building filled with smoke and flames. Terico had found the four-year-old boy outside the clinic, lying beside the body of the nurse who tended the patients. Both she and the boy were stabbed to death—the nurse had apparently tried to save whoever she could.

It was all in vain. Everyone's best efforts... none of it led to anything. *And I... I didn't even try. I just lay there, helpless. Unable to do a single thing.*
What was it all these people died for?

Terico finished covering the mass grave, burying forty-eight more citizens of the little town. He planted the shovel into the ground and leaned against its pole. His entire body ached, sore and in agony. He was in no condition to bury the corpses of an entire village.

The mist of Edellerston was heavy around him. A thick blanket keeping the stench of death tight around him. Constricting him.

Tightening his throat. Making him gag. Drenching him in sweat.

Blood dripped from his wounds, burning with an intensified vigor. Scratching at his wet and dirty skin. His clothes were splattered with blood and grime, but Terico didn't care to wash it off. What was there to care about? He had nothing. His parents were gone. His best friend was gone. His only love was gone. The entire village was gone. The only world he had ever known was gone. He felt he could just drop his shovel and lie down next to it. Never quench his parched, rough throat. Never fill his sore, famished stomach. Just let himself die. Just let it all end. Just forget everything that happened. Just pretend it was all a dream. Just force all the pain out of his heart forever.

No, Terico thought. *There is something more I can do… Much more I can do. Turan's still out there. And Suran might be, too. And Father would kill me if I just let myself die.*
Terico shut his eyes, pushing out tears from each of them. He could see his Father and Mother dying just a few meters in front of him. They did everything they could to stop Delkol, but he was far too strong. That man didn't need to kill them. He didn't need to kill anyone. He could have searched for whatever it was he was looking for without killing everyone. Yet he did. And nothing would change that now. Delkol and all but about fifteen of his Brotherhood lived while essentially all of Edellerston was little more than a black, smoke-stained blotch on the earth.

Terico pushed himself to a point south of the village, where he had gathered all the bodies he could find in that area. There were still two more mass graves to dig, and then about fifty more scattered bodies in the surrounding farmlands to bring together.

Just past the schoolhouse, Terico began digging the grave that would house all of his classmates and teachers, along with a number of shopkeepers and villagers who happened to be in the area at the time of the ambush. He focused on the task at hand, concentrating as hard as he could on the act of pounding the blade of the shovel into the dirt. If he thought about all his friends and all the things he did with them—all the things they talked about, all the games they played, all the tests they took together—he wouldn't be able to keep digging. He needed to bury them all. Bury away all the people he spent his time with. Bury his past. Bury his childhood. Let it all suffocate beneath a meter of unforgiving earth.

He became so focused on the task that he just kept on digging. The sky turned from a deep red to a pitch black, and still he kept on digging. Farther north, farther east, and deeper—farther and father toward the heart of the earth.

Terico's shovel slammed against something hard. He assumed it was a rock and pounded the blade a little to the right. Again he hit something hard.
There was something buried there.

He worked his shovel along the side of what turned out to be a brick wall. It went nearly to the top of the ground, where Terico dug to seek an entry to this underground chamber. Delkol had said he was searching for something called an Elpis—perhaps he hadn't found it, and it was hidden here? Terico had no idea what it was and what his father may have known about it, but if it was the reason behind the massacre, Terico was going to seek it out.

Sweating and bleeding and nearly collapsing from exhaustion, Terico kept digging across the top of the structure until he located a small square doorway. It reached the top of the ground, hidden with a small fake bush that acted as the handle. Terico dropped his shovel and pulled on the bush, lifting up a thick, heavy wooden door similar to those used for cellars, though much smaller.

Terico looked in and found a thin stone stairway that went nearly straight down. Several meters below, Terico could see faint traces of candlelight.
"Who's there?" cried out an old, echoing voice.

There was somebody down there. Terico didn't recognize the voice, but it may have been a villager who managed to hide from the Brotherhood.

"It's Terico. Terico Obisious."

"Obisious?" replied the stranger. "Just a second. I'll come on up." Terico stepped back and watched as a small man in a dusty green tunic walked up the staircase. He had dark green eyes, small ears, and straight chestnut hair. The man was probably in his late fifties, and it took a few moments for Terico to figure out who he was. Though Terico didn't know the man's name, he recognized him as one of the pub's most frequent visitors. In fact, Terico couldn't think of a time he ever saw this man outside of the pub.

"Evening," the man said. He took a long look around himself, pausing at each of the burnt-down buildings, and then staring a good minute at the pile of corpses Terico was about to bury. "Though certainly not a good evening. But glad to see someone else survived all this… Are there any others?"

"No, it's only us, as far as I can tell," Terico said. "But you hid down there when the Brotherhood attacked?"

"Yes," the man said. "I didn't know who was attacking, but the second I heard a commotion, I ran to my secret lair."

Terico frowned. Even if this man was pretty old, he didn't like the idea of a coward being one of the town's few survivors.

Not that I'm one to talk, Terico thought. But it was still suspicious

that this man—of all people—would escape such a thorough extermination so easily.

"Why would *you* have an underground chamber?" he asked the man. "Don't tell me it's just for a secret stash of alcohol."

The man shrugged. "Well, partly. But don't get the wrong idea, boy. I've lived a long, eventful life, and have gained a lot of enemies along the way. When you get this age, you get tired of the danger. It's good for someone like me to have a place to fall back to and hide away in for a while. It's the only way I've been able to stick around here for so long…

Not that it means anything now, though."

Terico wouldn't have pinned this man as having lived a dangerous life, but he imagined it could help explain the man's constant presence in the pub. Drowning away his hard memories.

"The name's Jujor, by the way," the man said. "I don't think we've met, but you probably know me as the resident poet."

Terico only knew him as the resident drunk, to be honest, but he knew better than to say this aloud. "I'm Terico. I was a student at that school." He pointed at what little was left of the building.

"The Brotherhood did this then…" Jujor said in a low voice. "The Shire Kingdom has become too powerful. I doubt our country's leaders will be able to deal with this quickly, though. The Fiefs Kingdom has enough to deal with already."

"*Something* has to be done," Terico said. "The king can't just let this slide. The entire village was destroyed!" It was difficult to speak with any energy, but Terico couldn't stand the thought of his country doing nothing about this.

"This is just a little town," Jujor said. "Very out-of-the-way. It's best that the Fiefs Kingdom continue building up its army. War in the Fiefs heartland is inevitable—it's just a matter of when Delkol will make his move."
"He's already made his move," Terico said. "He was here himself. He killed my parents by his own blade... I can't just let him go free. There has to be retribution for this."

Jujor looked to the ground a few moments, clearly shaken up. When he looked back up, he folded his arms and tilted his head to the side a bit. "And you think you're the one to bring him down, I take it." His voice was soft, nearly a whisper.

"I will kill him," Terico said. "Any way I can. I will kill him."

"Would that be enough?" Jujor asked. "What would killing Delkol do for you, Terico?"
Terico flung an arm back to point toward the pile of corpses, the vast majority of them belonging to children younger than him. "Their blood cries for atonement! That man... That monster can not live with the blood of our entire village on his hands!" He could see Delkol's smirking, amused face, as clearly as if he were standing right in front of Terico now.

"You may not believe me," Jujor said, "but I understand some of the suffering you're going through, Terico. I doubt killing Delkol would relieve you of any of that pain."

"I don't care about that!" Terico yelled. "If I suffer for the rest of my life, so be it. But I can't just do nothing. I have to... I *need* to kill him. How can I move on with my life, knowing that Delkol still lives?"

Jujor flattened his mouth a bit and just stared at Terico a few moments. "Okay. I see how it is... And to be honest, I'd like to do something about this as well."

Terico hadn't thought of what Jujor may have lost. Did he have family and friends who died as well?

"Delkol has taken away my one last respite of relief," Jujor said. He stared solemnly toward one of the burned-down shops. "That was easily the best pub I ever had the chance of drinking in."

Terico shut his eyes and felt the side of his forehead pulse with dismay. "Are you serious? Don't tell me the reason you moved here was so you could waste your days away at some pub."

Jujor cast a serious glare at Terico. "Don't belittle ale before you've had some yourself, boy. It works wonders for the heart."

Terico had tried a drink on a couple occasions in the past, and gagged on the putrid stuff each time. But perhaps if he grew old and bitter, his taste buds would be worn away enough to handle it just as well as Jujor.

Terico didn't intend to drive himself to ruin, however. There was still some sliver of hope for him, as long as he managed to bring Delkol down. If Terico could have his revenge, there was a world of possibilities for his future. He could find Turan and Suran, and he could live a normal life again, continuing his studies of alchemy and the Nexi arts. Perhaps Edellerston could even be rebuilt. These were all distant thoughts, but the first step Terico needed to take was clear.

Delkol had to fall.

"I don't care for your reasoning," Terico said, "but if you want Delkol brought down, you can help me. If you have any idea where he may have gone, please let me know." Though Jujor didn't seem like a reliable man on the surface, it was clear there was more to him in his past. No ordinary drunkard would have an underground hideaway like this.

"Tell me everything you know about what happened here," Jujor said.

Terico started at the beginning, telling how he was headed to school with Turan. How they encountered the Brotherhood, including Augurc Shire. That the school and other buildings were already burning, and Terico had gone to search for Suran. How Augurc captured Turan and escaped with him. And then how Terico searched for his parents and eventually arrived at the cathedral, where the town guards were fighting off other Brotherhood members.

"In the cathedral, I found Delkol just before he killed my parents," Terico said.

"Delkol demanded something from my father, but he refused to give it up. Father said doing so would lead to thousands of people dying... But after Delkol killed my parents, he went on to murder everyone else taking refuge in the cathedral. I wasn't able to move at the time, and Delkol didn't notice me during his massacre. I was under some corpses he flung through the air." Terico felt ashamed to admit his inability to stop Delkol, but he had to accept his failure if he was going to move forward with this.

Jujor listened to the story without interruption. He scratched his chin a couple times and nodded. "Did you hear anything else Delkol may have said?"
Terico remembered a bit of Delkol's conversation with one of the masked Brotherhood fighters. "He wanted to find something called the
Elpis. Probably what he and my father were referring to beforehand." "Ah, the Elpis stone," Jujor said.

"What is it?" Terico asked.

Jujor turned back to walk down the stairs, and motioned for Terico to follow him. There was a candle lit down below, so Terico was able to watch his footing as he walked down the steep staircase.

The room at the end of the stairway was very small, containing nothing more than a tiny bed and a tall bookcase full of liquor. The drinks were of many different colors, resting in glass bottles of all shapes and sizes. Terico looked a bit closer and noticed some food wrapped up between some of the bottles, as well as a number of old, weathered tomes wrapped in leather binding. The books weren't covered in dust, so Jujor was still making use of them, it appeared. Jujor pulled out some of the books and started flipping through their pages, presumably searching for information on the Elpis stone.

Terico sat on Jujor's bed and waited patiently for what seemed to be nearly a half hour. He hated to just sit there, but he felt it too difficult to head back up the stairs and return to shoveling. It was taking every ounce of his energy just to keep from falling asleep, but Jujor wouldn't let him help look through the books. The titles were partly scratched off from years of use, but Terico could make out some of them. *The Six Elements of Alchemy. The Pillars of Solilos and Other Ancient Legends. The Unicorn's Scroll of Sayings (Abridged).* There was nothing for Terico to do though but wait and wonder.

"Here it is," Jujor said at last. He held up a book titled *The Elpis Stone*.

Terico exerted every fiber of his being to keep from screaming. "Why didn't you check that book first?"

"Seemed too easy," Jujor said. "But at any rate, this book was compiled from a wide variety of sources, so there isn't much we can say for certain about the Elpis. It's a very powerful Nexi stone at any rate, but has been broken up into multiple pieces. Some say two, some say four, some say many."

"The village was destroyed just for a Nexi stone?" Terico asked. "Not just any Nexi stone," Jujor said. "This stone gives one the power of a god. Your father was very wise to not reveal anything about its location to Delkol. If there is a piece of the Elpis in this town, Delkol would be able to use it in his looming war against the Fiefs Kingdom. I don't know just how powerful the stone is, but the ancient tales all agree that it can be used to wipe out entire armies.

"In other words, imagine what Delkol and his men did to this village—and replace Edellerston with the entire Fiefs Kingdom. And perhaps every other kingdom he seeks to take over after that. It would be the end of an entire age."

Jujor stopped to let this sink in. Terico stared toward the flickering flame of the candle, and imagined the fires of Edellerston spreading across all of Fiefs—and then the entire world.

He remembered his thoughts following Delkol's massacre in the castle.
Delkol killed everyone, and nobody could even lay a finger on him. In fact, this was just a game to him. A very easy game. One that he always won, and always enjoyed winning.
"Do you think he found it?" Terico asked.

Jujor flipped to another page of his book. "I don't think so." He turned the book toward Terico to show him a page of writing accompanying what appeared to be some kind of map. "This is a special kind of map that can only be understood by cryptologists... such as *myself*. Of course, I'm a poet first, cryptologist second."

"Does it show where the Elpis fragments are?" Terico asked, leaning closer.

"Possible locations," Jujor said. "But as it turns out, Edellerston is sitting right on top of one of these little triangles."

"There are a lot of triangles on the map, though," Terico said. Just glancing at it, there had to be at least hundred of them spanning the entire continent and several islands.

"Only certain ones are accurate though," Jujor said. "And the tiny circle at the bottom right corner of that triangle means the stone is either in the sky or beneath the earth."

There was nothing but constant precipitation in the sky above Edellerston, but there *was* an extensive network of caves. "It must be underground somewhere. It's not in this little room of yours, is it?"

"No, I've never seen the Elpis before," Jujor said, "but I have a good idea where a fragment of it may be. Far below us there is an underground city known as Emoser Helena. When I was young, I worked in mines near a town a few days' journey from here. Though I never set foot anywhere near Emoser Helena, I learned from other miners all the legends regarding the city."

"You never searched for it, though?" Terico asked.

"No reason to," Jujor said. "The place had most certainly been looted clean centuries ago, and nobody was certain where its precise location was. This book shows that there is a city below here, and I imagine that is Emoser Helena. And I would bet my entire whiskey collection that we would find the Elpis there."

"I've been in the caverns many times," Terico said. "I've never gone too deep, though. The farther down you go, the worse the monsters get."

"Yes, I imagine the entire city is overrun with monsters," Jujor said. "Or rather, the forsaken. Back in my mining days, my team once dug a little too deep, and were attacked by forsaken... Not an experience I wish to repeat."

Terico knew the forsaken were monsters that were neither alive nor dead, and therefore were impossible to kill. They were creatures of nightmares, far worse than any monsters Terico had fought off with Turan on their brief incursions underground.

"If I can get the Elpis fragment, I'll have something Delkol is seeking," Terico said. "If it will bring me closer to him, I will definitely obtain it. Even if I have to fight through a swarm of forsaken to get to it."

"Much easier said than done," Jujor muttered. "If it weren't for Febraz, I would've been killed by those things. Though speaking of Febraz..."

"Who is this?" Terico asked.

Jujor turned from Terico and sighed. "He's an acquaintance of mine. He would have some soul catcher Nexi stones, which we *could* use to fend off the forsaken..."

"Soul catchers?" Terico had never heard of a Nexi stone called that.

"The forsaken have some semblance of a soul, and these stones are used to tear it out of them," Jujor said. "They're very rare, and very pricey. In fact, I doubt Febraz would give away a soul catcher for any simple sum of money."

Terico certainly didn't have any money, and he doubted Jujor had much either. "I will find a way to get one."

"Don't think you'll be able to steal one," Jujor said. "Nothing gets by Febraz without him knowing. His senses are sharp, even for a vampire."

"A vampire?" Terico said in a raised voice. "You're friends with a vampire?" Terico had never seen a vampire before, and he had counted himself fortunate. Every story he heard about vampires was a dark, foreboding one, almost always ending in misfortune for all parties that encountered them.

"It's okay, you'll see," Jujor said. "Tomorrow we can head to the city of Merze and find him. He's a trader there, and if I play my cards right he should be glad to see me again."

At last, a plan was formulating. Terico wasn't sure how much he could rely on old Jujor, but going to Merze and obtaining the soul catchers would give Terico something to do. If it would enable him to obtain the very stone Delkol was madly searching for, then it would all be worth it. It would surely ensure that they meet again, at the very least.

And I will be ready for him, Terico thought. *The next time we meet, you will draw your final breath, Delkol Shire.*

Jujor let Terico use his bed that night, considering how Terico exhausted himself while Jujor rested most of the day. The old man said he'd take care of burying the rest of the dead, considering there wasn't too much more to dig—it was mainly a matter of going through the farmlands and gathering the rest of the corpses.

Terico awoke the next morning and walked up the stairway to find Jujor with a cooking pot atop a small campfire. Breakfast turned out to be a horrendous, sloppy mush of some kind. It was a nondescript dark brown, and tasted like soggy rye bread.

"Eat it all," Jujor said. "You'll need your strength today."

"I think I'd be better off not eating it," Terico said. He forced another spoonful of the stuff into his mouth, and had to fight his gag-reflex to push it down his throat.

"That's the best I can afford, so don't complain," Jujor said.

"Perhaps you'd afford better if you didn't buy a dozen bottles of *every* kind of liquor in the kingdom," Terico said.

Jujor shoveled a couple bits of his slosh in his mouth, slipped out a small square bottle of dark violet liquid from a trouser pocket, and washed the breakfast down with a few deep gulps of hard liquor. He wiped his mouth and laughed. "Ah, good thing I have elvish scotch to get me through this."

After breakfast and at Terico's insistence, the two searched once more through the entire village for any other survivors, or any clues regarding the Elpis or the whereabouts of Delkol and the Brotherhood. Nothing turned up, so they walked back to Jujor's hideaway to gather supplies for the trip to Merze. Jujor had a pack which he stuffed a book and a couple small scrolls into, along with some foodstuff and a few small bottles of liquor.

"You have a sword?" Jujor asked.

"Yes, a strange one left by a Brotherhood fighter I killed," Terico said. He had searched the remains of his home for his own sword, but the Brotherhood had stolen it, along with all the Nexi stones and the potions and medicines Father and Mother had made. They did a thorough job of taking every usable weapon in the village, along with any magical items and medical supplies that could be of use to them.

"You'll just need some Nexi stones, then." Jujor handed Terico a small bag.

Terico untied it and heard the rocks inside shift in his hand. He opened the bag and found four lightly glowing Nexi stones—a deep blue one for water, a white one for light, a green one for vines, and a light blue one for ice. They were all very basic, but Terico understood that in the right hands, the simplest of Nexi could be used to overcome enemies who used even the strongest, rarest stones.

"You know how to use them?" Jujor asked.

"Of course," Terico said. He had taken plenty of Nexi exams in school, and though he wasn't one of the best in his class, he still felt he was competent. Fighting monsters had certainly given him lots of practice, much of which was a lot more practical than the tasks he was given at school.

"Good, let's get walking, then," Jujor said. "We won't get there until tomorrow afternoon, most likely."

•

The trip to Merze was uneventful, save for the disconcerting lack of moisture in the air once Terico was a few kilometers away from his hometown. Jujor explained that in most of the land it didn't rain as much as it did in Edellerston, and he felt it was safe to say that it was the only town where the air was *always* a bit wet.

Once they passed the vast fields surrounding Edellerston, Terico and Jujor continued down a windy dirt path that slinked through a thick Birchwood forest. The thin white trees were covered with vibrant green leaves, their brilliance enough to take Terico's mind away from his situation a little bit.

Most of the time, though, Terico's thoughts drifted to his parents, to Suran, to Turan, and then to Delkol. And at times he wondered about Jujor as well. The circumstances behind Terico's chance meeting with the old man were certainly unusual. So much so, that Terico couldn't help but wonder how much more to Jujor there was than he was letting on.

From time to time Terico tried starting a conversation with him, but Jujor wasn't one to reveal much of anything about himself. Instead he preferred to learn more about Terico, which made Terico feel a little uneasy.

"If you want my help, I need to know everything I can about you," Jujor explained. "It's not going to be easy, going against Delkol. But if we can get the Elpis before he does, we should be able to keep him from wreaking too much havoc."

A part of Terico wanted to focus on just finding Delkol and figuring out how to defeat him right away, but if what Jujor was saying about the Elpis was true, then there was a lot more than just Terico's vengeance at stake. If the entire Kingdom of Fiefs was in peril because of this Nexi stone, it was best that Terico do what he can to keep Delkol from obtaining it.

•

The temperature transitioned between moderate and cool once evening passed, so Terico didn't need a blanket to sleep. After he and Jujor stopped to rest to the side of the trail for the night, they helped themselves to some bread and cheese and continued their journey to Merze.

The trail eventually turned out of the forest and into long stretches of dark grass, weeds, and small bushes. Terico tried again to find out a bit more about Jujor. "I know you said you want payback for having the pub destroyed, but is there any more reason you have for helping me with this?
Have you lost anything to Delkol before?"

"I just wanted a peaceful, unassuming place where I could live quietly," Jujor said. "I've lost everything else in life, boy, so having the one piece of joy I had left taken away from me... I'd say that's enough to rile an old man to action."

Terico didn't feel like this was a full answer, though. "There has to be more to it than that. It's obvious you're knowledgeable in a lot more than just mining. My thinking is that the main reason for your underground chamber is to keep those old books of yours hidden. You know details about things few people have even heard about. And the fact you're so freely telling me all these things about the Elpis... I can tell there's a lot more to all this than you're letting on, but still— you're sharing a lot of valuable information with me. I'd like to understand why."

"Of course I'm not revealing everything," Jujor said. "All old people have their secrets, you know. But it's true, there are more reasons for me to help you than I've mentioned. But the main thing is... well, the town burned down, and there isn't much of anything left to do there. And to be honest, I see myself in you somewhat. It seems we were fated to meet, boy."

Terico decided it was best to not push Jujor further, though it was clear there was still more that needed to be unraveled about Jujor's past. He may have been a miner at one point, but he was likely a number of other—and more significant—things as well.

•

They arrived at the city a bit before noon, making better time than Jujor had expected. Merze turned out to be even larger than Terico imagined it would be. Dark stone buildings rose up three to four stories all around him. A great river ran through Merze, requiring all manner of wooden bridges to connect one side of the city to the other. Some were wide enough for a half-dozen carts to pull through, while others were just wide enough for one person to walk across.

Other than the disparity in size, the most striking difference between Merze and Edellerston was the lack of clouds above Merze. There had always been at least a few puffy clouds above Terico's hometown, but at least this day in Merze the whole sky was entirely blank. The sun seemed to illuminate the sky a blinding light blue, and Terico couldn't stand to gaze up at it very long.

Every step down the central cobblestone road sent a barrage of sights and sounds rushing at Terico. All manner of people walked by in every direction, speaking with one another, dealing in business, greeting each other, hurrying to their appointments. At one moment a group of tall, long-haired elves rode by on brilliant white horses, and at the next Terico spotted a group of human children starting a game of ball—right in the middle of the street, to Terico's amusement. People and carriages simply made their way around the children kicking a small orange ball back and forth.

To either side of Terico, traders sold all manner of goods, calling out their wares and prices to the passing masses. A one-legged man in his thirties sat atop his little wooden stand, selling thin quilted blankets. Beside him rested a long stand manned by a couple boys a little older than Terico, selling a variety of clay pots, cups, and other vessels. They had deeply tanned skin, and wore cloaks covered in thick multicolored zig-zags, along with black headbands and all manner of beaded necklaces. Terico wondered where they were from, but Jujor was already leading him onward, where Terico found a group of elven and human farmers working to sell a number of chickens, pheasants, and ducks they kept in small, individual wooden cages.

Jujor guided Terico down a thinner lane between long, vinespeckled brick homes, which apparently housed many families in separate rooms. Terico could hear some people holding a boisterous conversation, though he couldn't make out the words amidst the constant chatter of the people outside. For a moment he could smell the scent of freshly-baked bread, but it dissipated quickly. Terico tried to figure out what kind of bread it was, but didn't see any stands selling any baked goods.

They continued on through the city, eventually passing between a number of tents run by eigni—people who had light blue skin but no noses. One of Terico's teachers was an eigni, and a man very knowledgeable in the application of Nexi stones—but it was rare for anyone in Edellerston to see any others. At Merze, there were apparently many eigni—selling, buying, and trading their goods just as the humans and elves did.

"Looking for some good shoes, boy?" an eigni man asked Terico. The man was probably in his late twenties, and wore a red long-sleeved turtleneck shirt and long dark green skirt, along with a white ruffled tie clipped just below his neck. He held up a pair of shiny brown boots and cast a small, toothy grin.

"No, sorry," Terico said. Jujor pulled him forward so they could keep making their way through the crowds of people.

"Febraz is just ahead," Jujor said. "We will have to be careful how we approach him."

Terico thought over all the things he knew about vampires. They didn't like sunlight, didn't cast reflections in mirrors, and couldn't cross rivers or moving water in general. But most significantly, many of them preyed on people in the night, seeking to sink their fangs into the necks of unsuspecting passers-by and suck their victims dry. Supposedly vampires could live off the blood of animals, but from the stories Terico heard, it seemed most would prefer to kill humans and elves for their meals, giving themselves a boost of powerful energy in the process.

"Here he is." Jujor pointed to a closed tent just ahead of them.

Terico was a bit hesitant to meet this Febraz, but there was no turning back now. If he couldn't face a vampire, how would he be able to face the hordes of forsaken? Or the Brotherhood? Or Delkol? Perhaps Febraz would lash out at him, but he would be ready. Terico had his sword sheathed at his hip, and several Nexi stones in his trouser pockets. Perhaps Febraz was volatile—monstrous, even—but he had something Terico aimed to get, no matter the cost.

In front of the tent sat a small boy, likely no older than ten. His stand was covered with a variety of oddly-colored Nexi stones, as well as a number of chalices, goblets, and sparkling pendants. He wore blue and yellow robes, and had pointed ears. Terico knew vampires had slightly pointed ears, and he understood that they were nearly immortal, too. Was this little boy Febraz? For all Terico knew, this child was a thousand years old.

"Don't look so stunned," Jujor said in a low voice. "That's just an elven boy hired to run the stand. Febraz is in the tent, where it's nice and dark." "He can't go out in the light?" Terico asked.

"Not so loud," Jujor said. "Febraz's kind aren't looked at too warmly, you can imagine. Bad for business for people to know what he is... But to answer your question—no, he can go out in the light. He just doesn't like it, and would rather keep his identity a secret as much as he can. The longer it's a secret, the longer he can stay at one city, selling his wares."

"I see," Terico said. He walked up to the elven boy and glanced over the Nexi stones on the table. "Which one are we looking for?" he asked Jujor.

"It won't be out here, obviously," Jujor said. "We'll have to talk with Febraz personally."

"You know Febraz?" the boy running the stand asked.

"Yes, he's an old friend of mine," Jujor said. "Can we go see him?"

The boy looked down nervously. "I don't think so..."

Jujor turned to the tent and yelled, "Oy! Febraz!"

"Is that you, Jujor?" called out a voice from inside. "Please, I invite you to come in."

Terico was hesitant to follow Jujor into the tent, but he took a couple deep breaths and reassured himself that this would all be worth it in the end. As expected, it was dark inside the tent, lit by a single candle atop a small round table. There were three wooden chairs, the first of which was occupied by Febraz. He was a tall man with broad shoulders and pale skin as white as ash. Febraz looked to be in his twenties, but may have been much older.

"I see you've aged well," Jujor said.

"And I see you haven't," Febraz responded. He grinned, exposing two long vampiric fangs. The man had long black hair and light yellow eyes that almost seemed to glow in the dark. He wore all black and held a few wrinkled sheets of brown paper in his hands.

Jujor laughed and sat down across from Febraz, leaving Terico to take the seat between the two.

"It's good to see you again," Febraz said. "It's been too long."

"I kept meaning to send a letter," Jujor said. "Perhaps invite you for a drink. There's this great pub in... oh, never mind." Apparently he forgot for a moment that it had burned down with the rest of the village.

"You and your ridiculous drinks," Febraz said, his voice deep and smooth. "I have no taste for them, you know."

"Of course," Jujor said. "But it's the act of drinking together that matters, not the drink itself."

"Hm, well, I'll have to keep that in mind," Febraz said with his eyes half-closed. "Now how can I assist you, Jujor?"

"We're in the market for some soul catchers," Jujor said. "Think you can help an old friend out?"

"For a price, perhaps," Febraz said. "Whatever do you need soul catchers for?"

Jujor motioned a hand toward Terico. "Well, Terico and I will be heading underground soon, and will likely have a lot of forsaken to deal with. A couple soul catchers would help us fight them off as we go looking for something."

"You should know better than to go stirring up trouble with the forsaken," Febraz said. He placed an elbow on his table and rested the side of his head against his palm. "Now, what was it I saved your life from again? Ah, yes. *The forsaken.* Of course."

"This time will be different," Jujor said. "I'll have Terico leading the way, and we'll both have soul catchers. That is, if you lend them to us for a bit." Terico spoke up, looking toward Febraz. "So you saved Jujor's life?" Febraz gave a weary nod. "Yes, I happened to be in the mine that day Jujor's crew dug their way to a hive of forsaken. It was just on a whim, but I decided to save old Jujor's life."

"I wasn't old then," Jujor muttered. "And I've helped you plenty of times in return."

"Yes, yes," Febraz said, waving a hand up and down quickly. "But of the two of us, I'm the hero."

"We'll see about that," Jujor said. "Terico and I will be accomplishing big things in the near future. You'll be hearing heroic stories about us soon enough, if we can get a hold of some soul catchers."

"Very well," Febraz said. "I rather doubt you can afford to *buy* two soul catchers, so I'll have to think of some way you can pay me back for lending them out to you." He leaned to the side and pointed at Jujor's pack. "I imagine you have plenty of liquor in that bag of yours. Pull one out and have a drink."

Jujor sat up a little straighter and beamed. "You're taking me up on that offer, after all."

Febraz reached underneath his table and pulled up a corked bottle filled with crimson liquid. "I have my own drink, thank you very much." He pulled up a few ceramic mugs and pushed them so he and his guests each had one. The vampire picked up his bottle and pointed the end of it toward Terico. "Want some?"

Terico gave a deep frown and shook his head side to side.

Febraz laughed and started pouring some blood into his handpainted glass, which was covered in poorly-colored patterns likely drawn by a child. Terico wondered if Febraz had any children, and what exactly a vampire family would entail if that was the case.

While Jujor deliberated on what bottle of liquor to drink from, Terico watched the thin stream of blood pour from Febraz's bottle and splash into his cup. Terico didn't know where this blood came from or what species it had belonged to, but there was something a little strange about it all. Perhaps just the sight of someone pouring blood into a glass was bothering him, but there seemed to be something more troubling Terico. He stared at the blood, rising and falling along the inside of the mug as it dripped and sloshed into the vessel. It was very faint, but Terico noticed a slight residue left behind on the side of the glass. It would only last a moment, but the blood was briefly turning the inside surface of the ceramic mug from tan to a light gray.

Some kind of chemical reaction? Terico thought. As Febraz lifted his glass toward his lips, the realization struck Terico. In an instant, Terico was on his feet and wrenching the glass away from Febraz's mouth.

Febraz gasped, and Terico spilled blood on his sleeve and onto the table.

"What are you trying to do, boy?" Jujor asked.

"Liquid Coffin," Terico said. "This blood is poisoned."

"What?" Febraz asked. "I would have smelled something amiss if it were poisoned."

"It's an ancient poison used to kill vampires," Terico said. "An alchemical concoction that looks, smells, and tastes exactly like blood. It hasn't been regularly used for hundreds of years because the main ingredient was a very rare plant, and simpler poisons were developed later on."

"I've encountered poisons before, but never this Liquid Coffin," Febraz said. "How can you tell this isn't blood, though?"

"If you look closely, it reacts to the ceramic strangely," Terico said. "I wouldn't have noticed anything if it were poured into a glass cup, so you're fortunate you used this mug."

Febraz eased himself back in his chair. "I do see it now. Yes, blood shouldn't stick that much to the side, either. Very subtle..." He looked back up to Terico and smiled. "How did you notice that?"

"My father was an alchemist, so I read several books on potions growing up."

Terico sat back down and placed his hands on his lap. "There was a chapter on poisons for vampires, though I never expected I'd actually need to use that knowledge one day."

"And you probably never thought you'd use it to save a vampire's life, did you?" Febraz asked.

"To be honest—no, I didn't," Terico said.

Febraz turned to Jujor and nodded. "Good to see a boy with a head on his shoulders."

"I'm surprised, too," Jujor said. "But I guess now I can say I've saved your life, Febraz. We're finally even!"

"Maybe," Febraz said. "I wonder though... Why would this bottle be poisoned? It came from a friend of mine."

"You're letting people here know you're a vampire?" Jujor asked. "The general public doesn't suspect a thing," Febraz said. "But I do have a few friends I've come to trust over the years. This particular one has given me some rare blood from some of his adventures before. I have a feeling that he might have bought this bottle rather than obtained the blood himself."

"Ah, so the seller was just hoping to kill off some random vampires, wherever they may be," Jujor said.

"There is no way to be certain," Febraz said. "The seller could have been fooled just as well. It's interesting, just how many people can be deceived by one simple lie."

"And it leads all the way down to death," Jujor said.

The conversation paused a few moments, perhaps ending on a bit of a somber, more pensive note.

Febraz snapped a finger. "I believe our young Terico here needs to strike a deal with me."

"What do you have in mind?" Jujor asked. "You should give us the stones for free, for saving your life."

"Terico, I have two soul catchers," Febraz said, "but they cost a fortune. I think you would be capable of helping me out with a little something, so if you make a pact with me, I will gladly give you the Nexi stones you seek."

"A pact?" Terico asked.

"You will be marked," Febraz said. "It means you will be required to assist me with a single task, or forfeit your life. It won't be anything too much for you to handle, I imagine. But I've been hoping to find someone who can help out my d—" Febraz paused a moment. "Who can help me out. All you have to do is hold out you arm, and I will use a Nexi stone to create the mark of the pact."

Terico didn't like the idea of being required to fulfill any kind of task a vampire would have in mind for him. Though Jujor was friendly with Febraz, Terico really didn't know much about this man. For all Terico knew, being marked would make him Febraz's slave for life. Or perhaps the task Febraz would give him would put Terico's life unnecessarily at risk. What sorts of things would a vampire want him to do, anyways?

In the end, it didn't matter, Terico decided. If he needed the soul catchers, and this was the only way to get them—then he would likely do whatever it was Jujor asked. If it would bring Terico one step closer to killing Delkol, then he would do it.

He pulled his sleeve back and raised his arm toward Febraz.

"Do you realize what you're doing?" Jujor asked. "This isn't going to be a 'go to the store and pick me up some flour' kind of favor."

"I understand," Terico said, keeping his eyes on Febraz. "I will do whatever this man asks of me."

"Good, we have a deal then." The vampire slipped out a pallid white Nexi stone from his pocket. It glowed dimly in the candlelight, and looked about as pale and sickly as Febraz's skin.

Febraz placed the stone on Terico's left wrist. Within seconds, the rock dissipated into a misty white cloud. The sparkling flakes descended into Terico's skin, forming a black, intricate pattern. It looked like half of a spider's web with four arrows emerging from the top, reaching into Terico's palm and pointing toward his fingers.

"I will call on you when I need your assistance," Febraz said. He placed two light indigo Nexi stones on the table and grinned. "Have fun dealing with the forsaken, Terico. And be sure to keep an eye on Jujor for me, will you? I can never tell what that man's up to." "I'm right here, you know," Jujor said.

"Trying to hide things from you is a worthless endeavor," Febraz said. "But the more I let the boy know, the more even the playing field will be." Jujor stood up and nodded. "We'll have to try having a drink together again someday."

"Indeed," Febraz said. He turned to Terico and winked. "Be sure to keep a good hand on your sword's hilt at all times, Terico. You never know when you'll need to draw your blade."

Terico wasn't sure how to respond. He was now relying on a cryptic, bloodsucking vampire and a dodgy old man who continually grew a little more questionable to trust.

He wondered just how far down this path he would have to walk in order to obtain his revenge.

•

3

DEPTHS OF THE FORSAKEN

Once back in Edellerston, it didn't take long for Terico to lead Jujor to one of the cave entrances in the rocky hills just north of the burnt village. The sight of the town's remains was just as harrowing as it had been when the fires first died out, but it also strengthened Terico's resolve to not back down. It was a clear visual reminder of what he was fighting for, and why he was seeking out the Elpis.

Jujor had a red Nexi stone, which he caused to light the way down the cavern pathway. Terico led the way, however, and for the first hour most of the journey was fairly familiar to him. There were a number of stalactite formations that he used to go by when remembering which way to turn in order to keep heading downward.

From time to time Terico came across monsters, and Jujor left it to him each time to deal with them. At one point there were a few rockhoppers, which Terico tied up with a series of vines from his green Nexi. Later, a light yellow wisp tried possessing Jujor, but Terico managed to douse the ghostly light with the blue Nexi stone. He soaked Jujor as well in the process, much to the old man's umbrage.

The deeper into the cave they went, the more Terico wondered about the city as described in Jujor's old book. Jujor said it was a mystery why it was built so long ago, and why it was eventually abandoned centuries ago. Terico couldn't think of a good reason for Emoser Helena to be built so far below the earth. What would the people have lived off of? They certainly couldn't have grown crops without sunlight. Perhaps the Elpis stone played a part in the city's existence.

Jujor dimmed his red Nexi a bit to keep from straining himself, since it took a little effort to keep the light going. Terico offered to take it, but Jujor wanted him ready for any monsters that would jump out at them. At one junction Terico had to move aside a pile of large fallen rocks in order to continue down the path he and Jujor were taking. Terico had never been this far down the caves before, but Jujor felt they still had quite a ways to go before reaching Emoser Helena.

What may have been another hour passed—it was difficult to tell without the sun—and Terico started to feel a little drowsy. They had been walking down a thin, rock-floored path for so long, that traversing the jagged path had almost become a subconscious action. Terico had tried starting conversation with Jujor a couple more times earlier, but the old man was still avoiding any real answers about his life. Terico was curious to know more about the Elpis too though, so he decided to start there.

"So, why do you think the Elpis stone is down here?" he asked. "It's likely just a fragment," Jujor said. "And I can't be certain why it's in an underground city. There are all kinds of theories. To keep monsters away.
To provide light for the citizens. To create food for everyone down there. To create a protective barrier against outsiders. To hold up the earth around the city. Of course, all this brings up the question of why people would have a city down here in the first place. My guess is that the original intention of the city was to act as a place to keep the Elpis fragment hidden."

"How did the Elpis stone break apart?" Terico asked. "And when was it found in the first place?

"Most of the legends say the Elpis was the stone that the God of Hope used to create all the Nexi stones," Jujor said. "All the Nexi were buried deep in the earth so people would learn to work hard for their rewards, and to rely on divine powers in their daily lives. Don't know if any of that's true, but that's the general sentiment of the ancient stories.

"But where the Elpis was found and who found it is very unclear. When it was in the hands of a benevolent ruler, the people in the land lived without suffering or fear—the world was a paradise, if you will. But when a cruel, self-serving ruler used the Elpis, the entire continent fell into ruin. In some sources, it is said that the Elpis could be used to kill hundreds of people in a single instant.

"Eventually a man—some say the first king of Fiefs—managed to obtain the Elpis and break it into pieces. It's been hundreds of years since anyone has used an Elpis, because the fragments have been hidden away...

far, far away from one another."

"How did the king break the Elpis?" Terico asked.

"Again, the stories vary," Jujor said. "Some say he and a council of thirty-one alchemists managed to concoct a liquid that would break the stone apart into a hundred pieces once dipped in it. Others say a powerful elf, eigni, human, and vampire each sacrificed his or her life, enacting an ancient spell powerful enough to break the Elpis into four pieces. And one interesting tale describes the king summoning the ghost of a giant narwhal, which stabbed the stone into two halves with its tusk."

Terico didn't know what to think of any of these stories. He had heard many tales reminiscent of these ones as a child, and growing up he felt they were mainly just meant to entertain or help explain things about the world. But who knew? Perhaps some of these things did happen. The Nexi opened up the possibility for many astounding things, especially when rare, powerful stones were used.

His mind mostly on the Elpis, Terico continued to lead the way down the cavern trail with a wide variety of expectations settling in his thoughts.

Eventually he wondered what would happen when he did obtain the Elpis fragment, assuming it was still down there.

And what if Jujor is the one who gets his hands on the Elpis? Terico thought. Would the old man try to use its power? Was it possible that Jujor was coming down here for the sake of getting the Elpis for himself? He was an old man, and needed someone to help him fend off the monsters and forsaken in order to get to the stone. How long had Jujor known about the likelihood of the Elpis fragment being down below Edellerston? Was that the real reason Jujor moved to the village? And did he stick around in the pub in order to hear the tales of all the travelers passing through, in hopes of learning something more about the Elpis, or about the caves?

The sound of deep, gurgling screeches echoed in the distance, breaking Terico's train of thought. All at once, Terico heard at least a dozen monstrous cries, their grating noises overlapping one another in a horrendous racket.

"The forsaken," Jujor said. Terico looked back and saw Jujor's disconcerted expression. Even in the dim red light, it was clear to see how pale and worried the old man had quickly become. The sound was likely bringing back memories of his first and nearly fatal encounter with the undying creatures.

Terico unsheathed his sword and held it tight in his right hand, and picked out the indigo soul catcher from his pouch of Nexi stones.

The liquid shrieks grew louder, and for a few moments Terico thought he heard them coming from multiple directions. He stared down the dark cavern and readied himself to attack. The beat of his heart quickened, moving in harmony with the constant screeching of the forsaken.

Beneath the screams, Terico could hear the pattering of feet and claws. He took a deep breath, gritted his teeth, and raised his soul catcher forward. Seven forsaken charged into the light of Jujor's red Nexi. They ran on all fours. Fleshy, long-limbed, and wolf-like, the forsaken rushed in with the force of paws larger than a man's head. Dim red light glinted off their massive claws, their fanged teeth, their dark glossy eyes, and the metallic scales sticking out of their backs and limbs.

Terico aimed his Nexi stone toward the nearest of the forsaken. With all the energy he could muster, Terico forced a burst of indigo light to shoot out from the soul catcher.

The beast snapped its jaw at the light, and leaped straight for Terico, completely unhindered.

Terico stepped back and shoved his sword forward, jabbing his blade straight through the forsaken's neck. The creature snarled and swung a giant clawed paw for Terico's face.

"Turn!" Jujor yelled.

Terico leaned back and turned. A burst of flame blasted into the forsaken's body, forcing Terico to let go of his sword. A stream of indigo light crashed into the burning forsaken a moment later, but Terico couldn't watch to see if it worked.

He turned to the next two nearest forsaken and fired his soul catcher at one, while slipping out his green Nexi and aiming it for the second. Using two Nexi at the same time was difficult, but Terico was caught up in the heat of the action. The first forsaken snapped at the blast of the soul catcher, but Terico managed to tie up the legs of the second beast with vines.

The free forsaken pounced toward Terico, who grabbed the first Nexi his hand could reach. He wrenched the stone out of his bag and released its energy against the forsaken's torso. Ice covered the sprawling creature instantly, and the beast crashed atop of Terico before he could step out of the way.

The other forsaken bit off the vines tying its legs, having no problem with tearing off portions of its own flesh in the process. As Terico pushed aside the frozen—now only half-frozen— forsaken, he caught a glimpse of the other four creatures rushing for him.

"We're not strong enough to catch their souls right away!" Jujor said. "Disable them, and then use the indigo Nexi. Shut your eyes!" Terico complied just as blinding white light burst from a Nexi stone. He opened his eyes immediately after he heard the snap of Jujor's attack. Jujor wrenched Terico's sword from an unmoving forsaken at his feet, and tossed it to Terico while the rest of the forsaken screeched and moaned from the light. For their eyes, the flash had to be far worse than it would for a human being.

While one forsaken was still struggling with the ice on its body, Terico aimed his soul catcher and tried once again to defeat it. The indigo light dived for the creature, and a moment later Terico felt a surge of energy rush back up his arm. The Nexi stone glowed a little brighter, and the forsaken stopped struggling to break apart the ice covering it.

The creatures recovered from Jujor's attack, and Terico immediately used his white Nexi stone to blind them again. The nearest forsaken leaped for him anyways. Terico skewered the forsaken in the chest, and the creature boomed a raspy, watery laugh.

It *laughed.*

Before the forsaken could claw Terico apart, Terico blasted indigo light against it, pulling the soul out of the creature and into Terico's indigo Nexi. He shoved the forsaken from the blade of his sword and aimed his green Nexi for a forsaken charging at Jujor, who was releasing fire at another of the creatures.

Terico tied up the forsaken's legs and charged for it. He jabbed the creature in the back, but it reacted faster than Terico anticipated. The beast slammed the back of its massive paw against Terico's side, knocking him against the cavern wall and forcing the Nexi stones from his hand.

Another forsaken charged for Terico as he tried to regain his footing. His vision was dizzy and the upper half of his body ached with giant bruises, but he managed to grab the dark blue Nexi stone from his bag. He shot out water against the forsaken, pushing it back long enough for Terico to grab the soul catcher off the ground and aim it for the tied-up forsaken he had stabbed. Terico shot off the indigo light and caught the creature's soul, then turned for the forsaken recovering from the blast of water.

As the roaring forsaken regained its footing, Terico rushed for it with his sword drawn forward, his entire body burning with the intensity of the moment. The forsaken leaped for Terico, who turned to the side and slammed his blade straight into the beast's face. The creature fell to the ground, but was immediately back on its feet—now standing on only two feet. It stood nearly a half-meter taller than Terico, and that was even with its abnormally thin, lanky torso curved down from a shriveled, hunched back. The forsaken's face was nearly torn in half, black and red blood streaming from the gash stretched from one wolfish ear to the other. And still it swiped its claws toward Terico's chest.

Terico leaped back to avoid the creature's freakishly sharp talons, then blasted a stream of water against its pallid, fleshy body. It fell to all fours and shoved against the water, still strong enough to keep fighting. Another forsaken charged for Terico from the side. While still pushing back against the first creature with the dark blue Nexi in his left hand, Terico turned to the second creature, his sword drawn forward in his right hand. The forsaken leaped for Terico's head.

Terico drove his blade into the forsaken's heart, then shoved it into the stream of water rushing from his Nexi stone. The stabbed forsaken crashed into the other forsaken, and both collided with a giant stalagmite reaching toward the ceiling. Jujor ran toward the two creatures and used his indigo Nexi to catch both of the forsaken's souls.

The deep screeching and gravelly roaring stopped all at once, and Terico fell to his knees from sheer exhaustion. All seven of the forsaken lay still— a few of them covered in terrible burns—but completely still, nonetheless. The cave turned silent, but Terico felt his head ringing for several long minutes afterward.

"You used the Nexi stones a bit too much there," Jujor said. "You'll need to rest a bit."

Terico nodded, too tired to say anything. Jujor picked up the stones Terico dropped and put them back in the small bag tied at Terico's belt. Terico shakily looked over the forsaken lying around him. They had looked a lot like wolves when they ran in for the kill, but now it was clear they had a very human appearance. There were only a few patches of ragged fur poking out of their torn-up skin, and though their limbs were freakishly contorted, Terico could still tell they were arms and legs. The forsaken even still had on the tattered remains of clothing in various states of disarray. The very idea that the most sinister and lethal of monsters were in fact humans was... It was *disgusting*. But here they were, something not quite human, not quite monster—and not even quite alive. Even with a fatal blow to the face, these creatures lashed out at their victims, laughing all the way.

How had human beings fallen this low? Where had these men and women come from?

When Terico thought it over enough, it seemed the most likely explanation was that these were the citizens of Emoser Helena. They had somehow become creatures of the darkness. Jujor had Terico sit on the ground until Terico stopped shaking. He had never faced so many creatures all at once. The forsaken's hideous cries echoed in his head, as if even now they were still alive, still hoping to shred him into pieces.

He stared at the still-open eyes of the nearest forsaken—a man who couldn't have been much older than twenty before he transformed. His eyes were no longer human, the whites of his eyes now black, and the retinas and pupils a lightly glowing red—and still glowing, even now. The thought that the creature could still be alive in some form made Terico shudder, but he couldn't look away. He wished it hadn't fallen with its eyes open.

The forsaken closed its eyes.

Terico jumped to his feet and unsheathed his sword. The forsaken continued to lie there, motionless. For several long seconds, Terico held his position, his heart beating frantically. He waited for the forsaken to leap up at him, but the creature did nothing but lie there. It wasn't breathing, but Terico didn't think the forsaken breathed when they were alive, either.

"What's wrong?" Jujor asked.

"It closed its eyes," Terico said.

Jujor looked at the forsaken, keeping a safe distance from it. "And you're sure you captured its soul?"

"Yes," Terico said. He backed away from the creature cautiously, hoping to put some more distance between them.

The forsaken stood up on two legs and took a few steps back.

Terico raised his soul catcher, but the forsaken didn't do anything more. It simply stood there, its eyes still closed.

"Are you doing that?" Jujor asked.

Terico glanced back at him a moment. "What do you mean?"

"Well, technically we're the owners of these creatures' souls, now." Jujor took his indigo Nexi and stared at one of the burnt forsaken he had defeated. The creature stood up, placed its arms behind its back, and bowed toward Jujor. The image seemed to epitomize the definition of *surreal*, considering how only minutes ago it was an insane beast intent on tearing them limb from limb.

"We can control them?" Terico said. He gripped his soul catcher tight and looked to each of the forsaken he defeated. With just the force of his concentrated thoughts, Terico caused the four creatures to stand upright, then flex their clawed hands in and out in unison.

Terico smiled. "Things just got a lot more interesting."

•

It took some time to navigate the deeper chambers of the cave, but Jujor was tired and Terico was still recovering a bit from his overuse of the Nexi stones. Fortunately it took very little effort to keep the forsaken walking in front of them, making them act as bodyguards in the event that more of the creatures came to attack.

In the dim glow of Jujor's red Nexi, Terico caught sight of an open area at the end of the tunnel. He and Jujor followed their forsaken to what turned out to be a wide, deep pit. Grafted to the roof of the cave were eleven spiral staircases which worked their way down the massive hole. The steps were long and wide, and there were several meters of empty space between each of the metal stairways.

"This will lead us down to the city, I imagine," Jujor said. "It'll probably be a long way down."

"I guess we pick a stairway, then," Terico said. Each of the staircases looked pretty battered and dented up, and there was no telling which one might have a bunch of forsaken working their way up. Terico listened for any sign of the creatures below, but couldn't hear anything.

Jujor led his three forsaken down a walkway leading to the fourth metal staircase. It was one of the better-looking stairways, so Terico decided to follow Jujor down it.

"You should take a different stairway," Jujor said. "If a hundred forsaken rush up the one we're on, we'll both get killed. Might as well have one of us survive, if that happens." "A hundred?" Terico said.

"There's a whole city down there," Jujor said. "I imagine the citizens became these creatures somehow. Over the centuries they've dug tunnels far and wide, attacking miners in caverns for kilometers around. But as long as their souls aren't captured, they can live on forever, it seems. For all we know, there are a hundred thousand forsaken waiting below us."

Their army of seven forsaken didn't seem so useful if that was really what they were going to be up against. Fortunately they didn't need to fight all the creatures—they only needed to find the Elpis and get out of there.

Terico led his forsaken down the fifth stairway, which looked about

as safe as the one Jujor took. There was a good twenty or so meters between the two stairways, though.

He walked cautiously down the metal steps, and made his forsaken tread lightly as well. The staircase squeaked and grated with each step, but the echoes were light and dim.

"Hopefully these things hold," Jujor said. "I think there used to be a staircase between the ones we're going down."

Terico looked at the giant, dark gap between him and Jujor. There was no way to see how far the stairways went, and Jujor's light gave little for Terico to see by. He hoped that there weren't steps missing, though he felt he'd be safe following his forsaken. If there was a hole ahead, they'd fall for him. Terico made them hold their arms out so that they'd be able to grab on to surrounding steps in the event that one of them fell.

Minute after minute passed, and Terico felt a little more anxious with each turn of the giant staircase. The further down he went, the darker and quieter things seemed to get. There was always the constant creaking of the old metal steps, but the noise eventually turned dim in the back of Terico's head.

How long he walked down the stairs, he couldn't imagine. Perhaps an hour passed—perhaps two. But still he continued to walk down the steps, further and further into an underworld that seemed to be made more out of darkness, rather than stone.

It was difficult to concentrate, step after step, hour after hour. The utter monotony of the spiraling descent was tiring, and the fact Terico was accompanied by a group of forsaken gave the situation an especially foreboding atmosphere.

Every now and then he called out to Jujor, whose voice would always echo from the opposite staircase, generally from several meters above Terico's elevation. The old man was a bit slower than Terico, and that would put a good distance between them every ten, twenty minutes. Terico had to keep a bit of concentration on his forsaken, but he would still think of other things as well. Journeying through the caves reminded him of his times with Turan, and how they would sneak out of class to go look for rare rocks, plants, and creatures underground. Sometimes it was to earn a bit of money or to help someone out with some task, but the main reason for it all was for the sake of adventure.

Terico's journey with Jujor didn't have the same kind of feeling as his brief treks with Turan, however. Though Jujor had some wit about him, he lacked Turan's gift of gab and lighthearted nature. Plus Terico couldn't be truly certain where Jujor's loyalties lay in all this, while he never had to worry for even a second whether or not Turan had his back. At times Terico felt he and Turan were more like brothers than friends, just from the sheer amount of time they spent together.

Thoughts of the past reminded Terico of what this endeavor was for. If he could get the Elpis fragment, he'd be able to meet with Delkol—and likely be able to reach the murderer's brother Augurc as well. Terico would never forgive Augurc if anything happened to Turan. The sooner Terico found Augurc, the sooner he'd be able to stop the effects of the madman's experiments on Turan—assuming that was what his friend was captured for.

Jujor eventually called back to Terico, which let him know how far away the old man was. They were at about the same level again, so Terico got his forsaken moving again.

Yet another hour seemed to pass, and still they continued down the stairway.

•

Terico looked up over the railing to the endless spiral above him, then peered down to the infinite vortex below. A part of him wondered if he was caught in a loop that would magically go on forever. What if there was a point on the staircase that sent him back a few hundred steps, and he was actually just walking down the same few hundreds steps again and again and again?

He payed careful attention to the steps beneath his feet. It was too difficult to really see anything, but he could feel the bumps and dents in the thick sheets of metal. After completing a few more circles of the staircase, Terico noted a couple more unique-feeling steps—one that made a sort of loud pop when he stepped on it, and another that had a thick, jagged cut in the middle.

Terico watched for these two steps to come again. He walked on, following the plodding movements of the forsaken in front of him.

He started counting the steps, and he was almost at the four hundredth step when Jujor called out to him again.

"The echoing has changed."

Terico listened carefully, and sure enough, the sounds of everyone's footsteps was slightly different.

It took a while longer, but they soon reached the final step of their staircases without any problems arising. It was a relief to be on the ground again, though Terico knew there wasn't much reason to feel safe.

Though it was too dark to see far, Terico could tell he was standing in a massive, expansive cave. His footsteps didn't echo, and the ground felt a lot more stable beneath his feet. Jujor brightened the light of his red Nexi so they could see a bit further around themselves. The floor was flat and smooth at first, though later became littered with rocks and boulders. At first Terico thought these were just random stones, but on closer inspection he realized the ground was covered with rubble. It was hard to see much, but there was evidence of great stone buildings all around him—all in complete disarray. It was as if a great earthquake had wiped out the entire city.

"The whole place is probably like this," Jujor said. "We'll have to go deeper into the city to find the Elpis fragment, though."

They made their way between fallen buildings, their piles of stones reaching tens of meters in height at times. How Emoser Helena had been destroyed, Terico could only guess. If going by Jujor's stories though, it wouldn't be unlikely for the Elpis to have been involved.

Terico and Jujor sometimes paused to look in what was still standing of some of the structures, many of which had been built straight into the walls of the cave. Jujor was certain the Elpis would be glowing bright, so it wouldn't be hard to recognize it once they found a shining light. This was still a great city, however. It would take time to figure out where the stone was hidden.

The cave erupted with the blood-curdling screams of forsaken. All at once, tens of shrieks rang off the distant walls of the fallen city.

"We need to hurry," Jujor said. "Every forsaken in the city will hear this racket, and suddenly we'll have a thousand of them to deal with."

Terico, Jujor, and their seven puppet forsaken ran down the battered street of the city, weaving between the fallen stonework of the homes and shops the forsaken must have occupied back when they were human. Terico readied his sword and Nexi stones, but kept his eyes searching for the glowing light of the Elpis fragment.

Three—no, five—forsaken leaped from holes in a wrecked building about twenty meters ahead. Terico forced three of his forsaken to rush for them, while Jujor sent two of his to take care of the others. They caused their forsaken to claw away at their enemies, until all of them were wrestling and snarling amidst the piles of sharp rocks and rubble.

Another forsaken slipped out from a hole in a giant stone platform. Terico sent one of his forsaken to fight it, and another struggle ensued. All around him, the creatures were clawing at each other, sometimes tearing open great, bloody wounds—and even shredding apart entire limbs in the process.

Terico and Jujor used their indigo Nexi to catch more of the creatures' souls, and within a minute all the forsaken were weakened enough for all of them to fall under Terico and Jujor's control.

"Hurry," Jujor said. "We won't be able to keep this up forever."

Terico forced his forsaken to run to either side of him, following Jujor and his growing unit of forsaken. He could hear more of the creatures rushing for them from side roads and fallen buildings, the scraping of their monstrous claws giving them away beneath the constant noise of their screeches.

Terico and Jujor sent their captured forsaken off to fend against the new assailants. The creatures crashed into one another on all fours, swiping their claws against each other's faces. Terico followed Jujor's lead and continued capturing more forsaken as they ran through the battlefield. Those that they captured were often torn apart to varying degrees, but they could still run and fight with little hindrance from their injuries. Neither alive nor dead, nothing slowed the creatures from their ravenous bloodlust.

More and more of the forsaken ran for Terico and Jujor, some in groups of ten—some in twenty. The strain of controlling so many creatures was taxing, but Terico kept all his forsaken always running, always clawing. Again and again, he used his soul catcher to bring more of the forsaken into his ranks. Every now and then a forsaken or two would slip through and leap for Terico, but he would use his Nexi stones and sword to fend them off long enough for Jujor to capture them with his soul catcher.

The city boomed with the shrieks of tens of forsaken. Hundreds. All around him, Terico heard more and more of them charging toward them, howling, hissing, snarling, snapping their teeth. There were probably at least a hundred forsaken Terico was controlling now, and his whole body felt weak—each step he took, his limbs ached incessantly.

Keep moving, he told himself. *Don't stop for even a second!* "I see something!" Jujor said.

Terico looked to where the old man pointed. On the other side of a massive chasm, a small glint of light glowed with ever-shifting hues and colors. It wasn't blinding, but it was intense. The glow that emanated from the small rock spread far wider than the glow of any Nexi stone Terico had seen before. It was going to be difficult to get to it, with it so high up and on the other side of a giant gorge.

And with a thousand forsaken in the way.

"Just plow through them, Jujor!" Terico yelled.

Tens of forsaken rushed out of cracks in a long wall to Terico's left. He sent as many of his own forsaken as he could spare toward them and continued to run. Three creatures slipped by, and at the same time a couple more leaped from the third story of a half-destroyed structure above Terico. Meanwhile, Jujor controlled tens of forsaken to hack away at the hordes rushing from the trail ahead, while blasting fire at several more coming for him from behind.

Terico activated his light blue Nexi, freezing the ground in front of the three forsaken charging for him. As the creatures slipped on the ice, Terico

turned to the ones leaping for him from above. He used his dark blue Nexi to blast them away with water. His controlled forsaken continued to fight off tens of others, and Terico blasted away with his soul catcher to force as many more of the creatures to his side as possible. Jujor continued to push his way forward, only pausing a few seconds at a time to blind large groups of forsaken swarming around him. Terico rushed into the fray with a few dozen puppet forsaken encircling him. The wolf people tore at each other's throats, spilling blood around Terico in a hellish rampage.

Terico sprinted through the multitude of forsaken, swinging his sword in a mad, blind frenzy. Limbs, heads, blood, and gore flew from his blade and the claws of his forsaken army, as blasts of blinding light and fiery explosions pushed back tens of the undying creatures around him.

Terico and Jujor continued using their soul catchers, but the strain was too much to continue like this. There were still hundreds of forsaken between them and the cliff, and then a bottomless pit between the cliff and the Elpis fragment.

A forsaken lunged for Terico's throat. Terico avoided its claws and continued to fight his way forward, at times running across the sharp metallic-spined backs of the forsaken in the process. Which of the creatures were under Terico and Jujor's control at this point was impossible to tell— as far as Terico could see, the world was a sea of claws, fur, flesh, and blood.

A couple forsaken slipped past Terico's captured creatures. Terico used his green Nexi to bind one, then readied his light blue Nexi to freeze the other. The instant the first forsaken was bound by vines, the second creature immediately latched its teeth on the vine and pulled. It wrenched the stone straight from Terico's grasp, almost making him lose all his other stones in the process.

Another forsaken leaped for Terico from behind. Terico turned and swung his sword into the creature's chest. He stumbled back, crashing against the back of a forsaken standing upright. The beast turned and swiped its claws for Terico, who swung his sword for it with the first forsaken still impaled in it. Two more forsaken rushed through the multitude, straight for Terico.

He left his blade and sprinted forward, blasting the two with light from his white Nexi. The beasts leaped for him blindly, and one of them crashed atop of him with its torso.

Terico struggled against the frantic forsaken, which clawed the rocks to either side of him in a mad, screeching craze. Terico shoved against it, and the beast slammed the end of its paw against his arm, flinging away all of his Nexi stones. With his free arm, Terico reached for the soul catcher and forced one of his forsaken to leap into the side of the creature attacking him. The tens of forsaken to either side of Terico brawled unceasingly, tearing each other apart until their enemies were in pieces. Terico lost sight of all his remaining Nexi save for the light blue one, so he grabbed it and ran.

"Keep going!" Jujor screamed above the wild cries of the forsaken.

How the old man was holding up, Terico couldn't stop to tell. He ran onward, his heart racing, his lungs nearly giving out. On and on, more of the creatures rushed for him, screeching and yelping. Terico controlled as many forsaken as he could manage, stopping the legions of monsters dead in their tracks.

The end was in sight. The cliff was near, but Terico didn't have a feasible way of crossing the massive abyss. The gap had to be at least ten meters long, and Terico didn't have his green Nexi. He almost considered running back for it, knowing he'd be able to reach the Elpis with vines if he still had it. There was no way to find it now though, lost amidst the mobs of bleeding, growling creatures.

Terico kept running. He kept sending in more forsaken to protect him, kept capturing more of the beasts whenever the opportunity arose— but his mind was a whirlwind of chaos, sheer madness.

He sprinted toward the cliff, pushing past fighting forsaken with every step, many of the beasts crawling atop one another to get at their prey. Terico's mind was weary, barely able to formulate coherent thoughts as he struggled to maintain control of so many forsaken. His entire body burned and trembled from the pain and exhaustion of so much running, so much Nexi use, so much fighting, so much screaming, so much insanity.

With a light blue Nexi in one hand and the soul catcher in the other, Terico reached the edge of the cliff. He stopped and turned around, an entire wave of forsaken leaping for him from every direction possible. Terico's forsaken bashed and clawed against the hordes of mindless beasts, but it only temporarily slowed the swarms down.

Terico got an idea. *I have it.*

He forced all his puppet forsaken to turn to him and run as fast as they possibly could. Terico turned to the nearest forsaken and with all his might, blasted frozen air from his light blue Nexi stone.

His body nearly collapsed from the effort, but the forsaken froze instantly, encased in a large sheet of ice grafted to the floor and rubble of the cavern and side of the cliff. Terico guided the next several of his creatures to rush to the frozen forsaken. Terico froze the second forsaken to the end of the first, then froze the third to the end of the second. He had to use all his strength to make the ice strong enough to hold, and he had to get the forsaken to leap out with their arms and legs stretched as far as possible. It wouldn't take much more of this though for Terico to black out from overusing the Nexi.

Terico turned to the tens of forsaken leaping for him. He ducked beneath some, letting them jump off the cliff, then rushed for the creatures he froze to the side of the cliff. With the power of his indigo Nexi, Terico forced more of his controlled forsaken to rush up the slowly-forming ice bridge of frozen forsaken. He kept some of his beasts fighting off the enemy forsaken, though they were quickly being torn apart by the ravenous monsters. Terico made his way up his ice bridge and forced more of his forsaken to run up after him. The creatures would leap over Terico and run on to the end of the bridge, where Terico would freeze them to the ends of the previously frozen forsaken. The bridge was slick and narrow, and would likely only have the strength to last this one trip across.

But Terico only needed to reach the Elpis fragment. Once it was in his hands, it would all be over.

More and more of Terico's forsaken ran up the slowly-growing ice bridge, but several of the opposing creatures forced their way after them, and fighting between the beasts ensued atop the weak, crackling bridge. Terico slid down and shoved the beasts off, then ordered more of his puppet forsaken to leap past him and on up to the top of the bridge.

What seemed like a hundred more of the wolf-like creatures leaped out from the anarchy of beasts amongst the shadowy stone rubble. Terico turned and ran after the puppet forsaken ahead of him. Dizzy and nauseous, he felt as if he was slipping off the edge every step of the way.

He kept running, and with all his might he froze the forsaken running forward in front of him. He jumped atop of each frozen forsaken and kept freezing more of them until he reached the other side of the cliff. Moments after he collapsed on the stone ground, the swarms of fighting forsaken rushed onto the bridge of ice and beasts, collapsing it.

Terico took deep, painful breaths, but knew he couldn't stop to rest. Jujor was still out there, fighting off an entire city of the foul creatures.

Terico looked up to the Elpis fragment several meters above him. It was only a matter of climbing now, and there were plenty of nooks and protrusions to use as footholds. Standing back up made his vision black out for a moment. Fighting against the pain, Terico slipped his Nexi stones in his bag and climbed up toward the glowing Elpis.

His muscles strained and a part of him just wanted to shut his eyes and lose consciousness, but he kept pushing himself upward. As soon as he was in reach of the Elpis, Terico placed his hand on its smooth opal surface.
A surge of energy shot through his entire body. All his pain, fatigue,

headache, and injury vanished instantly.

Only to be replaced by an overwhelming blast of agonizing torture. Terico felt as if his insides were on fire, his lungs were breathing in water, his body was constricted in vines, and his mind was freezing in stinging ice. He felt as if he were screaming, but heard nothing. The entire world turned silent, and an all-encompassing light of changing colors consumed everything in Terico's vision.

He pulled his hand back, but the Elpis stuck to the palm of his hand. Terico fell backward, losing his grip and footing on the cavern wall.

But he didn't fall. The jolt of pain coursing through his body vanished as suddenly as it came, and Terico continued to lie in the air. It was obviously through the power of the Elpis that he was defying gravity, but he did not know how he was wielding it.

He turned down toward the endless masses of forsaken and took out his soul catcher and light blue Nexi. In the light of the Elpis, both of the Nexi stones shattered into dust. The power of even a fragment of the Elpis overwhelmed that of entire Nexi—even those as rare as the indigo soul catcher.

The thought came to Terico that with the energy of the Elpis, he should be able to take the souls of all the forsaken. He had felt the fire, the water, the vines, and the ice within the Elpis when he touched it. It made sense that the stone would have the power of all Nexi.

With a mere thought, the thousands of forsaken turned toward the cliff and sprinted right off the end of it. Every forsaken within Terico's sight ran as fast as they could, straight for the abyss beneath him.

With unnatural sight, Terico could see Jujor amidst the bloodstained rubble clearly, as if the old man were standing just a few meters in front of him. The darkness did nothing to hinder Terico's vision, as glowing light poured from his eyes, lighting everything he gazed at. Jujor looked badly hurt, but he was still standing.

This power... Terico thought. *This is how I will kill Delkol. I will kill him with the very power he sought for. The very thing he destroyed my entire village for!*
Every bone in Terico's body cracked simultaneously. He stumbled back against the cavern wall, then fell to the hard ground beneath him. He screamed and writhed in pain as he felt all the blood in his body freeze, and every pore of his skin erupt in flames.

He could hear Jujor yelling Terico's name, but it felt distant, as if a cry from some long-forgotten memory. Terico tried to let go of the Elpis fragment, but it stuck to him. He screamed and flailed, the pain coursing through his body like a waterfall of blades.

•

Terico opened his eyes, gasping for breath.

He was still underground, enveloped in darkness. He lay on cold, hard stone, but saw Jujor with the dim red glow of his Nexi nearby.

"Good, you're alive," Jujor said. "You weren't even breathing for a while, there."

It took a couple minutes for Terico to slow his breathing a bit and regain his composure. His mind pounded with a terrible headache, but otherwise his body wasn't in any more of that terrible pain the Elpis gave him. He looked in his hand and saw it wasn't there.

"Don't worry, I've got it," Jujor said. "I've got it in its own bag. It seems that it released some of its energy into you when you touched it. Have to learn how to control it to keep from being overwhelmed by it all.

Probably takes a Nexi master to even think of attempting it." "I'll need it in order to bring Delkol to me," Terico said.

"That's fine," Jujor said. "I'll give it back to you. But first we'll have to figure out a way back out of the city. There are sure to be more forsaken out there. And I'm in no condition to fight anymore." "Were you hurt?" Terico asked.

"I got clawed in the back," Jujor said. "I've already taken care of it though, while you were unconscious."

Terico looked around and saw he was back on the other side of the cliff. "How did you get me back over here?"

"You dropped this." Jujor slipped a green Nexi out of his pocket and handed it back to Terico. He apparently used vines to bring Terico across the ravine.
After Terico explained how he lost all his Nexi stones, Jujor took a light blue Nexi from his pouch and gave it to Terico.

"Thanks, Jujor," Terico said. "You've helped me a lot already."

"It's thanks to you we've got the Elpis fragment, though," Jujor said, smiling. "This opens up a whole world of possibilities.

Terico wondered what possibilities Jujor was thinking of, but decided not to bring it up. It was still unclear what Jujor's goals were in all this, and the fact that he possessed the stone at the moment forced Terico to not do anything rash or suspicious.

"Judging by the size of the fragment," Jujor said, "I'd say we have a quarter of the stone. There are three more pieces out there, but who knows how many Delkol has."

"He may already have the other three," Terico said. "We'll have to make sure he never gets this one."

A light gray light shined from the mark on Terico's wrist and palm. Terico blinked a couple times, unsure of what to make of it.

Within a few seconds, the light spread across the rest of his body.

"The mark!" Jujor said. "It's—"

Terico vanished before he could hear the rest of Jujor's cry.

•

A moment later, Terico appeared in a bright space, and he shielded his eyes from the painful light.

"What's wrong?" asked a familiar voice. It sounded like Febraz. "It's bright," Terico said. "Where am I?"

"We are in my tent..." Febraz said. "There is only one candle lit." Terico slowly inched his eyes open and realized he really was inside the shadowy darkness of Febraz's tent. It just seemed bright when compared to the pitch black of Emoser Helena. He saw he was sitting on one of Febraz's chairs, and outside Terico could hear the continuous chattering of the

marketplace. It was strange, to say the least, to be back in a normal city filled with normal people so suddenly. Well, save for Febraz.

"So why am I in your tent, exactly?" Terico asked.

"I activated your mark to bring you back to me," Febraz said. "I realize this is pretty sudden, but I need your help with something."

Apparently Febraz was able to bring him all the way back to Merze via the magical mark the vampire gave him. The fact Febraz already needed Terico was peculiar, and it was unnerving that Terico was whisked away like this without warning.

"But now Jujor's left all alone in that cave," Terico said. "And he—"

And he has the Elpis fragment, Terico was about to say. But the less people knew about what Terico was doing, the better.

"As long as he has the soul catcher, he should be fine," Febraz said. "I do apologize for this, but we did agree that you would help me when I called for you. Complete this task, and the mark will disappear and you will be free to continue whatever it is you are up to."

This was it, then. Time to find out what this vampire had in mind for Terico. After all he had just been through, Terico didn't think Febraz could really come up with a task that was so terrible.

Febraz took a sip of blood from his crudely-painted mug, then set it back down on his table.

He looked down at Terico with sharp, glowering yellow eyes. "Can you *please* help my precious little daughter win a competition?"

•

4

A DEADLY GAME

It wasn't quite what Terico expected to hear, but he waited for a further explanation before giving a reaction. The competition Febraz had in mind could have been any number of things.
"I am certain you will be able to handle this," Febraz said. "Areo is a strong girl and will be all right, as long as the fight is kept fair." "Fight?" Terico asked.

"Yes," Febraz said. "My sweet little darling is turning one hundred this year, so she can take part in the Rite. If she passes, she will at last be able to reunite with me, here under the sun."

There were several things in these two sentences Terico wasn't quite understanding. His thoughts stumbled with what to ask about first.

"Wait... one hundred?"

"Ah, it must sound old to a human," Febraz said. "One moment." He set his mug of blood down on the table and glanced around his dark, candlelit tent. Terico looked around as well, finding a variety of wooden chests and crates. There were a few sheathed swords atop some of the boxes, and a number of odd, shiny trinkets here and there. Febraz got up and picked up a small, framed picture lying atop one of the crates. He walked back to the table and handed Terico the picture before sitting back down.

"This was painted about four years ago," Febraz said. "She used to have such nice long hair, but I suppose her mentor wanted her to have it cut." Terico lifted the picture a bit closer to the candlelight and tilted it so he could see the image. It was a portrait of someone's face, though if Febraz hadn't said this was his daughter, Terico would have probably guessed this was a boy. This Areo had a rather jagged, masculine face, with dark brown eyes and short brown hair. She didn't look very happy. "She used to be human?" Terico asked.

"Yes, until she was seventeen," Febraz said. "Her blood parents died of illness when she was only six, so she had to live on her own for quite some time. We crossed paths one day when I was staggering down the road, almost fatally injured, and she gave me a rabbit she had caught in a trap. The animal's blood rejuvenated me, and I learned how she had survived the last four years on her own, selling rabbit pelts for her bread. We ended up sticking together, and I raised her as best an outcast vampire could."

"But then you made her a vampire when she was seventeen?" Terico asked.

Febraz gave a light sigh and clasped his hands together atop his table. "She caught the same illness her parents had died from. She never wished to become a vampire, and even as she lay dying, she asked me to just let her go…"

"You didn't though," Terico said.

"Of course not!" Febraz said. "I loved her far too much for that. She was upset at first, as you might imagine—but time heals all wounds, as they say. She's become one of the vampires city's best hunters."

"So she's in Istal?" Terico asked. He had heard stories of the city of vampires, deep in the forests west of Fiefs Kingdom.

"Yes, she had to go there after becoming a vampire," Febraz said. "Couldn't go out in the sunlight anymore. I would sneak into Istal whenever I could in order to see her, but for a long time she struggled with connecting with anyone there. It was against the vampiric code for me to make her a vampire, you see. I am not a Seeker, so I had no authority to do so."

"You were an outcast already, though?" Terico asked.

"Well, not technically," Febraz said. "I just never quite fit in well at

Istal... Most of my kind are a bit more serious about life than I am." Terico nodded, waiting for Febraz to continue.

"But yes," the vampire said, "I was officially outcast after I made Areo a vampire. She was shunned for not being what people call a *legitimate* vampire, and eventually went into hibernation to get away from the constant mistreatment."

Terico didn't realize vampires could hibernate. "How long was she asleep?"

"At least seventy years," Febraz said. "When she woke up, Istal

society in general had become slightly more accepting of her kind, and she managed to make a friend and find a mentor willing to help her train for the Rite.

"I suppose this is what you need to know about the Rite. There is a Nexi stone that holds transformative qualities. It is very rare, and only a few vampires a year are able to receive one. Those who pass the Rite use this stone in order to be able to walk in sunlight. Areo has been training several years now in order to receive this stone. So if she wins the competition, we will finally be reunited!

"Since I can not go to Istal myself without putting Areo's success at risk, it would be best to send someone in my place to help Areo out. You were quite resourceful the other day when you saved my life, so I decided you would work perfectly for this."

"Recognizing a poison doesn't have anything to do with this, though," Terico said.

"I trust you, boy," Febraz said. "And aren't you the type of person who wishes to help out people in need?"

Terico didn't have a choice in the matter anyways, so there wasn't much point in arguing with Febraz. "All right, I will help her out, though it seems a little wrong to help out in such a serious competition. You said it was a fight?"

Febraz nodded. "A fight to the death."

"What?" Terico yelled. "Isn't that a little much? Even for vampires?" "No, these Nexi stones are very, very rare," Febraz said. "Only the strongest of vampires will be able to make it out in the world on their own, so the Rite is really just a precursor of what is to come. We aren't a very beloved people amongst non-vampires, you may imagine."

There were plenty of reasons for that, of course, but Terico knew better than to bring them up now.

Terico moved the subject elsewhere. "You can go in the sunlight. Does that mean you have one of those stones?"

"I won one in the Rite well over three hundred years ago," Febraz said. "I was a rather good fighter back in the day."

This man was over three hundred years old? Terico would have never guessed it.

"Don't look so surprised," Febraz said. "Age doesn't hold the same meaning for vampires as it does humans. Time passes, but we don't change so much.

Take Areo, for example. She may be almost a hundred years old, but she hasn't aged a day since becoming a vampire. She still has the heart of a seventeen-year-old, too. So bring her back to me safe and sound, okay?"

"Okay... so I just need to make sure Areo doesn't get killed." Terico lifted his hand with the black tattoo embedded on it. "And then this mark will disappear?"

"Yes," Febraz said. "It holds a spatial connection to both Istal and my tent. Once we are finished here, I will have the mark send you to Istal. Once Areo has defeated her enemy in the Rite, take her hand, and then the both of you just need to place a thumb on the mark for about ten seconds. You will return to my tent in an instant, and the mark will vanish. I will count on you to make sure Areo returns to me in full health."

Terico bit his lip a few seconds, letting his mind think over the mission. It seemed that it was more up to Areo to not get killed than it was up to him. "So... what if things don't work out?"

Febraz closed his eyes and gave a big, stupid-looking smile. "I doubt you would wish to find out what I would do... *if things don't work out.*" He spoke this last phrase slowly, giving each word special emphasis.

Terico really didn't wish to get on a vampire's bad side, and if all he had to do was help this man's daughter come home safely, then it was worth going through this brief endeavor. He just had to count on Jujor being able to get out of the underground city on his own, and on being able to find the him afterward somehow. More than anything, Terico hoped Jujor wouldn't try using the Elpis fragment for whatever plans he had in mind.

"How do you want me to help your daughter, exactly?" Terico asked. Febraz opened his eyes and placed a softly glowing black Nexi stone on his table. "Areo's mentor is blind. He trained her to fight in the darkness. In other words, to rely on senses other than sight. Istal is lit by white

Nexi that grow on the mangroves in the dense forest. If you use this black Nexi, you will be able to absorb the light in the arena."

"I see." Terico took the stone and placed it in his small belt pack with his green and light blue Nexi. "It still seems like cheating, though."

"Who cares," Febraz muttered. "Areo has been through too much hardship in that city as it is. She will be much happier back here with me." Terico doubted this, considering Areo wasn't nearly as young as he had made her out to be. But this wasn't Terico's concern. He just needed to get this business finished so he'd be free of the mark, and back to looking for Jujor and the Elpis fragment.

"Keep a good eye on her after the Rite, too," Febraz said. "There are

still those in Istal who do not look kindly to citizens who weren't made vampires the official way.

"I understand," Terico said.

"Great!" Febraz said. "Then off you go." The vampire snapped his finger, the noise much louder than Terico thought possible.

The mark on Terico's wrist glowed white, then in an instant, he vanished from the vampire's tent.

•

The city of Istal was unlike any Terico had ever imagined. All around him, giant mangroves grew over ten meters tall, their thick, leafy treetops blocking out all sunlight. As Febraz had described, the sprawling trees were decked with small white Nexi stones, basking the wide dirt street in a light, constant glow. In the distance, Terico could see grand wooden structures with sparkling gold trimming and thin red towers. Everything glowed in the soft, white light of the mangroves' Nexi stones, as if the city was lit by hundreds of tiny full moons.

Terico headed down the path toward Istal, a little nervous at the prospect of entering a city entirely populated with vampires. It was probably a little strange to be worrying this much when he had fought through entire legions of forsaken only a few hours beforehand, but Terico did feel out of his element in such a foreign setting. He was also very tired, his body ached terribly, and he didn't have a sword on him. There were his three Nexi stones, but those would only help him so much if he was outnumbered in a fight with vampires. The fact they were nearly immortal was certainly a benefit in their favor, and some of them could have decades more experience at fighting than Terico ever would.

The complete silence around Terico lent an ominous atmosphere, but he walked on toward the city, ready for anything. Or at least most anything. *Just have to bring that girl to Febraz, and then it's off to searching for Jujor*, Terico thought. He recalled the picture of Areo and tried to keep it fresh in his mind, considering he'd need to recognize her before doing anything else. *I suppose I shouldn't think of her as a girl, though, but as a woman.* Though she looked seventeen, she was actually almost a hundred, Terico remembered. But then again, she slept through a lot of that. Would she be in her twenties? And then Febraz was saying that vampires don't really age, so perhaps she was just always going to be seventeen in every way? It was all rather perplexing. Terico wondered how Areo felt about it.

He gazed at the mangroves, which grew so thick and so close

together, they didn't even let in sunlight from the sides of the road. Much of the trees' roots grew above the ground, intertwining with one another like a barrel of entangled brown snakes. The immense system of roots formed dark, tall walls to either side of the pathway, acting about as good a barrier as any stone wall of comparable size, Terico imagined.

It was a little odd that there weren't any people going to and from the city, but when Terico thought more about it, he decided Istal probably wasn't visited by many travelers. The city perhaps had strict regulations for who could leave it, too.

Terico passed a number of wooden homes, all of them well-kept and orderly. The sight didn't match what he had expected—the image of gloomy, wrecked, abandoned structures. Perhaps that sort of abode was more common for vampires prowling near cities other than Istal.

Eventually Terico reached a fountain of water that stood a few meters in front of a great wooden stairway, which led up to a long building with an oddly curved roof. It was difficult to tell what the structure was for— perhaps some kind of governmental building.

Something leaped atop his back. Terico fell to his knees and yelled out in surprise. Fangs sunk into his neck, and he felt his whole body grow suddenly weak as the assailant sucked blood from him. With one quick burst of fury, Terico shoved the vampire off his back, turned around, and struggled to maintain his balance.

He looked down at what appeared to be a six-year-old girl wearing a bright purple dress with white, lacy trimmings. She had large yellow eyes and long violet hair. Terico stared incredulously as a trickle of blood dripped from the side of her lips. The girl stared up at him, her expression just as bewildered.

"I just wanted a little blood," the child squeaked. "We don't get human visitors very often."

"Don't do that!" Terico said, placing a hand over the two tiny fang marks the girl left in his neck. He felt his heart beat to the pace of a stampede of wild horses. "I don't want to turn into a vampire!"

"I'd have to inject blood into you to do that," the girl said, frowning. "And I'm not even a Seeker. I was just wanting a little drink."

Terico adjusted his footing and took a few deep breaths. He didn't feel so dizzy anymore, and it seemed the girl had only gotten a couple gulps of his blood down. "Still, you surprised me. Make sure you ask next time."

The child put on the most deadpan expression imaginable. She glanced to the side and muttered, "You just would've said *no*."

Terico sighed. "You don't know that."

The girl jumped to her feet, wide-eyed and with a huge, toothy grin spread across her face. "Can I suck some of your blood?" "No!" Terico yelled.

"You filthy brat!" the girl yelled back, waving her arms frantically from side to side.

"You pint-sized blood-sucker!" Terico replied.

"You blue-haired, stupid-faced, helpless little infestation of weakness and pointless little human dumbness!" The girl was jumping up and down at this point.
"Is something wrong?" came a man's voice.

Terico turned around and found a vampire who looked to be in his forties. This man wore dark brown robes with a thick yellow sash, and had a red bandana covering most of his black hair. He had thin eyes and a quizzical look about him.

"I..." Terico had no idea where to start.

"I just wanted some fresh blood!" the girl said. "It was the most delicious blood I ever had! And this dumb *boy* has so much of it, that he shouldn't mind sparing *just a little.*"

The man turned back to Terico and smiled. "Analicia is a feisty child. She was turned into a vampire just a couple years ago. A very rare case of a sixyear-old becoming a vampire, but she would have died otherwise." Terico didn't really understand the system used for choosing who gets to—or has to—become a vampire. But he had more pressing business at the moment.

"But I am curious," the man continued. "How did a human get here in the first place? Have you met with the grand council?"

"No, I was sent here by a vampire," Terico said. He decided it was best to not say it was Febraz if he could help it. "I'm hoping to find a woman, er, girl named Areo."

The man grinned. "Areoseps Kanto?"

Terico didn't know what her full name was, but there probably weren't too many *Areo*s in the vampire city. "Yes, pretty sure." "She's my big sister!" the man said.

Terico looked at the man for any sign of a resemblance, but quite frankly there wasn't any. And this man had to be at least twenty years older than Areo, at least in appearance. Perhaps he became a vampire much more recently than her, though.

"Don't look so surprised," the man said. "Most vampire families aren't related by blood the way human families typically are... My name is Jenba, by the way. Areo and I have been training under the same mentor for the past four years. Areo's one of the combatants in the Rite today. I imagine you came to see her fight?"

"Yes, when does it start?" Terico asked. "And where will it be?" "There's a large field with hills on the side for people to watch on," Jenba said. "It's near the center of the city, by the grand council edifice. It will start in a couple hours."

"Good, there's still time then," Terico said. "Can you take me there? I need to speak with her if I can."

"I suppose," Jenba said, his expression difficult to read. "How do you know Areo?"

Terico wondered what he should say. This Jenba seemed friendly enough, and perhaps Areo had told him all about Febraz already. It seemed safe to trust him. "It's a long story, but I was marked by a vampire named Febraz, who says he is Areo's father."

Jenba chuckled. "Oh, wow. I think Areo's head will erupt when she hears this."

As Terico imagined, it sounded like Areo didn't quite reciprocate the feelings her father expressed toward her. "I guess you know about Febraz then."
"I've never met the man myself," Jenba said, "but I've heard plenty of... *interesting* stories about him—most of them from Areo herself. But let's start heading to where the Rite will take place. We can talk on the way there."
"Hey!" the small girl cried. "Don't leave me behind."

"Children shouldn't watch the Rite," Jenba said. "Go back home and finish your chores, or something."

"No way! I want to—"

Jenba snapped a finger at the girl, his snap even louder than the one Febraz had done. The child turned and ran in an instant.

Terico smirked. "So, vampires have the ability to snap really loud, eh?"

Jenba tilted his head a little and raised an eyebrow. "No... I suppose I'm pretty good at it, but it has nothing to do with being a vampire." Terico wasn't so sure of that, but didn't care to argue about it.

•

On the way to the arena, Jenba explained a little about the style of fighting he and Areo were trained in. By relying on senses other than sight, they could not only fend off enemies with ease in the dark, but were unpredictable in their movements, disorienting their opponents.

"So you have been with Areo for a while then?" Terico asked.

"Yes, not long after she awoke from her hibernation, Areo and I began training under Master Nivakil," Jenba said. "She's progressed so quickly though, that she's already prepared enough for the Rite." "You think she'll win then?" Terico asked.

Jenba looked up to the long, overhanging branches of the mangroves. "To be completely honest, it will be difficult. She is no doubt a better fighter than her opponent, Krug. But it is likely the Rite will be set up in a way to work in Krug's favor."

"Why?"

"Persecution isn't as bad as it once was, but there are still many vampires who would never accept Areo as a *true* vampire. She was just an accident, they would say. And so they will probably try to make sure she doesn't win the Rite."

"That's murder," Terico said. "This *is* a duel to the death, right?" Jenba nodded. "This is an opportunity for elitists to kill Areo without actually getting their own hands dirty."

After showing him around the city for a bit, Jenba took Terico to the empty dirt field where Areo would be fighting. There were a large number of vampires gathered together to watch the Rite, sitting in long metal benches embedded into the steep hills on either side of the arena. There was probably room for at least a thousand people, but there were still spaces available in some of the lower rows.

A short man in thick leather armor stopped them when they approached the arena. He looked even more pale than most the other vampires, which Terico didn't think could be possible. "Hold up, now.

You're not a vampire..."

Terico shook his head. "I know Areo, though. I'm... a friend of a friend." *Sort of.*

"He's with me," Jenba said. "There won't be any trouble." "I certainly hope so," the guard said.

Terico followed Jenba on down to an open area on the third row, not far from the middle of the arena.

"Security is probably a bit more worried about this Rite than most," Jenba said. "Some in the crowd will probably be... very upset if Areo wins." "Great," Terico said, suppressing a sigh. The last thing he wanted was a riled up arena of angry vampires to deal with.

There was still some time before Areo and Krug would arrive, so Terico continued some of his conversation with Jenba. "You said you were Areo's brother, then?"

"We do everything together," Jenba said. "It will be sad to see her go, assuming she wins. Of course, it will be even more sad if she loses."

Terico found it odd that Jenba wasn't counting on Areo to win. "Shouldn't you have a little more faith in her? You don't seem to have too much hope that she'll win."

Jenba turned to Terico and raised an eyebrow. "We have to be realistic in this world, Terico. That's how Master Nivakil trained me and Areo—to analyze our situations with a clear mind. We can't pretend that things will all work out all right if there's a good chance they won't." Terico frowned. "So you always prepare for the worst, then." "Not if the worst is highly unlikely," Jenba said.

Terico sat on his hands quietly and slumped forward, letting his thoughts reflect on Jenba's words a bit. It seemed that "the worst" had been precisely what happened to him quite regularly over the past week. His parents murdered, his village destroyed, Turan captured, Suran missing, being marked by a vampire, fighting through hundreds of forsaken, getting tortured by the Elpis, getting separated from Jujor... and now this.

This diversion better not cost my life, he thought.

The crowds nearby grew quiet as a group of vampires pushed their way through, and stopped in front of a woman holding a dark gray sack. They forced her to open it, and then confiscated a red Nexi stone.

"We'll return it to you after the match," the leader of the outfit said. He was a man with spiky red hair and a goatee, and was dressed in a similarlyhued suit. "We don't want any interference for this match."

Terico leaned over to Jenba to whisper to him. "Some of the elites you were talking about?"

Jenba turned around and nodded. "Look sharp. They're coming this way."

The red-haired vampire folded his arms behind his back and grinned, baring his fangs.

A man in a top hat beside him pointed at Terico. "I sense three Nexi stones."

"Evening, human," the red-haired man said. "We'll need to hold on to your Nexi for the duration of the Rite. We'll return them to you afterward."

Terico didn't like the idea of giving up his Nexi to these six random vampires, especially when he was supposed to use the black one to tip the event in Areo's favor.

"You run the Rite?" Terico asked.

"We work in conjunction with those who do." The red-haired man motioned to a number of vampires sitting at a table at one end of the arena. "They agree this will help ensure the match goes smoothly."

He held out his hand, and Terico took a long look at it, trying to decide the best course of action. Causing a scene here wouldn't help matters any, and Terico wasn't in fit condition to fight with six vampires at the moment.

Terico gave up his three Nexi stones.

"Thank you for your cooperation," the man said with a light smile. He and his five followers continued to make their way through the stands, guided to a few more Nexi stones by the vampire in the top hat.

Terico wondered how he would be able to help Areo without Febraz's black Nexi. *Perhaps Areo will just win the match in ten seconds flat, and I won't have to worry about it?* Perhaps that was the kind of wishful thinking Areo and Jenba's mentor warned them to avoid.

"There he is." Jenba pointed out to the opposite side of the smooth dirt field. "He's our mentor. The one with the cane."

Sitting at the front row was a weathered-looking vampire with dark rings under his dim yellow eyes, which seemed to be staring off toward nothing in particular. Terico recalled he was blind—hence the cane. The man was dressed a bit like Jenba, but also wore a flat-topped, triangular black hat of some kind, embroidered with golden lettering in an ancient language Terico didn't recognize.

"Would you say he's like a father to you and Areo?" Terico asked. Jenba laughed. "No, definitely not. I don't know if I've ever met a man less cold and harsh than Nivakil. But he's a true master when it comes to the hunt. In sparring matches, most don't take him seriously because of his blindness. They *always* end up regretting it."

Terico wondered what effect such a teacher would have had on Areo. She was apparently a pretty tough girl before she ever met Febraz, considering how she lived on her own as a child. But Terico imagined rigorous training under someone like Nivakil could leave a significant impact.

The lights of the white Nexi above the arena turned several times brighter all at once. The vampiric multitude covered their eyes and muttered obscenities under their breath. It took a few moments for Terico's eyes to adjust, but it was only a mild annoyance for him in comparison.

"What's going on?" he asked.

Jenba gritted his teeth and stared menacingly toward the table where the people running the Rite sat. "So that's how it's going to be."

"What?"

"They're making it extra-bright so it will be more difficult for Areo to win," Jenba said. "It will just look like an accident to everyone here, since the Nexi can glow a bit brighter than usual from time to time..."

"Won't the brightness hinder the vampire she's fighting, too?" Terico asked. "It's clearly making everyone here uncomfortable."

"Areo is fighting Krug, one of Hidif's trainees," Jenba said. "Hidif is an elite who can afford to train her pupils in special facilities lined with extra-bright Nexi, meant to simulate the light of the sun to some degree. Areo and I couldn't afford any of the special training that most Rite combatants receive, and we never had access to any of the facilities Krug has fought in these past eight years."

With the mangroves above glowing this bright, it would be difficult for Areo to win, since she never trained to fight in a setting this bright. Hidif perhaps trained Krug for the select purpose of having him fight under these rigged conditions.

A few minutes passed before the participants for the Rite walked into the arena. Terico spotted Areo entering in front of the table the judges sat at. Just like in the small portrait Febraz showed him, Areo had a rather jagged face, and sharp, pointed brown eyes. She was squinting from the bright lighting, and didn't appear to be carrying any weapons save for a single Nexi stone. Her hair was a bit more ragged than in the portrait, and she now had some off-white highlights—a sort of cream color. These ran down the center of her hair, and down the locks of hair in front of her ears.

Her outfit was even more peculiar to Terico, though. It was a black and red long-sleeved turtleneck with a sort of caped skirt attached to the belt, but precariously cut open in the front. She also wore long black boots and a thick gold-colored belt.

"Do your best, Areo," Jenba called out to her.

She walked toward the benches and looked up to him. "I will." She looked to Terico and asked, "Who is this?" Her voice had a callous feel to it.
"Ah... I'm Terico. Your father kind of asked me to come watch your Rite, and... report back to him."

Areo shut her eyes and slowly shook her head. "Febraz, Febraz. Let me guess. He wanted you to help me win the match."

"Sort of," Terico said. "Yes."

Areo opened her eyes and frowned. "I have to win on my own, Tairigo." She squinted from the light of the mangroves again.

"I understand... Ah, here's an idea though." Terico turned to Jenba and slid off the man's bandana.

"What are you doing?" Jenba asked.

Terico tossed the bandana to Areo. "You fight best in the dark, right? You might as well just blindfold yourself."

Areo tied it across her eyes and nodded. "Krug will probably use a white Nexi, thinking the extra light will hinder me further." "How many Nexi do you have?" Terico asked.

"We each only get one," Areo said. "I'll be using a tan one."

Terico understood this stone was a bit harder to control than most. "Best of luck, then."

For a moment he expected Areo to say she wasn't one to rely on luck, but she simply turned away without responding. She walked toward the center of the field, a few meters from where her opponent was standing.

Krug was a very thin, lanky man, who appeared to have become a vampire a couple years younger than Areo. He wore all white, and the sleeves of his shirt and trousers were very long, wide, and billowy. As Areo guessed, the man held a bright white Nexi in his hand. Terico wondered how effective it would be with Areo blindfolded.

At any rate, the man stood tall and confident. He had short, slickedback blond hair and a rather all-knowing look on his face. If Krug was concerned about the Rite at all, he was doing a good job hiding it. Terico doubted he would go easy on Areo though, considering this was a life and death situation.

The two vampires faced each other a good four meters apart. At the front table, one of the judges announced that the Rite would begin at the ringing of a small golden bell one of the others held. It would be a fight to the death, and the one left standing would earn the Nexi known as the Rite stone, allowing the winner to travel the world as he or she pleased. A warning was then given that if there was any indication of cheating—by either the contestants or by friends in the audience—then the perpetrator would be killed on the spot.

There was nothing more for Terico to do but sit and watch then, he decided. He clasped his hands together and sat forward, keeping an eye on both Areo and Krug. The two combatants readied their Nexi stones.

The bell rang, and Krug immediately rushed for Areo, who waited a moment to gauge Krug's footsteps. Simultaneously, they forced their fingernails to lengthen and thin into long, needle-like claws, at least ten centimeters long.

Areo leaped back just as Krug swiped for her neck. Krug slid forward after her and swung again, his motions fluid. Areo hopped to the side and jabbed her claws for Krug's chest. While still stepping forward, Krug leaned back and twisted to the side, avoiding Areo's attack with ease. Areo skidded to a stop and lunged for Krug. She was quick. Krug blocked Areo with a grid of claws, then slid around her to tear into her back. Areo dashed forward, too fast even for Krug's seamless movements. Areo's quick and precise motions alone were impressive, but the fact she could duel this well while blindfolded made the feats that much more stunning. Yet after a couple minutes of this, it was clear Krug was starting to wear Areo out. While Areo's movements were rigid and straightforward, Krug's motions were slick and refined. His dodges and counterattacks constantly melded into one another, clear evidence of a much more sophisticated level of training. Areo needed to finish him off now, because it seemed clear she wouldn't outlast him if the fight dragged on much longer.

Krug kicked for Areo's head. She ducked and swiped for his leg still on the ground. Krug leaped forward, his vampiric strength propelling him higher than a human could manage. He swiped his claws for Areo's back in the process, but Areo rolled forward before he could reach her. Upon landing, he spun in place and slipped out the white Nexi from his sleeve.

He ran for Areo as she turned back around. She took her tan Nexi from a small pouch on her belt and aimed it for Krug. The earth in front of her erupted and formed into a giant arm and hand, a bit larger than a grown person. The hand of hardened dirt reached out for Krug, who swerved to the side and sliced through the hand's thumb and index finger with his claws. He continued toward Areo, who leaped back as Krug blasted a burst of light from his Nexi. Even from the stands, Terico had to cover his eyes— the potency of this white Nexi was stronger than any he had ever seen before.

Areo stumbled to the right, straight where Krug was already sliding toward. She leaped back immediately, but Krug still managed to claw across her torso, tearing through her clothes and drawing deep bloody marks from her left shoulder to her right hip.

 As Areo skidded to a stop, Krug sprinted for her again. She swiped her claws for Krug's face. He leaned back—as he did so, Areo swiped for his stomach. She tore through his cloak, but Krug spun to the side and thrust claws straight through Areo's outstretched arm. Screaming, Areo used her Nexi to force a giant hand to burst out of the earth between her and Krug. The hand of dirt slammed against Krug, who flew back a couple meters before stumbling to his feet.

Areo gritted her teeth and turned back to Krug. How she could stand and fight after getting her arm skewered in five places was beyond Terico, but must have been a testament of her vampiric tenacity. Blood poured down her arm, soaking through her long sleeve. Krug licked the ends of his claws, looking even more energetic and confident than before. Terico recalled that blood gave vampires more power, and he began to worry a bit more for Areo's life.

And if Areo dies, I'm in trouble too, Terico remembered. *She better have a secret ability she can fall back on, because her speed and blind fighting aren't cutting it against this well-trained of an opponent.*
Terico blinked a couple times, then found Areo was already closing in on Krug. She jabbed her claws at him, then pounced for his head as he dodged her attacks. Krug leaped back, then leaned forward and ran beneath Areo, who tried swiping her claws into the back of Krug's head.

Krug turned around as Areo landed. Areo immediately spun around and lunged for him again. Krug ran back and raised his white Nexi. The blast of white light he emitted lasted several seconds, and it took a couple seconds longer for Terico's eyes to adjust enough to see again. He looked back to the field and saw Krug had put several meters' distance between him and Areo during the whiteout.

A stream of water erupted from Krug's Nexi stone, colliding directly with Areo's stomach. She fell back a couple meters before sliding across the ground, leaving a bloody mess across the dirt floor. The water dissipated, and Krug cast a wide grin out to the audience. It took a couple more seconds for most of the vampiric audience to recover from the prolonged blast of light, at which point a wave of gasps and quiet chattering filled the arena. The question everyone was asking was obvious—how was Krug using a dark blue Nexi, when he was just using a white one?

Jenba stood up and raised his hands in the air. "What's going on here?"

"Did he sneak in a second Nexi stone?" Terico asked.

A crazed look on his face, Jenba looked down to Terico. "That's supposed to be impossible. The contestants are always inspected to make sure there's no foul play. The judges would find a hidden Nexi right away." Terico watched as Areo struggled to get back to her feet, one arm draped over her stomach. She fell back to her knees, struggling to breathe. Areo's mentor Nivakil stood up, his blind eyes directed toward the table at the end of the field. A moment later, an older-looking vampire from the judges' stand arose.

"What is this?" the judge yelled. "Only one Nexi stone per candidate is allowed."

Not far from Nivakil stood a tall, young-looking woman with long, light blue hair. "My pupil is using only one stone, of course. Krug has such a deep connection with Nexi, that he is capable of altering the color and ability of every stone he wields." Her name was Hidif, Terico remembered. She carried a strong voice which pierced through the whisperings of the crowd, and seemed to hold herself in a self-confidence even greater than Krug's. She was hauntingly beautiful, dressed in a fine, orange and yellow silk dress—and she likely had the power to back up her air of authority, too.

Krug held up his dark blue Nexi stone for all to see, then wiped his left hand across its smooth, glowing surface. After giving the stone a few rubs, Krug slid his hand away to reveal the deep red glow of a red Nexi. The crowds gasped, and for a moment Terico wondered himself if this was a legitimate ability some people could have. His gut instinct was telling him there was a likelier explanation to this, however.

"As you can see," Hidif continued, "none of the rules have been broken. Krug utilizes a single Nexi stone, yet is not limited to a single magical ability. He is easily my strongest pupil, and likely the strongest contender for the Rite in at least three centuries." Terico could hardly stand this woman's dialogue. Especially when she carried the posture and expression of a sadist.

Krug rubbed the stone again, turning it back into a dark blue. Crowds of vampires applauded vigorously, impressed with what appeared to be a whole new world of potential—a power entirely unheard of.

"Very well," the judge said, sitting back down. "Finish the match."
Krug's mentor turned to Nivakil and flashed a long, pleasant smile at him. Areo's mentor simply sat back down, his irritated expression unchanging. Terico looked back to Krug, who walked casually toward Areo. She stood back up and flexed her claws—she was still going to fight. How she was going to keep Krug from impaling her in this state, Terico couldn't imagine.

It's too suspicious, though, Terico thought. *Changing the stone back to dark blue again... Why not just keep it red? Perhaps... perhaps even while it was red, it was still actually a dark blue Nexi.*
The realization hit him—a memory of a page from one of Mother's herbology books. There was a rare leaf called chralthis that could be rubbed on a Nexi stone to temporarily change its color. Con artists would sometimes use it to make everyday Nexi such as red and dark blue appear to be rare stones that would fetch a much higher price. Of course they'd be found out within the hour, but if they were traveling they could sometimes get away with it.

I'd bet half the farms in Fiefs that Hidif gave Krug some chralthis in order to fool everyone, Terico thought. *The stone he has now is a dark blue one, which his mentor probably threw to him while everyone was blinded by the four, five seconds of white light. Those vampire elites confiscating everyone's Nexi stones likely wouldn't have asked her to give up her Nexi. If anything, they're all working together, and their task was to make it appear impossible that anyone could have given Krug another Nexi.*
So Krug likely had his white Nexi up his sleeve, or managed to throw it to his master during the whiteout. Either way, Terico knew he'd be able to prove their foul play—but would an arena of vampires listen to him in the middle of the match? He had been warned to not stir up any trouble, and Areo was adamant about needing to win on her own. Terico wasn't sure if she would be able to under these circumstances, though.

Areo side-stepped each of Krug's jabs toward her heart, avoiding what Terico understood to be the most effective way of killing vampires, save from a complete beheading. Though Areo was bleeding and badly beaten, she was still quick enough to avoid Krug's attacks, and was still able to read his movements without seeing them. Playing this defensively wasn't going to win her the match though, and it was only a matter of time before she wore herself out.

With a flick of her Nexi stone, Areo forced another arm of hardened dirt to burst from the ground and reach for her opponent. Krug turned and blasted the arm to bits with a jet of water from his Nexi, then continued the blast toward Areo. She forced a large, thick mound of earth to emerge in front of her, deflecting the highly pressurized water.

Before Terico could realize it, Areo was suddenly within striking distance of Krug. She slit his neck, but Krug pushed her back and proceeded to claw at her wildly. He scraped across her right thigh, down her chest, and across the left side of her face. Instead of pulling back, Areo slammed into Krug, jabbing several claws into his chest. In the process, she got almost all of Krug's claws impaled through her stomach, the bloody ends of the claws poking out her back. She headbutted Krug and pushed out of his claws, nearly falling back to the ground in a dizzy nausea. Her entire body was dripping with blood, and she had to keep an arm wrapped around her stomach.

Screaming, Krug lifted up his Nexi stone, which was white again. Or rather, was the white one he had used before, Terico imagined. A burst of light emanated from the stone, again lasting a few seconds longer than was typical.

When the light faded away, Terico saw Krug was wielding a green Nexi. Again, the crowds thought he had shifted the white stone's power to that of a green one—but Terico was almost certain Krug was just getting new ones from his mentor while everyone was blinded.

Krug aimed the stone for Areo. She ran toward Krug, but struggled against her injuries and the intense light of Krug's white Nexi, which likely still pierced through her bandana to some degree. Before Areo could reach him, Krug caused vines to fling out from his stone and wrap around Areo's body. The vines bound her tight, forcing her legs together and her arms and claws flat against her sides. She struggled to tear through the vines with her claws, but Krug continued to create more and more vines to warp around her, keeping Areo from being able to even move them.

Another arm of dirt emerged from the ground behind Krug. He turned and leaped away from the giant hand's attempt to grab him. Krug avoided each of the earth arm's attacks, then used a brief opening to tear apart the hardened dirt with his free clawed hand. Areo tried creating another arm of dirt, but it didn't hold. The tan Nexi stone was a difficult one to wield, and it was probably a miracle Areo had been able to use it at all in her current state. She would have been dead had she been anything but a vampire, of course—but she still surely felt the pain of what would have been fatal injuries for most anyone else.

"At last, it's over!" Krug yelled, his voice gurgling with blood leaking from his neck. He flung Areo up a bit and caused his Nexi's vines to hold her upside-down. With a flick of his wrist, he raised her a little more so that her neck was level with Krug's raised free hand. He was going to slice straight through her neck—cut her head off entirely.

Jenba stood up, his mouth open. Terico stared breathless as Krug pulled his arm back, readying his swing for Areo's neck. The entire arena turned silent.

And Areo grinned.

Krug thrust his claws to Areo's neck. In one sudden movement, Areo scrunched her body up and tilted her head down toward her chest. Krug's longest claw flung into Areo's mouth. She clamped her teeth on the claw and jerked her head to the side hard. The claw snapped clean in half, its pop echoing across the arena.

Krug stumbled backward, screaming from the pain. Areo immediately worked the claw end in her mouth so she could slice it across the vines binding her. In three jerky, difficult motions with her head, she worked the snapped claw against the vines enough to free one of her arms enough. Once able to move her arm, she tore apart the vines with her own claws, making light work of them in seconds.

Krug caused more vines to entangle her, but Areo was quick to claw away at them. In a sheer frenzy, Areo ripped through Krug's attacks and clawed at his face. He slipped back, screaming, but Areo continued to push through his continual onslaught of vines.

Areo jabbed a claw through the web of vines straight through Krug's right hand, forcing him to drop his Nexi. She sliced through the remaining vines and lunged toward Krug as he instinctively clenched his impaled hand. Krug swung his claws at Areo as she approached. She dropped to the ground and swung a leg against the back of Krug's legs, tripping him backward. With a flick of her wrist upward, a thin stalagmite of earth erupted out of the ground directly behind her opponent. Krug fell directly on top of its pointed end, which burst straight through his back and out his chest.

He lay atop of the stalagmite, motionless, his heart impaled.

For several long seconds, the masses watched to see if Krug would move. Areo fell to her hands and knees, her strength utterly spent. She crawled up to Krug and jabbed all her claws into his neck. All at once, she twisted her claws into different directions, ripping off Krug's head entirely. Terico gazed in silent awe as Areo drank freely from the blood pouring from Krug's severed neck. Many of those in attendance cheered and applauded Areo's victory, but Terico could only stare.

Areo stood up and faced the audience on Terico's side of the arena. Her clothes were tattered and torn, and her body was covered in splotches of blood—yet there wasn't a single wound on her body. Her face, torso, arms, legs—every centimeter of her was free of the deep gashes and holes Krug had driven into her. The blood she drank had healed her... regenerated her.

She looked up to Terico and Jenba and slipped off her bandana. Her eyes closed against the bright light of the mangroves, and a weary smile spread across her face.

A part of Terico was impressed by her resilience and tenacity.
Another part of him felt terror.

5

THE DOWNWARD SPIRAL

At Terico's insistence, Areo checked in Krug's sleeves to find a white Nexi, a dark blue Nexi, and the chralthis leaf used to temporarily change the color of the water Nexi stone. After a brief explanation regarding how Krug ended up with three Nexi stones, the judges were quick to send guards to Hidif's location. The mentor was quick to slip away, however, lost amidst the upset crowds in seconds. Terico noticed that the elite vampires who stole his Nexi stones went conveniently missing as well.

In the end, the match satisfied the majority of the audience, though many were still visibly upset about the turn of events regarding Krug and his mentor. The prospect of a vampire who could change the properties of a Nexi stone ended up too good to be true, to the disappointment of many others.

What mattered to Terico though was that Areo got through the match alive, which left him needing to simply get to her and send her back to Febraz before any elites decided to take out their anger on her. He watched as the judges presented her with a sickly pink Nexi stone, presumably for her to wield in order to live in the sunlight. There wasn't much more to the ceremony than that, and the crowds began to disperse as soon as all the judges stood up to leave.

Terico followed Jenba down to the torn-up field of the arena, cautious to walk around the holes Areo had formed with her tan Nexi. When Jenba reached Areo, they each nodded and shook hands. Terico thought it a bit odd how formal they were being about such a momentous occasion, but knew better than to question their ways.

Their mentor approached from behind, his eyes staring blankly past Areo. "You succeeded."

Areo turned around and looked down to Nivakil, who stood just slightly shorter than her. "Yes."

"Given the circumstances," Nivakil said, "most would probably say your victory was quite surprising."

"Most likely," Areo said. "The judges likely expected Krug to win from the start."

"They are all fools," Nivakil said. "Your victory was not surprising at all. I never doubted you would win."

Jenba leaned back in shock. "What? Are you serious, master?"

Nivakil simply stared back, his face like an empty void. Terico had the feeling that this man was always serious.

"I'm just surprised, is all," Jenba said. "You always tell us to never count on anything."

"You should always fight this way, yes," Nivakil said. "If you take your enemy for granted, no matter how weak he may appear to be, you will let your guard down and suffer from careless mistakes. I've trained your sister to fight this way since *lesson one*, and it's been clear for some time now how important winning this Rite was to her."

Areo gave Nivakil a light bow. "I owe my victory to your training, master."

"Yes," Nivakil said, "and you have put into practice every aspect of my counsel. You are ready to travel the world as you see fit."

Jenba looked surprised by his mentor's comments, and Terico gathered that praise escaped Nivakil's mouth only on the rarest of occasions. It made Terico think of his father for a moment. He was a bit like that, too. "Make me proud, Areo," Nivakil said.

In his head, Terico could hear his father say, "Make me proud, Terico." It was a moment that took him away from his present worries, and it left him feeling out of place in this vampiric city.

In this entire world.

"I will," Areo said.

Jenba sighed and folded his arms. "I will... miss you, big sister."

Terico still thought it sounded strange for this middle-aged man to be calling Areo his older sister.

"I will see you again," Areo said. "I just wish to see more of the world for a time." She turned to Terico and tilted her head to the side a bit. "I imagine my father is anxious to see me, at least."

Terico nodded. "He made it abundantly clear that I needed to bring you back to him."

"I suppose that means we'll be traveling together a while," Areo said. "Not too long," Terico said. He held up the mark on his wrist. "This will magically send us to Febraz's tent in an instant."

Areo's eyes widened. "He *marked* you?" She shut her eyes and palmed her forehead. "He really goes too far sometimes..." There wasn't much to argue there.

Areo opened her eyes again and placed her hands on her hips. "I apologize for the... inconvenience. I hope this hasn't troubled you too greatly."

Terico wanted to say it wasn't a big deal, but that wouldn't be very truthful. Febraz separated him from Jujor and the Elpis fragment at a very inopportune moment. "Don't worry. I'll be fine."

"I do thank you again though," Areo said. "I'll go pack my things, and then you can be on your way again."

"And make sure you change your clothes," Nivakil said. He looked Areo up and down, which was odd, considering his blindness. "You're an unsightly mess... Not to mention the indecent exposure laws you're nearly breaking."

Areo folded her arms across her chest while Jenba fell into a fit of laughter.

Terico insisted he go with Areo back to her house, just to keep good on his promise to make sure she got back to Febraz safely. While Areo got ready to leave, Terico waited with Jenba and Nivakil in the entry room of the tiny home. It was a small, unassuming place, with no sign of decoration or embellishment anywhere. There was a fireplace and a pot sitting on a small table, which had a battered chair on either side of it. But not much else.

It didn't take long for Areo to come back with a small bag that, for all Terico knew, held all her worldly possessions. She wore an outfit very similar to the one she had for the Rite, though this wasn't torn or stained in blood.
Her skin and hair were wiped free of any blood as well.

"Anything more to deal with here before you leave?" Nivakil asked.

"No, everything's gone," Areo said. "Someone will be moving in tomorrow."

Apparently she had been planning for some time to leave this life behind her. It was a sentiment Terico felt he understood, considering the turn of events of his past week. It was strange to see other people's lives changing as much as his, but there was also something reassuring about it, somehow.

The four walked outside and went back behind the house so Terico and Areo could disappear without causing a stir.

"Are you excited to see Febraz again?" Terico asked.

"I'm a bit upset with him," Areo said, "but to be honest it will be nice to see him again. I can always count on him... to care, you know." She grinned. "I can't count on him for much else."

Terico smiled too. "Luckily his mark has been working effectively. He said we both just need to place a thumb on the mark, and hold it there for about ten seconds."

Before either of them could do so, a group of vampires converged around them from either side of the house. It was the six elites who had gone around confiscating everyone's Nexi stones amongst the audience.

"You fought well today, Areo," said the red-haired vampire, the leader of this group. "We're going to have to demand you give up your

Rite Nexi, however."

Areo raised her eyebrows and gave a long, slight smile. "Um... you folks *did* see the match today, didn't you? I think you might want to rephrase that last sentence. I'll assume it was a slip of the tongue if you head on back the way you came."

The lead elite glowered. "So you get one kill and suddenly you think you're unstoppable. You do realize there are six of us, and only four—" He glanced to Terico. "Correction. Only *three* of you."

He looked back to Areo and grinned. "And as it turns out, we're backed up by some of the top officials running this city. Because the fact is, child, you don't deserve the Rite Nexi."

Every word oozing out of this man's mouth unnerved Terico. Somehow Terico didn't even count as an opponent to these vampires, and somehow a ninety-nine-year-old could still be called a child. And Areo won that Nexi stone even *with* these elites conspiring against her.

The red-haired vampire laughed. "Looks like I've upset the little human. I sure hope he—"

Terico punched him in the face.

"Hasty," Nivakil muttered.

Areo's and Jenba's claws elongated simultaneously, and a barrage of glowing lights shined from the enemy vampires' raised Nexi stones.

In moments, the six elites were on the floor, screaming their heads

off. Terico staggered backward in surprise, realizing that each vampire had a hand severed off—the hand holding a Nexi stone.

Nivakil shook the blood off his claws, then caused them to shrink back into normal-sized fingernails. "I expected more of a fight."

From what Terico could tell, Areo and Jenba had each clawed the face of the vampires closest to unleashing a Nexi power—but somehow Nivakil managed to completely lop off a hand of each enemy in a matter of seconds. And Terico hadn't even seen the man prepare to attack, as he had Areo and Jenba.

Nivakil walked to the nearest elite, who was writhing from the pain of his bleeding, severed hand. "Oh, quit crying. It should mend soon enough, and your hand will regenerate in a week's time."

Terico picked out his three Nexi stones from the pockets of the vampire in the top hat. "Febraz will probably want his black Nexi back..." Nivakil walked to Terico and placed a hand on his shoulder. "I did call your move hasty, didn't I? But it did give us an opening. And to be brutally honest, you only did what the rest of us were wanting to do." The mentor didn't grin, but there was a grandfatherly glint in his eyes. "Thanks," Terico said.
"I'm glad to have met you." "Thanks for coming by, Terico," Jenba said.

Nivakil turned to Areo and nodded. "Best you get going now. Remember everything I've taught you, and you will do well. Oh, and let Febraz know that if he ever wants to start another ruckus here, he's welcome to sneak over to my place."

"Thank you for everything, master," Areo said. She turned to Jenba and smiled. "Good-bye for now, little brother."

"Have fun in the sunlight," Jenba said. "You could probably use some, now that I think about it."

Once they had finished their good-byes, Terico got Areo to place her thumb on his marked wrist, and placed his own thumb beside hers. At the count of ten, Terico would leave behind the vampiric city and all the troubles it brought him.

I have enough to deal with, regardless, Terico thought shortly before he and Areo disappeared.

•

They appeared in Febraz's tent a moment later. Terico looked down at his wrist to find it clean of the dark symbol Febraz had marked on it.

He looked back up and noticed several candles lit on the table, giving the tent a bit more light than there was before. But instead of finding Febraz, a young man in white sat atop the back of the chair, his feet resting on the seat. Terico recognized the uniform—this was a member of the Brotherhood. He had the requisite white mask with the mark of the inverted cross over his right eye, but also had an eerie, crescent-curved smile painted on the mask.

"What is this?" Areo asked, her voice livid. Terico glanced down to where she was looking, and found Febraz lying on the ground. He was almost entirely covered in the sticky swamp-like substance that comes from the brown Nexi stone. His eyes and nose were left uncovered, and he looked panicked... And for good reason, Terico realized—the area over his heart was also uncovered, and the Brotherhood fighter held a long sword directly above it. In fact, the tip of the blade was resting atop Febraz's chest. All the Brotherhood member had to do was push the blade down, and Febraz would die impaled.

"Welcome back, Terico," the assailant whispered behind his mask. "If either of you make a move, the vampire dies immediately."

There was something peculiar about the way this person spoke. He had a young, tortured voice, but there was something more... But Terico couldn't focus on that—the Brotherhood were after him, apparently.

"What are you doing? Leave Febraz out of this."

The assailant simply stared back at Terico through the mask's thin, nearly invisible eye holes. Terico's mind flooded with questions. How did the Brotherhood know he was alive? And what did they want from him? Did they know he was after the Elpis fragments?

The masked boy started trembling... vibrating. Terico held his breath and stared at the assailant's sword, precariously shaking atop Febraz's heart. Areo crouched down a bit, her fingers curled and twitching. For several long seconds—perhaps even half a minute—the Brotherhood member kept shaking in complete silence. Terico could see Areo tense up further and further, and it was only a matter of time before she lunged for the assailant's neck. Terico wasn't sure if even Areo could be quick enough to stop this masked boy before Febraz would be killed, though.

"What do you want?" Terico asked, his throat dry and tight. "Just let Febraz go, and I'll meet your demands." The sight of this trembling Brotherhood member, his smiling mask, his sadistic hostage setup—it was all so horrifically surreal.

The assailant tilted his head to the side a bit. "Good, he's important to you." The Brotherhood fighter continued to shake, the tip of his blade digging a little deeper into Febraz's bleeding chest.

"Stop it," Areo said, her eyes wide, her body motionless, and her voice just above a whisper. She seemed to be exerting all her might to keep from screaming. "Stop it now."

"No, this is good," the assailant said. "This is what Terico needs." "What are you talking about?" Terico asked. "If you have a problem with me, then fight *me*! Leave Febraz out of this."

"I will fight you, Terico," the masked boy said, his voice cracking. "I will fight you... but only once you've been brought down to my level. Only once you're an empty husk without a single soul in the world to turn to!

The assailant plunged his blade into Febraz's heart.

"No!" Terico screamed.

Areo flew for the assailant's face, her claws already extended several centimeters. The Brotherhood fighter leaped back and ripped his bloody sword out of Febraz, then swung it up against Areo's claws.

Terico slipped out his green Nexi and launched vines for the masked boy. A jet of water blasted against Terico's stomach, bashing him hard against a wooden crate. His vision blurry, Terico could barely make out the clash between the masked boy and Areo. He heard the scraping of sword against claws, then a cry from Areo.

Terico forced himself to his feet, and remembered Febraz had some swords in his tent. Terico found a long, slender one and grabbed it. He rushed forward as the Brotherhood fighter sliced off several of Areo's claws. She stumbled back, screaming, and Terico slammed his blade against the fighter's sword.

The masked boy pushed away, then kicked Terico in the stomach. "Let me kill this vampire girl first, since it seems you know her. I'll fight you later, Terico!"

Terico rushed back for the assailant, fighting back the pain in his stomach. The assailant lifted a brown Nexi and blasted it. Terico dodged and swung for the boy's side. The masked boy blocked with his blade, then with his free hand used a dark blue Nexi to blast water at Terico's sword. Terico's arms flung back and he lost his sword in the process. With the flick of his wrist, the masked boy shot swamp material at Terico's feet, planting Terico to the ground. Febraz's sword was out of reach.

"Watch it, mate," the assailant said. "I'd hate to scar that pretty face of yours."

Turan.

Before Terico could respond, the boy turned to Areo, who was back on her feet and raising her tan Nexi stone. Terico quickly took out his black Nexi and wielded it. The flames of the table's candles dissipated instantly, their flickering lights flying into the Nexi stone.

He couldn't see anything, but he could hear Areo unleashing a frenzy of dirt and claws at the assailant. The boy screamed, and boxes tumbled over, spilling their metal contents across the floor. In the meantime Terico worked his feet out of his shoes, then stumbled across the floor in search of the sword he had used. The floor erupted beneath him, and Terico rolled against another crate as a portion of the tent ripped asunder, letting some light in.

Areo fell back to the ground, a deep gash across her stomach. The masked boy limped out into the light, his right leg badly injured—perhaps crushed by a dirt hand formed by Areo. The assailant hurried through the frantic crowds, the people turning and gasping at the violent scene. Areo struggled back to her feet, but instead of chasing the masked boy she turned to Febraz.

Terico ran into the crowds, his sword raised. "Out of the way!" He pushed through the screaming masses until he caught sight of the masked boy, running a few meters ahead down the road.

"Stop!" Terico yelled. "I know who you are. I know it's you, Turan!"

The masked boy kept running, but turned his head back to look at Terico.
"You're wrong. Turan is dead! I am Augurc's newest, most powerful soldier. I am Lynx!" He sprinted down a thin side road, and by the time Terico reached the diverging path, the masked boy was nowhere in sight.

Terico kept running, kept searching—but he found no sign of the Brotherhood member anywhere. Just like a lynx, the masked boy had slipped away silently, just as suddenly as he had appeared.

By the time Terico got back to the tent, he found a large gathering of civilians and a couple city guards in red and black uniforms looking over the scene. There was no sign of Areo or Febraz, however. People yelled foul comments regarding vampires, and others asked in worried voices about what the commotion was about—and what the danger entailed.

Areo must have ran off with Febraz. Terico turned away from the scene before he would get pulled into a long investigation. His mind filled with morbid images.

Febraz is dead. He is dead because of me.
Turan is a Brotherhood member. He wants me to suffer.
Areo is now hiding somewhere with the corpse of her father. The very day she gained the Rite Nexi... and this is how she is reunited with Febraz...
Questions erupted in Terico's mind. Why did Turan kill Febraz? Why was Turan a Brotherhood fighter? Was he already experimented on by Augurc?
What did that man do to Turan's mind?

Augurc and Delkol Shire. Two heartless brothers, both doing everything they could to destroy everything in Terico's life.

Why was this happening? When would it ever stop?

Terico gripped the hilt of his sword a bit tighter.

It will all end when they're dead. Delkol must die. Augurc must die. The Brotherhood must die. This constant bloodshed and agony... It has to end.
In any way possible, I have to end it!

.

Terico eventually found Areo at the end of a dark alley, hiding behind a pile of rotten firewood. She had her teeth clamped in Febraz's neck, and tears trickled down her face. The deep wound in her stomach was healed, but she otherwise looked in a miserable state.

Upon seeing Terico, she let go of Febraz's neck and wiped the blood from her mouth. She let her dead father drape across her lap and looked up at Terico with exhausted, bloodshot eyes.

They stared at each other for a few seconds.

"I'm sorry, Areo," Terico said. He couldn't think of anything more to say. Nothing he could say would make anything better.

"I wanted..." Areo began, but she had to wait a bit before continuing. "I wanted to be with him again... in the sunlight."

Terico couldn't imagine how long Areo had been waiting for this day. Putting all her effort into passing the Rite, all so she could return to the world outside of the vampiric city. To visit with her father again, without having to worry about harm befalling Febraz in Istal. And now everything she had worked so hard for was taken from her. In an instant. Without any warning.

"My parents were taken away from me by the Brotherhood as well," Terico said. "It was also... very sudden."

Areo wiped her eyes and shut them tight. "My father... Febraz was the only one who was there for me. When I was all alone, just a little child... He gave me something to live for."

Terico nodded and sat down beside Areo. "Keep living for him. That's all we can do for our parents. They... tend to place the lives of their children above their own."

As Terico's thoughts turned to his parents, he imagined Areo reflecting on all the time she spent with her father. Clearly there wasn't a perfect relationship between Febraz and Areo, but there was still a strong bond between them, stronger than a simple tie by blood.

Somehow Terico had to keep moving on. Areo was in the same boat as him now, so he hoped he would find a way to help her move on as well.

•

That night they buried Febraz in a secluded grove outside of Merze. Overcome by exhaustion, Terico fell asleep beneath the trees, and didn't wake up until it was well past sunrise. He presumed Areo got some sleep as well at some point, since she looked a little better off than she did yesterday.

"Are you going to be okay?" Terico asked as they headed back to the city.

"I... don't know," Areo said. "I don't know what to do now."

They returned to the marketplace in silence for the most part. Terico just needed to buy some shoes, having lost his in Febraz's tent. After selling his black Nexi stone to a merchant, Febraz bought some strapped leather shoes and some food for the trip to Edellerston. Terico hoped to find Jujor at the old man's underground hideaway, but was prepared to go back down to Emoser Helena if necessary. Hopefully Jujor was still alive, and hopefully he still had the Elpis fragment.

It was a lot to hope for, but Terico was still certain there was more to Jujor than met the eye.

Terico and Areo headed back to the ruins of Edellerston. It was a tiring, gloomy journey, and there wasn't much Terico was able to do for Areo on the way there. He explained his situation with the Elpis, and how he intended to bring down Delkol and his Brotherhood. Areo said her mentor strongly discouraged acting out in revenge, but still accompanied Terico regardless. She just needed someone to be with, Terico imagined, but he didn't mind. It was the least he could do, considering how it was his fault for her father's death, to some degree.

Why Turan killed Febraz was difficult to understand. It was clear Turan simply wanted Terico to suffer, and the best way to do that was apparently by killing everyone Terico knew. There weren't many people left who Terico knew though, considering how his home village was wiped out.

But what am I supposed to do now? Terico wondered. *Turan's mind has been ruined by Augurc somehow. Is there any way to save him?* Knowing that Lynx was Turan, Terico had to decide how he would act if they ever met again. Would Terico be willing to fight his best friend? Was there a way he could reach out to Turan? And what if Areo is still with him? Would she lash out for revenge? She said it was best for her to never seek revenge, but would she actually follow her mentor's advice in that regard? How could you live, knowing the murderer of your loved one was still alive and well? What if Areo did decide to have her deserved revenge? What if

Areo killed Turan?

What if I *kill Turan?* Terico thought. *Could I ever do that? Could I ever live with myself, having killed my best friend?*

Terico gritted his teeth and balled his hands into fists. *The fact that I'm even considering this is wrong. I have to save Turan somehow. Perhaps I can use the Elpis to heal him.*

It wasn't wise to count on the mysterious Elpis for so much, but Terico couldn't think of any better ideas at the moment. It gave him something to work toward, at the very least. One day he would kill Delkol, and at last he would be free from the pain in his heart.

I don't know what you'll do in the end, Areo, Terico thought. *I'll help you however I can, though.*

•

A couple days passed before Terico and Areo reached the remains of Edellerston. The journey was uneventful, but Terico was able to hold a bit more conversation with Areo as they worked through the white tree forest. He learned a bit more about life in Istal and some of the difficulties Areo faced as an "unofficial" vampire.

She shared a couple stories about some of the things she did with Jenba when they weren't training, such as the card games they would play, and the penalties they would dish out to one another upon losing. One time Jenba buried Areo a few meters underground for a week, and one time Areo made Jenba swim naked to the bottom of an icy lake. Terico thought this was all rather cruel, especially for siblings—but apparently they made it through these punishments unscathed, and even enjoyed them in some strange way.

As they journeyed, Terico tried sharing some of the food he bought with Areo, but learned that vampires really did live solely off of blood. Areo said she wished she could still eat human food so she could remember how things tasted, but it had been so long since she had any that she didn't miss it too much. She had a number of vials and bottles of blood in her small pack, and would down a few gulps each day. Apparently it didn't take much for her to get by, though she explained it took a lot of blood for her to regenerate. Technically she didn't need any at all to live on a day to day basis, but having a bit each day gave her the energy she would need to fight in the event she would need to.

They reached Edellerston in the afternoon, and it was cloudy enough there that Areo didn't need to constantly squint. Though she was perfectly capable now of walking in the sunlight, her sight was still slowly adjusting to it. After living by just the dim light of the mangroves for so many years, it wasn't surprising that the outdoors would be hard on her eyes for a while.

Terico led the way to the fake bush that acted as the doorway to Jujor's hidden underground room. He pulled on the bush to open the way to the stairway passage. To Terico's relief, the stairway glimmered with faint candlelight emanating from the dark room below.

"About time you got here," Jujor said.

Terico smiled and walked down the lopsided staircase, leading Areo down with him. "Glad you made it out of the cave, Jujor." Once at the bottom, Terico found Jujor sitting on his bed, holding his book on the Elpis stone. The old man looked tired, but alive and well.

Jujor looked at Areo a few seconds, then grinned at Terico. "I see you've been doing well for yourself, boy."

"Hardly," Terico muttered. "You're all right, though?"

"The forsaken gave me hell," Jujor said, "but that's nothing new for me. I got back here the same day we got the stone, and have been waiting for you to show up."

"Glad you made it out all right," Terico said. He looked back to Areo. "I should introduce you both. Jujor, this is Areo. She is Febraz's daughter, and just passed the Rite to get the transformative Nexi.

"And Areo, this is Jujor. He helped me find the Elpis fragment in the underground city. Febraz saved his life once when Jujor worked as a miner."
Jujor smiled at Areo. "It's good to finally meet you, Areo. Febraz has told me all about you. Sometimes wouldn't *stop* talking about you." He looked to Terico and resumed where he left off earlier. "Speaking of Febraz, I've gathered that he's the reason we were separated. I'm assuming that's why you randomly vanished back there? Some sort of business you had to perform for him?"

"The mark summoned me to him," Terico said. "I'm afraid things didn't end well for him though..."

Jujor looked at Terico sadly, his face turning pale, strained. "He's gone then? That's..." He looked down to the floor. "I was afraid this would happen. He had stayed in Merze longer than was safe for a vampire."

"It wasn't that," Terico said. "He was killed by T—" He stopped short. "By a member of the Brotherhood."

"The Brotherhood again?" Jujor muttered. "Why would they bother with Febraz?"

Terico didn't want to delve into this subject with Areo there. "I don't know. Delkol and his followers don't seem to need a good reason to kill people." Jujor sighed and looked up to Areo. "I'm sorry for your loss, child. I hope Terico's been of some help to you."

"He has," Areo said. "Terico fulfilled Father's wish to bring me back to him."

Terico felt a pitiful guilt fester in his heart. He didn't think he deserved any kind of praise with Febraz dead, and with his best friend turned a member of the Brotherhood. A part of him would have preferred Areo's spite to her praise, and a part of him felt he would have handled Turan's death better than the fate Turan ended up with.

Areo went on. "Terico says you have a piece of a stone called the Elpis."

"Yes, I have it right here," Jujor said. He untied the small pouch on his belt and poured out the Elpis fragment onto his bed. It glowed bright yellow, then silver, then orange, and so on through all the colors of the Nexi. It was perfectly smooth save for the end of the back side, where it was split from the other three portions of the Elpis. Terico was glad to see it here, and know that Jujor hadn't used it for some ambiguous purpose. It sounded like Jujor hadn't touched it, which may have been wise considering the torture its power had put Terico through.

"And this has the power to bring down the Brotherhood?" Areo asked.

"It has the power to do a lot of things," Jujor said. "Is that what you would use it for?"

"I... I don't know," Areo said. "My master said it's unwise to be driven by a desire for revenge."

"It's something most people seem to wish for deep down, though," Jujor said. "We all wish for justice to be served. Blessings for the righteous, punishments for the wicked."

"That's only natural," Terico said. "Why should it be any other way?" "I'm not saying it should," Jujor said. "But Areo's master has a point well worth considering. The road toward vengeance is a bloody one, and often connects to many other bloody roads. Kill one man, and five people will wish to avenge him. And if they kill the murderer, who's to say five people won't want him avenged as well? And so the five who killed him are killed, and there's five people for each one of those killed seeking revenge."

"Of course I've thought of this," Terico said. "But you said yourself that Delkol could kill thousands of people if he gains the Elpis. You said he could destroy all of Fiefs with that power."

"Is that why you want to kill him?" Jujor asked.

Terico frowned because he knew what his honest answer would be. "Does it matter?"

"Perhaps not," Jujor said. "But make sure you understand what you're getting into, Terico. You know what it's like to lose people you love. I expect that every member of the Brotherhood has at least one friend or relative in this world."

"I know," Terico said. "I won't let this fact stop me from doing what's right, though."

"But how can you know what's right?" Areo asked. "What *is* right?" Terico thought over Areo's question, not quite sure where she was going with it. "What I decide is right." There was nothing he could completely trust in the world, save for his own instincts. Nothing was more clear to Terico than the need for Delkol and the Brotherhood to pay for their sins against the world.

And if Terico needed to obtain the Elpis stone in order to do so, he would stop at nothing to find each of the Elpis fragments.

With the aid of his map and documents, Jujor decided the next likely place to find an Elpis fragment would be in the eigni city of Vursa. Terico was intrigued by the prospect of going to a city of eigni, but still took the mission of finding the Elpis piece seriously.

"We can take a boat there from Merze," Jujor said as they made their way through the outlying farmlands around Edellerston. "The eigni have long had a strong connection with the Nexi, so it wouldn't be too surprising for them to have an Elpis fragment hidden somewhere in one of their cities."

"Shouldn't they be using the Elpis?" Areo asked.

"It was likely hidden several hundred years ago," Jujor said. "If anyone there knows of the Elpis, they would probably just regard it as a legend at best. Whoever broke the Elpis apart put a lot of effort into turning the stories of the stone into just that—stories."

"It's just strange that we'll be finding something in a city that could have been using the stone for hundreds of years now," Terico said.

"Don't you remember the forsaken back in Helena?" Jujor said. "I rather doubt that was a natural evolution, boy. The Elpis is incredibly dangerous— even just a fourth of it. You should know from experience."

"I don't even understand what happened back there," Terico said. "First my injuries healed, and then I felt all this energy, and all this pain..."

"The full power of the Elpis is said to be more than that of all the Nexi stones in the world," Jujor said. "The fact you didn't die outright is probably a miracle in and of itself. It's a good thing you're—" He stopped, and Terico waited several seconds for Jujor to continue.

"I'm what?"

"You have a strong connection with the Nexi, apparently," Jujor said. "But I would be very hesitant about using the Elpis ever again, boy. It was difficult to see from far away, but you seemed to be undergoing a complete transformation."

Terico had been too overwhelmed by the pain to notice anything changing about himself at the time. "What do you mean?"

"Well... you almost looked downright demonic," Jujor said. "I'm not sure if you were affected mentally or emotionally when you used the

Elpis, but I was rather worried for a minute there."

Terico kept walking, staring out at the distant fields around him. He wasn't sure how to take all this. He had transformed when he used the Elpis? He thought over everything he did when he had access to its power. He had managed to heal himself and save himself from falling, and then sent all the forsaken running off the cliff. Terico had been in the right state of mind the whole time—it was simply the pain of the Elpis's power that overwhelmed him. And he had a feeling he'd be able to handle the power the next time he accessed it. Knowing what he was getting into would better prepare himself for the Elpis's energy.

Once he had all four fragments, Terico knew he'd be able to bring down Delkol. The world would be a better place without Delkol. And once the Brotherhood was crushed, Terico would be content to give up the Elpis stone's power. He understood that power could quickly drive a man down a self-destructive spiral of cruelty and tyranny.

Terico would only use the Elpis to put an end to the misdeeds of the Shires. He could go back to a normal life once that was done. At least—as normal a life as he could manage at this point. It was apparent that this quest for justice would not go smoothly, but Terico had long accepted that.

•

The three reached Merze in the afternoon a couple days later. Areo was concerned about how they would find a boat willing to take them to Vursa, considering how difficult it was for outsiders to enter the eigni city without anything to prove they had official business there. The eigni island cities generally liked to keep out of foreign affairs, especially when tensions were high between the nearby Fiefs and Shire Kingdoms.

Jujor assured her that he had connections with the eigni, apparently through the professor who taught some of the Nexi classes at Terico's school. Jujor's only concern was in finding a small boat, because Jujor didn't want anyone finding out about the Elpis. The less people who knew where they were going, the better, he claimed. Terico didn't think the three of them attracted that much attention, but he couldn't fault the old man for wanting to proceed cautiously.

They walked up and down the wooden piers of the harbor, speaking with about a dozen sailors who ran small boats. Some of them weren't planning to set sail that day, and others asked for a price too steep for Jujor to afford. But most simply had no reason to go all the way out to Vursa, which was a foreign, perhaps foreboding locale to them in the first place.

At last they came across a man with spiky blond hair, leaning back against the side of a small wooden boat with one mast, and probably only a couple rooms below deck. The sailor looked to be in his mid-twenties, and wore a loose, light gray shirt and trousers, along with a curious headpiece made of dark green metal. It wrapped across his forehead like laurels, and joined in the middle with a smooth, dark blue Nexi stone.

"Hey, travelers," he said, pointing a hand toward them. "Welcome aboard the greatest ship in all of Merze! Or rather, in the entire world. Not only does it float on water, but it offers the most beautiful views!"

He stood up tall and pointed both hands toward himself, then winked at Areo. "Of course, the ocean is pretty nice to look at too."

Jujor laughed. "I like this guy."

"I don't know," Terico whispered. "He sounds pretty desperate." "In more ways than one," Areo added.

"We're hoping to sail to Vursa," Jujor said, shaking the man's hand.

"Good to travel with you, kind sir," the sailor said, nearly a third of his face filled with a grin. He spoke in a clear, loud voice that only a man of the seas could command. "My name is Borely Sen, but you can call me Captain Borely. Or just Borely! I'm not so finicky. I've been called much worse!"

"You'd take us to Vursa then?" Jujor said. "How much for three passengers?"

"Anything at all!" Borely said. "Hop aboard and we'll be on our way... to adventure!" At this he raised a hand out toward the sun in the far horizon.

"Anything?" Jujor said. "How about fifty—"

"Three hundred fifty, and you've got yourself a deal!" Borely said, clapping his hands together.

"That's... more than *anything at all*," Jujor said.

"But for a chance to hold the lovely maiden's hand, I'll bump it down to three hundred!" Borely slipped by Terico and gently took Areo by the hand, and gave her a light, aristocratic bow. Areo stepped back and jerked her hand away.

Borely chuckled and leaned over to Terico to whisper to him. "You two aren't— you know—an item, are you? "

"No," Terico said. "But—"

Borely turned back to Areo and placed his index finger beneath his chin. "What's your name, heavenly goddess? I still need to come up with a name for my ship, and they say the name of a beautiful woman will ensure a safe journey across the tumultuous waves of the sea!"

Areo simply stared back at Borely, her eyes completely giving away her annoyance toward this man.

Borely leaned back and sighed, tilting his head backward and placing a hand to his heart. "Oh, to hear her sweet voice—I look forward to it with all the anticipation of my soul."

"Right, right," Jujor said. "So two hundred fifty, plus we'll throw in a free presentation of Areo's speaking ability at some point." "Two hundred ninety-nine," Borely said.

"Two hundred sixty, final offer," Jujor said.

"Two hundred seventy-five, and a private dinner with the maiden," Borely said.

"Fine," Jujor said. Borely instantly took Jujor's hand and shook on the deal. "What?" Areo screamed. "I'm not here to be bartered, you know!"

"Ah, what a sweet, soothing voice," Borely said, leaning back and wincing from the outburst. He turned to the plank connecting the little ship to the pier and skipped up it.

"Right then. Time's a wastin'!" He turned and beckoned everyone to come aboard. "Setar wasn't built in a day, and it will take three times that to get there by boat!"

"We're going to Vursa though," Terico said.

Borely stared at Terico blankly for a few seconds before snapping back to his default jovial expression. "Right! Vursa it is, then."

•

6

LIFELESS CITY

Captain Borely had enough small cots for each of them to sleep in that night, but Terico didn't feel like he got more than an hour's worth of sleep total. He certainly doubted he ever had more than ten minutes of actual rest all at once. There was just something unnerving about sleeping on a boat. It never stopped moving, and the constant motion made Terico tense. At any moment the endless waves of the sea could come crashing down on the little ship, and the constant creaking of the weathered wooden planks and groaning of the rusty metal girders did very little to calm Terico's apprehension. The fact that the captain seemed so oblivious didn't help matters either.

When morning came, Terico wearily walked up the stairs to the deck. He found Areo leaning against the railing at the very front of the ship, looking out to the horizon, while Borely manned the helm situated a ways behind the mast. There was a good breeze, and the sky was dotted with a few pleasant clouds, including one that dimmed the sunrise.

There wasn't much to look at on Borely's boat. Above deck there was the mast, the helm, and a room at the back where basic materials and ship equipment were stored. The sail was a nondescript gray, and the ship in general was maintained just enough to keep it afloat, it seemed. Or maintained as best it could be, but could only look as good as it did considering how old it probably was. Terico imagined Borely was a fairly new sailor, so it would probably be difficult for him to afford anything better.

Terico walked over to Borely, who leaned against the helm and gave Terico a quick salute.

"How did you sleep, Terico?" Borely asked.

"I've slept better," Terico said.

"First time at sea, I take it?"

"Yes." It wasn't so long ago when Terico stepped outside of his home town at all, in fact. And he certainly never rode a boat in Edellerston.

"How's old Jujor sleeping?" Borely asked.

"Fine," Terico said, remembering the old man's horrendously loud snores. Jujor apparently knew a fair amount about sailing, and had agreed to run the boat for part of the night so that Borely could get some sleep. Jujor went back to sleep once Borely woke up, at which point Terico knew he wouldn't get another wink of sleep.

"That's good," Borely said.

Terico thought the captain would say something more, but the man kept quiet for once. Yesterday it had seemed there was no end to the one-liners at Borely's disposal.

His thoughts wandering over the events of the past couple weeks, Terico stared at the waters stretching out in every direction for as far as his eyes could see. The air was crisp but stank of the salty waters, which Terico had a hard time imagining people being able to get used to.

He had once felt the fields and farmlands surrounding Edellerston extended forever, but standing on a small boat in the middle of the sea was a much more imposing sight. At the very least, it was a lot more troubling of a sight. There was still the possibility this rickety old boat would decide to just start sinking—and then what would Terico do? There was a rowboat in the storage room, but Terico doubted somewhat that they'd actually be able to use it to reach land before dying of thirst. Well, except for Areo.

"So, she's quite the lovely one," Borely said, staring out toward Areo. She was still looking out into the waves, too far away to hear Borely's dialogue. Terico was a little startled by the captain's timing. "Um, okay."

Borely leaned over to Terico as if to tell a secret. "She's definitely the loveliest lady to grace this humble deck. This is probably her first time aboard a ship, I'd wager. She looks like she hasn't seen much sun at all, really."

"I suppose," Terico said.

"Is she an elf, by the way?" Borely pointed at his ears a moment. "I didn't notice before since she's got her hair over her ears, but this morning

I thought I saw some points."

"She... doesn't talk about herself much," Terico said. He doubted Areo would want him letting random people know about her being a vampire.

"That's true," Borely said. "Tried a dozen times to get a good conversation going with her, but she's an aloof one! Plays hard to get... Not that I mind— I like women like that. I'll be sure to learn more about her when we have our private dinner tonight."

"Oh... kay," Terico said. He really didn't care where this was going. And he rather doubted that Areo would ever actually have this private dinner Borely spoke of.

"I'm surprised that you two weren't a couple," Borely said. "Pleasantly surprised, of course. But does that mean you have a girlfriend back home then?"

Terico stared out at a small, delicate cloud in the distant horizon. He still had no idea what may or may not have happened to Suran. Did she die in Delkol's attack? Was she captured? Could she have suffered the same fate as Turan? Or worse? All this time, she could be suffering, and Terico not know a single thing about it. What if she needed him right now? He was out in the middle of the sea, and Suran could very well be undergoing the darkest of horrors at the Brotherhood's expense.

He could still remember the time he spent with her the day of the attack. How she had brought his mother elven herbs for the sick. How she had prepared breakfast for everyone. And how she spoke so kindly to him, always concerned for his well-being. Terico hadn't been able to ask her to spend the day with him during the upcoming festival—which would have long passed by now had it actually happened. Had the village not been utterly decimated.

It was all a moot point now, but some of Terico's greatest guilt that day came from not being able to find Suran when the Brotherhood attacked. He should have gone with her when she left to help her brother with something. Had he been there with her, he could have protected her.

"I take that as a *no*," Borely said.

Terico remembered the question, but didn't really want to get into it. The fact that he wasn't there for Suran when she needed him most was painful enough as it was.

Do I really deserve to ever be anything to her? he thought. *If she is still alive, that is.*
The day passed slowly, and there was little for Terico to do but reflect on his many mistakes and reaffirm his decisions and intentions for the future. Somehow he would make things right as best he could. It seemed clear that his world could never be as it once was, but there was still much he could do. If he could find an Elpis fragment in the eigni city, he'd be one step closer to achieving his goals.

He thought back to the power he briefly wielded in the underground city. It was only a matter of time before he would have it again. And with more of the fragments combined, the power would only be greater—exponentially greater.

The possibilities the whole Elpis stone presented were likely too magnificent for Terico to even comprehend. What limits would there be to his power then? Would there be any at all?

Would he be able to shape his world precisely as he wished? Perhaps his world *could* be as it once was.

•

Areo had met plenty of fools over the course of her long life, so this wasn't the first time she had to put up with someone who got on her nerves. And in all honesty, there were people she knew who were even more ridiculous than Borely was. But the thing that bothered her most was the fact Borely *wasn't* a complete idiot who didn't know when to quit. She could tell it was just a facade, and she really didn't wish to see him keep acting like this for the rest of the boat trip.

And so, to Terico and Jujor's dismay, she accepted Borely's invitation to a private dinner.

If Borely was surprised as well, he managed to hide it behind a cool smile and all-knowing gleam in his eyes.

He brought Areo down to the room she had shared with Terico and Jujor, and set up a makeshift table by laying a large, circular slab of wood atop one of the cots. He pushed the other two beds to either side of the table, apparently intending them to act as chairs. Then after setting a candle down in the middle of the table, Borely took one of the lit candles hanging on the wall and used it to light the one on the table. With everything arranged as he saw fit, he hurried back upstairs to procure whatever it was he intended to provide for the dinner.

Of course, Areo wasn't going to be able to eat anything Borely would bring, but she doubted he would mind. He came back a minute later with a bottle of wine in one hand, and some foodstuff wrapped in cloth in his other hand. It turned out to be a smoked fish, some kind of dark bread, and a hunk of pale cheese. Areo didn't recognize what these foods were precisely, and it had been a long time since she had been exposed to the smells of human cuisine like this. Perhaps it all would have smelled nice to her before she became a vampire, but at this point she merely felt indifferent.

"Wish I had better," Borely said, "but this will work nicely, I believe."

"That's very kind of you," Areo said. "I really would just like to chat for the most part, though."

"Oh, that's great!" Borely said. "I'd love to learn more about you, Areo."

"Really?" Areo asked. "That wouldn't be very aloof of me, though. Wouldn't you prefer I play hard to catch?"

"Oh, wow," Borely said, grimacing. "You heard all that?"

"I have pretty good hearing," Areo said. "But if you want to learn more about me, I'd like to know who it is I'm dealing with here." She pointed a hand toward Borely. "Who are you? I find it a bit strange that a man your age is aimlessly wandering the seas all by himself."

Borely placed his hands on the bed to either side of him and leaned back a bit. "Ever since I was a kid, I've been traveling the seas. Of course, I wasn't alone then. My parents ran a large cargo ship, and I helped them out along with my older brother. And that's how I've always spent my days—can't think of much else I could be doing."

"You're alone now, though," Areo said. "What happened?"

For a moment Borely looked at Areo with an almost thoughtful look in his eyes. "Well, that's how things go... Back when I was nine, the port of Merze was a more dangerous place than it is today. Vampires would sneak onto boats at night, and once the ships were far from shore, they'd attack in the middle of the night. And sometimes... the people they turn into vampires go mad."

Areo felt her throat go tight. Borely was speaking generally, but it was clear he was referring to what must have happened to his family's ship. "Sometimes..." Borely continued, "Sometimes even a brother will turn against you. A boy turned vampire can lash out against anyone— even his own parents. And just tear away at everyone. Kill every single person on the ship... and force you to kill him."

Areo looked down to the table, letting this revelation sink in. She had killed people before, including Krug just a few days ago—but the thought of having to kill your own sibling was unthinkable. She didn't have any brothers or sisters while growing up, but she had Jenba in Istal. Would she be willing to kill him if her life depended on it? It was the sort of decision nobody should ever have to make.

There was also the dilemma on her mind regarding Borely's outlook

on vampires. The average human had a negative view of them to begin with, and the slaughter of Borely's entire family would surely have left him bitter, at the very least. There was no telling what he would do if he found out Areo was a vampire.

But to lose his parents, and then have to kill his own brother—all at the age of nine. Areo could only imagine how Borely was able to move on after such a life-shattering experience.

"I'm sorry," Borely said, forcing a smile back on his face. "I didn't mean to just share a sad story. I've done quite fine for myself, really. I keep to the seas and try to keep my family proud as best I can. It's not the most glamorous of professions, but it's nice to help people get to where they need to go. I meet all sorts of people, and it's always nice to look out at the seas and skies."

"I see," Areo said. She doubted Borely's life was as carefree as he made it out to be, though. It was rather unlikely that Borely had an easy time making a living as a young orphan in the harsh environment of a shipyard. It probably took him many years of hard work to obtain this ship, as brokendown as it was.

Borely poured a couple cups of wine and set one down for Areo, then took his and gulped it down quickly. "Ah... there's been ups and downs, but that's how life is, you know? I'd have to say this particular trip is a high point in my life."

Areo glanced to her right. "Oh, really."

"Yes, I'm glad to have met you," Borely said. "I hope things have been going well for you lately as well."

She had agreed to share a bit about herself, but she obviously couldn't tell him some of the most basic things about who she was. "No, I'm afraid not. I lost my parents when I was young as well, but there was a man who raised me as a father later on. He was recently killed, unfortunately."

Borely turned somber, and to his credit Areo felt this was one of his more genuine expressions. "I'm sorry... I didn't realize..."

"It's okay," Areo said. It was surprisingly thoughtful of Borely to try apologizing for his behavior, but there was no way he could have understood Areo's situation. He still didn't know the truth, and Areo didn't intend to drag him any further into things. "I will be fine. It just... leaves this empty feeling."

Borely nodded. "It lingers. For a while it hurts, and some days you just don't care about anything anymore. You just want it all to end. But... it passes eventually. Perhaps not entirely, but enough for you to go on living. To make the most of things. You're never certain, but you feel that there is a way to move on. Perhaps the path you end up taking is the best one, perhaps it isn't. But you take it and hope for the best." A long smile spread across his face. "Or something like that."

Areo shook her head, but couldn't help but smile a little as well. The advice was both overly simplistic and a bit meaningless, making the whole monologue fairly ridiculous. But it was a nice sentiment, nonetheless. "Thanks, Captain Borely."

"Not a problem, madame. But you can call me Borely, if you wish. Though if you must use an adjective, there's always *Handsome Borely*. Or *Ravishing Borely*. Or from you, I wouldn't mind hearing *Sweet Borely* or *Dearest Borely*."

Areo frowned. *Certainly can't call him* Subtle Borely *any time soon*, she thought.

"I'll think about it."

•

Terico was able to get more sleep that night, mainly due to the fact he had gotten so little the previous night. The constant shifting of the ship still bothered him at some level, but he was able to keep his thoughts directed elsewhere for the majority of the rest of the trip.

By noon Jujor was up again, and to pass the time he brought up a deck of cards to play with. He sat down near the helm so Borely could play as well. Terico and Areo sat down with them.

"You all know how to play individuals?" Jujor asked.

Everyone said *yes*—as far as Terico knew, individuals was one of the betterknown card games.

"Great, I'll deal," Jujor said. He handed each of them eight cards.

Terico looked his cards over, finding three dead trees, two princesses, a hawk, a mountain, and an archer. Three of the images were major constellations, so Terico needed to get five others in order to complete the set and win the game. It was a game where each player needed to deceive the others in order to get the specific cards they needed.

As the game went on, it seemed pretty clear Areo was ending up with most of the major constellations.

"Did you play individuals a lot with your brother?" Terico asked.

"Yes," Areo said. "He was much better at it, though. I preferred playing central village."

Jujor drew a card and looked his hand over. "It seems Terico has had some practice as well. You played with your classmates at school, I take it?" "From time to time," Terico said. "I wasn't very interested in card games, but Turan liked them a lot." Terico stopped, not really wishing to talk more about his past. On days they didn't have any escapades into the caverns planned, Turan often dragged Terico into a game of cards after school with whoever else they could find. Sometimes Suran and her brother Lanek would play, if they didn't have things they had to do at home.

Terico's thoughts drifted to times he would go with Suran and Lanek to help them out with tasks their parents gave them. Their parents were

mechanics, and spent much of their days designing parts for airships, a kind of transport that floated in the air like a balloon, but looked more like giant ships. Supposedly Suran's parents had constructed an entire airship in the city of Plien, but Terico never saw anything more than the metal parts he helped Suran and Lanek craft at their workshop.

"It's your turn, Terico," Borely said, breaking Terico's train of thought.

"Oh, pass," Terico said.

"You look a little distant there," Jujor said.

"I'm just... thinking," Terico said.

"A good habit to have," Borely said. "What's on your mind?" "Just the things I used to do," Terico said. "My old life, I guess." "Where are you from?" Borely asked.

Terico pushed his cards together into a little stack and gripped them with one hand. "Edellerston. It's destroyed now, though."

"Oh..." Borely said. He glanced to Jujor and Areo. "Is that where all of you were from?"

"For a while," Jujor said. "I've lived at a lot of places, but Edellerston was where I spent my last fifteen or so years."

"I... grew up near Otosel," Areo said. As Terico expected, she didn't mention living in Istal.

"I'm just curious how you all ended up together on this little voyage," Borely said. "And why you're going to Vursa, of all places."

"It's best we don't give the purpose of our journey," Jujor said.

Borely sat up straight, a great smile beaming on his face. "Oh, really?"

"I'm serious," Jujor said. "It's best you not get involved in this." "Oh, I've figured it all out already," Borely said, folding his arms.

Jujor's eyebrows fell flat, and his lips tightened into a deep frown. "No, you haven't."

"It all goes back to the Brotherhood," Borely said. "There's been a lot of talk about them, lately. War is inevitable, and it sounds like the Shire Kingdom's armies have begun to assemble for a full-scale invasion. But the Brotherhood has been getting things ready for them, striking lots of key locations to prepare the way for the main armies.

"So I'm guessing the Brotherhood attacked your home town. And I'm also guessing the Brotherhood killed Areo's father. And therefore it's probably safe to say that the Brotherhood is up to something in Vursa now. I've heard that airships have been sighted heading back and forth between there and the Shire Kingdom."

"I'm not going to respond," Jujor said.

"There's no reason to hide anything from me," Borely said. "I'm on your side in this. I don't have anything personal against the Brotherhood, but I've heard enough stories of their murders and destruction in general.

I'd be perfectly glad to bust a few of their skulls for the greater good." "You can fight?" Terico asked.

Borely set his cards down, then put his hands into fists and raised them up in front of himself. "I've had to protect my ship's goods more than once. I can handle things in the heat of a battle."

"You can help us out if you want," Terico said, "but suffice to say we may be entering a dangerous situation." There was the chance they could run into the Brotherhood, considering they were searching for the Elpis fragments as well. They were apparently going by accurate data—enough to know there was one at Edellerston somewhere, at least. And there was the possibility there would be monsters similar to the forsaken in Vursa as well. That is, if the Elpis was there at all. Jujor himself wasn't entirely certain about the locations marked on the map in his book.

"Great!" Borely said. "I would do anything to make sure Areo's mission is a complete success."

"It's not my mission," Areo said. "I'm just helping Terico and Jujor." And from what Terico understood, trying to decide if she wanted to personally help bring down the Brotherhood.

"Our mission isn't what you think it's going to be," Jujor told Borely. "If you come with us, you'll have to vow to keep everything a secret. Otherwise... you'll be *made* to keep quiet."

Borely's smile weakened a little, and Terico turned to note the stern look on Jujor's face. It was actually a bit frightening.

It was another moment that made Terico wonder about who Jujor truly was. The old man hadn't done anything bad so far, but would his true colors show once more of the Elpis was obtained? Terico felt wrong for second-guessing Jujor like this, but he wasn't about to let anyone ruin his plans for revenge against Delkol.

There was no certainty that Areo and Borely were truly on Terico's side in all this, either. He had to remind himself that there were no guarantees at this point.

Anyone can turn against you, Terico thought. *And anyone can die at any given moment.*

•

It was evening by the time they reached the small island that contained the city of Vursa. The port was full of ships, but there wasn't anybody in them. The piers were completely deserted as well.

Terico had thought Istal was a quiet city, especially when compared to the hectic marketplaces of Merze—but Vursa was even quieter. With the sun already set and a chilly breeze passing by, Terico almost felt like he was walking into a graveyard.

Once Borely tied up the boat to the dock, Jujor led the way into the city. Terico was bombarded with sights he had never imagined. His eigni professor back in Edellerston had said Vursa was a colorful city, but Terico thought that just meant some of the buildings would be blue, some green, some yellow, and so forth. Instead, every building was painted a hundred different colors, and it was only upon closer inspection of individual structures that the sheer intricacy of the artwork was revealed.

Terico walked toward a two-story building with large oval windows, and looked over the many mosaics and murals on the walls. Running along the steps to the doorway were stylized curves of at least a dozen different colors, and it took a few seconds for Terico to realize this was lettering in the ancient eigni language. All around the windows and door and running across the bottom and top of the building were delicate mosaics of red, yellow, blue, and black—a mixture of strange, shadowy flowers with crashing waves and rays of sunlight. Amidst the rest of the walls were larger depictions of golden glowing ships sailing a violent sea, a tired-looking eigni man wreathed in flames, a group of scrolls with intricate red-inked maps of various eigni islands, and a group of eigni gathered atop a tall rocky hill to wave orange and purple flags in the air.

Terico didn't know what any of these particular images referred to, but they were all very realistic-looking. And the more Terico looked at the walls, the more pictures he found hidden amidst the rest of the imagery. The paths they walked on were also covered in images and patterns, but much of this was faded. Some portions appeared to have been repainted in recent years, while other areas seemed to be in the middle of having new artwork drawn over the older material.

But everywhere Terico looked, there were hundreds of new paintings to see. Whether they were homes, shops, or governmental structures, every building was covered in immaculate artwork. Some buildings had paintings of individual eigni—presumably the people who lived in those houses. Terico could tell which buildings were shops, on the other hand, because their imagery primarily depicted the wares they sold. The painting styles varied from house to house, perhaps telling something about the people who lived in them. Terico wondered how all this affected the way eigni interacted with one another.

Down near the port, many of the shops depicted boats, ship parts, fish, and fishing gear. But there were also those covered with paintings of clothes, advertising the many unique styles the eigni wore. Others had paintings of the peculiar meals the eigni ate, most of which Terico couldn't identify at all. Some he wasn't even sure if they were a meat or vegetable.

Terico didn't know too much about the eigni save what he knew of Professor Kanto, a rather blunt man who would rarely stray from the material he intended to teach each day. It was presumed by Terico and most of the other students that eigni were generally this way—strict and to-the-point—but the incredulous devotion to the arts on display here gave Terico a very different notion of them.

"This. Is. Amazing," Borely said, emphasizing each word. "Even the tiles on their roofs are painted with different things."

Terico looked up to the steep roof of one of the upcoming buildings, and saw a large image of a wide stringed instrument he didn't recognize. As he walked closer to the building, Terico realized that all of the tiles had small, individual paintings of various instruments painted on them. Somehow the tiles were arranged to make it appear to be one giant image from far away.

"It's all very nice," Areo said, "but where are all the eigni?"

Terico had been so caught up in the artwork that he hadn't noticed the complete lack of people living in this city. "Maybe they're all at their homes." He walked up to a nearby house and knocked on the door. There was no answer, and knocking on a few other doors didn't warrant any results either. Each of the doors were locked, and Terico couldn't see anyone through the windows.

"Something has happened here," Jujor said. "We'll keep looking and see if we can find anyone."

They continued down the main city path, and Terico did his best to look for anything out of the ordinary. Closer to the center of the city, the buildings became a couple stories larger, and many of them were embellished with grand sculptures. They were mostly statues of large fish, sharks, and other creatures of the sea, and each was covered in patterns of many colors, just like the buildings. The sight of the city in general was a bit dizzying, and Terico wondered if he would really find anything hidden amidst this chaos of clashing and complementing colors.

It didn't take long for them to make their way around the entire city, to Terico's surprise. Vursa was much smaller than he thought it would be.

"So, nobody here at all," he said. "Do you think the Brotherhood came here?"

"All the buildings are intact," Jujor said. "I didn't find any signs of an attack at all…"

"Perhaps the eigni were threatened?" Borely said. "They may have chosen to leave rather than fight."

"The eigni do generally try to keep out of wars," Jujor said, "but I rather doubt they'd just give up their whole city like that. And I don't see anyone here in their place."

"Should we just look for what we came here for?" Terico asked. "We'll head underground," Jujor said. "I bet the eigni went to their underwater structures. We're more likely to find what we're looking for there, anyways."

"Oh, they do live underwater then," Terico said.

"Not all," Jujor said, "but many do. Their buildings are held up with the power of orange Nexi stones. Very few non-eigni have stepped foot below sea level here, but I know a good way down."

He led them to an out-of-the-way side road between tall buildings, then turned past a few more.

"Why would you know a secret way to the underwater part of this city?" Terico asked.

"Because I know everything," Jujor muttered.

"Really?" Borely said. "Can you tell me my future?"

"Swimming with the fishes if you keep asking dumb questions," Jujor said.

Terico was a little concerned with Jujor's agitation, but it was understandable if the old man was worried. This city certainly didn't feel welcoming, and there was no telling what they would find down below. Jujor walked to one of several sheds attached to the back of a building, and slid open the latch to the second doorway. Inside was a long, spiraling staircase, though unlike the ones in Emoser Helena, this was made of white stone, and lit by dim red Nexi every dozen or so steps. These steps weren't painted, which Terico figured was because most people probably didn't access this stairway.

For several seconds, Areo looked back toward the dock in the distance. Terico looked as well, but couldn't see anything but the tiny ships and buildings.

"Something there?" Jujor asked.

"I hear an airship," Areo said.

"Let's get going then," Jujor said. "If the Brotherhood is involved, we don't want them aware of our presence."

•

After several minutes of walking down the tight staircase, Terico came in sight of water. The red-lit walls around them transitioned to transparent glass, and suddenly they were surrounded by the dark water of the sea. Terico reached out his hand to touch the glass, but it was farther away than it appeared, placing it just out of his reach. How the eigni constructed such a long tube like this, he couldn't guess. He hadn't known there were people capable of engineering such a marvelous feat.

They walked on down the stairway for some time—perhaps another ten minutes or so. It wasn't nearly as long as the staircases going down to Emoser Helena, but it was still very long, and very surrounded by some near-infinite kilograms of water.

Once at the end of the stairway, the four reached a passageway that opened up into a hall that rose seven or eight meters tall. The floor was made of the same soft white stone as the stairs, and had red Nexi every few meters grafted into the floor to light the way. The tall glass walls curved up to the rounded-off ceiling, so all around them was water. Terico saw a school of bright teal fish pass by overhead, and couldn't help but smile for a moment.

This was the sort of magic, the wonder of exploring new places, that had always called Terico to adventure while growing up. He had always looked forward to the day he could leave Edellerston and see the world. To have adventures with Turan he could never have just in the nearby caverns. The way life turned out couldn't have been any more different than Terico imagined, but he could at least recognize some of the joys this journey could bring. He could not dwell on the feeling long, knowing that some danger had befallen all the eigni of this city—but it was something to be traveling down this underwater tunnel, heading to a city few outsiders had ever stepped foot in.

The hall expanded into a series of glass-encircled pathways. These led to tens of giant glass domes filled with buildings similar to those found above ground, save for the lack of intricate paintings. These structures were cleaner, simpler, and more tightly organized.

Some of the domes seemed to house entire neighborhoods, while a few looked almost as large as the entire city above ground. Altogether, Vursa was clearly larger than Merze, and drastically larger than Istal. Terico entered one of the nearest domes, in awe of how high the glass walls stretched above the rooftops of the homes and shops. He could make out some of the orange Nexi stones embedded in the glass, glowing bright and giving the structure the strength needed to keep the city from caving in with water.

"Here's some eigni," Areo said. She pointed down the path, and Terico had to squint to make out some of the light blue figures in the distance.

He hurried down to them and raised a hand to the nearest one—a bald man in his fifties or so, wearing bright red trousers, and a sleeveless shirt that seemed to be made of green and black bandages.

"Hello," Terico said. "Sorry to bother you, but—"

The eigni walked on past Terico. The man didn't respond in any way, or even look at Terico.

Terico jogged back a few steps and stood in front of the man. "Wait, I just had a couple questions."

Though the eigni was staring straight at Terico, it seemed as if he didn't actually realize Terico was there. Yet he managed to walk around Terico and continued on his way down the straight path.

"Long day at work?" Borely said, raising an eyebrow.

"Let's try someone else, I guess," Jujor said, clearly confused by the eigni's actions.

They walked down to a black-haired eigni in his early twenties, who wore some kind of one-piece suit made of randomly-sized patches. He was sitting on the front steps of his house, staring up at the distant waters.

"Can we ask you something?" Terico asked.

No response.

"Are you all right?" Jujor asked.

No response.

"Have you completely lost your mind?" Borely asked.

No response.

Areo bent down to one knee and grabbed the man by his shoulders. She shook him vigorously for several seconds, but the eigni simply remained sitting on the step.

Areo stood back up and folded her arms tight. "He held himself up just fine, and he's clearly breathing..."

Terico walked over to an elderly woman in a yellow blouse and white trousers, but she didn't respond to any of his inquiries either. Instead she kept on walking, oblivious to Terico's calls for her assistance.

Shortly afterward he spotted two boys and a girl heading to a nearby house, and hurried over to stand in front of the doorway, blocking their path. The yellow-haired children wore matching green shirts and black skirts, and were probably siblings, Terico took it. They simply stood there, waiting for Terico to step aside. When they didn't respond to anything he said, he picked up the nearest child and asked him to say anything.

The boy, probably five or six, just looked at Terico, entirely blankfaced—a sharp contrast to Terico's exasperation with the situation.

"They're all mindless," Jujor said. "I wouldn't be surprised if what we're looking for is involved with this."

Perhaps it was possible for someone with an Elpis fragment to do something like this, though Terico had no idea why someone would turn the citizens of an entire city into mindless drones. They didn't seem to be doing anything, other than walking or sitting around.

"We'll have to find it," Terico said, "and reverse this spell that's been cast over everyone."

"Hey, over here, quick!" came a child's voice from a ways behind him.

Terico turned around a found a young eigni boy with short white hair. He looked about ten years old, and wore small orange shorts and a black turtleneck shirt without sleeves.

"Hurry!" the boy said. "Come hide here."

More anxious to speak with a real eigni than worried about the ambiguous danger the child referred to, Terico jogged over to the boy, quickly followed by Areo, Borely, and Jujor. The boy led them down a path between homes and around to the back of a shop, where several piles of wooden crates had accumulated.

"What's happening here?" Terico asked the boy.

"There was an official up ahead," the boy said. "You can't let them find you. If you see anyone wearing dark red robes, stay far away from them."
"Eigni council members wear red robes," Jujor said.

"Yes," the boy said. "They've done something terrible to the city. I think I'm the only one that was able to fend off their spell. It turns everyone mindless... makes them do whatever the council wishes. Everyone's under the government's control now."

"How did this happen?" Terico asked.

"I don't know," the boy said. "I've been trying to find out myself, but the council members keep finding me. They're all armed with daggers, so you have to be careful.”

“We’ll be careful,” Terico said, “but we need to know everything we can about what’s happened here.”

“Let’s start with who we even are,” Jujor said. He introduced himself, then Terico, Areo, and Borely, and explained that they were concerned with the Brotherhood being involved with what happened in Vursa.

“My name is Kitoh,” the boy said. “I don’t know about anyone other than the council being involved in this. And I don’t know how they’ve turned everyone mindless.”

“Do you know where these red-robed eigni meet?” Terico asked.

“In the largest dome, there’s the grand council room,” Kitoh said. “There are a lot of council members guarding the way, though.”

Borely punched a fist into his palm. “That’s where we come in, kid.”

“If it’s well-guarded, that’s probably where we need to head, anyways,” Terico said.

“We don’t know if we’ll actually find what we’re looking for, though,” Jujor said. “The eigni naturally have a strong connection with Nexi power, so there are many possibilities for what has happened here.”

“We’ll have to find out,” Terico said. He hoped they would find the Elpis fragment there, but regardless, he intended to help the people of this city. The situation in Vursa seemed nearly as terrible as the one he witnessed in Edellerston, and he didn’t want to see that grisly scene ever repeated again.

•

The group followed Kitoh down the glass tunnels leading to the largest dome of the underwater city. Upon reaching the dome, they made their way between buildings, careful to watch for any eigni wearing the dark red robes of the eigni government. Eventually Kitoh stopped them a ways from what he pointed out to be the building the city’s grand council regularly met in. It was a giant silver building with a red dome on top, and was surrounded with a white brick fence at least five meters tall. At the nearest entrance stood eight eigni men in red robes.

Terico unsheathed the long, thin sword he had taken from Febraz's tent. "Be careful," Jujor said. "I'd prefer we don't start killing off the leaders of the eigni's largest city."

"We can't just let them control the people like this," Terico said.
"Let's see if we can figure out precisely what's going on first," Jujor said. "Don't you find it strange, for example, that the council members are the ones that are armed? Normally they'd leave this sort of work to trained guards."

It was a good point, and it did make the whole situation a level stranger. If the council was controlling all the eigni, wouldn't they force guards to protect their base of operations? And for that matter, why wouldn't they have all the civilians perform some kind of work for them? Everyone was just mindless for some reason. Perhaps the Elpis was tampered with, and this was just how everything ended up somehow.

"Right then," Borely said. "We'll just have to knock them out cold then." He took out some metal knuckle gloves from his pockets and slipped them on over his fists. The metal covered both his knuckles and his palm, giving him something to grip on to. Terico noticed a small orange Nexi stone embedded in the palm of each of the fighting gloves—a setup that could prove quite lethal when activated.

"Don't use those Nexi stones," Terico said. "You might punch a hole straight through these eigni."

"Worry not, Terico my boy," Borely said. "My control over these Nexi is flawless."

"I'm afraid I don't have any Nexi," Kitoh said.

"Here, you can use this," Terico said, handing the boy his green Nexi. Terico had been given a light blue one that he could fall back to in case his sword wasn't enough. "Just keep a safe distance away from them."

Once everyone was ready, Terico charged down the path to the main street and on toward the entryway—a large open arc carved into the thick fence. Areo, Borely, Jujor, and Kitoh followed from behind, raising their weapons and Nexi stones.

A moment later, the red-robed eigni unsheathed their long, pointed daggers. Several of them took out Nexi stones of their own. Two of them fired streams of water, and a third shot a series of vines. Terico slashed away at the vines while the others got out of the way of the jets of water.

One of the eigni turned his blast of water toward Areo, who raised her tan Nexi and released a torrent of dirt from the stone. It formed into a barrier and deflected the water away. At the same time, Borely reached the nearest council member and punched away the man's dagger.

Terico pushed through the vines and ducked beneath a blast of water. Another set of vines rushed past him from behind, and he realized these were Kitoh's vines, heading toward the group of council members. An eigni immediately shot off fire from a red Nexi, engulfing the vines in flames. Terico quickly cut off Kitoh's vines before the fire could rush down to burn the child.

Jujor ran past Terico and slammed his sword against the dagger of the largest eigni. As the eigni slipped out a tan Nexi to fire at Jujor, Borely leaped in front of Terico and punched the eigni in the head, knocking him out cold.

Borely turned to the next closest eigni, avoided the man's dagger swing, and landed a solid punch into the eigni's stomach. The eigni stumbled back a bit, a thin yellow glow around his body revealing the protective barrier he had activated with a yellow Nexi. Borely caused his right fist to glow orange, then slammed it again into the enemy's stomach. The eigni flew back several meters before rolling backward against the stone ground several times, finally lying flat on his stomach in an unconscious heap.

Another council member pushed through to Terico and jabbed his dagger for Terico's chest. Terico parried the attack, then slammed the flat side of his sword against the man's arm, knocking away the enemy's dagger. With his free hand, Terico slipped out his light blue Nexi and shot off a gust of frozen wind at the eigni councilor.

One eigni threw his dagger at Terico, who turned in time to swat it away with his own blade. Two council members rushed for him from either side, one with a dagger glowing bright orange. A third eigni aimed a red Nexi for him.

Borely rammed a shoulder against one eigni, while Areo wrapped an arm around the second eigni's neck. While Borely fought off the eigni wielding the Nexi-strengthened blade, Areo forced the other eigni down to the ground, and briefly lengthened her claws to bat away the man's dagger. She forced her fingernails back to normal before Borely could notice. At the same time, Terico fought off the blasts of fire with bursts of cold air from his light blue Nexi. While Terico fended the eigni off, Kitoh's vines slunk across the ground. They wrapped around the eigni's feet, then pulled against the councilor, slamming him to the ground. The back of his head impacted the stone floor, knocking him unconscious.

Jujor pushed a white Nexi against the face of another eigni, and managed to knock the man out cold with his sword's hilt while he released a burst of light from the Nexi stone.

Soon enough all of the red-robed eigni were taken care of, and Terico and his companions were able to catch their breath. One eigni was still conscious, and Terico bent down to one knee in order to speak with him. "What are you people doing here?" Terico asked. "Why are you controlling everyone in the city?"

The councilor gazed toward the sea above, his eyes unmoving.

"Why are all the civilians mindless?" Terico yelled.

But still the man didn't respond. He was just as unresponsive as everyone else in Vursa.

"It seems the councilors are under control as well," Jujor said. "I'm not sure why they would be capable of fighting like this, but not be able to speak."
"Or even seem to realize what's going on," Terico said. He pushed the man back down and sighed. Nothing about this city was making any sense.
    Borely picked up one of the Nexi stones the councilors had used.
"Spoils of war, at least?"

"Not necessarily," Jujor said. He picked one up and looked it over. "There's a small triangle scratched into this one. It's a method people can use to ensure that only one individual can use a particular Nexi stone. A way to keep enemies from using your own Nexi against you."

"It looks like they're all marked like that," Borely said, looking over a couple more. He held up a dark blue one and tried using it, but no water came out. "We'll just have to keep fighting with what we have," Terico said.

"Let's make our way inside before more councilors show up."

Once they were ready, they hurried down the path leading to the

main entryway into the building. The doors were several meters tall, and made of a thick metal. It was locked, and the councilors didn't have any keys when Terico and his associates checked the pockets of the red robed councilors.

"I can handle this," Borely said, raising a fist back as far as he could manage. "Everyone step back!"

Worried the doors were going to shatter into a thousand jagged metal shards, Terico led the others back a good ten meters or so while Borely readied his massive punch. The captain's right fist glowed an illuminating orange, shining too bright for Terico to look directly into.

Borely bashed his fist against the thin crease where the two doors met, pounding his arm straight through. The doors bent inward with a brief screech, forming an opening just large enough for Borely to walk through when ducked down a bit. The effect was a bit anticlimactic, but it worked nonetheless.

The five entered the building and walked quickly down the main hallway. To either side of them were blue statues of eigni men and women, the sculptures curiously wearing actual red robes just as the real eigni councilors did. The floors were of the same material as the paths outside, though there was much more of an echo in this hallway. Terico thought the building in general had the smell of strong-scented soaps, but he could never find where the smell was coming from.

When they spotted eigni in red robes approaching from connecting hallways, they usually managed to slip into a room in time to avoid having to dispose of the eigni councilors.

Eventually they reached the central room of the main hallway, which was a large square room that housed a single long table. It was oval-shaped and shined a glossy black. Surrounding the table were what Terico guessed to be about fifty light gray chairs. Other than the table and chairs, there was nothing in the giant room but tall, empty white walls.

The door on the opposite side of the room opened, and a large eigni man in red robes walked in. He carried a staff with a large indigo Nexi at the end of it, with a pink Nexi embedded just beneath it. He also wore a golden vest draped over his shoulders—perhaps marking him as the head of the city's council. A dozen red-robed eigni followed him in, silently forming two lines of six to either side of him.

The council leader approached Terico and his companions, his staff echoing a hollow thump with every second step. The eigni man gave a calm smile when he stopped about ten meters away from Terico. "Good evening, visitors. What brings you to my quiet, peaceful city?"

At first Terico thought this eigni was a portly man, but on closer inspection he seemed much buffer than he first appeared. The man was bald, but had a black goatee, dark brown eyes, and a deep, powerful voice.

"What happened here?" Terico asked. "How come *you* can talk just fine?"

Jujor pointed toward the Nexi at the end of the man's staff. "He has everyone's souls, I imagine. Though how he got it to work on eigni, I can't really guess."
"Now, now," the large eigni said. "Let me first welcome you to my fine city and introduce you to the new order that has been established." He raised a hand to the side. "I am Ganto, the emperor of Vursa. The grand council of traitors are now under my command, and through them—this entire city of fools obeys my every whim. The latent energy within every eigni flows from the civilians, to the councilors, and on to me, rendering me much more than an emperor... I am an *invincible god*."

Terico unsheathed his sword. "So you're controlling everyone. For some mad lust for power."

Ganto looked unperturbed by Terico's raised weapon. "For the improvement of society. How many other cities can claim to have no crime, no hunger, and no sadness? Nobody fights. And nobody gets hurt. And when anyone seeks to disrupt this utopia, I can simply strike down our foes with my unlimited supply of Nexi.

"Quite the improvement from the grand council's ways. Pretend there is nothing amiss in the world. Act like there are no threats to our people. Dismiss any notion that something terrible could ever happen to this city. And never, ever take action. Not one of these councilors would heed my warnings. Not once—not even *for a second*—did they consider what I had to say."

He pointed his staff to some of the councilors to either side of him. "But look at them now. *Now* they listen. *Now* they take action. *Now* they actually *do something* for this city."

Though Ganto looked about as composed as one could probably hope for in a leader, Terico couldn't help but think the man had gone completely mad.

"That is the situation in Vursa," Ganto concluded. "We have achieved a peace unrivaled in all the world. You may return to wherever you are from in order to share this news with others, but I'll have to ask that you don't come back here. There is no need for outsiders in Vursa. We can't risk this city getting contaminated by the troubles of the outside world."

"Okay..." Terico said. "That was probably the most ridiculous little speech I have ever heard in my life."

"Can I bash this guy's skull in?" Borely asked, raising his fists. "I'm afraid he'll open his mouth and start talking again."

Jujor sighed as he unsheathed his sword. "So much for talking things through. We could've at least found out a thing or two about how his power works."

Ganto frowned and raised his staff toward Terico. "So you all have a death wish, it seems. My judgment will be swift and just." He slammed the end of the staff against the ground, and his whole body became enveloped in pink and indigo light. The glow steadily grew brighter, and it quickly turned impossible to see Ganto within the light at all. The pink and indigo mass shifted, growing larger and larger. It grew several meters wide, then almost a dozen meters tall—nearly reaching the top of the building.

"What's going on?" Terico asked.

"He's using the power accumulated from the eigni souls via the indigo stone," Jujor said, "and activating the pink stone for some kind of transformative power. He's... turning into something."

"Some of the most powerful eigni are capable of transforming into creatures," Kitoh said. "But *this* is... This is big..."

Terico and the others had to take a few steps back to put some distance between them and the steadily growing mass of light. An earsplitting roar emanated from the glow—the roar of some terrible, giant beast.

Terico had dealt with monsters before, but never one this large. The plant monster he had fought with his father and Turan was big, but the thing looming within this foreign light was even larger.

Once the glow faded, Terico stared up at a massive, lumbering dragon.

It was a dark blue creature with clawed, bat-winged arms and bony legs that bent at three points. The dragon hunched down to leer its long head toward Terico. The creature as a whole was grotesquely muscular, and a giant fin at least three times Terico's size grew from the beast's back, giving it a vaguely amphibious appearance.

The beast's tiny red eyes leered down toward Terico. It grinned a long smile that stretched far down either side of its face, reaching back to its beefy neck. There had to be well over a hundred needle-like teeth running up and down the beast's jaw.

"Perish," Ganto said, his voice much deeper and louder in his dragon form.

He lunged for Terico, who leaped to the side and bashed his sword against the dragon's neck. The blade bounced off the beast's tough scales, not even leaving a scratch. Ganto swung his his head against Terico, flinging him back onto the table.

Borely rushed for the other side of Ganto's head, and landed an orange Nexi-powered punch against him. The dragon was only slightly deterred, and quickly turned its giant maw toward Borely. Areo ran to Borely and pushed him out of the way just as Ganto released a massive blast of fire from his mouth. The fire scarred the floors black—even melting part of the stone away—and blew a hole in the wall. It even scorched the wall on the opposite side of the adjacent hall.

Terico pushed himself up and ran to Ganto's left leg. He took out his light blue Nexi and blasted cold air at the dragon. Ganto turned and simply flung his long, winged arm down at Terico. With only a moment to react, Terico leaped against the sharp, webbed wing and slammed his sword into it. He held on to the sword to keep from being thrown back through the air.

Kitoh sent vines toward the dragon's snout, perhaps hoping to clasp Ganto's mouth shut, but the beast released another burst of fire, the power of the blast strong enough to send sweat rushing down Terico's body and even blind him for a moment. A brief glimpse above Ganto's shifting wing showed Terico that Jujor had grabbed Kitoh with some vines of his own, saving the eigni boy from Ganto's fiery inferno.

Terico saw Ganto was hardly even feeling the blade piercing his wing, so he forced his feet against it and pulled his blade out. Terico landed on his feet and tried shooting another gust of cold air at the dragon's feet, in hopes of freezing it to the ground. The air in the room was far too hot for it to have much effect though, and Ganto was quick to adjust his footing and face Terico again.

Borely slammed a punch against Ganto's right leg, but the dragon immediately kicked him aside, knocking him back against the far wall. He slumped to the ground, groaning from the pain.

While Jujor shot off a jet of water from a dark blue Nexi at Ganto's neck, Areo ran up the dragon's tail and forced her claws to lengthen. The dragon leaned hard to the right and slammed back a winged arm toward her, but she slammed her claws into the dragon's back and leaned behind the other side of the tall, arcing fin of the beast.

Terico ran in front of Ganto and slammed the end of his blade into

the dragon's chest. The hard scales protected the dragon here as well, but Terico felt he found a weak point in the beast's armor. He ripped his sword back out and rolled away from Ganto's swinging left arm. Terico avoided the curved claws running along the top of the wing, but was bashed against the ground by the wing itself. Terico forced himself back to his feet and slammed his sword for the same point he had attacked before, hoping to penetrate the beast's insides.

Ganto ran forward just as Terico swung his blade. Terico fell backward and barely managed to keep hold of his sword. Just before Ganto could trample over Terico, Jujor shot a blast of water at Terico, shoving him just to the side of Ganto's giant clawed foot.

His whole body bruised and beaten, Terico struggled to get to his feet. He looked up and found Areo making her way up the rest of the dragon's back. She reached the back of Ganto's neck and slammed her claws into it. The claws pierced into the beast's neck, but weren't long enough to reach through to the other side.

Ganto thrashed his neck back and forth to shake Areo off. She gripped her feet hard against Ganto's scales, but her claws slipped out and she fell back, crashing onto the table and tumbling against a chair.

All of their attacks were having little effect on the beast. It was only a matter of time before Ganto flattened them, or burned them into ashes.

"Jujor, the Elpis!" Terico yelled. "Use it now!"

Ganto breathed fire toward the old man, who shot a blast of water against the fire. Walls of flame flew past Jujor on either side of him, his stream of water just barely strong enough to hold back the blinding flames directly in front of him.

"I can't!" Jujor yelled back. "Only you can!"

Kitoh ran toward the back of the dragon and released a wide stream of vines for Ganto's back. The dragon swung his long tail against Kitoh before the boy could react. He rolled several meters away, losing the Nexi stone in the process.

Everyone was getting beaten down, and Terico was in poor condition to fight this oversized beast. "Throw it to me, Jujor! Now!" "It's too dangerous, boy!" Jujor yelled.

The dragon lunged for Jujor, snapping its hundred teeth for the man's head. Jujor leaped aside and jumped over the melted portions of the floor. Terico knew Jujor was referring to the torture the Elpis put Terico through back in the underwater city, but he was just going to have to deal with the pain and get a firm grasp of the Elpis stone's power. "This dragon's more dangerous! Now hand it over!"

At last Jujor relented, throwing the glowing fragment straight to Terico's open hand. Terico immediately felt the surge of energy heal his wounds, filling his entire body with an incomparable vigor. He felt his hair lengthen, his vision turn clearer, his joints loosen, and his muscles strengthen. Glancing at his hands, he saw his skin turn a light gray, and his clothes turn black with gleaming gold trimming. Swirls of glowing light enveloped him, shifting through all the colors of the Elpis.

The dragon leaned its head back from Terico a bit, surprised by the power emanating from Terico's body. "These pests... Kill them all!"

At Ganto's command, the twelve council members raised their daggers, split into three groups, and ran toward Borely, Kitoh, and Areo. The dragon then turned to Jujor, who wearily raised his sword and a dark blue Nexi.

Terico suddenly needed to be at four places at once. He flew to Kitoh, the one closest to the mindless council members. Terico raised the Elpis toward the four eigni and blinded them with a burst of white light. Without stopping, Terico flew on to Borely's position, and with his sword charged with dark blue energy, Terico swung a violent wave of rushing water against the four councilors. Terico immediately flew back toward the long council table, slamming through the four blinded eigni near Kitoh in the process.

Before the four remaining councilors could reach Areo, Terico held the Elpis toward them and blasted a torrent of brown swamp material at them, stopping them dead in their tracks—and covering them so they couldn't use a Nexi against Areo. Terico instantly turned to Jujor and shot toward him. Ganto snapped his teeth at Jujor, who stepped to the side and slammed his sword into the dragon's right eye. Terico expected the beast to lean back, roaring in pain.

Ganto leaned his head down and bit off Jujor's head. The dragon sank his teeth all the way to Jujor's chest, tearing down to his heart and severing off Jujor's left arm.

Screaming, Terico bashed his sword into the side of Ganto's head, charging the blade with all the orange Nexi energy he could muster. The dragon still didn't cry out in pain. Ganto thrashed his neck back and forth until he managed to throw Terico off of him.

Terico kept a firm grip on his sword, and managed to keep afloat in the air. He could feel the Nexi elements starting to erupt all throughout his body.

At one moment it felt as if his organs were melting from a great oven, the next moment his insides felt frozen, and the next moment he felt wound up in vines forcing the very breath out of him. Terico fought back the torment and flew back down for the dragon. Most of the redrobed eigni were back on their feet, but so were Borely, Areo, and Kitoh— albeit shakily. Terico needed to kill Ganto immediately. This would all end with Ganto dead.

"I will find your weakness!" Terico screamed. He forced white sparks of light to emanate from his sword, powered by the lightning of the white Nexi.

Ganto turned and exhaled a gigantic ball of fire. Terico dove beneath it, then blasted straight for Ganto's chest, his sword raised straight forward. Like a strike of lightning, Terico shot for Ganto's heart. The sword pierced through the dragon's scales, but Ganto still didn't cry out in pain. The beast clawed at Terico with his long, thin arms. Terico ripped out his sword and dodged Ganto's attacks.

Have to kill him, Terico thought, his entire body engulfed with blinding, ravenous pain. *Have to kill him now!*

Screaming, he forced his sword to turn silver. Feather markings shifted rapidly within the blade, and Terico felt the jagged tips of the feathers tearing apart his insides—slitting open his esophagus, thrashing apart his intestines, scraping against his bones, clipping his muscles into pieces. His head pounding and his eyes streaming with tears, Terico sunk the silvercharged sword into the dragon's neck.

Ganto roared, but began thrashing about once again. Before Ganto could grab Terico with his decrepit clawed hands, Terico released purple Nexi energy into his sword. The blade vibrated furiously, tearing deeper and deeper into the dragon's neck. Terico shoved the blade left and right, in and out. The sword screeched against scales and released torrents of blood as it dug through layers of thick muscle.

Terico avoided Ganto's swipe and continued swinging the vibrating purple sword further into the dragon's neck. With one last burst of Elpis energy,
Terico reactivated the silver Nexi power while continuing to pour purple Nexi into every jab of his blade.

His head felt like it was going to rip apart in an explosive headache, but Terico pushed his blade through the other side of Ganto's neck. Screaming in agony, Terico swung to the right, tearing through skin, muscle, and bone. While still powering the blade with silver and purple Nexi energy, Terico swung back to the left, slicing through the rest of the gigantic dragon head.

Ganto's severed head fell to the ground, and the rest of the dragon's monstrous body fell to a heap behind it. The madman's staff slid out of the dragon's open jaw, the two Nexi stones still glowing bright.

Terico fell down as well, dropping his sword but keeping a firm grip on the Elpis stone. Though the transformation he went through had dissipated, he couldn't stop shaking. Couldn't get himself to stand back up. Couldn't see. Couldn't move on his own. Couldn't even breathe. He could hear Borely, Areo, and Kitoh continuing to fight the eigni councilors. But why were they still fighting? With Ganto dead, they should be back to normal.

At last Terico's blurry vision returned to normal, and though he was still trembling uncontrollably, he managed to get on his knees and grab the hilt of his sword, which was back to its normal color.

Terico looked to Areo, finding her clawing away some vines released by one of the red-robed eigni. Kitoh leaped atop the back of another one, and Borely blocked the thrust of another eigni's dagger.

Each of the councilors dropped to the floor simultaneously, blood rushing from their mouths. They gagged on their own blood, and in seconds turned silent and still. They all simply died, seemingly for no reason at all.

The door behind Terico opened. He turned to find a tall, hooded figure in black armor stepping into the wrecked council room. The man wasn't eigni—he was human.

"They say imitation is the greatest form of flattery," called a familiar voice. "Though I have to say, it is amusing to see you killing others with the same skills I used to kill your parents, and everyone else in that shoddy cathedral." *Delkol.*

Terico widened his eyes and leaped to his feet. He raised his sword and gripped his Elpis fragment tight.

The man who murdered his parents, destroyed his village, and brought an end to everything good in Terico's life. Delkol Shire stood just a few meters in front of him. The man flipped back his hood, revealing a thin, all-knowing smile. Staring at this man replayed the entire tragedy of Edellerston in Terico's head.

It all came down to this.

"First things first," Delkol said, raising a green Nexi stone. Vines shot across the room and into the open neck of Ganto's dragon corpse. Terico considered running over to cut apart the vines, but within seconds they squirmed through

Ganto's insides and ripped out what Delkol was looking for. It was a small, golden Nexi stone—sometimes called path finders, thanks to their ability to lead people to what they were seeking. Terico only knew it from tales of legend.

"Perfect, perfect." Delkol caused his vines to slide back into his green Nexi, zipping the gold one straight back to him. He clenched both Nexi stones and dropped them into his pocket. "All those eigni, and that inner Nexi energy they mentally possess and generate. From the civilians that supply the energy, to the councilors that refine the energy, and on to my puppet dictator, who never even realized I had this gold stone growing inside his body, powered by the eigni of an entire city..."

He turned to Terico and grinned, unable to contain his sheer glee in the situation. "Likewise, thank you for doing everything I've intended for you to do, Terico. My golden Nexi is already leading me to the remaining Elpis fragments, and in my mind I can see it as clearly as I see it now, resting right there in your clenched fist. You've been a very helpful boy,

Terico... But your usefulness has finally ended!"

He held up an Elpis fragment, causing shifting colors of light to glow all around him.

His eyes turned entirely black, save for small white pupils—staring straight at the Elpis piece Terico held.

•

7

HATRED AND HOPE

The entire council room filled with light—a glow that constantly changed color. A whirlwind engulfed the chamber, and Terico struggled to keep from falling back. Accessing the power of his Elpis fragment, Delkol transformed into a demonic personage. His skin turned light gray, while his hair and scar turned a blinding white. His clothes and armor also changed in appearance—first they turned black, then gained thin, swirling white patterns. It was an imposing sight, and Terico didn't like the idea that he looked similar to this when he used his own Elpis fragment. He was going to have to access its power once more though. This was, after all, the very reason he had gone to all the effort of finding the Elpis in the first place. It was time to use its power to destroy Delkol.

It was time for Terico to have his revenge.

He forced the energy of the Elpis to flow through his body. Though it strained him to access the power again so soon, Terico wasn't going to let himself back down now. In an instant, Terico felt his body shift back to the painful form he took when he fought off Ganto. It felt as if something was clawing away at his throat from inside, and for a couple seconds his body felt entirely drained of life, nearly sending him to his hands and knees. He barely managed to keep on his feet though, and to keep his sword gripped in his hand. Terico pointed his blade at Delkol focused all his thoughts on killing the man who destroyed everything his life had entailed.

Delkol laughed. "You can hardly even stand, and yet you wish to oppose me?"

"You killed them," Terico said, his voice louder than he expected it would be. "My parents. You killed them right in front of me... You didn't notice, but I was there."

"Ah, but I did notice!" Delkol yelled. "I left you alive on purpose. Your father knew where the Elpis fragment in Edellerston was, so I thought perhaps you might know too. And if not, I knew that old man assigned to watch over you would probably help you find it. My Brotherhood was struggling to locate the Elpis there, so I decided to set up a little back-up plan... And just as I hoped, you came straight to me as soon as you obtained it! It will only be a matter of days now before I have all four pieces of the Elpis!"

Terico swung his sword at Delkol, releasing a blast of white lightning. Delkol instantly caused a barrier of earth to emerge from his Elpis and protect himself. The lightning burst the dirt wall apart, and Delkol walked toward Terico, completely unfazed by Terico's attack.

For a second it felt as if Terico's entire body had filled up with squirming worms, and he stumbled back from the strange, sudden torment. Before he could recover, his Elpis fragment began to burn his hand, as if Terico were gripping a white-hot coal from a fiery furnace. He screamed and nearly dropped the Elpis on instinct, but he forced himself to keep a firm grip on it.
There was no way he was going to let Delkol steal it from him.

"I can make the same deal I tried to make with your father," Delkol said, continuing to walk casually toward Terico. "Give me the Elpis, and there will be no need for me to kill you or your friends over there."

Terico glanced back at Areo, Borely, and Kitoh, who had gathered a few meters behind him. They were in no condition to keep fighting, and really— neither was Terico. But he couldn't just run away. He couldn't just do nothing. Not again.

Ignoring the pain pulsing through his body, Terico ran toward Delkol. With the flick of his wrist, Delkol caused a long lance made of silver feathers to slide out of his Elpis stone. It launched at Terico, who accessed yellow energy from his Elpis to create a protective barrier around his body. The tip of the lance deflected off his forehead, and Terico swung his blade to erupt a wave of flames toward Delkol.

Delkol immediately flew upward to avoid the fire. A large blast of water shot at him, which he barely avoided. Terico turned and realized the water came from the Nexi stone in Borely's headpiece. Delkol tilted his body and dived away from the thick jet of water, unknowingly heading straight for a formation of dirt quickly shifting into a giant hand. Delkol spun in place at the last moment and swung his silver-glowing sword through the earthen fingers encircling him. Vines from Kitoh's Nexi stone rushed for Delkol's feet, and for a couple seconds Delkol stumbled through them a bit before slicing them apart with silver feathers jetting out of his blade.

Terico sprinted toward Delkol again, and watched as the man struggled to keep to his feet. Delkol groaned as about a dozen silver feathers tore out of his flesh at random points, releasing tiny streams of blood to flow across the pallid floor. He was suffering from the Elpis as well.

For a second Terico felt as if his body was cracking apart like broken glass, and it surprised him that he didn't fall straight to the ground. But he kept pushing forward, while Delkol fell into a strange, high-pitched coughing fit.

Screaming from the surge of energy emanating from his body, Terico forced his sword to glow orange, then charge with sparks of white light—just as he saw his father do. He leaped toward Delkol, flying several meters in the process, and swung his blade with all the power he could possibly contain within it.

Delkol stood straight again at the last second, his eyes entirely white and searing. A sphere of dark purple energy burst in all directions from Delkol's Elpis, flipping all the chairs and the massive table behind him, and sending Terico flying back all the way to the far wall of the building, several meters past Ganto's dead dragon body. The blast knocked Terico's sword away, but he managed to keep a firm grasp on his Elpis stone. Terico fought to stand up again, but his limbs felt light, immaterial—as if his body didn't even exist. He knew he couldn't stop using the power of the Elpis as long as Delkol still wielded his own Elpis fragment—but Terico knew he would die if he went on much longer.

I'll keep going, he thought. *I can't stop now. I'll kill him, even if I have to die in the process!* Areo, Borely, and Kitoh ran to Terico's position, while Delkol fell to his hands and knees. Delkol screamed for several seconds at a time, his body enveloped in a crackling, purple steam. Borely helped Terico to his feet, while Areo turned to Delkol and raised her tan Nexi stone.

"We have to leave," she said. "The Brotherhood may already be overrunning the city and port. You can get the Elpis from Delkol later."

"No!" Terico screamed. "Delkol is... weakened!" He shoved Borely aside and stumbled toward Delkol, raising his Elpis as best he could. His vision turned blurry, and for a moment he felt as if he would throw up all his insides at once. Terico groaned and fell to his knees, then fell to his face before he could find the strength to move his arms forward.

No, I can't stop here, Terico thought. *I have to kill him! Now!*
Terico pushed himself back to his feet, and looked up to find Delkol floating in the air again. Hundreds of silver feathers circled around Delkol continuously, as if he were surrounded by a whirlwind. Thick tendrils of purple light slid out of his Elpis stone, and pockets of loose purple energy snapped at random points around him, growing considerably louder with each crack.

"It's no use, Terico," Delkol said. "You may have the blood necessary to use the Elpis, but you lack the will to use it well!"

Kitoh ran past Terico, raising a staff in the air—it was the staff Ganto had used.

"Kitoh, wait!" Areo yelled.

Indigo and pink light enveloped the small boy, shrouding him completely. The mass of light shifted, growing larger and larger—a sight Terico had just witnessed when Ganto...

Just as Terico realized what was happening, he found himself staring up at a massive blue-scaled dragon—much like the one Ganto had turned into. Apparently, when the right Nexi stones were involved, an eigni could turn into such a creature. And if Kitoh was powerful enough to fend off the power that turned the rest of the city into mindless Nexi suppliers, then it made sense the boy would be capable of this kind of transformation as well.

Kitoh blew a torrent of fire at Delkol, who sent all his floating feathers rushing straight for the massive dragon. The fire breath melted away all the silver feathers, and Delkol fell back to sending tendrils of the vibrating purple energy flying for Kitoh.

The dragon beat away several of the tendrils with his long, bony arms and wide, batlike wings, but Delkol produced many more tendrils, and began pummeling the giant beast with snapping strikes of energy. Kitoh roared and nearly fell back, forcing Terico to fly out of the way before the dragon would step backward onto him.

Delkol tried creating more of the violent purple energy, but floated down to the ground, dropping his sword and clenching his head with both hands. He still held on to his Elpis fragment, but yelled uncontrollably from a terrible pain infecting his mind.

Terico grabbed his sword off the ground, then rushed back through the air, flying straight for Delkol. It was too difficult to place any Nexi energy into his sword, so Terico simply swung the metal blade at Delkol. Just before Terico could connect with the man's head, Delkol forced a large wing of silver feathers to burst out the side of his sword, blocking the attack. The wing bashed Terico in the side, knocking him back several meters.

Areo and Borely ran past Terico, sending a wave of hardened dirt and blasting a jet of water at Delkol. Flying backward, Delkol avoided the attacks, then turned toward the exit when Kitoh leaned down and released another wave of fire.

Delkol fell to the ground and ran for the exit, groaning in pain from his Elpis use. He cut off his connection to the intense power, undoing the effects of his grotesque transformation. He pocketed his Elpis fragment and ran into the hallway before Terico could get back on his feet again.

No! Terico thought, fighting to stand back up. He was exhausted— far more exhausted than he had ever felt in his life. *I can't give up... I have the Elpis!*
But it was only a fragment. It wasn't the whole thing. That was the problem, he realized. He needed more of the Elpis. The power was too difficult to control well when it was broken apart like this. That was the point. Nobody would be able to do too much damage to the world while it was still fragmented. Even Delkol struggled to use the Elpis to its full potential.

It's not over, Terico thought. *I will find him again. Soon! If I don't find him, then he will come to me, using his golden Nexi. And I'll be ready for him. I'll have more of the Elpis than him.*

 And I'll kill him!
 I'll finally kill him!

At last... I will kill him...

•

It strained Delkol to even move, but he forced himself to keep running down the glass-walled hallway through the underwater city. He hated to leave behind a piece of the Elpis stone, but there was nothing he could do about it at this point. The power of his Elpis fragment had overwhelmed him, and it was too difficult to deal with three fighters and a dragon under such conditions. More importantly, the eigni of the city were likely starting to awake from their mindlessness, what with Ganto dead. The city guards would realize what happened, and find Delkol's airship stationed at the dock. The airship was well armed, but it wouldn't take long for Vursa defenses to at least damage it.

His Brotherhood wouldn't be able to destroy Vursa the way they burned Edellerston to the ground, and the eigni masses could prove useful once again some time in the future. The last thing Delkol needed was to be stuck in this city. And now that he had the golden Nexi, it wouldn't take long to locate the other two Elpis fragments. Delkol could always return to Terico to retrieve his Elpis later—preferably when Delkol had three of the other pieces.

It's only a matter of time, Delkol thought as he made his way up the spiral staircase. *After so many centuries, the Elpis will finally be whole again. The king of Fiefs will have no choice but to stand down then.*

No... I won't even give him the choice. He and every member of that royal court must pay with their blood. They have denied me. They have denied my father. They have denied my grandfather. For hundreds of years now, they have denied every rightful heir to the throne. Denied them even the chance to speak up on the matter!

Outcast us! Forced us out of their fertile country and into a pitiful wasteland! None of us have forgotten the many injustices the Shires have had to suffer. None of us will just sit idly and let the Fiefs have their way forever. It's finally time for retribution to be payed.

It's time for all the decay and iniquity of the Fiefs Kingdom to crumble beneath my power.

All these years of preparation will soon pay off... And at last I will claim my rightful place as king over all the land!

He let his hatred for the Fiefs Kingdom drive him on up the stairway. Livid with rage against the iniquities of the Fiefs, Delkol planned all the steps he would take to bring down every single person associated with them. In his mind, he could clearly see himself powered by the infinite Nexi energies of the full Elpis. No army in all the world could stand against him then.

I wish you were still here to see me now, Father, Delkol thought. *To see my rise to power. The return of the Shires in all their former glory...*

But with the full Elpis, the glory of the Shires would be even greater than it had ever been.

With this knowledge so deeply ingrained in Delkol's heart, there was no doubt in his mind that nothing would keep him from achieving his goals. His brother Augurc would never consider challenging him again, for one thing. The ministers of his kingdom were easy to please, as long as his

Brotherhood continued to bring back riches from their conquests. And that foolish boy Terico would pose little threat. Delkol acknowledged Terico's power via the Elpis, but there was little mystery to that boy's mind.

Delkol reached the portion of the city above ground, and hurried straight to the dock. There were already eigni out and about, but most still looked tired and confused. Delkol kept behind the crudely-painted buildings so the civilians wouldn't notice him. It was simplest to just avoid the attention of the masses, and therefore keep the city guards from figuring out what had happened.

He soon reached the dock, and caught sight of his airship already floating a ways in the air. Just as Delkol hoped, the captain was smart enough to raise the airship as soon as it was clear the eigni were in control of their own minds once more. Delkol ran past the confused civilians gathering at the dock, and pushed past the line of eigni standing on the pier. They were speaking amongst themselves, some of them asking questions about what had happened the last couple weeks, the others having difficulty remembering specifics. Amongst them were eigni pointing up at the giant dirigible, and Delkol noticed a couple yellow-uniformed guards running amongst the crowd.

Delkol shoved his way through the yelling masses and reached the end of the pier, where his airship was lowering a rope ladder for him to climb. He leaped off the pier and grabbed onto the ladder, which quickly began to raise back up. The eigni cried out and pointed at him, but the city defenses hadn't gathered together yet. If Ganto was even a little intelligent, he would have confiscated and hidden the city's weaponry, just in case some of the eigni regained their self-awareness somehow.

Once Delkol was pulled into the ship, he walked confidently past his Brotherhood followers and on to the bridge.

"Release fire Nexi on all the boats," Delkol ordered. "As soon as the ships are burning, we leave this city."

Terico had to have come to Vursa by boat, and Delkol intended to keep him from getting near any other Elpis fragments. It was never Delkol's intention for the boy to obtain more than one piece of the Elpis, and it was vital at this point for Delkol to not take any more chances. He recognized his failure to retrieve the Elpis piece from Terico, and vowed to himself to kill the boy outright the next time they'd meet.

The captain skillfully guided the airship over each of the tiny boats below, while members of the Brotherhood dropped red Nexi from openings in the back of the airship. Delkol leaned his head out a side window to watch each of the ships erupt into flames, the fires guided by the Brotherhood members dropping the stones.

"Good," Delkol said. "Now lead the airship away before Vursa defenses can begin launching Nexi at us." He kept an eye on the scene below. The civilians ran off in their predictable panic, but the guards were too slow to organize themselves for an effective counter-attack. Most of the guards were probably still underwater, hurrying up the stairways to the upper city.

Once the airship was a safe distance from the city, Delkol sat down on the central chair of the bridge—a tall, red-cushioned chair made of jagged white wood, resting on a small raised dais. He took out his golden Nexi and smiled at its brilliant glow.

Show me where another Elpis fragment is, he thought. *One other than my own. One other than Terico's.* Not even needing to close his eyes, Delkol could clearly see the capital city of the Fiefs Kingdom in his mind. An image of the castle appeared vividly in his head, followed by a hallway leading to an underground chamber.

"Tch, of course," Delkol muttered. "They have a piece of the Elpis in their very castle. I wonder if even the king knows about it, though?" He sat up and slipped the gold-colored Nexi back in his pocket.

It was going to take some effort to get his hands on that Elpis fragment, Delkol knew. He had an inside man working for him in the Fiefs castle, who would at least be able to help Delkol sneak into the premises. He would need more firepower to act as a sufficient diversion, however.

"Send carrier pigeons to each of our other airships in the area,"
Delkol ordered his second-in-command. "We'll all meet together east of Yehvel."
There were three other Brotherhood airships conducting operations in this region.
It would take a day at most for them to gather and prepare for the attack, and
then it was only a matter of traveling to Setar, which wouldn't take long by airship.
Augurc's ship would also have the death bird, which Delkol could use to fly down
to the castle with.

As long as Delkol used each of his pawns correctly, there would be little trouble
for him in obtaining this piece of the Elpis. The thought of the power that two
pieces would bring him filled him with confidence. What chance would the
castle's royal guard have against him then?

Delkol smiled at the possibilities the Elpis would further bring to him.
"Once in Setar, we will make clear our intentions for the Fiefs Kingdom."

•

Terico awoke and found a dark night sky above him. He was lying on a thin
mattress, and his body felt like it had been crushed by an avalanche of boulders. A
splitting headache turned his vision blurry, and for several minutes Terico simply
stared at the spinning sky, half-hoping to die.

"Are you awake, Terico?" It was Kitoh's voice, but Terico couldn't bother to
move his head to look at him.

"Somewhat," Terico said, barely managing a whisper. Speaking was painful, filling
his throat with needles.

"We were worried," Kitoh said. "You hardly moved at all when Borely carried you
up. We thought you might have used the Elpis too much." Terico didn't respond.
If anything, he wished he used it a little more. If only he was a little more
powerful, he would have been able to bring Delkol down.

"He's gone, I'm afraid," Kitoh said, as if reading Terico's mind. "That man you
were fighting escaped in an airship, it sounds like."

"Why aren't we... on the boat," Terico said. Glancing around, he could see eigni
walking around and talking with one another.

"It... burned down," Kitoh said. "All the boats in the dock were set on fire."

Terico shut his eyes and gritted his teeth. He tried to clench his fists as well, but his arms were too sore to even move.

Delkol... Everything you do...
"The Elpis," Terico said. "Do I have it?"

"Yes," Kitoh said. The boy knelt down beside Terico so he could see him. "I'm assuming you mean the rock glowing different colors... The one you used to gain all those strange powers..."

"It's a piece of the Elpis," Terico said. "But it... it..."

It didn't matter anymore, did it? It would be a long time before Terico got off this island. With everything in the dock up in flames,

Terico was stuck in Vursa until another ship came. Jujor's book on the Elpis probably burned to ashes along with Borely's ship. And even if it survived, Jujor wasn't around anymore to interpret all its data. On top of this, Delkol now had a Nexi that would lead him straight to the remaining pieces of the Elpis. Delkol and his legions of Brotherhood followers would obtain three pieces, and then head straight back to Terico.

And what would he do then? Three pieces of the Elpis would render Delkol's power much greater and much more stable than Terico's. As determined as Terico was to kill Delkol, he knew he would be no match for Delkol under such circumstances.

Jujor... Why did you have to die, old man? You were the only one of us who knew what we were doing. And all this time, I always questioned what you wanted out of all this. Why... Why did it have to end like this? I never understood why you helped me with this. Why you were willing to risk your life for this... or give up your life for this...
From the moment Edellerston burned down, he was there for me. Jujor never turned against me. Even when he had the Elpis fragment for himself, he waited for me to come back to him.
So why... Why couldn't I help him when he needed me most? Why couldn't I save him? Even with the power of the Elpis... Why are my efforts never enough?!
There had to be more Terico could do. He couldn't let Jujor's death be for

nothing. If there was a way to get off this island, he was going to find it——and he was going to act immediately. Even though he couldn't move, he was going to at least sort things out.

"The city," Terico said. "Is everything back to normal?"

"Yes," Kitoh said. "It's kind of surprising, actually. Everyone's trying to figure out what they've been doing the last couple weeks, and there is a lot of worry about the grand council... but otherwise everyone is just getting back to their homes, having their suppers, going to bed. This is my family's house here. My parents are lending mattresses for everyone."

"Your family?"

"Yes, it's just me and my parents. We're all fine, same with Borely and Areo."

"Where are they?" Terico asked. He hadn't heard Borely or Areo at all since he woke up.

"They're here," Kitoh said. He helped Terico sit up so he could see them. It made Terico wince to sit up, but he managed to keep from crying out in pain.

Areo was sitting on a mattress, her legs brought up to her chest, and her arms wrapped around her legs. Borely lay on his side on another mattress, his elbow against the ground, and his head propped up in his palm. The two were staring off into opposite directions.

"Something wrong with them?" Terico asked.

"Well..." Kitoh's voice rose a bit. "I think they're upset."

"Yeah," Borely said. "*Upset.*"

"Okay, angry then," Kitoh said under his breath.

"I think I'm missing something," Terico said.

Borely sat up straight and faced Terico with a grim expression. "Oh, you don't know?" He raised an eyebrow and frowned deeply, then leaned back and raised a rigid arm, pointing at Areo. "*She's a conniving, bloodsucking vampire!*"

Terico sighed. "Yes, she's a vampire... But she's perfectly fine. She won't bite you." Terico understood that most people didn't have much experience around vampires, and he himself had plenty of misconceptions about them until he actually went to Istal. There were plenty of bad vampires out there of course, but there were plenty of good ones too. It now seemed a bit ridiculous for people to react in the sort of way Borely was.

"I don't know," Areo said, shutting her eyes. "If he goes off on another yelling rampage, I might suck him dry to get him to shut up about it."
Borely stood up and raised his arms in the air. "You lied to me! I came here for you, you know! And then, from out of nowhere, you're fighting that dragon with these long vampiric claws! All this time you were a vampire... What you did was just *wrong*. I was willing to fight anything for you... I *did* fight anything for you! I fought mindless eigni politicians, a dragon, and a near-invincible demon man! And did I mention the dragon?"

"Yes, and you nearly died," Areo said. "We know."

"And for what?" Borely yelled. "For lies. You deceived me. All this time you've been deceiving me. All this time you were just playing with me, scheming against me—and all while I was... I was *interested* in you!"

Areo gripped her legs tighter and tilted her head farther away from Borely. "If you were so interested in me, you should have at least noticed I was a vampire. The fact I ate nothing the entire boat trip should have been a good hint."

"You were in the sunlight, though!" Borely said. "How was I supposed to know vampires could use a Nexi stone to go into the sunlight? Regardless, you should have at least admitted you were a vampire when I was talking about them."

Areo looked back at Borely and stared wide-eyed. "It was obvious you hated vampires, so why would I tell you I'm a vampire?"

"Obvious?" Terico said. "What do you mean?"

"I didn't tell you about this," Borely said, "but my family was killed because of a vampire. They turned my brother into a vampire... and then he killed my parents. And then I killed him. And everything ended in one giant bloody mess. That's how it always goes when vampires are involved." "Are you trying to blame all this on me?" Areo asked.

"I lost my boat because of you!" Borely said. "That little boat... was passed down from generation to generation in my family. It was all I had left after my parents and brother died. And now it's gone. Everything's gone." Terico could understand where Borely was coming from with this, but the arguing had to stop. It made sense for Areo to keep her identity a secret, so Terico couldn't blame her for that. Borely just needed to accept Areo was a vampire and move on, because blaming her for his situation wasn't going to help anyone.

"I'm sorry for your loss, Borely," Terico said. "But you chose to come here with us. I realize you did not know the full story behind Areo, but you have to let it go. Try putting yourself in her place, if you can. Would you admit you were a vampire under her circumstances? It's not the thing you say when someone has let you know his family was killed by vampires."

"It's... it's just too much to accept," Borely said, shaking his head. "You could put yourself in my place as well, you know. I don't care if you think Areo is nice. There's no way to be certain with vampires."

"Or anyone else," Terico said. "None of us here know that much about one another, after all. But we've just been through quite a bit together, haven't we?"

"Yes," Areo said. "We have... gone through a lot recently." "More than I ever wanted to go through," Borely said.

Terico closed his eyes and just breathed for a bit, trying to alleviate the pain in his head as best he could. When he opened his eyes he turned to Kitoh and nodded. "I'm sorry you had to see so much bloodshed today." "It's okay," Kitoh said. "I'm just glad the city is back to normal again..."

It was one positive outcome of this dark series of events. Terico smiled a bit, and Kitoh smiled as well. Even if Terico wasn't able to defeat Delkol or retrieve the Elpis piece, at least he was able to help Kitoh save the city. Kitoh had his parents again, and life could return to how it was once more.

Perhaps it was still possible for Terico's life to return to how it was once more as well. He still clung to that hope, as small as it was.

"About Jujor..." Terico said, not sure how to word his questions.

"We've buried him," Areo said. "But we kept his sword, and the items he brought with him." Areo let go of her legs and set them down flat in front of her, then grabbed a small pouch sitting beside her. She opened it and dumped its contents onto her mattress, revealing a few gleaming Nexi stones.

One of them was a color Terico had never seen before. A teal Nexi.

"What does the teal one do?" he asked.

Areo tossed the stone to Terico, who was too weak to catch it in the air. It bounced off his shoulder and landed on the mattress, near his right hand. "Oh, you're still recovering," Areo said. "Are you going to be okay?"

"I'm doing better," Terico said. "I'm just very sore, and very tired. And I have a bad headache. It will go away eventually... But right now I need to figure out how we're going to find the remaining Elpis fragments.

If this teal Nexi will help us, I'm going to use it."

He picked it up and slowly raised it in front of himself. Areo and Borely both got up to get out of the way, just in case the stone released something dangerous.

"Are you sure you should try it?" Borely asked. "I mean, we're all recovering from the fight down in the council room, and you shouldn't drain yourself even further."

"I don't feel so drained," Terico said. "Beaten up and weakened, yes. But the Elpis gave me the energy I needed to wield Nexi power. I need to find out what Jujor's Nexi does. He never used it around me, but it must have some purpose if he always had it with him."

He activated the power of the Nexi, causing it to glow a little brighter. Nothing came out of the stone, and Terico didn't feel his body affected in any way.

"Is anything happening?" Borely asked.

"No," Terico said. He tried accessing the Nexi's power again, but still nothing seemed to happen.

"One moment," came a woman's voice. Terico looked around, but there wasn't anyone nearby, other than Areo, Borely, and Kitoh. And that wasn't Areo's voice. It sounded a bit older—though the person it belonged to probably *wasn't* older, of course.

"Who said that?" Borely asked. He and Areo were glancing around as well.

"I don't know," Terico said.

"Okay. What is your status, Jujor?" the woman asked.

The voice was so close, but there was nobody there. Terico looked

at the teal Nexi and wondered if somehow he had summoned a spirit that was speaking to him. The spirit had mistaken him for Jujor, it seemed.

"I'm not Jujor," Terico said. "I'm Terico... But who is this? Are you a spirit?"

There was no response for ten, twenty seconds, and for a moment Terico worried the spirit left. If she had some connection with Jujor, Terico intended to figure it out.

"Where is Jujor?" the woman asked, her voice consistently terse and to-the-point.

Terico wasn't sure where to speak to, so he simply spoke out to the empty air in front of where he sat. "He has been killed, I'm afraid... How do you know Jujor?"

"He is dead..." the woman said, a hint of sadness in her voice. She didn't say anything more.

"He died fighting an aide of the Brotherhood," Terico said. "An eigni who worked with Delkol Shire."

"You are still in Vursa." The woman's tone made it more like a statement than a question.

"We are," Terico said. "But I still don't know who you are, or even what you are... I'm Terico Obisious, and I've been traveling with Jujor in order to find the pieces of the Elpis stone, in the hopes of bringing down Delkol and the Brotherhood." Terico decided it didn't matter at this point if Borely and Kitoh knew the truth about his objectives, considering how they had witnessed the power of the Elpis firsthand.

"I know all about you, Terico," the voice said. "Jujor has kept me wellinformed for years now."

"For years?" Terico asked.

"Allow me to explain," the woman said. "My name is Rilv. I am the head servant of the Fiefs royal court, and commander of the kingdom generals. Jujor was an operative of the royal court who reported directly to me. We corresponded through the use of teal Nexi stones. The teal Nexi is very rare, and the connection between each of them is strong enough to send one's voice from one stone to another. I am currently in the royal castle of Setar."

"So you're not a spirit," Terico said. "And you're in *Setar*?" It was incredulous, the very notion of speaking with someone all the way in Setar, the capital of Fiefs Kingdom. Of course, the Nexi made the impossible a reality—but Terico had never heard of a power like this before. It really sounded as if this woman, Rilv, was right there speaking with him. "Yes," she said. "I relay pertinent information to the king when needs be, but I am generally left to discern on my own what actions need to be taken to ensure the safety of the kingdom."

"Why was Jujor watching over me?" Terico asked. "Why would I be important to the kingdom?"

"At first Jujor was primarily assigned to keep in touch with your father," Rilv said. "Your father was stationed in Edellerston for the purpose of making sure nobody would ever locate the Elpis fragment below ground."

"My father worked for the royal court?"

"Not officially. But it was in our interests to always be aware of his location.
He was one of the few in the world capable of accessing the power of the Elpis. And as his son, you are also one of those few. In recent months, the ruling brothers of the Shire Kingdom have been seeking the Elpis fragments, and it has been important for the court to take effort in keeping the Shires from obtaining them."

It was all so much for Terico to take in all at once, but one question jumped to his mind. "If you knew all this... why was it Delkol and his men were able to march straight to our village and destroy it? If you knew all about the Elpis piece there, why didn't the Fiefs army help protect it?"

"We did not believe Delkol knew of the possibility of an Elpis fragment in Emoser Helena," Rilv said. "And in hindsight, it was a mistake to not station more guards in Edellerston. However, we did not wish to draw attention to the village. On top of this, our country's armed forces have had to deal with many hit-and-run attacks staged by the Brotherhood in dozens of significant locations. I imagine you would be less familiar than most with the state of our kingdom in recent months, considering how remote of a location Edellerston was situated in."

Terico didn't feel any better with how the Fiefs Kingdom had handled the situation with Delkol, but it was true he didn't have a good understanding of the country's state of affairs.

"So you know we have an Elpis piece," Terico said. "Delkol also has one.
And now he has a golden Nexi that will lead him to the other two."

"Time is of the essence then," Rilv said. "We will need you to come to Setar as soon as possible."

"Our boat has been destroyed, unfortunately," Terico said. "All the ships docked here were destroyed."

"A ship would take too long," Rilv said. "We will send an airship to pick you up, along with any of your companions who wish to assist."

An airship! This was precisely the sort of thing Terico wished to hear. "How soon can it arrive?"

"A couple new operatives are currently traveling by airship not far from your location," Rilv said. "I have the means to speak with them via teal
Nexi, and can ask them to pick you up within seven hours."

"That's perfect," Terico said. "What will I do in Setar, exactly?" "We have an Elpis fragment in our possession," Rilv said. "It is hidden in an undisclosed location, but can be brought out to you upon your arrival. Once we give you the fragment, our wish for you is to use the power of the Elpis for the sake of killing Delkol Shire. Doing so could prevent a full-scale attack on the capital, which we have reason to believe may ensue within the week."

"I... have no problem with that," Terico said. It was a little troubling to think his goal to kill Delkol was precisely what the government wished him to do. In some ways, it felt like his whole life was being orchestrated by outsiders. Terico thought of his father, then of Jujor, then of this unknown woman speaking to him. Everyone was connecting Terico to the royal court—a strange premise when there had never been anything in his life, or in all of Edellerston, that would concern the outside world, let alone the Fiefs governing rulers.

"Good, I expect to meet you by tomorrow evening," Rilv said. "If there is nothing else, I have several matters of business to attend to." "Okay," Terico said, not sure what else he could add.

The teal Nexi glowed a little dimmer, and the mysterious woman didn't say anything more. Terico felt his connection with the stone dissipate, and his whole body turned numb for a few seconds. He wasn't sure if this was an effect of using that particular Nexi, if he was still recovering from the Elpis poisoning, or if his body was just reacting from the shock of so many revelations all at once.

So Jujor worked for the royal court. And father was connected as well. And the kingdom has held an interest in me all this time.

But why? I can use the Elpis, but why?

And now he was going to be ferried by airship to the capital city. Straight to the royal castle. It was... strange. Incredibly strange. Even after all the chaos Terico went through that day, this was still a lot to grasp. His thoughts turned back to the Elpis. Delkol could be heading straight to the capital in order to get his hands on the Elpis fragment held there. Rilv understood this, of course—but was she prepared to hold off the Brotherhood? Setar had to be the best-defended city in the kingdom, and if the Elpis fragment was in the castle, it should be especially unlikely for Delkol to reach it. But there was no telling what Delkol had planned. The man had a piece of the Elpis himself—perhaps he could just blast apart the castle all on his own, rampaging to his heart's content.

There was nothing for Terico to do now but wait. The best thing to do would be to rest and recover from the pain his Elpis fragment caused him. "So we'll be heading to Setar," Borely said. "I'll come along, if just to get back to Fiefs."

"I'll come too," Areo said. "I still wish to help."

"Thanks," Terico said. "There's still a chance we can work this out. But at the very least, it won't be long before the rest of the Elpis fragments are obtained."

Kitoh's parents arrived shortly thereafter, and Kitoh was able to explain the day's events to them. Terico thought the boy's parents took everything rather well, and was a bit surprised at how... *unsurprised* they were when Kitoh detailed how he managed to keep control of his mind while the rest of the city fell prey to Ganto's power. Or when Kitoh explained how he used a Nexi stone to turn into a giant dragon.

"You have done well," Kitoh's father said. He was an eigni about Terico's height, with wiry black hair and a thin, pointed mustache. He was dressed in robes with thick, multicolored stripes running vertically. He looked to Terico and smiled. "Kitoh has always had a vibrant connection with Nexi energy. Even before he began his schooling, he had better control of Nexi stones than most adults."

Kitoh's mother tussled the boy's thick white hair and took him by the shoulder. "What you did was very brave, Kitoh. We're so proud of you." Kitoh's mother was as short as her husband, but had long, wavy white hair, and wore a long red coat and black trousers.

"It's thanks to him we were able to find Ganto," Terico said. "And he likely saved all our lives when he turned into a dragon."

Kitoh looked to the ground, afraid to make eye contact with anyone. He whispered a thanks, but had a nervous frown on his face.

"Shy lad," Borely said.

Kitoh's father nodded. "He's always been a quiet boy, but... as you might imagine, it is difficult to live a normal life when everyone sees you...

the way they see Kitoh."

Terico could imagine there would be a great weight of responsibility, and an even greater weight of expectations. The fact Kitoh was largely responsible for saving the city would only add to this, Terico realized.

"You'll probably keep quiet about all this then," Terico said.

"It's up to Kitoh," the boy's mother said. "It seems nobody is certain about what happened since Ganto took over, so nobody has to know if he doesn't want anyone to."

Kitoh didn't respond, but it was assumed he didn't want to let the city know of his role in saving everyone. Terico thought it was good of the boy to not seek any praise or reward, but felt a bit bad for him. There would likely come times when his assistance would be readily noticed, and there would only be more expectations and responsibilities for him to deal with. Choosing to not help everyone would lead to disdain and derailment, while choosing to help everyone would put him in constant danger. And all the while eigni of all ages would envy the boy's power, or seek ways to use Kitoh for their own purposes.

Terico wondered if Kitoh had any friends in this city. It seemed that a child as powerful as Kitoh would be either feared or shunned. And given the boy's personality, Kitoh would likely just accept the poor treatment, rather than fight against it.

"You are all probably hungry," Kitoh's father said. "How about I fix up something for all of you to eat."

"It sounds like you have a lot ahead of you," Kitoh's mother said. "Sorry there's no room for you all to sleep inside."

"No need to apologize," Terico said. "We're just glad to have somewhere to recover."

Kitoh's box-shaped house looked just big enough for perhaps two small rooms, Terico realized. It was fine for him and Areo and Borely to sleep outside, though. This area was secluded, and none of the eigni passing down the road in the distance noticed them there.

While Kitoh and his parents busied themselves inside, Terico remained sitting up, fiddling with the Nexi stones Jujor left behind. It was going to be difficult without Jujor, but it seemed the old man still had a way of helping Terico know where to go next. As long as Rilv was trustworthy, there was hope Terico would be able to obtain the rest of the Elpis.

Areo and Borely both sat on their mattresses in silence, simply thinking to themselves. Terico realized they probably just weren't going to be able to speak to each other again. It likely wouldn't be much longer before they parted ways, though Terico did wonder if they'd be able to work together if the situation called for their cooperation. There was a chance everyone would have to fight with the Brotherhood in order to obtain the Elpis piece in Setar.

 Kitoh and his parents returned with a plate of food for Terico and another for Borely. Areo explained that she had already eaten, so after a few rounds of reassuring them she wasn't hungry, Kitoh's parents relented and let her sit in peace.

The meal was some kind of pinkish soup with chunks of fish and papery brown things floating around in it. Stirring it with his wide white spoon, Terico saw the soup was as thick as a stew, but cold, almost icy. Terico took a bite and nearly threw it back up on reflex.

He gulped it down and took a couple deep breaths. "What is this, exactly?" "Needlefin salmon, renkun, nephlatipi seaweed, mevarala snapper, and plores," Kitoh's mother said. "We knew humans eat these fish, so we thought it would be a safe choice."

"Any chance we can... have the fish cooked?" Borely asked. "Not to say we don't like this, or anything."

"Oh, I heard this once," Kitoh's father said. "Humans always cook their food over a fire before eating it. Including fish."

"Well, we cook fish," Terico said. "But we don't cook everything..." The fact the eigni didn't know such a simple fact seemed difficult to believe, but he realized he didn't know a lot of basic things about the eigni, either. Kitoh's parents likely lived in Vursa their entire lives—not so different from how Terico lived in Edellerston his whole life, until recently.

Terico used a red Nexi stone to heat up the fish pieces on some rocks he washed off with a blue Nexi. Once the fish was cooked, he and Borely tried the soup again. The strangely-colored liquid was still difficult to swallow, but the fish had a taste that was a bit unique—a bit juicier than the fish Terico had back at home. But it had a good taste to it.

Once he finished eating, Terico lay back down on his mattress. The airship would likely arrive in about six hours, so he asked Kitoh's parents if they could wake him up in five. Kitoh's parents said they weren't tired at all for some reason, and agreed to wake Terico, Areo, and Borely up before the airship would arrive. They were glad to help in what small way they could, considering Terico and the others helped restore things as they were to the city at large.

Terico fell asleep quickly, his thoughts drifting from Kitoh and what would be in store for him from now on, and then to Jujor and all the things the old man had given up for Terico over the years.

More and more people were becoming involved in Terico's quest for revenge, and Jujor's words on the subject made Terico wonder if all this fighting would truly be worth it in the end.

The road toward vengeance is a bloody one, and often connects to many other bloody roads, Jujor had said.

That's fine, Terico thought. *I will accept the consequences. Turn the road into a sea, and I will dive in if I have to.*

•

Kitoh's parents woke Terico up just as they said they would. Terico felt far too tired to wake up, and the sight of stars still in the sky only seemed to make him more exhausted. Areo was already up, and Terico wondered if she had even gone to sleep at all. Now that Terico thought about it, he wasn't sure if Areo even needed to sleep.

Kitoh walked out of the house and joined his parents.

"I guess this is good-bye then," Terico said. "Thanks for all your help, Kitoh."

Kitoh looked to the ground and didn't say anything.

"Is something wrong?" Borely asked.

"We spoke with Kitoh," the father said, "and we suggested to him that he go with you. Our city has been saved thanks to the three of you, and to your companion who died fighting Ganto. While you go on this quest to stop the Brotherhood, you would greatly benefit from Kitoh's assistance."

"Kitoh's already done more than enough for us," Terico said. "We couldn't ask him to go with us. We'll be traveling a dangerous road..."

"We believe Kitoh was meant to help you," the mother said. "It is important in out city to repay our debts. If you are taking part in events that will change the world, it feels right that Kitoh would be there, helping."

"Of course, we leave it up to him," the father said. "But that is our proposition, and our suggestion."

All of this was about the last thing Terico expected a child's parents to say in such a situation. Did they really think Kitoh would be perfectly safe out there, traveling with strangers, fighting against dangerous enemies? Most parents would do everything they could to keep their child out of danger's way, Terico thought.

"Well, it probably wouldn't be for too long, and we'd bring you back home afterward," Terico said. "But like I said, it won't be a safe journey, and I don't feel you're obligated to help us more than you already have. But I'll go ahead and ask anyways, if that's what your parents wish... Do you want to come with us?"

"No," Kitoh said, looking to the side.

"Why?" Kitoh's father asked. "Most boys your age would be excited to help."

"I'm... afraid," Kitoh said in a soft voice.

"I'm sorry," Kitoh's mother said, placing a hand on the boy's head. "If you wish to stay, that's fine."

"What is it you're afraid of?" the father asked.

Kitoh looked to the ground for a few seconds before responding. "It will be dangerous. I'm afraid of dying... But mostly I'm afraid of myself.

I... I turned into a monster. I don't want to have so much power..."

Terico could understand what the child may have been thinking. Kitoh saw firsthand what a terrible man could do with the power to turn into a dragon. And he also saw said dragon die a grisly death at Terico's blade. The memories of that terrible fight would never leave that boy, but the fact that Kitoh turned into a dragon very similar to Ganto would make the experience even more harrowing. Kitoh knew what it felt like to house the strength of a massive beast, and to blow fire capable of melting through everything in its path. The sheer destruction Kitoh could bring was more than a boy like him would ever want to be capable of. As the father implied, Kitoh wasn't like most boys his age.

"I know what you mean, Kitoh," Terico said. "If you remember, I also transformed when we fought Ganto and Delkol. It's a frightening transformation, and the power I wielded was... probably more than any one person should ever have. But I kept hold of who I was. I knew what I was fighting for. And even though I looked different and felt different..." Terico motioned to his heart. "I *wasn't* different. And I think you are stronger than you think, Kitoh. And I don't mean strength as in Nexi power or ability to fight. You have the will to be precisely who you want to be."

Kitoh looked up to Terico. The boy's eyes were open wide, and Terico noticed just how weathered and beaten-down the child looked. It was clear Kitoh hadn't been able to sleep at all.

"You've been through a lot," Terico said. "Choose for yourself what you do next, but just know that I think you're already a commendable eigni. Don't come with us because your parents want you to, or because your society expects you to. Just do what you wish."

Kitoh nodded, and a faint smile crept up the sides of his thin lips. "Thank you, Terico. I think... I think I'll go with you. I'd like to see if I can find a good way to help more."

Terico smiled, a part of him amazed that someone that young could be that selfless. "Right, then. We'll wait for you to get what things you wish to bring."

Kitoh returned to his home, and after a couple minutes came back with a small pack. He still had a worried look on his face, and Terico wondered how certain Kitoh actually was about coming with them. Perhaps it was impossible for the boy to be completely sure. How often was Terico completely sure of the choices he made? Kitoh had just gone two weeks on his own and had been all right, though, so perhaps he thought he'd be fine away from home for a while.

Once his parents finished their good-byes, Kitoh joined Terico, Areo, and Borely and headed down the city street to the dock. There weren't many eigni walking the street at this hour, but there were some crowds looking over the burnt-down boats and working to recover items and materials lost in the water. Unfortunately

Borely's entire little ship was lost to the sea, so there wasn't much chance of finding anything left intact.

Terico and his companions kept a good distance away from all the eigni at the dock. They waited in silence for the airship to arrive, and it wasn't for another hour or so before it came into view. It was a small, clunky-looking dirigible. A loud mechanism of random metal parts, none of which seemed to match each other in color or texture. Terico led Areo, Borely, and Kitoh down an intact pier, where they awaited a rope ladder to lower from the airship.

Once the ladder was down, Terico worked his way up the creaky ropes—a long, difficult climb in his exhausted state. There was a good wind that morning, and Terico had to keep still at times to maintain a strong grip.

He soon made it to the top and grabbed a hand that reached out to help him aboard. Terico stepped into the dark, torchlit room and took a few seconds to catch his breath. He looked from the thin, slender arm he held and up to the face of this operative. It was Suran.

•

8

UNEXPECTED REUNION

Terico could hardly believe his eyes. Standing just in front of him, holding his hand—was Suran. The fact she was even alive was a miracle in and of itself, but to see her now... and *here*, of all places...

"Suran... you're alive," Terico said, almost disbelieving his own words— even with her standing right there. Ever since the attack on Edellerston, he had expected the worst for Suran. And in light of recent events, it felt strange to have such a positive turn of events in his life.

Suran smiled and took Terico's other hand. "My brother and I took a secret passage from our workshop to the caves, where we hid for a few days... We eventually went to our airship in Plien though. My brother is on the bridge, piloting it right now."

"I'm glad you're all right," Terico said. He heard Areo, Borely, and Kitoh make their way into the ship, but didn't look back.

"Ah, you two know each other?" Borely asked.

"Yes," Terico said. "Go ahead and roll up the rope ladder and close the hatch. I'll be back with you in a minute." Terico led Suran out of the room and into a dim, narrow hallway, which squeaked and vibrated with loud machinery.

He stared into Suran's bright hazel eyes, overcome with the fact she was right here with him. "I... never found your body, or Lanek's. I was afraid the Brotherhood captured you."

Suran trembled a little, and her smiled faded away. Her eyes watered a bit as she spoke. "We came back to Edellerston. Once we felt it was safe, we searched the entire village. Everything was burnt down, and there was nobody there. No bodies anywhere... We searched for you, and for our parents, and for Turan... we searched for anyone. But there was nobody.

We thought... you had died, Terico. I'm so sorry."

It was just like Suran to apologize, though she had clearly done nothing wrong. Terico let go of one of Suran's hands and placed it on her shoulder. "I had left already. I traveled with an old man named Jujor. We went to Merze, and then to an underground city below Edellerston. I had already buried everyone beforehand."

Suran frowned. *"Everyone?"*

"I'm sorry," Terico said. "Your parents were killed by the Brotherhood. I believe everyone we knew was killed that day." The exception was Turan, of course, but Terico didn't want to bring up what happened to him right now.

Tears flowed down Suran's face, and she had to catch her breath for a few seconds. "Mother and Father..." She looked down and sniffed a couple times. "I... I'm sorry. Lanek told me they were most likely dead... But I had hoped... *I hoped...*"

She stepped closer to Terico and wrapped her arms around his back. Terico draped his arms over her shoulders and held her close, letting her cry on his shoulder.

"I understand how you feel," Terico said. He closed his eyes and could see his parents' deaths transpire right in front of him. Mother charging Father's sword with Nexi energy. Father fighting off Delkol. Delkol setting Father ablaze with fire, then swiftly beheading Father and Mother in one stroke. "I'm sorry," Suran said, looking up at Terico. "You've lost your parents too..." She tried to hold back her crying, but the tears still dripped from her eyes. "It's just so... It's just not right. How could this happen?

How could anyone do this?"

Terico shook his head. "It's unthinkable, and yet it happens." He couldn't think of what else to say. He didn't care how Delkol and his Brotherhood could be so heartless as to eradicate an entire village. There was no legitimate reason for it, and Terico intended to make them pay with their blood.

He held to Suran until she recovered from her grieving. Terico's heart ached for her, and for a minute he wondered if he had ever truly mourned for the loss of his own parents. He had cried over the complete massacre that composed his village after the attack, but he busied himself with burying the dead right away. And all his thoughts had already turned to having his revenge on the Brotherhood. From the very onset, he latched onto the goal of killing Delkol.

I can mourn for the dead later, Terico thought. *Once Delkol is dead and his Brotherhood destroyed—then I can mourn.*

•

Once Suran was feeling a little better, Terico took her back to meet Areo, Borely, and Kitoh. But before Terico could begin recounting what he had been through the past couple weeks, Suran had everyone follow her to the bridge, so that Lanek would be able to hear everything as well. The airship was a small one, and it made Terico feel even more ill at ease than Borely's boat did. The high winds rocked the airship just as much as they did the boat, but the fact Terico was hundreds of meters in the air gave him a constant disconcerting feeling.

The bridge was at the front of the ship, and was a small room with a metal floor and lots of dark, crooked machinery. A boy Terico's age sat in a chair overlooking a wide variety of bent levers, thin chains, and a variety of hooks and clamps. The boy was Lanek, an elf with hair as long as his sister's, though his hair was a light turquoise rather than red. Terico had a class on Nexi control with him and Suran, and before and after class Lanek was nearly always in the middle of a group of cheerful classmates, usually composed of girls.

Even in this rusty airship, Lanek presented himself in an air of elegance. He wore a dark turquoise uniform that complemented his hair, along with black trousers, gloves, and boots.

"Welcome aboard the *Seven-Three*," he said. "Or as I prefer to call it, *The Finest Hour*."

"Glad to see you're okay," Terico said.

"Well, I'm glad you're glad," Lanek said, tilting his head and lowering his eyelids a bit. "I know *Suran* is glad."

Terico had never spoken with Lanek too much, but each time he did Lanek always seemed a little... *suspicious* of Terico, if that was the right word for it.
"Yes, it's wonderful," Suran said, walking toward her brother. "Terico has always been a good friend."

Lanek grabbed Suran's arm and pulled her close. He spun her around, wrapped an arm around her stomach, and had her lounge back on his left leg, her head resting against Lanek's right shoulder. Suran laughed and Lanek grinned, tilting his head atop of Suran's.

Lanek turned serious and whispered in Suran's ear. "Your eyes are bloodshot. Has he made you cry, Sister? I can toss him out the window if you wish."
     Suran nudged Lanek in the stomach and slipped out of his arms.
"Oh, Lanek. You need to stop treating me like a little kid."

"I'm sorry," Lanek said. "You're just too sweet and adorable, though."
Borely leaned to Terico and whispered, "You said they are siblings, right?" Terico sighed. "Yes, they just get along really well..." Or something. Lanek was just strange.

Lanek crossed one leg over the other and folded his arms. He looked over Terico and his companions and smirked. "I suppose I should learn your names. A colorful little group you've assembled here, Terico."

"This is Borely, Kitoh, and Areo," Terico said. "It's a bit of a story how I met each of them."

"A sailor, a powerful eigni child, and a vampire who has passed her Rite," Lanek said.

"Um... yes," Terico said, raising an eyebrow. "You've met them before?"

     "No, of course not," Lanek muttered. "But I *have eyes*."

     "Wait a second," Borely said. "You could tell Areo was a vampire?"

     "Well, yes," Lanek said. "It's kind of obvious."

Borely's face turned a bright red, though it was difficult to tell in the room's poor lighting.

"Still, it's surprising you could tell all this from looking at them," Terico said.

Lanek held an arm to the side nonchalantly. "The man's dressed like a sailor. Smells like one, too. As for the boy, well—I don't imagine you'd drag along a nine, ten-year-old without good reason, and it is said the eigni have a natural connection with Nexi. He must have a particularly good connection, and is helping you find those Elpis fragments you love so much. As for the girl, well—I suppose she could be a hundred years old for all I know. But at any rate she's a vampire, as evidenced by the pale skin, the pointed ears she's trying to hide, the way she keeps her fingers slightly curled, the way she keeps her mouth clamped shut, and the... *unseemly* clothing she's wearing. And she must have passed her Rite if she's been able to travel with you in the daytime all this while."

It was a terribly meticulous observation, which surprised Terico a bit. Lanek had never been one to stand out in class, but it seemed now that he likely just didn't hold much interest in the things the teachers taught.

Borely turned to Areo and frowned. "I never did find out how old you really are. Maybe you *are* a hundred years old."

"Almost," Areo said. "Give me a few more months."

"You're *ninety-nine?*" Borely yelled. "You have to be kidding me!"

Lanek leaned his head back and clenched his teeth. "Not so loud, please."

Borely shook his head and threw his hands up in frustration.

"No need to throw a fit," Lanek said. "From what I understand, the number of years a vampire lives doesn't have much effect on her *age*, if you follow." He turned to Terico and leaned forward a bit, shifting to a new subject. "Fortunately I have recently received from Rilv an overview of what you have been up to. You have a piece of the Elpis?"

Terico pointed to the pouch at his belt. "I have one, and Delkol has one."

Lanek tossed Terico a stone, and he caught it.

"Now you have *twooooo*," Lanek said slowly, raising two fingers. Terico looked at the small rock, and found its glow constantly shifting from one color to the next. Like the piece Terico had, this was perfectly smooth save for the end where it was broken off. It really was an Elpis fragment.

"How... How did you...?"

"Oh, it was nothing," Lanek said, closing his eyes and holding his hands out to either side of himself.

"Brother exaggerates," Suran said. "When we went to our airship, we met with a woman named Rilv, who works for the royal court. She told us that Delkol likely destroyed Edellerston in order to find a piece of the Elpis, a powerful stone the government has tried to keep secret. She asked us if we could use our airship to go look for an Elpis piece at the ancient ruins of an island called Reipol. Lanek was anxious to do whatever he could to stop
Delkol, so we accepted the mission."

"Not *anxious*," Lanek said. "I simply... needed something to do."

"We searched several islands before finding the right one," Suran continued. "We eventually found one with some very tall mountains and found some old stone ruins hidden in the snow. But when we found the

Elpis fragment... we were attacked."

Lanek's expression grew surprisingly grim. "Knight's armor... without the knights. Just collections of floating armor from some longforgotten era of the past. Phantoms, as it were. Phantoms guarding their treasure."

"You fought off phantoms of knights?" Terico asked, surprised Suran was involved in such a dangerous situation. He knew she and Lanek were talented with Nexi stones, but he had never thought of them as the fighting type—especially Suran.

"We had to," Suran said. "I felt bad for them, but they were trying to kill my brother."

"And *you*," Lanek added. "Those foul demons slashed open your right thigh, if you remember. Spilling your precious blood across the snow, scarring your slender, beautiful leg… I'll never forgive myself."

Terico looked to Suran's leg—which was covered by her skirt, of course.

"I'll be fine," Suran said with a smile. "Brother bandaged me up, and I'm already well enough now to walk. He seems to forget he was the one nearly killed, though."

"A couple of the buffoons had the nerve to try dropping a boulder on me while I was busy fighting the others," Lanek said. "Sister pulled me away with vines in time, but a chunk of the rock chipped off and bashed me in the back of the head. Knocked me out cold for hours, Suran tells me." He rubbed the back of his head and sighed. "Doubt the lump will *ever* go away, though."

Terico stifled a laugh, but Lanek still seemed to notice Terico's amusement.

Lanek glared at Terico but continued his account. "So in the end, Sister finished off the knights and obtained the Elpis, then helped me back to *The Finest Hour*. Eventually we let Rilv know of our success, and were told to just lay low for a while. She was still trying to work out where other pieces of the Elpis could be, it seems. But last night we were told to fly over to Vursa and pick you lot up. It seems you're an important part of

Rilv's plans, seeing as she wants you to have the Elpis fragments."

"It must mean that Terico can use them," Suran said. "Isn't that right, Terico?"

"Yes. I'm not sure why, though."

"All I know is that *I* wasn't able to use it," Lanek muttered. "At any rate, that's our story. I'm guessing the government got you to search for the Elpis piece you found."

"In a way," Terico said, remembering Jujor technically worked for the royal court. It was strange to think of him that way, though.

"How did you escape the Brotherhood's attack?" Lanek asked.

Terico recalled Delkol's words of how Delkol intended to leave Terico alive. It was a terrible fact, knowing Delkol had used him for the sake of locating a piece of the Elpis. That Terico was spared by the man who killed Terico's parents.

"I fought the Brotherhood," Terico said, "but I eventually got hurt and fell to a place that kept me hidden. After they finished destroying the town, I searched for any survivors. There was only Jujor, a man who helped me find the Elpis piece I obtained. He has since died, however."

"Nobody else survived then," Lanek said, stating the fact more than asking about it.

"No," Terico said. "I'm sorry, but your parents were killed."

Lanek shut his eyes and clasped his hands together. "I assumed as much. We didn't find any sign of their survival when we searched the village..." He didn't say any more, but kept very still. The silence lasted for what seemed half a minute.

"We'll keep working on their airships for them," Suran said in a quiet voice. "And build new ones they would be proud of."

Lanek opened his eyes and smiled. "Yes. We'll stick together, through times of joy, through times of pain. And through times of pain we'll turn into joy." He stood up, gave his sister a hug, and sighed. His expression turned very tired, very worried. "This world... this world we live in..."

"We'll make it better," Suran said, her voice turning weak. "We'll make it a place... where we can all smile again."

•

At Suran's insistence, Lanek agreed to show Areo, Borely, and Kitoh around the airship, including their quarters where they could rest over the course of the journey. Lanek set the ship to continue on its own, but asked Suran to remain on the bridge while she spoke with Terico.

"I'm sorry about my brother," she said once everyone was out. "He's overprotective at times, and is still upset from when I got injured."

"It's nothing," Terico said. "I'm happy you're both all right. And a little amazed with all you've been through since... we separated."

"I am too," Suran said. "It's a little hard to believe. I never expected to go on an adventure like this. It's all so strange... And you've been through so much, too. Merze, Emoser Helena, Istal, and Vursa. And with so much danger in such a short period of time."

"And it's not over yet," Terico said. "But once we reach Setar, I'll have three pieces of the Elpis to Delkol's one. Once I'm finished with him, I'll have the full Elpis, and the Shire armies should call off their attack." "What will you do then?" Suran asked.

"I'm not sure," Terico said. He had been so focused on killing Delkol that he hadn't thought much about what he'd do afterward. He just wanted to live a calm, simple life for a while.

He remembered Turan, though. If Terico could find Turan, he would want to try using the Elpis to heal him somehow. With the full Elpis, it was said anything was possible, and Terico felt he'd be able to undo the effects of Augurc's experimentation on Turan.

"But you're sure about the Elpis," Suran said. "And about... Delkol?" "What do you mean?" Terico asked.

Suran glanced away. "I know you wish to kill him. And... I don't know how to feel..."

"He destroyed the village," Terico said. "He killed our parents. I saw him slaughter the weak, the defenseless, the ill, the elderly, the young. Even children and infants. He took pleasure in this, Suran. He enjoyed killing *everyone.*"

"I understand," Suran said. She looked up to Terico with a frown, slightly trembling. "I just worry. I worry he will kill you. And I worry you will kill him, and... you'll change. You've already changed, and I'm afraid.

I don't know where this will all lead."

Terico felt his heart start to beat a little faster, a little harder. Had he changed? How had he changed? Perhaps he did change, but it only made sense he would. Who wouldn't change after watching his entire hometown go up in flames? After watching nearly everyone he knew die right before him?

A part of Terico was upset with Suran's words, but he understood she was just concerned. Terico couldn't let his quest for revenge consume him—it seemed like an obvious thing to say. But what else could he focus on right now? He had to bring Delkol down. It was likely he was the only one who could.

"I'll be okay," Terico said. "I promise. I'll get the third Elpis piece, wait for Delkol to come to me, and I'll defeat him. Once I have the full Elpis, I'll threaten the Shire armies, and they will return to their kingdom. Then I'll leave the Elpis to Rilv, who will probably want it broken apart again and hidden at new locations. And then... we can do what we wish.

We can live somewhere safe, quiet." "We?"
Suran asked.

Terico hadn't even realized what he had been saying. "I mean... in a general sense. Us and whoever else would be with us."

Suran smiled. "It sounded like you meant something else there."

"Ah..." Terico said, glancing away. He looked at all the controls of the ship, a little surprised at just how many there were. Hanging above some of the controls were thin white ropes, which Terico assumed were meant to be pulled for certain tasks.

"You and Lanek must have worked a long time on this airship."

"We only helped our parents with some of the parts," Suran said. "There were workers in Plien who put the ship together. When Lanek and I went there, there wasn't much left we had to do to get it airborne. And as you can see, it was a really quick job..."

Terico turned back toward Suran and smiled. "I think you did great. You've always been a hard worker. And everything you do, it's always for others." "Oh, that's not true," Suran said, blushing slightly. "I do things for myself."

"Hardly," Terico said. He felt nervous to go on, but knew it might be a while before he could let Suran know how he felt about her. "But that's one of the... many things I've always liked about you, Suran."

She looked to Terico's eyes a few seconds, a little confused. "Oh... thank you."

"I wanted to tell you some important things that day," Terico said. "Back before we were separated. After defeating a monster plant, I came home with my father and Turan, and you were there cooking food for us. You had brought my mother some herbs to help treat some patients at the clinic."

"I... I remember," Suran said.

"When you were heading to your workshop, I spoke with you," Terico said. "I wanted to ask you to go with me to the Long Shadow Festival."

"Oh, the festival," Suran said. "That would have been a while ago."

"Yes," Terico said. "But I was hoping to tell you more. I wanted to tell you how much I liked you."

Suran's eyes widened a bit, but she didn't say anything.

"I still like you," Terico said. "Seeing you again, alive and well—I can't keep this to myself anymore. I like you very much, Suran."

Suran stood there in silence, just starting at Terico for several seconds. She then glanced around a bit, her blush turning a little redder. "I... I'm surprised, Terico. I mean, I've always been your friend, but... I never realized... I didn't know you liked me that way before."

Terico chuckled, though a strange mix of emotions were building up inside him. "That's why I'm telling you now. I've always been nervous about letting you know."

"Oh, I see," Suran said. "I... thank you, Terico. But I don't know. I'm just still so confused. Until now I didn't even know you were alive, and...

Can I think about what you said?"

"Of—of course," Terico said, suddenly feeling a bit foolish for everything he said. Perhaps it was all far too soon to say anything. But he still felt it was important to say...

The door to the bridge opened, and Lanek walked back in. "All caught up on things, are we? I hope all is as it should be."

"Yes," Suran said, still blushing. "I'll be back in a minute." She walked to the hallway in a jittery, nervous way.

Lanek sat down in his chair and frowned deeply. He pointed to his eyes and glared at Terico. "I'm watching you, boy."

Which Terico thought was pretentious of him, considering they were the same age.

•

Time passed, and Terico spent much of his time going over details of his travels with Suran and Lanek, and hearing more from them about how they'd been keeping things running on the airship. The vehicle apparently required constant attention, and there were still things they were working to improve in various ways. Terico had trouble following it all—he had never understood much about mechanics, with all its gears, steam, and latches. It just wasn't something he was exposed to, like Suran and Lanek were.

As the hours passed, Terico noticed that Areo and Borely would never stay in the same room as one another. Perhaps it was pointless to try working something out between the two, since they were likely going to separate as soon as the airship reached Setar. Terico was curious to find out if either of them had worked out what they wished to do once at the capital city. Perhaps Borely would go find some work at the riverside port, and perhaps Areo would go off to travel on her own.

Terico found Areo in the quarters Lanek had lent to everyone to rest in. She was sitting on one of the small cots that filled up most the room, leaving only thin slots for people to walk between. There was a strained look on Areo's face, which she hid shortly after Terico walked in.

"Good day," she said.

"You looked troubled," Terico said. "Not that I blame you. We may be facing the Brotherhood some more."

"I'm only contemplating a few things," Areo said, turning to the far metal wall.

Terico sat down on a cot opposite of Areo so she was looking at him again. "What about?"

"Just some things Jujor said," Areo replied.

"He said a lot of things," Terico said. "And I was never too sure if many of the things he said were true."

"He was a bit mysterious," Areo said. "I only knew him for a short period of time, but I'm glad I met him. Jujor was a good man, and a friend of my father. I wish I could have known him sooner."

"It's strange," Terico said. "Jujor lived in my town my whole life, but I don't think I ever really spoke with him until the day it was destroyed. And now I feel he really was an important part of my life... I wish I could have known him better."

"You never know when people will die," Areo said. "It's something my mentor always made clear. You can't assume you will still be alive the next day. You have to live each day to the fullest."

Terico placed his elbows on his knees and clasped his hands together. "That's a harsh way to live."

"I had a harsh mentor," Areo said, still straight-faced. "You'd know— you met him."

"I remember..." Terico said. "You were thinking about some things Jujor said, though?"

"I'm trying to decide what to do," Areo said. "My father was killed, and I knew I couldn't just do nothing. After so many years of training to pass the Rite, I was looking forward to seeing Father again. To be honest, I was hoping to get advice from him... I wanted to know what to do with my life in general. I wanted to leave Istal—to travel the world for a while. But then what? I didn't know, and I still don't know. I'll never hear

Father's voice again, for as long as I live..."

"It's what Jujor said about revenge," Terico said. "You're still trying to decide if you want to seek out the one who killed your father."

"Yes," Areo said, sitting up a little straighter. "My master said to avoid seeking revenge. And Jujor's words implied that revenge wasn't worth the trouble. And it's something I've been thinking about quite a bit lately... I imagine myself killing that masked boy, and I feel nothing. I don't think killing him would satisfy me. No amount of blood can replace my father. I wish to do something, but I feel that whatever I do would be meaningless."

Terico let each of Areo's words sink in. He immediately disagreed with each of her statements. In Terico's point of view, killing Delkol would relieve him of immeasurable pain. Obviously revenge wouldn't bring Terico his parents back, or restore the village. Terico wasn't so naïve to believe that killing Delkol would erase all of Terico's sadness, or even all his hate.

But there would be justice. Terico could imagine killing Delkol, and obtaining that reassuring feeling that an unspeakable wrong had been avenged.

Terico thought of sharing this with Areo, but he knew to hold back. It was Turan that Areo would need to kill if she desired revenge. And Terico was still determined to find a way to save Turan. It wasn't Turan's fault that he killed Febraz—he only acted in accordance with the experimentation Augurc performed on him. If Terico could keep Areo from killing Turan, then all the better.

"It's difficult to know what to do sometimes," Terico said. "If you can help us keep Delkol from obtaining the Elpis, then I think you will have dealt a greater blow to the Brotherhood than killing one boy would. I believe Febraz would be pleased with any effort you make on his behalf."

"I just hope to keep the Brotherhood from making more people suffer as I have," Areo said. "But regarding my father, he would be pleased with me no matter what I did. I don't think there was a time he was ever truly upset with me."

Terico smiled a little. "My parents were that way too. I mean, they didn't approve of many of the things I did growing up... I tended to sneak off and throw myself into danger on a pretty regular basis... But they were the type of parents who could never be *really* angry at me."

"I can tell," Areo said. "You have a good heart."

"Thanks," Terico said. "I think everyone on this ship has a good heart."

Areo frowned, surely thinking of Borely.

"I know a lot of the things Borely said were uncalled for," Terico said, "but I'm sure you understand the reasoning behind his words."

"Of course I understand," Areo said. "It doesn't make any of them right, though."

"Indeed," Terico said. "And I'm sure he will work that out as well."

He stood up and walked to the door, while Areo simply sat still and quiet.

When Terico opened the door to leave, she spoke up. "It's ridiculous how he's handled himself. Borely acts like an idiot, but there *is* more to him." "There's more to everybody, it seems," Terico replied. He shut the door behind him and found his own words haunting him.

More to myself as well? he thought.
She says I have a good heart. But would a good heart seek to kill?

•

At the end of the hallway Terico found the room he and the others had entered when first boarding the airship. There were thin, rectangular windows looking out to the distant fields below, but Terico didn't wish to look out them like Borely was. It was unnerving enough as it was just walking around in this airship, knowing the fragile structure was being held up by an even more fragile balloon. He trusted in Suran and Lanek's ability to finish putting the ship together, but the fact they had to rush through things at the end was an ever-present thought in Terico's mind. He stood about a meter from Borely and looked back toward the hallway.
"An interesting view?"

"Pretty intense," Borely said. "Really makes you feel like a bird, seeing things from this vantage point. I've been up in tall crow's nests at the top of ship masts, which I think is a bit more worrisome at times. At least when there's a good storm. Then again, I wouldn't want to be in this airship in a big storm, either."

Terico hadn't thought of that. What if a lightning storm erupted around the airship? The balloon would surely explode, and send everyone in the airship all the way to the landscape below. Certain death for everyone. He tried to not think about the possibilities any further.

"Hopefully the weather stays clear," Terico said. There were some clouds out, but there wasn't anything too menacing looking.

"Hopefully," Borely said. He turned around to face Terico. "Anything you needed me for?"

"I just wondered how you were doing," Terico said. "You've been dragged into a lot more than you bargained for, I imagine."

"It's strange how things can just... not go the way you want them to,"
Borely said. He forced a weary smile. "I mean, it wasn't so long ago that I was thinking I had found myself a nice little adventure, some interesting travel companions, and a chance with a beautiful woman! Instead I lose my boat and all my belongings, the old man I was just getting to know ends up dead, and the woman turns out to be a vampire." Borely kept smiling, but shook his head solemnly. "I mean... how does that *happen*? The feeling is just... It's like you meet up with a friend you haven't seen in ages, and instead of shaking your hand, he punches you in the stomach.

As hard as he can."

"I know what you mean," Terico said, a little amused by Borely's analogy. "I mean... with things not going the way you want them to. But you know, things can get better."

"I get that you've been through a lot," Borely said, "but you've got to understand... That boat was everything to me. That was like my family to me. All I had left to connect myself to them."

"There's still yourself," Terico said. "Well, I guess it's not much comfort to say 'At least you're still alive' in a situation like this. But I'm sure you'll figure out where to go from here."

"I know," Borely said. "I can't help but be frustrated, though. Normally I'd just hit a pub for a few hours, but Lanek's told me there isn't a drop of liquor in this airship."

"You can get a drink when we're at Setar," Terico said. "Is that what you like to do though when not sailing the sea?"

"Never a dull moment at the pub," Borely said. "Usually a few games of chance for me to jump in on every time I visit. Luck might not be on my side outside the pub, but more often than not I've got a gift once I'm inside. And whether I win or lose, I always meet some interesting people." It was certainly a different sort of life than Terico was used to, but he could understand Borely's need to spend time having fun with people whenever he had the chance. If Borely transported cargo for most of his living, that would mean lots of long, lonely treks on his small ship.

"I suppose you've met some interesting people here too, at least," Terico said. "I'm sorry luck hasn't been on your side, though."

"I'll live," Borely said. "And I intend to bounce back once I get to Setar. I can make Areo pay me back for my boat, and then be on my way."

Terico felt he should have seen this development coming, but it still sounded absolutely ridiculous. "You're going to make Areo pay you for your boat?"
"She deceived me," Borely said. "It seems reasonable to me."

"You've got to get over it, Borely," Terico said. "Vampires have to keep their identity hidden as best they can. People just don't trust them." "For good reason," Borely said.

"No," Terico said. "I disagree. And even knowing your family was killed by vampires, I think you shouldn't be judging Areo based on what others have done to you."

"You don't get it!" Borely yelled, holding his hands out to the sides. He stared at Terico with his eyes wide and his teeth clenched for several seconds before continuing. "A vampire turned my brother into a vampire, and my brother killed my parents! And then I killed my brother! You can't understand what that's like! You understand the pain of death, but you can never understand the pain of having the blood of your own brother on your hands! And it's all because of vampires that this endless torment has been forced upon me!"

Borely took a couple deep breaths before continuing. "You think I should just get over it. You think I should just let go of this past and pretend everything's fine. It's not so simple. Every time I look at Areo now, I remember my brother. I see my brother as a vampire. I see myself shoving a blunt fishing knife into my brother's heart. Again and again and again!"

It took several long seconds of silence for Terico to believe Borely was finished. The man stood up tall and turned back to the window he had been looking out of before.

"You're right," Terico said. "I don't know how you feel. I never will, since I've never had any siblings... But the thing is, I don't *need* to understand what you're going through. I can't fix these problems for you, so there isn't much use in trying. But the fact is there's nothing wrong with Areo and you know it. You'll just have to let that settle in your head for a bit."

Terico turned and left, leaving Borely to decide how long he'd consider Terico's words.

•

Time was drawing near. It wouldn't be long before the airship reached Setar, Lanek explained. Terico's thoughts constantly turned to the Elpis stone, and he repeatedly found himself shifting the two pieces he had in his hands. Even without accessing the power of the Elpis, Terico could feel something strong in the stones. They carried a weight in them that didn't exist in regular Nexi stones. They weren't heavier, really—but there was something more to them.

Terico walked around the bridge, past the two seats occupied by Lanek and Suran. In the far back corner of the room, Terico found Kitoh sitting on the hard metal floor. The boy sat cross-legged, and had a scared look on his face. Every now and then Kitoh would glance around when the airship shook a little more than usual, then take a deep breath once things returned to normal.

"You going to make it?" Terico asked.

Kitoh looked up and nodded slowly. "I hope so."

"You'll probably be fine if the airship falls apart," Terico said. "You can turn into a dragon and fly down to safety."

Kitoh looked down to the ground and held his breath. He looked absolutely terrified.

"Are you afraid of heights?" Terico asked. "I am myself, I admit."

"It's not that," Kitoh said, his voice so soft Terico had to lean down a bit to hear him better. "I don't want to turn into a dragon again..." "I see. It must be..." Terico struggled to find the right word.

"Bloody amazing." Lanek spun his chair around so he was facing them. "If I could turn into a dragon, I'd probably fly around and burn things every day."

"Which is probably why you don't have that power and Kitoh does," Terico said under his breath.

"I have to say," Lanek went on, "that you're not what I expected from an eigni boy who could turn into a dragon. But I suppose this only makes you all the more endearing."

Suran turned her chair so she was facing Terico and Kitoh as well. She glanced to Lanek. "I doubt turning into a dragon is a simple matter. It might be painful... And it might be frightening."

"Dragons have no need to be frightened," Lanek said. "They're huge. They can fly. They breathe fire."

"They're not invincible, either," Terico said. He did see that Lanek had a point, but there was obviously more to Kitoh's worries than the mere physical danger involved of fighting in general.

"I'm not worried about dying," Kitoh said, still looking to the ground. "Or getting hurt."

"Then what's wrong?" Lanek asked.

"It's... the fact I *can* turn into a dragon," Kitoh said. "I shouldn't be able to."

"Why?" Terico asked. From what he understood, Kitoh was one of the most powerful eigni in Vursa—and certainly the most powerful one his age. And the fact Kitoh was the only one who fended off Ganto's Nexi power was proof enough of his superior capabilities.

"Very few eigni can do it," Kitoh said. "And those that can... they're all very powerful, very experienced adults. It's... not right that I should be able to do this much. It's *wrong*."

Terico wasn't sure what he could say that would actually help Kitoh. The boy didn't really want to be here in the first place. And Terico didn't think there was anything Kitoh could really do other than accept the fact the boy had a great deal of power and use it as he deemed best.

Suran walked over to Kitoh and sat down beside him. "I don't really think this is a matter of right and wrong. Whether or not you have any great power, you can choose to do whatever you wish. But the fact you have a great power doesn't mean anything about who you are. My brother and I are good with machinery, but that doesn't define who we are. And even though we're siblings, our personalities are actually rather different." "Thankfully," Terico said.

"There's nothing wrong with being good at machinery," Kitoh said. "As a dragon, I can hurt lots of people. I'm afraid."

"That's good," Lanek said. "There are grown men out there who have power, but don't truly understand what that means. They have power and think that means they can do whatever they want."

Suran wrapped an arm around the back of Kitoh's shoulders and smiled. "It's okay to be afraid. I think we've all been worried lately. That's perfectly normal."

"I don't know if I'll be able to fight," Kitoh said. "Everyone's expecting me to, but I don't know if I can do it."

"It's all right," Suran said. "When the time comes, I'm sure you'll find the courage you'll need."

Terico weighed his own feelings in his heart. He was deeply concerned for what was to come, of course. There was no telling what the Brotherhood was planning at the moment.

"We'll all have to find that courage when the time comes," Terico said.

Terico felt he should be well past the stage of overcoming his fear of fighting Delkol and the Brotherhood. And yet there was still a piece of fear lodged deep in his heart.

Perhaps it was just a sliver, but it was still there.

9

CLASH IN THE SKIES

A few hours passed before Lanek directed everyone's attention to the landscape ahead. Terico looked out the large window at the front of the bridge and found a city in the distance. It was difficult to see any individual buildings, including the royal castle where the king lived, and where an Elpis fragment presumably resided. Everyone looked out at the bright panorama, staring down in curious silence.

Terico had gotten a little used to the sensation of being this high up in the air, so he let his gaze linger a little longer at the distant scene. There was a wide river that ran between the expanse of green hills, down through the city, and on past the farmlands below. The lines of crops were dizzying to look at for long, so Terico focused more on Setar, its grand structures slowly becoming a little more clear to the eye.

"Amazing," Suran said. "The very size of these buildings..."

Terico thought it was all very impressive, but it had to be even more fascinating for someone like Suran, who was more knowledgeable in engineering. And in her case, she had only been outside of Edellerston on a few brief occasions in her life. Seeing the capital city would be a special event for her.

"It's certainly a large city," Terico said. "It looks really chaotic from up here."

"To be expected," Lanek said. "The castle and its surrounding premises are rather well organized, but there's only so much that can be done for a city at large. Especially one as old and expansive as Setar."

"It has its own kind of beauty," Suran said. "I don't think I'd ever want to live in such a big city, but it is nice to visit."

"Poor time to visit it, though," Lanek said. "If things don't work out with Terico and the Elpis, we'll probably be caught up in Delkol's invasion."

Terico would have liked to assure that everything would work out, but there was no telling what Delkol had been up to since escaping Vursa. Areo, Kitoh, and Borely continued to look out the window in silence, each of them impressed by the view the airship offered. Terico hoped Kitoh would be up for whatever lay ahead, and that Areo and Borely would be able to handle things as well.

Eventually Terico was able to make out the castle at the city's center. It was a tall structure of dark red stone, portions of which were painted yellow or purple. It was encircled by six thin red towers that stood even taller than the castle, each of which were connected together by a deep brick wall. Further out, Terico spotted a portion of the river redirected to form a moat around the central portion of the city, which included the castle grounds as well as a great deal of the city's larger buildings. Outside the protection of the moat were thousands of tiny wooden huts and patches of farmland— far too many for Terico to ever count.

"Lanek, are you there?"

It was a familiar voice, though it took Terico a moment to remember it belonged to Rilv, the head servant of the royal court.

Lanek leaned back in his chair and slipped a teal Nexi stone from his pocket. "Good afternoon, madame."

"Scouts have reported four Brotherhood airships approaching the city from the east," Rilv said. "Most of the royal fleet is away, gathering reinforcements from neighboring cities, and the remaining ships have been sabotaged by a double agent. It will take some time to get any of them in the air—I need you to hold off the airships in the meantime. Or simply take them down."

"Oh yes, how simple," Lanek said. "Four airships against one that's fortunate to even be airborne... Suddenly *The Finest Hour* takes on new meaning."

"So you can't handle it then?" Rilv said.

Lanek gripped the Nexi stone and sighed. "To be realistic..."

"You have the tools necessary to achieve victory," Rilv said. "Deal with those ships and I may accept your earlier proposition."

"Very well," Lanek said. "I guess *I'll try* then. Is there anything else?"

"No," Rilv replied. "If any airships get close to the castle, we will be able to launch Nexi stones at them. But I imagine the Brotherhood has a plan, as evident by the fact there is a traitor in our midst."

"Just leave it to me." And with that, Lanek put the Nexi stone away and stood up to run the controls of the airship.
He turned it toward the region east of the city, leading the airship toward a few dots in the sky that Lanek identified as the Brotherhood airships.
"Delkol is probably on one of those ships," Terico said.

"Sounds likely," Lanek said. "Everyone get ready—they'll start firing at us as soon as we're in range."

A part of Terico wanted to activate his Elpis stones and attack the airships himself, but he couldn't be certain Delkol was on one of them. He didn't want to exhaust himself and then be left vulnerable for when the time came to face Delkol.

Suran sat down in her chair and moved it toward some of the controls about a meter from Lanek. She placed her hands above four different levers, which Suran had told Terico were used to control each of the four Nexi cannons equipped to the airship. There were many Nexi at her disposal, so as long as Lanek piloted the ship properly, Suran would be able to both attack and defend via her mental connection with the Nexi stones.

"Two ships coming toward us," Lanek said. "The other two are continuing toward the center of Setar."

Terico could see the city far below, and realized it would probably only take a few minutes for the Brotherhood ships to reach the castle at the speed they were going. Now that they were closer to Terico, he could see these airships were massive— several times larger than the one Suran and Lanek built. Great white dirigibles each with a thick, inverted black cross painted down their sides. The dark metal machinery of the jagged ships tied beneath the blimps hung menacingly, at least a half-dozen Nexi cannons hanging from each side of them.

"One will attack while the other tries to slip past," Suran said. "If Delkol can locate where Elpis pieces are, he'll know Terico is here. They'll try to board the ship to retrieve the Elpis."

"Everyone prepare to fight then," Lanek said.

"But what about those other two ships?" Borely asked. "They're already getting away."

Lanek didn't respond, and Terico wondered if he should go after them. Rilv said the city did have defensive measures, but the Brotherhood had to know that. They had to have a strategy in mind, and it left Terico uneasy.
What was Delkol's plan? Was he trying to lure Terico out of the airship? Perhaps Delkol was hoping Terico would go after those two airships.

Kitoh ran out the bridge and down the hallway, gripping a couple bright Nexi in his fist.

"Kitoh, wait!" Areo called. She turned and ran after him.

"Hold on!" Borely yelled, running after her.

Terico followed to find out what was going on. He chased Borely and Areo down the clanging hall and into the airship's entry room. Kitoh forced up a lock at the very back of the room, then began sliding open the shaking metal doorway.

"Stop!" Areo yelled.

Kitoh turned back a moment, then leaped out of the door. He fell through the sky a couple seconds, then activated his Nexi stones. The boy turned into a great dragon, just as he had at Vursa—only this time he was flying. He would have been too large to fit in the airship's entry room at this point, and was probably at least a quarter the size of the dirigible as a whole. Kitoh used his massive wings to turn himself around, then flew toward the doorway and maintained a speed similar to the airship's.

"I'll go with you!" Areo yelled over the rushing winds. "Just drop me off at one of the airships, and I'll take care of the Brotherhood!" Once Kitoh was close enough, Areo leaped out the door and landed atop the dragon's back. She nearly stumbled over the other side, but managed to hold a strong, careful grip with her claws. Once secured, she situated herself so she sat against the front of the giant fin protruding from Kitoh's back.

Kitoh was about to take off, but Borely yelled out to them. "Hold on! I'm not letting you sneak away that easily!" Before Terico could stop him, Borely leaped out, arms and legs flailing in the air. He screamed at the top of his lungs, and for a moment it looked like he was going to miss the dragon entirely.

Kitoh swerved to the left and dived down a bit to scoop Borely up with the back of his large, thick neck. Still screaming, Borely tumbled backward, pushed by the tumultuous winds. He crashed straight into Areo, who grabbed onto Borely and slid her way in front of him. She forced Borely to wrap his arms around her stomach to keep him from flying off into the air.

"What are you thinking?" Areo screamed. "Are you insane?"

"Someone has to watch you!" Borely yelled. "You're too suspicious to be left alone at a time like this!"

Terico could only make out a groan in Areo's response, before Kitoh swooped down beneath the airship and flapped his giant batlike wings to propel himself forward. If Kitoh could drop Areo and Borely off at one of the two ships heading to the castle and then attack the other one himself, it would buy Suran and Lanek some time as they dealt with the other two ships.

Terico shut and locked the doorway, then ran back to the bridge to watch the approaching Brotherhood airships. Suran still had her hands at the controls, while Lanek guided his airship to the best spot to take on the two enemy ships. The odds were against them, but Lanek said their ship would be faster and more dexterous than the giant Brotherhood dirigibles. Terico knew though that in the end, it would come down to his skill with the Elpis stone. Delkol was seeking it, and a final battle was certain to ensue in some form.

And I have one more piece than him, Terico thought. He knew this wouldn't spell an instant victory, and knew better than to become overconfident. Delkol certainly had a plan in mind, and Terico had to make sure to not fall for it.

"One more minute," Lanek said, his rapt attention on the nearer of the two enemy airships.

"I have it," Suran said, staring wide-eyed at the same ship. She adjusted one of the levers ever so slightly, and Terico could hear the clanking of a shifting cannon at the front of the airship. From here it wasn't possible to see the tilt or direction of the cannons, but Terico assumed Suran had a good, intuitive handle for it, and her mind's connection with the ship's Nexi stones would act as a guide for her as well.

With her mind, she used a Nexi to fire one of the cannons, launching a great red Nexi stone for the nearest Brotherhood ship. Terico watched the large glowing stone tumble through the air, rushing straight for the back half of the dirigible.

A swarm of dirt rushed out of one of the enemy ship's cannons, quickly forming into a massive wall of earth that curved a good distance in front of the back half of the balloon. The red Nexi exploded into a great ball of fire, blasting apart the hardened earth floating in front of the dirigible. The detonation blew apart the shield, but had no effect of the airship itself.

"A brilliant shot," Lanek said. "But they have an equally competent Nexi user in their midst."

"I'll break through their defenses," Suran said, already working with a second lever.

The Brotherhood ship shot a series of dark blue Nexi stones, then set them off about a dozen meters from *The Finest Hour*. At the same time, Suran released a tan Nexi, which she caused to form a protective barrier in front of the airship. With a limited amount of dirt at her disposal, she had to direct portions of the the dirt to just the right spots in order to block the four blasts of water. The end result was a formation of strained, hardened earth that twisted and turned sharply in several directions. As the earth was shot, the water and dirt broke apart and plummeted toward the ground.

The second Brotherhood ship continued onward in the meantime, slipping toward *The Finest Hour* while Suran was busy defending against the first ship. The moment she had the opportunity though, she turned to a lever to control the cannon on the starboard side of the airship.

"Keep an eye on them both," Lanek said.

Suran responded by firing a tan Nexi at the second enemy ship, which continued approaching from the side. Terico thought it risky to use up a tan Nexi for an attack, considering its important role for the airship's defense— but he decided to trust Suran's judgement for now. The large tan stone transformed into a long stone spike, flying straight for the dirigible. Terico doubted it would pop like a balloon, but the damage the stalactite would cause could bring it down, he imagined.

The enemy ship fired a couple light blue Nexi toward the spike, detonating them a few meters in front of it. The spike was going to freeze and shatter into small harmless pieces, Terico realized.

Just before it crashed into the bursting ice Nexi, the giant earth spike exploded into a massive ball of dust. Apparently there was a red Nexi stone lodged in the tan Nexi cannon, and Suran detonated it just before the spike of earth was destroyed. Terico watched as a thick smoke screen enveloped the area between *The Finest Hour* and the enemy airship, as well as most of the enemy airship itself. Now her plan was a bit more clear—her goal was to create as much dust as she could, as close to the nearer of the two Brotherhood ships as possible.

"Now, Lanek!" Suran cried.

"Already going," Lanek said, pulling on a rope with one hand while adjusting a lever with the other.

The airship took a sharp, sudden dive to the right, and Terico fell to the ground hard. He managed to grab onto one of the thick legs of Suran's chair, which was grafted to the metal floor.

"Oh, and hang on," Lanek added as an afterthought.

"Thanks for the warning," Terico said.

"Always be on your toes," Lanek replied.

Terico pulled himself up and saw the first Brotherhood ship firing several red

Nexi, hoping to keep *The Finest Hour* from slipping behind the thick, lingering smoke screen. Suran quickly fired a couple green Nexi from the front of the ship. As soon as they were in the air, she caused their vines to spread out in all directions and intertwine with one another. In seconds a thick, expansive wall of sprawling vines appeared. The red Nexi crashed against it, blowing it apart and burning the vines to ash. Lanek guided the airship behind the smoke screen before the first enemy ship could attack again.

The moment it stabilized, Lanek forced the airship to speed toward the second enemy ship, which was still making its way through the cloud of dust. Terico held on to the back of Suran's chair, anxiously watching for the second airship to appear. Lanek drove *The Finest Hour* onward and turned it hard to port.

The Brotherhood ship emerged from the dust, its side facing toward *The Finest Hour*. Lanek had guided his airship upward a ways, however, leaving the enemy ship vulnerable and blind about a dozen meters below.

"Fire!" Lanek yelled.

As he gave the order, Suran quickly adjusted the two forward cannons and fired a couple red Nexi at the giant blimp below. She and Terico peered out the window to watch the two fire stones crash into the dirigible. Suran caused the fire to spread quickly, sending the entire blimp bursting into flames. Lanek piloted *The Finest Hour* back a ways, trying to keep the remaining dust and the ensuing thick black smoke between his airship and the remaining Brotherhood ship.

"Nice!" Terico said. "That was brilliant, Suran."

Suran smiled but was quick to return to her seat. "There's still another one to deal with."

"Three, actually," Lanek said. "We don't know how Terico's ragtag team of misfits is holding up."

The airship jerked to the right slightly, and a terrible clanging noise erupted from the hallway.

"Terico!" an echoing voice screamed.

Terico ran to the hallway and found masked members of the Brotherhood entering the back of the airship. They had apparently used vines to reach the ship, and then forced a large opening in the floor via orange Nexi.

"Boarding party," Terico said. "Four—no, five of them."

"Go with him, Suran," Lanek said. "I'm in position to fire once the smoke clears. I can pilot and defend at the same time."

Suran got up and joined Terico, who unsheathed his sword and charged down the hall.

"Use the Nexi that Rilv gave us," Lanek called back to Suran. "And don't die! Tell Terico I'll kill him if he lets you get hurt!"

The way Lanek said it made it sound like a joke, but Terico felt pretty sure Lanek would make good on that promise in such an event. Terico wasn't going to let any of the Brotherhood near Suran if he could help it though, regardless.

He and Suran rushed into the back room of the airship and found the five Brotherhood members, each of them dressed in white clothes and silver armor. Their white masks each bore the symbol of the inverted black cross over the right eye, but only one mask had the additional smile painted from ear to ear.

"Terico!" the boy yelled. He tilted his head a bit and tossed an orange Nexi in the air a couple times. "And isn't this a pleasant surprise...

It looks like *Suran* is still alive and well."

"Terico..." Suran said in a hushed voice. "Is that... Turan?"

The boy clenched his orange Nexi tight. "Turan is no more! Turan died, but has been reborn as Lynx!"

"He was captured by the Brotherhood," Terico said. "Augurc has brainwashed him. If we can capture him without killing him, I might be able to find a way to save him."

"Your orders, Lynx," said one of the masked fighters.

"Kill Suran, the girl!" Turan replied. "I will pin Terico down and make him *watch*!

And then... I'll break every little bone in his body!"

•

Areo held tight to Kitoh's back while Borely held on to Areo. The sailor wouldn't stop screaming, and it was difficult to tell if it was out of fear or enjoyment. Flying through the air on the back of a dragon was exhilarating, but Areo had to keep focus on the two airships slipping away in the distance. One of them was turning so its cannons would face toward the approaching dragon.

"Watch for Nexi fire!" Areo yelled.

Kitoh didn't respond, perhaps afraid to speak in this form. The boy flapped his long, leathery wings to bring himself higher, where it would be more difficult for the airships to fire at him.

"Hang on," Areo called back to Borely. "And quit screaming."

Borely laughed. "I had always hoped to die in a glorious way. Can't think of anything more spectacular than *this*!"

"Don't die, you idiot," Areo yelled. She squinted toward the nearest airship, the sky annoyingly bright and the winds only making things worse. The blasts of several cannons boomed through the air.

Kitoh turned to the left, avoiding a large red Nexi stone. It exploded above him, forcing him to dive downward. Two more red Nexi stone approached, detonating in front of him. Areo gripped Kitoh's back tighter, but for a second it felt like Borely was losing his grip. He managed to keep hold though, even as Kitoh flailed to the right of the bursting fire. The dragon rushed forward to avoid a fourth stone, then corkscrewed to the left to keep away from the burst of flames erupting from a fifth and sixth red Nexi.

"Hurry and drop us off at the farther airship," Areo told Kitoh. "We'll fight them off from within, while you handle this ship." She wanted Kitoh to be able to return to the elves' airship in case the boy couldn't maintain his dragon form for much longer, so she didn't want to force him to chase the enemy ship getting further and further away. She also needed to make sure the Brotherhood didn't reach the castle, guessing they had some special means of breaking past the castle's defenses.

Kitoh rushed for the second airship, pushing his wings harder with every stroke. The first airship launched a series of dark blue Nexi at Kitoh, and once the second airship was in range, it also began firing ice Nexi. The Brotherhood's tactic was readily apparent—Kitoh was struggling to fly through the frozen air.

Areo felt her whole body grow cold as more of the dark blue Nexi burst apart mere meters away. With each detonation, the Nexi released torrents of frozen air and water in all directions. Kitoh struggled to push through, and for a moment he had trouble getting his wings to flap properly. The dragon fell several meters, scaring the breath right out of Areo and Borely.

Fortunately Kitoh managed to keep himself together and continue flying. He flapped as vigorously as he could, working his way above the pockets of frozen air released by the light blue Nexi stones. Areo couldn't stop shivering, and neither could Borely, who she worried would lose his grip around her stomach.

One ice Nexi rushed by just a few centimeters to Areo's left, and she nearly flung herself to the right in reaction. Instead she held on tight, and counted herself lucky that the stone wasn't set off when it was right next to them. Otherwise they would have all been frozen, leaving them to plummet to the earth helplessly.

Kitoh pushed above the range of the Nexi cannons, then soared toward the second Brotherhood airship. Once near enough, the dragon dived down toward it, pulling up just as he reached the bottom of the ship. Kitoh positioned himself so he was directly underneath the ship. He flew along at the same speed as the airship, and turned his head back to Areo, as if waiting to hear what to do next.

"We'll break in," Areo said. She considered having Kitoh breathe fire at the ship from here, but she wanted him to save his energy for the ship he would have to face alone.

Careful to keep hold of Kitoh's back with one hand, Areo took a green Nexi stone from her pouch and aimed it for the side of the ship. It didn't look like there were any ways in from below, so she and Borely would just have to break in from the side. If the sailor could break through the massive doorway to the Vursa council room, he could break through a door to the airship too.

She caused several thick vines of her Nexi to wrap around a railing, then reminded Borely to hang on tight again. "Be ready to fight the moment we break in."

"No problem," Borely said.

Once the vines were secure, Areo let go of Kitoh's back and leaped off. She gripped her Nexi stone tight with both hands and caused the Nexi to reabsorb its vines. With the vines clung tight to the siding of the airship, Areo was propelled through the air and pulled up toward the railing. Borely was a heavy weight to carry, but he managed to keep a firm grip on Areo. Once at the railing, Areo grabbed on to the side of the ship and pulled herself up to a set of steps leading to one of several metal doorways. She glanced back down once more to see Kitoh heading back to the other airship, flying low to make it difficult for the Brotherhood ships to shoot him down.

Once on the steps, Borely let go and walked up to the doorway. He looked flustered, but Areo didn't comment on it. She brushed off her waist and hips, a little upset Borely had to hold on to her so tight for as long as he had.
"You better not hold back," Borely said, raising a fist toward the doorway. "I hate having to count on you, but you'll have to watch my back."
Areo glanced away. "Watch your own back. I won't slow you down."

Borely turned back to the door and charged his fist with orange Nexi energy. He landed a solid punch, sending the entire door flying into the entry room. Areo charged in after Borely, rushing straight for the nearest Brotherhood member she caught sight of. A masked man turned around and started to yell something. Areo clawed apart his throat and ran on to the next nearest Brotherhood fighter, leaving the first to drop dead behind her.

At the same time, Borely ran for a Brotherhood fighter knocked to the ground by the metal door Borely had punched in. Areo glimpsed Borely punching the masked man just as he was getting up. Borely shattered the man's mask and knocked him out cold.

Areo saw the room was very long, running for tens of meters forward and backward. There were long rectangular windows and several small tables covered with the controls used to operate the ship's cannons. There were six Brotherhood members left to deal with, Areo quickly counted. These were competent fighters, and Areo no longer had the advantage of surprise on her side.

Borely was closer to the next nearest Brotherhood fighter. He dodged a burst of fire released by the masked man, then slammed a Nexi-powered punch into the man's chest. The man flew back, straight through one of the large windows. Borely immediately turned to the next Brotherhood fighter.

Vines grasped the sides of the broken window, and the masked man Borely had punched leaped back into the room. He had his fire Nexi raised toward Borely, who was turned away from him.

"Watch it, Borely!" Areo yelled.

She rushed for him and pushed him away from the enemy's blast of fire. The flames nearly caught on to her, but she jumped back in time to avoid the attack. In one swift motion, she spun in place and leaped for the enemy. The man ran to her and raised his red Nexi. She sliced the man's hand clean off before he could activate the Nexi stone. Still stepping toward the man, Areo finished the motion by plunging her free claws into his heart.

By the time she turned around, a long-haired Brotherhood member had released a stream of swamp material, while a short Brotherhood fighter ran toward Areo with two daggers raised. Areo ran aside of the brown Nexi substance and charged for the fighter armed with daggers. In one glimpse, Areo realized one dagger had a purple Nexi attached to its hilt, while the other had a yellow Nexi.

Areo slipped out her tan Nexi and released a burst of dirt at the fighter. Closing her eyes, Areo leaped into the cloud of dust and listened for the assailant's exact movements. With two footsteps to go by, Areo lunged for the fighter, listening for the swipe or thrust of a dagger. The Brotherhood member swung a dagger—the one with the purple Nexi, which created a spherical shockwave to clear away the dust. The blast of energy disturbed Areo's swipe toward the fighter's neck, and she ended up clawing at the assailant's mask.

The mask flung off of the fighter, revealing the face of a woman—she had short black hair and large, piercing green eyes. Areo continued her attack, slashing again for the woman's neck. The Brotherhood member activated the yellow Nexi of her other dagger, and Areo's claws slammed against the yellow glow that enveloped the woman's body. Areo stepped back to avoid the swipe of the woman's other dagger.

At the same time Areo heard an object collide with the ground just behind her. She leaped back as hard as she could, jumping over what turned out to be a brown Nexi stone—the one used by the Brotherhood member from before. The stone blew apart, releasing a deluge of swamp substance. The second Brotherhood member guided most of it toward Areo, who quickly released a burst of dirt from her tan Nexi. She coated the swamp material beneath her feet and hardened the dirt, allowing herself to run back from the thick, dark waves.

The woman with daggers ran around the rushing swamp, much faster than Areo had expected. At the same time, Areo heard footsteps coming from the side. She glanced and found a third Brotherhood fighter avoiding a blast of water fired by Borely, then sprinting on toward Areo. A tall masked bald man—an elf, Areo noted from the pointed ears. He wielded a long metal staff.

While Borely beat down the man controlling the swamp, Areo caused a large arm of earth to erupt from the dirt she left atop the swamp. She turned back to the woman with the dagger, who swung a wave of purple energy at Areo. While dodging the attack and going by the sound of the man's footsteps, Areo caused the dirt arm to grab the man's leg. The woman continued toward Areo, who readied her claws for the kill.

A blast of water slammed into Areo's back, flinging her straight for the woman with daggers. The elf apparently had a water Nexi embedded in the end of his staff, Areo realized. She crashed against the woman, who shoved a dagger toward Areo's heart. Areo slipped her claws into the the woman's hand at the last moment, forcing the assailant to drop the dagger.

The two crashed against the far wall, the enemy's head bashed hard

against the thick dull metal.

Before Areo could claw at the enemy, a very large red Nexi fell to the ground about a meter away from them. An attack meant to take her down, even if it cost the Brotherhood woman's life.

The woman was dazed. Areo grabbed the dagger with the yellow Nexi from her and turned around. She leaped over the red Nexi just as it detonated into a massive ball of fire. Areo activated the yellow Nexi, creating a barrier around her body just as she was engulfed in the flames. The ear-piercing detonation flung Areo across the room for several meters, sending her crashing past where Borely and two other Brotherhood members were fighting. She tumbled across the floor, then rolled until the fire covering her body dissipated. By keeping the energy of the yellow Nexi active, Areo managed to keep from getting burnt by the all-encompassing flames.

She glanced back to where she had been, finding a massive hole in the room, now filled with dark smoke and patches of blue sky. Both the woman and the elf Areo fought were gone.

Borely batted aside vines flung by one Brotherhood fighter, then spun in place and slammed a hard punch into the stomach of the other fighter, who had charged for Borely from behind with a sword. The first fighter raised a tan Nexi, aiming it toward Borely from behind.

Areo flung her dagger into the man's back. She ran to him and clawed apart his neck before he could fight back. Meanwhile Borely continued to fend off the other Brotherhood member, who activated an orange Nexi in the hilt of his sword. Borely leaped back, smart enough to know he wouldn't be able to block the man's swings with his fists, even with his thick metal knuckles charged orange as well.

The moment he had an opening, Borely stomped forward and slammed his forehead against the enemy's forehead, activating the blue Nexi in his headpiece in the process. The jet of water sent the masked man flying back several meters, clear across the room. He crashed against the wall, just beside the door to the airship's hallway.

A large, muscular man walked into the room and stopped at the entry. A small vest left most his chest and abdomen bare, and several glowing green Nexi were grotesquely grafted to his arms. The man had a wide bandana to keep his long black hair back, and a pallid scar curving across his nose. His face was essentially a series of frowns—one from his bandana, another from his scar, and a third from his actual frown. He stared at the chaotic scene before him with cold, soulless green eyes.

> Areo had never seen this man face-to-face before, but she knew of him—Augurc Shire, one of the two brother leaders of the Shire Kingdom. He was considered subordinate to his older brother Delkol, but Augurc was the one with the darker reputation. Even in Istal, Areo had heard stories of the man's sadistic experiments and monstrous creations.

The masked Brotherhood member Borely had blasted across the room crawled toward the newcomer. "They're strong..." He struggled to get to his knees, but was too injured to do so.

"No," Augurc said. "You're weak." He grabbed the man by the neck and lifted him up. Augurc held the man with his right hand, which Areo saw had an ice Nexi embedded in it.

The man's entire body froze instantly. Augurc continued to hold the man, and it took a few seconds for Areo to realize Augurc was forcing more and more icy air into the frozen corpse. For a moment the masked body glowed a bright light blue.

Augurc looked to Areo and Borely a few seconds. "You would have made interesting test subjects." His voice was monotone, lifeless.

He lobbed the frozen body toward Areo and Borely. Areo stepped back, but saw it was going to miss by a couple meters.

Upon landing, the body shattered into hundreds of small pieces of ice. Each of the pieces immediately sprouted several long icy needles, which jetted out and connected with one another. In seconds, there were thousands of these jagged protrusions, weaving a massive web of ice with needles that grew increasingly longer with each passing moment. Areo ran back and forced Borely back with her, but the freakish ice mass was growing far too quickly to escape from in time.

Areo handed Borely the tan Nexi and began clawing away at the jetting needles of ice with all the vigor she could muster. Meanwhile Borely controlled earth to push away as much ice as possible, hardening the formations of dirt to create a barrier between them and the spreading web of ice. The long, thick needles dug into the earth walls, quickly tearing it apart. Areo continued to furiously swipe apart the razor-sharp icicles, but her mad frenzy was wearing her out, and there was no end in sight to the ever-expanding web of ice.

Amidst the frozen entanglements, Areo noticed thin vines rushing through the holes and cracks of the ice formations. Augurc was guiding tens of vines toward Areo and Borely, hoping to ensnare them while they fought off the ever-growing ice needles. Borely managed to block off the vines reaching toward him, but Areo had too many icicles to fend off for her to claw apart the vines slithering toward her feet.

"Smash the ground!" Areo yelled.

Borely charged the orange Nexi for one of his fists and did as Areo directed. He quickly knelt down and punched a wide hole straight through the metal floor. The floor was thick and had multiple layers, so it took Borely a few punches to break through all the way. As Areo beat away the icicles, the web of ice grew increasingly tighter as long needles started filling in all the gaps. Once Borely tore the holes in the floor open enough for them to fit through, Areo immediately slipped out her green Nexi.

She quickly created vines to wrap around the portions of metal connecting the different layers of floor together. At the same time, Augurc's vines reached Areo's feet, then began encircling her legs.

Areo leaped down the hole and let her body dangle in the air beneath the airship. She clawed apart Augurc's vines while keeping a firm grasp on the vines from her own Nexi. Borely jumped down the hole and grabbed on to Areo's vines before he could be impaled by the expanding ice formation. He climbed down the thick green ropes until he was about a meter above Areo.

"Well, now what?" Borely asked.

Areo looked to the other Brotherhood airship. It looked like Kitoh was still battling with it, avoiding the Nexi stones the Brotherhood launched at him.

"Just hold on," Areo said.

Borely formed a thick barrier of earth over the hole above them, keeping the web of ice from reaching down to Areo's vines. Areo kept a close eye on the hardened dirt, watching for any sign of the ice needles breaking through. She didn't know what to do until Kitoh came back for them, other than hang on tight. The winds were furious beneath the airship, which had fortunately slowed down a bit following Areo and Borely's ambush. She hoped that the two of them had at least managed to make things difficult for this airship to reach the castle.

A figure lowered from the side of the airship, about a dozen meters away. It was Augurc, standing straight in the air with his arms held out to either side of him. Vines from his many Nexi stones connected his arms to the railing of the ship. He caused his vines to effortlessly reach for pieces of the airship's underbelly they could easily wrap around, and guided himself slowly toward Areo and Borely.

Incredulously, Augurc looked unfazed by the fact he was hanging from the bottom of an airship hundreds of meters up in the air. The wind pushed him far to the side at times, but still he continued to make his way forward. As he approached, he raised his right palm and caused an icicle to emerge from the Nexi stone embedded in it. The ice formed into a long, jagged spear that extended at least a meter long.

Like extra appendages, Augurc's vines pulled him toward his prey. His spear of ice at the ready, the man floated toward Areo and Borely, an entirely disinterested expression etched on his face.

"Give me my tan Nexi," Areo said. Borely tossed it down to her, and she immediately released a thin tendril of dirt toward Augurc. The man slashed away at the hardened dirt, his jagged icicle slicing through with each stroke of his arm. And all the while, his vines continued leading him toward Areo.

Borely shot off a jet of water from his metal laurel's Nexi, but Augurc easily caused his vines to slide him to the side of the blast. Augurc's control over the green Nexi in his arms seemed unconscious—as if it took more effort for the man to breathe than to control the vines from his arms.

It was difficult to think of anything more to do, dangling hundreds of meters above the ground, hanging from the vines of a single green Nexi.
Borely shot off jets of water several more times at Augurc, but to no effect.
Augurc dodged every attack effortlessly, and continued to approach them.

Areo looked back and found an airship bursting into flames. She looked down and squinted into the bright blue sky, searching for any sign of Kitoh. After a few seconds of this, she glanced back to Augurc, now just a few meters away.

She turned back and found Kitoh, soaring straight for them. The dragon flapped his wings as fast as Areo could imagine him being able to, but it was going to take a few more seconds for him to reach them.

For a moment it looked like Augurc was going to fling himself down to stab Areo with the giant icicle protruding from his hand, but he caused his vines to bring himself upward at the last second. The man sliced through all of Areo's vines in one swoop, too quick for Borely to shoot with his dark blue Nexi.

Areo immediately guided the cut ends of her vines to latch on to Augurc's legs. She and Borely fell a few meters, but held on thanks to Areo's control of the vines. Augurc cut the vines wrapped around his legs, and Areo and Borely fell again.

They crashed onto Kitoh's back. Areo held on carefully with her claws while Borely grabbed Areo's leg and started screaming once more. This time though, Areo was pretty certain he was screaming in excitement.

Once she and Borely were situated safely on Kitoh's back, sitting in front of his fin, Areo looked back to the airship Augurc continued to hang from. "Now's our chance to take down that airship," Areo said. "Augurc isn't on board, and there isn't anyone running the cannons."

Kitoh turned back to the airship, flying high above it. Once near the dirigible, Kitoh swooped down and breathed a giant field of fire across the top of the great balloon. The blimp erupted in flames, and Areo directed Kitoh back down to the ground below, recognizing the boy's energy was wearing thin.

Areo looked back to where Terico and the elves were situated. It was difficult to see their airship, or the other two of the Brotherhood's airships. She had to simply hope they would pull through, and believe that Terico would manage to defeat Delkol if the time came for them to meet once more.

•

Terico and Turan clashed swords, leaving the other four Brotherhood members free to charge for Suran. Furious, Terico shoved Turan back as hard as he could. He leaped back to Suran's position and swung his sword at the nearest masked fighter. The tall, lanky man blocked with his own sword, then activated an orange Nexi in his hilt. Terico slipped back before the man could slice the blade of his sword clean in two.

Turan lifted a brown Nexi stone while Suran shot off a vibrating purple wave at the Brotherhood fighter nearest to her, knocking him off his feet— she apparently had the Nexi stone for loose energy. A masked fighter with a large axe used a yellow Nexi to guard himself against the burst of energy, and continued rushing toward Suran.

Dodging Turan's blast of swamp material, Terico leaped in front of Suran and slammed the blade of his sword against the axe pole of the man charging for her. Terico glanced right and saw the tall swordsman pointing a dark blue Nexi at Suran.

She leaped away before the man could hit her with a jet of water. Terico pushed back against the axe of the Brotherhood member he fought, but the burly man was too strong. Suran suddenly jumped in front of Terico and slammed her purple Nexi against the axe man's stomach.

The man shook back violently, and Suran slipped to the side to allow Terico to slide his blade through the man's chest.

A series of vines immediately rushed for Terico, guided by Turan a couple meters away. Terico hacked away at them, but glanced back to Suran, noting how heavily she was breathing. She was struggling to stand, having used so much Nexi energy. Not only had she just finished shooting off a bunch of cannon Nexi, but she was utilizing a rare purple stone to fight these Brotherhood members.

She blasted away the swordsman approaching her before collapsing on her knees. Another Brotherhood member raised a red Nexi and fired at her. Terico found a brief opening from the rushing vines and ran in front of Suran. Just as the flames rushed around him, Terico slipped out his dark and light blue Nexis and created a barrier of ice to protect him and Suran from the flames.

Vines wrapped around Suran's legs, and before Terico could even turn around she was dragged away—straight toward Turan.

"No!" Terico shot off the formation of ice, slamming it against the masked fighter wielding the fire. The tall fighter with the sword leaped in front of Terico before he could chase after Suran. Terico blindly ran straight through the man, shoving his blade through the enemy's stomach before the man could swing his sword. Terico ripped his blade out the man's side and continued running after Suran.

Turan dragged Suran to him and wrapped more vines around her body to keep her from struggling. The vines stood her up straight beside him, and as Terico sprinted toward him, Turan rubbed a gray Nexi stone across the blade of his sword.

Turan stood behind Suran and placed his glowing gray blade against Suran's throat. The masked boy looked at Terico, the sadistic painted smile mocking Terico in his helplessness. Terico stopped about three meters away, but kept his sword raised.

"Stop!" Terico yelled. "Don't do it, Turan."

"My name is Lynx!" Turan replied. "But speaking of Turan, I wonder who it was that wouldn't stop for *him*. It was his supposed best friend. *Terico*. I saw it all. When he needed his best friend most, Terico *abandoned* Turan! I saw Turan... screaming Terico's name. Crying for help..." His muffled voice cracked a bit behind the mask, but then turned livid—far louder than Terico expected. "*Needing someone to save him from this agonizing fate!*"

"Turan, I'm sorry," Terico said.

"Of course!" Turan screamed. "Now you're sorry! I'll make sure you're plenty sorry! I'll—"

"It was a difficult decision!" Terico yelled. "I thought our friends at the school needed help. I thought you'd be okay... I thought things would work out..." He stared at Suran's pale face, struggling to breathe from the tightening vines. Terico considered reaching for his Elpis pieces, but knew Turan was watching his every movement. It would take a second to activate the power of the Elpis, and by then it would be too late.

"You thought things would just *work out?*" Turan yelled. He slid his blade toward Suran's neck.

"No!" Terico screamed.

A sphere of purple energy exploded from Suran, blasting apart the vines wrapped around her. The shockwave sent Turan flying back to the large hole in the floor he had made when breaking into the airship. Suran collapsed on her hands and knees, her last bit of energy spent on creating that one final blast with her purple Nexi.

The detonation pushed Terico back a couple meters, and knocked Turan's mask and green Nexi away in the process. Stumbling back, Terico grabbed the green Nexi from mid-air and immediately launched a series of vines toward Turan, already falling out of the ship.

I won't abandon you again!

"Grab on!" Terico yelled as loud as he could. He sent the vines rushing out the opening, unable to see how far down Turan had already fallen. There was no way for Turan to save himself, having just been hit that close by a full-powered blast of loose Nexi energy, and without his green Nexi stone to grab on to the airship with.

Terico continued to create more and more vines from the stone, driving them down as fast as his strength could manage. Several heartracing seconds passed before Terico felt an added weight to the vines. Terico gripped his Nexi stone tight and held on. He guided the vines back into the stone, pulling them back up into the ship. At the very end of the vines Terico found Turan hanging on, his body limp and beaten down. He still held on to his gray-glowing sword, but his grasp was tenuous. Terico dragged him onto the ship and sighed in relief. He fell to his knees and set the green Nexi down, but still kept a grip on his sword.

His mind went blank a few moments. He simply stared at Turan's barely conscious body while Suran crawled over to kneel beside Terico. He looked to her and felt his whole body start to tremble. At one moment he thought Suran was going to die, and the very next moment he thought Turan was going to die. It drove him to tears to see them both alive. Suran clasped her hand in Terico's and gave a small, exhausted smile.

Turan lifted his head and stared up at Terico. Turan's dark brown eyes were ringed with deep black marks, and his scraggly blond hair was speckled with blood. It was strange to see him without his mask again. To Terico, it almost felt like he was back in Edellerston again, and everything was back to normal. Turan coughed up blood and shook violently, still reacting from the purple energy Suran hit him with.

"I'm dying," Turan said, crimson lines trickling from his lips.

Terico stood up and walked over to Turan. Suran followed beside him, limping along wearily.

"Don't strain yourself," Terico said.

Suran closed her eyes and smiled. "I'll be fine." She took a more serious expression and added, "It's Turan we should worry about. There's a medical kit on the bridge I can get for him."

"I... I'm sorry," Turan said before coughing up some more blood. "I was wrong."

"It's okay," Terico said. "Augurc did something to your brain, perhaps heightening certain emotions you had at the time. But it will be all right.

We'll help you through this, Turan."

"I... I've hurt you, Suran," Turan said, tears trickling down his face. "I'm so sorry."

Suran smiled as if it were nothing. "I'm just tired is all. I'm just glad you're alive."

"We still need to heal you though," Terico said, helping Turan roll over so he lay on his back. "Where do you hurt?"

The airship turned hard to the right, then shook violently. Terico fell backward and slid a couple meters before managing to grip a seam in the metal flooring. Suran grabbed on to the floor beside Turan and helped him hold on, even in her weakened condition.

What's Lanek doing? Terico thought. The airship shook again, and Terico realized the ship was descending. The Brotherhood airship was landing attacks on *The Finest Hour.*

The ship stabilized slightly, and Terico turned back to Suran and Turan.

Suran stood up and turned her head back to check on Terico. "Are you—"

Turan stood up and stabbed Suran through the chest.

"No!" Terico screamed.

He ran straight for Turan, who pulled his gray blade out of Suran's chest and shoved her to the ground. Turan stood still, staring at Terico wideeyed, as if surprised by what he had just done.

Then he grinned.

Terico swung his blade at Turan, ready to hack him to pieces. At the last moment, Turan leaped backward, letting himself fall out the hole in the airship. He had his green Nexi again, Terico realized.

Through the window, Terico saw the Brotherhood airship, flying by only a dozen or so meters away. It fired several cannons straight at *The Finest Hour*, but a barrier of earth appeared to block most of them. One connected, however, and the ship began to descend more rapidly.

Terico looked out the hole in the airship to find Turan far below, hanging on to vines connecting him to the Brotherhood ship. A part of Terico wanted to use the Elpis and go after him, but right now Suran needed him.

Suran. The moment she was stabbed, Terico's entire body had seemed to freeze over, and yet he still reacted. His heart stopped, but still he forced himself to move. He ran back to Suran's limp form, almost falling over amidst the shaking of the airship. He knelt down beside Suran and looked over her bloody wounds. The blade had pierced all the way through her chest, and on out her back. She was still managing to breathe, however—a frail hyperventilation, terrifying in the fragile balance it held.

Tears streamed down Suran's face. "T-Teri...co..."

He took out his Elpis pieces and accessed their power. His body surged with the violent energies flowing through every pore of his skin. The transformative effects quickly took hold, but the power building up in Terico felt far greater than he imagined. With two fragments of the Elpis, Terico's power was many times greater than it was with one.

I can heal her, Terico thought. He knew from experience there was healing energy in the Elpis—he had healed himself in the underground city, and was strengthened when fighting Ganto and Delkol. The pain was almost unbearable, but he survived. He could survive again.

Suran looked up at Terico, a frightened look on her face. Seeing Terico in this form must have been shocking.

"It's the Elpis," Terico said. "I'll use its power to heal you." He placed a hand over the bleeding wound in her chest, wincing at the grisly sight. Focusing all his concentration on Suran's wound, Terico shut his eyes and willed the Elpis power to shift to healing energies.

Terico's body turned boiling hot, then freezing cold, then tight and constricted, then overwhelmingly weak and nauseous. With each passing moment, the plagues of the various Nexi powers swept through his body. He struggled to seek out the healing energy, the pain of the Elpis far greater than it was the last two times he used it.

Hot tears slipped from Terico's eyes, and the blood spilling over his hand turned frigid, icy. He cried Suran's name, exerting every bit of his mental focus on healing her of this wound.

For just a moment, Terico felt as if his pains were erased, his entire body lightened and free of of the Elpis's agony. The pain of a blinding headache afflicted him immediately afterward, but Terico forced his mind to latch back on to the previous energy. He felt the healing return, and quickly willed the energy to flow from his arm to Suran's wound.

Suran fell into fits of convulsion, screaming at the top of her lungs. Terico's immediate reaction was to pull away, but he knew with a certainty this was the energy that would heal her.

"I'm sorry, Suran!" Terico yelled above her cries of agony. "Hold on just a little longer!"

Suran arched back and reached out with her arms, struggling to break away from the torment the Elpis inflicted on her. Terico held her down to keep his hand firmly over the bleeding injury.

Can't lose her now... Not now... Not when we're so close... Not when we're finally together again! Not when I've already lost everything else! Suran's screams grew louder, and her limbs contorted into painful, disjointed positions. The Elpis energy continued to flow to Suran's body, the process draining to Terico's mind and soul. He slowly felt as if his very existence was leaking away. For a moment he felt as if continuing this would cause him to disintegrate from the inside—to crumble apart and fade away forever. And yet he kept pushing himself to heal Suran, to do whatever was in his power to save her.

Perhaps a minute of this passed before blood stopped leaking from the thick opening in Suran's chest. Terico's body trembled from the rush of energy flowing out of his body, but managed to lift his hand away to look over the wound. Using his sleeve, he wiped away as much blood from the wound as he could.

The incision was gone—there wasn't even a scar left. With his clean hand Terico felt only smooth, healed skin, and noted the steady beat of Suran's heart.
He put away the Elpis stones and cut off his access to their power.

The sudden release of energy gave him the overwhelming urge to lie on his back and die, but he kept his focus on Suran and her injury. She writhed in pain for a few more seconds before settling down. Her screams faded to gasping cries, and within a couple minutes she was breathing normally again.

Terico looked her over, and as far as he could tell the wound was gone. He checked her back and saw the slit there was gone as well. The fact Suran was breathing normally again seemed to imply her lungs were healed, and Terico felt her pulse to check her heart was still beating properly. He wasn't sure if she had been stabbed in the heart, but without the Elpis Terico doubted he would have been able to heal her in time.

"How are you feeling?" Terico asked. He felt terrible himself, struggling to even sit up at this point—but he had to be certain Suran was fine before he could worry about himself.

"I'm okay," Suran said, her eyes half-open. "But Turan... stabbed me."
"Does it still hurt?" Terico asked.

Suran looked up at him a few seconds. "No... I feel fine... I'm just tired... So very tired..."

"That's all right," Terico said. He knew Suran had exhausted herself already from Nexi use, and the strain of the Elpis energy would have certainly worn her out even further. "You can rest all you want now."

He looked out the window and saw the airship was still descending. The machinery of the ship had grown louder, and it was clear there wasn't much chance of it staying airborne much longer.

Terico lifted Suran off the ground and carried her with him down the hallway. It strained him to carry her, despite how light she was—but he wasn't going to leave her alone for even a second at this point. He needed to get Suran to Lanek, then find a way to save the airship. Terico wondered if he would be able to find a way to fix *The Finest Hour* with the power of the Elpis. It would likely take a lot of effort to figure out a way to do so, and by then he would have exhausted himself far too much to be able to fight Delkol.

The third piece is at the castle, Terico remembered. *I can fly there with the two pieces I have, and then the third fragment will give me even more power. I'll be able to take Delkol down easily then...*
Terico stumbled to the bridge, where Lanek was frantically working with several different levers. He turned back for a moment, quickly noting it was Terico and Suran entering the room. He returned to his controls and pulled on a rope as hard as he could, working to stabilize the drifting airship.
"What happened to Suran?" he yelled as he went back to a lever.

"She was hurt, but I healed her with the Elpis," Terico said. "She should be fine."

"You let her get hurt?" Lanek screamed. He was absolutely livid, yet continued to operate the controls as if he were having a friendly chat. "I'd kill you, but we're probably all going to die in just a minute anyways." "The ship's going to crash?" Terico asked.

"Too late to save it," Lanek said. "There were far too many jets of water to defend against while piloting the airship."

"Get on my back and I'll fly us out of here," Terico said.

Lanek turned around and looked up at Terico in callous disbelief.
"You fly."

"I fly. Now come on." Terico turned and ran back down the hallway. He heard Lanek's footsteps following behind him, and continued to the gaping hole in the entry room. The airship tilted backward, making it easy for Terico to run down while carrying Suran. He gripped his Elpis fragments tight and accessed their power upon reaching the edge of the hole. The burst of torment erupting in the very center of his chest made him cry out in pain, but he managed to stop and bend to one knee so Lanek could climb on his back. Terico felt his body transform, and he filled with the pain and energy of every Nexi in the world. For a moment Terico felt he would utterly collapse beneath the weight Lanek placed on his back. Lanek was about as thin and light as his sister, but carrying both him and Suran was too much for Terico to handle in this state.

He strained himself to seek out the orange Nexi energy within the constantly shifting powers rushing through his body. For a moment it felt like his mind was going to shatter, but just as he was about to collapse he managed to grab hold of the strengthening Nexi power bursting within him. Suddenly carrying Suran and Lanek was a simple matter, and Terico was able to concentrate on levitating off the ground.

"Hang on," he said to Lanek. Terico looked down to Suran's tired face, straining to keep her bloodshot eyes open. Though he had saved Suran's life, Terico still felt uneasy about her.

She's just worn out, he thought. He forced himself to concentrate on the task at hand.

The airship shook more violently, and tilted even further backward. Terico let himself fall out of the hole, jumping forward to make sure Lanek didn't hit the edge of the jagged flooring.

The three plummeted out of the airship, falling only a little faster than the quickly descending airship. The ground was much closer than Terico expected, and he needed to start flying immediately. This ability was much more second-nature, apparently an inherent aspect of the transformation the Elpis brought him.

He flew down to the green fields below at a safe speed, then glided a good distance from where the airship would crash. As soon as Terico reached the ground, he stopped using the Elpis power, regaining his normal form once again. He knelt down so he could lay Suran down gently, and so Lanek could get off of his back.

"Are you okay?" Terico asked Suran.

She barely managed to nod in response. Too tired to speak, she shut her eyes and fell asleep on the spot. Terico and Lanek watched to make sure she was still breathing, and checked for any further signs of injury.

"She seems fine," Lanek said, "but I'll want to take her to a clinic to be certain. Wearing herself out this badly probably warrants a visit in and of itself."

Terico agreed, and sat down beside Suran so he could recover himself. His whole body was worn out, and the fact his best friend had stabbed the girl he loved was painful to think about. And in the end Turan managed to slip away, still vengeful and blind with hate. Terico wanted to believe it was all Augurc's fault, but the fact Turan wanted

Terico to suffer because Terico left him back during the attack on Edellerston... There was a sense to it. And a part of Terico felt he couldn't really fault Turan for wanting revenge.

Turan didn't want to simply kill Terico, though. He wanted to kill everyone Terico loved. He wanted Terico to hate his very existence. This was how Turan felt, Terico realized. Turan's life was a constant hell. Surely Augurc did experiment on Turan, but Turan was able to recognize what he had become. Turan still knew what he was doing—he wasn't mindless—and yet to some degree he had lost his mind to the lust of revenge. Terico thought over Jujor's and Areo's words on the subject. How different was Terico's quest for revenge?

I can't just stop, Terico thought. *Not now. Not when everyone is depending on me to bring Delkol down. He's still out there... He's probably in one of those airships, heading for the castle. I have to get there before him.* Terico turned to Lanek, who was watching his airship crash into the ground. It collapsed in a tremendous heap in the distance, loud and terrible.

"Rest in peace, *Finest Hour*," Lanek said. "What a short, unfortunate life you lived."

To Terico it was just an airship, but to Lanek and Suran it was something they had spent a great deal of time and effort on. It was also a treasure of their parents, as well as a symbol of their past, long lost to the cruelty of Delkol and his Brotherhood.

Everything goes back to him, Terico thought. *Delkol. The man who killed my parents. Destroyed my home town. Wreaked havoc in every land he stepped foot in. And through his Brotherhood, he has hurt the lives of every living person I know. Suran. Lanek. Areo. Borely. Kitoh. Turan.*

It will never end. It will never end until he's dead.

I have to find him now!

If there was a golden Nexi that could lead people to what they sought after, Terico could access that power via the Elpis. He already knew he could see great distances with the power of the Elpis—if he could combine that ability with the golden Nexi energy, he would be able to find Delkol.

Upon activating the Elpis fragments, the instantaneous surge of energy tore through his body. Terico nearly collapsed to the ground, but managed to keep to his feet.

"What are you doing?" Lanek asked.

Terico gripped his forehead and shut his eyes tight. An all-encompassing white light was surging within him, blinding his eyes—blinding his entire body. He screamed uncontrollably. One moment an icy wind blew through his bones, and the next moment he felt as if his blood were turning hard— solid and heavy. Just standing up was difficult, but Terico pushed himself to access the power he would need to find Delkol.

He opened his eyes and still felt blinded for several seconds. A Brotherhood airship came into focus for a moment, then turned blurry and fragmented. The sky split apart, and for a second Terico felt his own body was being ripped in half, tearing from his left shoulder to his right hip.

He gripped the Elpis pieces tighter and turned around, facing toward the capital city. His vision went dark, then turned into an image of the castle. It was blurry at first, but once it cleared Terico felt as if he were standing just outside the castle grounds. He noticed something flying past one of the red towers. Terico gazed at it, and his vision focused in on what turned out to be some kind of giant hawk. It was difficult to tell at first, but Terico quickly realized the demonic creature was made entirely of bones and bloody strands of muscle. How it was able to fly, Terico couldn't imagine—but it flapped its skeletal wings vigorously, propelling it from the castle and toward the area where *The Finest Hour* fought the Brotherhood airships.

Terico stared closer at the gruesome bird, bringing his vision closer to it. There was someone riding on top of the reigned beast.

Delkol.

And as Terico focused a little more, he could make out the gleam of Nexi stones in Delkol's hand. Two stones—and they continually shifted from one color to the next.

The airships were just a diversion, Terico realized. While Rilv's units were scrambling to prepare the city to defend against the approaching airships, Delkol sneaked to the castle with the help of his secret agent and obtained the Elpis piece hidden there.

I can't let him get away, Terico thought. He forced his mind to let go of the golden Nexi power and shut his eyes for a few seconds. His head was ringing violently, and a part of Terico wanted to fall to his hands and knees and retch out all the organs in his body. His insides quivered and turned soft, as if they were dissolving into liquid.

He forced himself to fly into the air. Lanek was yelling something at him, but he sounded distant. For a moment Terico wondered if Lanek was dead, then wondered why he was flying away. Something snapped in the back of his head, and he clawed at it, screaming from the pain erupting in his mind. His vision turned blurry for a few seconds, and once it cleared Terico realized he was lying on the ground, his clothes and body torn up in bloody gashes.

His body was suffering from Elpis poisoning. Even with half the Elpis, it was too difficult for him to use it too much, especially when he was completing difficult tasks. Saving Suran from death and pinpointing Delkol's location were taxing on Terico's very being, it seemed.

He cut off his mind from the Elpis energy and fell into a violent coughing fit. The agony struck at his heart and lungs the hardest, but at the same time his mind felt like it was being stabbed with a thousand tiny needles all at once.

As Terico drifted to unconsciousness, his thoughts somehow remained coherent, focusing entirely on Delkol. Terico could see the man's smug expression perfectly. His short, light brown hair flapping in the wind. His icy blue eyes, gleaming wide and eager. The macabre scar running across his right eye, from his forehead to his cheek. And that smirk. That all-knowing, pretentious smirk.

You think you've won! Terico thought. *I'll kill you. I'll kill you. I'll kill you.* He fell unconscious, all his thoughts sinking deeper and deeper into a thirst for revenge.

•

10

HIS ENTIRE HEART

Terico woke up to find himself lying in a bed. He stared up at a ceiling painted a dark blue, about the same color as his hair. His whole body ached, even worse than it had after using the Elpis in Vursa. It strained his eyes to glance around, and he had to wince when he looked too far to one side or the other. He was apparently in a clinic, one quite nicer than the one in Edellerston. The green blankets he lay in were light and cool, and he was dressed in clean clothes—a loose, white shirt and trousers.

"Hey, he's up," Borely said, standing up from a small wooden chair in the corner. Areo and Kitoh got up from their chairs and followed after him. They walked to the side of Terico's bed and stood quietly for a few moments.

"How are you doing?" Areo asked.

"I'll live," Terico said. He glanced to the other side of the room and noted a second bed, which he found occupied by Suran. Save for the slight rise and fall of her breathing, she lay perfectly still beneath her blankets. Her eyes were closed, but she still looked exhausted.

"What happened?" Terico asked. He was struggling to piece together everything that had happened. He knew he used the Elpis, and that he was chasing after Delkol...

He tried to sit up, and Areo helped him position his back against the wall behind him.

"Lanek found you just outside the castle grounds," she said. "He brought Suran with him, and she's still unconscious. It's been about fourteen hours since the airship attack, but nothing has happened since." Borely handed Terico a couple leather pouches. "Here's your Nexi stones, and the Elpis fragments."

Terico opened the lighter of the two bags. "Two pieces of the Elpis.

And now Delkol has the other two."

"The castle was attacked," Areo said, "but we don't know any specifics yet. Rilv said she'd explain the situation once you were up again."

"Everyone's okay though?" Terico asked. "The three of you look well. And Lanek?"

"He's fine, but is... away," Areo said. She looked down to Terico, her expression grim. "And Suran... The doctor is still concerned about her condition, I'm afraid."

"She'll be fine," Terico said, his memories of yesterday's events starting to piece back together. "She was stabbed, but I healed her. I used the Elpis to save her."

"Explain more," said a man's voice. Terico turned to find a man dressed in the light green and black garb of a city hospital worker. He was a tall man in his forties, and had short, black hair and a full goatee. His ears were slightly pointed, perhaps marking him as a half-elf. "I need to understand precisely what happened to the patient."

Walking beside him was a woman only slightly shorter than the doctor. She seemed in her late twenties, and had sharp, thin eyes and silver hair that reached her shoulders. Terico inferred from the regal purple and white uniform that this was Rilv, the head servant of the royal line.

"It was just as I said," Terico explained. "The Brotherhood boarded our airship, and the two of us had to fight them all off. Suran was stabbed in the chest by one of them, but I used the healing energies of the Elpis to save her shortly afterward."

"There was no wound for me to examine," the doctor said. "And no scar left behind."

"It disappeared," Terico said. "And there shouldn't be a problem anymore. She's breathing fine, isn't she?"

"She's alive," the doctor said, "but she's extremely weak. Barely able to maintain consciousness for more than a minute at a time, and with several hours needed to recover each time. Her brother said she was worn out from Nexi use, but if that were the case she should have recovered by now... Do you remember if there was anything peculiar about the sword used?"

The questioned triggered Terico's memory of the blade glowing gray. "There was a gray Nexi stone. He rubbed it against the full length of the blade, turning it gray."

"A gray Nexi stone?" Borely said. "What does that do?"

Terico had never heard of a gray Nexi, let alone seen one used before. It must have been a very rare stone.
"A poison," Rilv said. "Incurable." "Wh...
What?" Terico cried.

"She will not live long," Rilv said, as terse as she was when she spoke via the teal Nexi.

Terico turned to the doctor. "No, there has to be a way to heal her."

The man sighed and shut his eyes a few seconds. "I'm sorry, boy. The gray Nexi's energy is the power of death. It seems you slowed the effect a bit with the Elpis, but she is still dying nonetheless. Had it been a regular poison of some kind, there might have been a chance—but the gray Nexi has affected her entire bloodstream, and in turn every vital organ in her body. I'm afraid there is no possible cure... It's only a matter of time."

"No," Terico said, pushing aside his blanket. "No, that's wrong. I can use the Elpis." He struggled to turn himself so he could get out his bed, then strained himself to walk over to Suran's. He held on to the side of her bed to keep from falling to the ground, and had to take a couple slow breaths to recover.

"You can barely stand," Rilv said. "You can not use the Elpis again in this state. And with only two of its four pieces, you won't be able to last long.

You will kill yourself."

"I have to try!" Terico yelled. "I'm not going to just let her die!" "You healed one wound," Rilv said, "but can you heal every organ in her body? On top of this, her entire bloodstream has been infected by the Nexi energy. You would have to heal every drop of blood in her body."

Terico thought over how long this would take him. Hours, he realized. The agony would be unbearable, and he likely *would* die if he made such an attempt.

No. I can't just do nothing. Not again. Not now. I have half the Elpis. I can save her. It has to be possible. I'm not going to lose her now!

He took his Elpis fragments and placed one in each of his hands.
Though he felt half-dead himself, he had to try. There was energy in the Elpis that could strengthen him—if he could access that energy right away, he might be able to hold out long enough to find a way to heal Suran.

"Stop," Rilv said. "You must rest."

Terico ignored her and gripped the Elpis pieces tight. His body filled with a hundred energies, each of them destroying him from the inside. He screamed, but forced himself to clasp the Elpis pieces tighter. All the wounds across his body erupted with searing heat, as if a tremendous fire was rushing out each of his cuts and pushing against each of his bruises.

Terico collapsed to the ground, sitting against the side of his bed. He fell into sudden gasps of slow breaths, his lungs heavy and dense.

Rilv walked to him, bent to one knee, and wrenched the Elpis fragments from him. Terico couldn't fight back, barely even conscious of what she was doing.
"I will return these to you after you recover," she said. "You probably need to rest at least a day before using the Elpis again. It is pertinent you regain your strength before Delkol's armies close in on the city."

Terico took long, shivering breaths. His body felt cold and tight, as if he were buried beneath a frozen avalanche. He couldn't respond to Rilv. He couldn't argue. He couldn't yell. He couldn't scream at the sheer wretchedness of his situation.

Suran is dying, and I couldn't do anything.

"I need to explain the current situation to you," Rilv said.

Suran is dying.
"I will be brief, as I have many matters to return to," Rilv continued.

Why is this happening?
"Delkol Shire has obtained the castle's Elpis fragment. He escaped with the remnants of his Brotherhood, which has joined with the Shire armies in preparation to invade Setar."

Just when we were back together... Just when things finally started to look up for us...
"Using the power of the Elpis, Delkol killed nearly every royal guard he came in contact with. Before escaping the castle, he murdered the king and each of the royal dukes. At that point, every soldier and servant he caught sight of was killed."

I have the power to save her... I have so much power, and yet I'm failing her!
"Fiefs Kingdom is now without a leader, and the Shire armies will likely be ready to invade within the next two to three days."

Why can I not do this one thing? Suran needs me more than ever... She needs me, and I can do nothing.
"The traitor within the royal guard has escaped with Delkol, who now has half of the Elpis. It is likely that it was through this agent that Delkol was able to enter the castle in secret. He is likely also responsible for Delkol learning about your father and the Elpis fragment in

Edellerston, as well as the likelihood of an Elpis in Vursa."

I won't stop. I won't stop trying to save you, Suran. As soon as I can, I'll use the Elpis to heal you. I'll destroy the poison. You'll be healthy again, and live a long, wonderful life. I'll heal you, no matter what it takes.
"It is up to you, Terico, to use your half of the Elpis to defeat Delkol. If you can kill him and retrieve his two Elpis fragments, this war can be stopped before the city suffers extreme casualties."

We can still be together, Suran. I can heal you. There has to be a way to heal you.
"I am conducting every possible effort to bring in all the reinforcements I can, but time is short. Delkol has amassed a large, well-trained army, and many of our most valuable resources have been undermined.

On top of this, the death of the king has hurt the morale of our troops. The massacre of at least half the royal guard and over a hundred servants has also been a terrible blow." *I won't fail you, Suran.*

"Terico. Do you understand how vital you are to the preservation of our kingdom?"

Terico looked up at Rilv, his vision blurry. He realized his eyes were clouded with tears, and wiped them out right away.

"Do you understand, Terico?" Rilv repeated.

"You're being too harsh," Areo said. "You can't order him around like this right after being so blunt about Suran's condition."

"He must understand that there is no hope for that girl," Rilv said.

"No hope?" Terico said. "You're wrong! I still have the Elpis. There's still hope for Suran. Just give me some time, and I'll heal her."

"She is a lost cause, and you need to move on," Rilv said. "You must understand that you are the only one who can defeat Delkol with the power of the Elpis. You will be one of the most important factors in this war, and your success or failure will greatly affect the outcome of this battle."

"Why?" Terico yelled. "Why am I the one who has to do this?"
"Do you not want to kill Delkol?" Rilv asked. "He is the leader of the Brotherhood, and therefore the one responsible for this girl's state."

"I know!" Terico said. "But why? Why is it just me and Delkol who can use the Elpis?

Rilv tightened her dark, knifelike eyes a little further. She stared down at Terico a few seconds before responding. "You have royal blood. Only those descended of the royal Fiefs line are capable of accessing the power of the Elpis. You and Delkol are both descendants."

"Royal blood?" Terico asked. "My parents weren't royalty. We lived in *Edellerston.*"
"Your grandfather was King Levae Fiefs. He had an illegitimate child—your

father. To keep him a secret, your father and grandmother were moved to the remote village of Edellerston. Your father adopted the last name of his mother. He grew up and had a connection to the Elpis hidden there. The royal head servant who preceded me deemed it pertinent to have someone watch over your father, just in case it ever became necessary to gather the Elpis together. Eventually Jujor was the one assigned to Edellerston, and he deemed you to have an even greater connection with the Elpis."

Terico struggled to believe such a story, though the more he thought about it, the more everything started to make sense. And yet his whole life he never suspected a thing. His parents never acted anything like royalty. Nobody in Edellerston had even been to Setar, as far as Terico ever knew. He hardly ever knew a thing about the current events of the Fiefs government. The very notion that Terico was connected to all this was incredulous.

And he wasn't just connected to it.

"I'm... a member of Fiefs royalty," he said. The very fact these words were coming out of his mouth seemed ridiculous. He had never aspired to any such thing. The thought never crossed his mind—not even *once.*

"And the king is dead," Rilv said. "This means you are the only heir to the throne."

Terico shut his eyes and clenched his forehead. He couldn't believe this was happening. It didn't *make sense.*

"I have no intention of being king," Terico said.

"Of course. Now is hardly the time to instate you as king," Rilv said, folding her arms. "You have not been prepared for such a responsibility, and the threat of Delkol's invasion warrants greater attention. I will lead the armies for the time being. In the meantime, you must rest in preparation to fight Delkol. Focus on killing Delkol and retrieving the full Elpis. Once that is taken care of, we can deal with matters of royal succession afterward. It is best we focus on our very survival for the time being.

"Give me back the Elpis," Terico said. "I'll only use it once I'm ready." "You will die if you use it too soon," Rilv said. "It would be unwise to take that risk."

"I may not be king, but I am royalty," Terico said. "As the royal head servant, you must comply with my demands."

"My greatest priority is the safety of the kingdom," Rilv said, standing up a little taller. "I strongly suggest you allow me to hold the Elpis fragments for the time being. I will return them to you once you have recovered."

Terico stared at Rilv's placid eyes for several long seconds. This obstinate woman was going too far.

What, does she want the Elpis for herself? What is going through that head of hers?
He wondered if he could really trust her. There was no way to be certain where her loyalties lay.

"You failed to protect the Elpis piece held in this castle. I won't risk you losing these two pieces as well." Terico held out a hand. "Return them to me, head servant."

Rilv simply stared at Terico, as stone-faced as ever. Terico thought she wouldn't comply, but she at last responded with a small, curt bow. After setting the Elpis pieces back on Terico's bed, she turned and walked out the door, swift and proper.

•

Terico lay back in bed, each minute feeling like hours. Areo and Borely tried to keep Terico company for a while, but Terico simply had nothing to say. They eventually left with Kitoh when Terico stopped responding to their inquiries. He couldn't care for any of the things Rilv had revealed.

His family was Fiefs royalty all this time. He was now heir to the throne. The king and dukes were all murdered. And all the armies of the Shire Kingdom were closing in on the city.

And Terico didn't care. It all meant nothing to him. Not when Suran was dying.

The doctor said she likely had at least a day left to live. He would come back from time to time to check on her, but he never said anything more to Terico regarding her condition.

Hour after hour passed, and all Terico could do was lie still and watch Suran. With each passing minute, he wished to try to use the Elpis once more, but he knew he wasn't ready yet. His body would just crumple beneath the torment of the Nexi energies if he accessed the Elpis's power again too soon. He had to be patient.

It was the hardest thing in the world, watching his greatest love slowly die right before his eyes.

He gazed at her shut eyes, and over her face in general. She lay so quiet and still, Terico constantly worried if she were alive or not. He would get out of bed from time to time to check on her. When it looked like she wasn't moving at all, he would check her pulse. He placed an ear over her heart and listened for its faint, distant beating. The pulse of her small, weak heart was slowly fading away.

It was still too early for him to attempt using the Elpis again. He stroked her long red hair, then felt the outline of her thin, pointed elf ear. It brought back a childhood memory of when he was about five, when he first played with Suran.

She was the first elf his age he ever played with, and after they finished climbing a tree he asked if he could feel her ears. She let him, but only if he let her feel his ears. His short, rounded ears made her chuckle, and Terico couldn't get her to explain what was so funny. His ears were *normal*, he told her. It was *her* ears that were funny. Of course, she didn't think that way, and Terico had to learn for himself how much a different perspective could change things.

Terico lay back down and thought of all the people he had come in contact with since leaving Edellerston. He wondered if he had been able to see the point of view of each person he encountered. Turan, Jujor, Febraz, Areo, Borely, Kitoh, Lanek, Suran. Everyone had encountered a great deal of suffering since that fateful day Delkol attacked. They all found ways to cope. They all found ways to move on. They all struggled and fought and gave their all for what they believed in.

But Delkol. What was his perspective? To some degree, all the misery Terico's friends and associates had suffered was a result of this one man's quest for power and domination.

Why? Terico wondered. *How does this drive him to murder countless victims?*
If Delkol could use the Elpis, then it meant the Shires were descendants of the

Fiefs from centuries back. Terico knew the Shire Kingdom was founded when the Shires were exiled from the Fiefs Kingdom and conquered some of the surrounding territory, but he didn't know the Shires were royalty.
Perhaps Delkol simply felt he was the rightful ruler of the Fiefs Kingdom.

It was all so ridiculous, and Terico didn't want to think about it any longer. There could never be a legitimate excuse for Delkol's actions. He had to be stopped—there just was no way around that.

But the time to face Delkol would come later. If what Rilv said was true about the gathering Shire armies, it wouldn't be long before Delkol would make his move. But the more pressing matter was Suran and how to save her.

Terico spent the hours either staring at the ceiling or watching Suran, always thinking of how he would use the Elpis to heal her. He knew how to transfer the healing Nexi energy to her, but he wasn't sure how to apply it to each of Suran's poisoned organs. The gray Nexi had affected each system of her body, weakening her in every way possible. Terico wondered if he'd have enough energy to heal Suran's entire body. It had taken so much out of him just to heal the wound of the sword that pierced her...

"Terico..."

It was Suran. Terico got out of his bed and stood beside her. "I'm here, Suran."

Her eyes were still closed, her entire body as still as as can be. "Terico..."

Half a minute passed, but she didn't say anything more. Terico placed a hand on her head and held his breath. He bent down a bit so he could listen as closely as he could. Suran exhaled slightly, but Terico couldn't make out any words from her breath.

"I'm here," he said again. "You're going to be okay. Just keep resting..."

She lay there, quiet and motionless, an embodiment of pure innocence. Her breaths were slow and shallow, even more so than was typical of sleeping.

She's dying, and there's nothing... nothing I can do yet. He knew he was still too weak to use the Elpis right away. Making another attempt to heal her this soon would only wear him out more, and he would need all the energy he could get in order to save her.

Suran slid a small hand out from her blanket. Terico clasped it and looked down to Suran's eyes, which were still shut. Suran's hand was so cold, it made Terico shudder when he first held it. He gripped it tight, letting her frigid energy seep into his hand.

"My... mind is far away," Suran whispered. "Tell me... a story." "About what?" Terico asked.

"Us," Suran said, her voice tired and scratchy. "Happy."

There were plenty of happy times Terico spent with Suran and their classmates. In a soft voice, Terico shared some of the happier memories he was able to quickly remember.

He started with a story of when they were seven years old. Suran

and a friend of hers had found a tiny rabbit in the forest caught in a simple snare. They wanted to free it, but were afraid the frightened animal would bite them, or that they would hurt its leg while trying to untie the rope. They found Terico and Turan and asked them to help save the rabbit. At the time Terico didn't think there was much purpose in this, since another animal would just get caught later anyways—but Suran couldn't help but sympathize with this specific rabbit. Turan pointed out that they had all eaten rabbit in the past, but still Suran wanted to free this bunny, regardless.

Once in the forest, Terico held on to the animal while Turan untied the rope. Terico managed to calm the rabbit and let Suran pet it, which filled her with emphatic glee. Terico couldn't help but smile, too. Though it might have been wrong to mess with the trap, Terico was glad to make Suran happy. Even as a child, he recognized something special in Suran's smile.

There was a faint trace of one on Suran's face as Terico told the story.
Terico moved on by recounting when they had participated in a play for the
Heavenly Lights Festival. They were all twelve at the time, and their class was
assigned to perform the tale of Yemadi for the village. In an attempt to put a fresh

spin on the yearly performance, the class had everyone play the roles of characters of the opposite gender, with the exception of Turan, who played as a giant worm demon. Terico ended up with the part of a castle maid who happened to hear the worm's wicked plot, while Suran got the lead role of Prince Yemadi.

It was likely the most ridiculous play the village had ever seen, but most of the class managed to get through their lines without dying of embarrassment. The crowds roared with laughter whenever Turan squirmed onto the stage in his absurd worm costume, and would applaud whenever a new character appeared. Just the anticipation of seeing which girl would play as the blacksmith or which boy would play as the fortune teller was enough to hold everyone's interest. The one to get into the play most wholeheartedly though was Lanek, who volunteered for the role of Yemadi's love interest, Princess Iminia. He was probably the only one who looked just like the character he played, actually. Some of the villagers even questioned Lanek's gender for a few days, to his amusement.

The details of the story made Suran smile a tiny bit more. Her breathing was still very slow, and her hand was still nearly cold as ice.

Terico moved on to another story. About a year ago, Terico's parents had fallen gravely ill. They were sick in bed for several days, and Terico took time off of school in order to care for them. One day Terico left to buy some food, and when he came back he found Suran in the house, tidying up the mess that had grown over the past few days. She ended up helping Terico prepare a soup for his parents.

Once Terico's parents were asleep, Suran took Terico outside so they could chat. Suran was worried Terico was going to get sick himself if he didn't get enough fresh air, and wanted to let him know he could always go to her if he needed help. They walked to a field of yellow flowers, bright even under the night sky. Terico had trouble thinking of things to talk about with Suran, so they simply looked up at the sky for a while, searching for constellations and falling stars. It was probably that night when Terico realized just how much he liked Suran, though he had no idea how to go about telling her. So they simply enjoyed their time together, gazing up at the sea of stars.

"As always, you were concerned for the well-being of others," Terico said. "It made me really happy to be with you that day. And I was always glad to see you at school. I always wished we could do more together."

Suran's faint smile had faded slightly, her nearly sleeping face turning a little more thoughtful.

"And we will do more together," Terico said. "You'll be well soon enough.
And once the Elpis is gathered, my work in this city will be done.

We can go wherever we wish."

She didn't say anything more, but drifted slowly back to sleep. Terico knelt down on the floor, too tired to keep standing. His hand still gripping Suran's, Terico shut his eyes and lay his head against his arm.

·

Hour after hour passed, but Terico could not fall asleep. Though the Elpis had drained him of all his energy, Terico didn't feel tired enough to sleep. Even as night drew on, he remained kneeling by Suran's bed, holding tight to her cold, tender hand. Darkness fell over the castle, and Terico kept all his thoughts on Suran and how he'd heal her.

Her tiny heartbeat pulsed from her wrist, so faint that Terico was afraid to move his hand away—as if the slightest disturbance would douse what little fire was left in Suran's heart.

The door to the room opened, but Terico didn't bother going to his bed. He listened for who approached, hearing only one person treading the thick wooden floor.

It turned out to be Lanek, who didn't bother lighting any of the wall torches. He looked down to Terico and pursed his lips.

"A part of me would still love to kill you," he whispered. "You must realize... that girl is the most important person in the world to me."

Terico looked up to Lanek. "Where have you been?"

"Working with the doctor," Lanek said. "We're searching through every text on the gray Nexi stone we can find. To call that stone *rare* would be a... vast understatement."

"I'm sorry," Terico said. "You asked me to protect Suran... but I failed."

"Yes, you did," Lanek said. "And I really do wish to yell at you for it. For hours on end. Or at least to slap you."

Terico stared at the elf, knowing better than to object. A part of Terico felt he deserved any retribution Lanek wished to deal him. If Terico hadn't saved Turan from falling out the ship, Turan wouldn't have stabbed Suran. It was thanks to Terico that Suran was in this state, dying a little more with each passing hour.

Lanek walked to Suran and placed a hand on her forehead, stroking her bangs a few times. "I need to keep searching for a cure, if there is one. You keep resting, Terico. If Suran wakes up and you're awake, you let her know she's going to make it. And when the time comes... you better heal her."

"I will," Terico said.

"I realize you and Suran have been good friends for many years now," Lanek said. "And I understand that... there's only so much I can do for her as her brother." He bent down to give his sister a kiss on the forehead, then turned away and took a long, slow breath. "When the time comes, please save her, Terico. I've already lost my parents. I can't lose my dear sister, too."

Lanek walked back to the door, his last words giving away his tears. Terico said nothing, but focused on his grip on Suran's chill palm.

•

The night passed without Suran waking up again. Kneeling on the floor for so long was painful, but Terico was too focused on Suran to let the pain in his knees affect him. Terico listened intently the entire night, but Suran didn't speak up again until morning.

"Terico..." she whispered. She was still too fatigued to open her eyes.
"Yes," Terico said in a hushed voice. "I'm still here."

"I'm..." Suran began, but she couldn't finish her sentence.

"It's okay," Terico said. "Don't push yourself. Just rest a little longer... I'm going to use the Elpis to heal you. As soon as I can, I'm going to heal you."

Suran lay still, her mouth open slightly for several seconds. "Talk..."

She needed Terico to speak to her. He thought of telling more stories of the good times they spent together, but instead felt he should finally tell her all the thoughts that had built up in his heart. For hours now, his mind had been entirely focused on Suran and all his hopes and dreams for her.

"There's so many things..." Terico began, struggling to find the right words to say. "So many things I wish to do with you, Suran. I will heal you, and then the battle will end, and everything will work out. In the end, everything will be all right.

"They might try to make me be king afterward, but I will turn them down. I don't seek power, or the strain of an entire kingdom's troubles. I would rather live somewhere quiet and peaceful. I would like it if we lived in a small town like Edellerston again. It wouldn't be the same, of course, but we belong in the countryside somewhere. We can leave all this behind. The royal courts, the wars, the Elpis, the power struggles, the constant death... We'll leave it all behind.

"We'll live together in a village, and the world will never trouble us again. We can get married... Nothing will break us apart. We'll always support each other. Every day, you can call me dear. Then I will call you dearest. And you will call me dearest forever... And... I'll call you dearest of all times, all places."

Terico couldn't say any more. His throat was so tight, it hurt to even breathe. Tears dripped onto his hand and Suran's hand, still clasped together. Terico had wanted to be strong for Suran, but he couldn't control himself. All his feelings for her were pouring out, and he couldn't stop himself.

"Once this is over, let's get married," he said.

Suran gave the slightest hint of a smile on her face. "I would... like that."

"I'll give you my... entire heart." Terico was too overcome with emotion to say anything more.

He knew what he had to do. As soon as his energy was back, he would use the Elpis to fight off the poison infecting Suran's body. He wouldn't let up until she was in perfect health once more. Even if he had to give up his entire heart.

•

The morning slowly crept toward noon, and Suran's condition continued to grow worse. Despite Terico's presence, Suran's hand only grew colder. Her pulse slowed down even more, leaving four seconds of emptiness between each heartbeat.

The doctor eventually returned to check on Suran once more. "The poison is affecting her a bit faster than I anticipated."

Terico stood up and gritted his teeth against the pain in his legs. "How long does she have? How soon do I need to use the Elpis?" "You shouldn't use it before you're fully healed," the doctor said.

"But how much time does Suran have left?"

The doctor sighed. "It's difficult to say. I've never had a patient infected by gray Nexi energy before."

She could be hanging to her final breaths then, Terico thought. *This man doesn't know how much time Suran has left to live. I have to heal her now.*
"Okay," Terico said. "I'll keep watching over her."

"Very well. Make sure you get some sleep..." The doctor looked concerned, but he also looked very weary—he may not have slept at all either.
As soon as the doctor left, Terico took out his Elpis fragments and gripped them tight, one in each fist.

I'll start by healing her mind and heart, Terico decided. He placed one hand on her forehead, the other over her heart.

"Don't worry," Terico said softly. "This might hurt, but the Elpis will destroy the gray Nexi energy inside you."

He knew he wasn't in very good condition to use the Elpis again, but there was probably no time left to wait any longer. One can only wait so long before breaking down.

I can do this, Terico repeated in his head. He activated the Elpis stones, causing them to glow brighter. The energy rushed up his arms and flooded his body with every pain imaginable. The fact he was still recovering from his use of the stones the day before only made the agony worse.

With all his might, Terico focused on directing the Nexi energies to Suran's mind and heart. He shut his eyes and exerted all his strength to separate the healing forces from the rest of the Elpis powers. Upon accessing the healing magic, Terico forced the energy to flow from his body to Suran's.

Suran's eyes shot open and she screamed at the top of her lungs. Terico wanted to cover her mouth to keep her from alerting the castle's nurses, but he couldn't move his hands away from Suran's mind and heart now. He continued to pour Elpis energy into Suran, his body trembling from the torment of the Elpis. Suran writhed beneath her blankets, tears streaming down her face.

Terico felt the healing energy collide with the gray Nexi energy in Suran's body. There was far more of the poisonous energy accumulated in her than the Elpis energy Terico was transferring to her. The gray energy negated all of Terico's efforts, then rushed up his arms and flooded his body with the effects Suran was suffering. Immediately Terico's arms went limp, too weak to even hold up.

In seconds, Terico's whole body turned weak and lifeless, and it simply became impossible to fight the Nexi energy, let alone the torment of the Elpis. He fell back and collapsed on the ground, unable to move at all for several seconds. His mind disconnected from the Elpis, and once he could move his hands he pushed the Elpis fragments away. The pain coursing through his body remained several seconds longer, and Terico almost felt certain he was going to die.

It didn't work, he thought, shutting his eyes tighter. *It didn't work at all.*

Suran's cries died away, and she lay still and quiet once more. Terico wanted to get up to check on her pulse or to see if she was breathing, but his limbs failed him. The brief burst of gray Nexi energy in his body was heightened by the energies of the Elpis, and his entire body felt numb, unresponsive.

The effects faded away after a few minutes, however, destroyed by lingering traces of the Elpis's healing powers. As soon as Terico was able to move to his hands and knees he pushed himself back to Suran's bed.

I can try again, he thought. *I have to keep trying!*
He picked up the Elpis pieces and struggled to stand on his feet again. He felt too weary to do so, and decided he had to rest a few minutes to recover.

Once he was able to stand, Terico felt for a pulse, and after several seconds felt only a single faint heartbeat. Suran held on to life with only the slightest of grips, her body threatening to give in to the poison at any moment.

"Stop!" a woman yelled. Terico glanced to the door to find Rilv entering the room.

"This is my only chance," Terico said, turning his focus back to Suran.

"You don't have the energy to save her," Rilv said. "You need to rest until you have fully recovered."

"She will die by then!" Terico yelled.

"You were supposed to rest," Rilv said. "You need all your energy for when Delkol attacks."

So this was Rilv's hope, Terico realized. She just wanted Suran to die while Terico slept, and then have Terico continue to rest and prepare for Delkol's invasion.

"Leave," Terico ordered. "I need all the concentration I can get." "You can't keep using the Elpis like this," Rilv said. "You will die." Terico ignored her and placed both hands on Suran's heart. He gripped the Elpis fragments tight and accessed their energies once more. In seconds, the power overwhelmed him. He could feel the gray Nexi in Suran's body fighting against his Elpis energy, utterly overpowering it. There was a moment of utter torment, then a moment of complete emptiness, and then a moment of pure grief.

I need more, Terico thought. *My power isn't enough. Even if I were fully rested, I wouldn't be able to fight off this poisonous energy. I need the full Elpis.*
His body turned limp and weak once more, forcing him back to the ground. He dropped the Elpis pieces to either side of him and rested his back against the side of his bed. Every centimeter of his body drummed with a stinging pain, and his headache seemed to pulse from head to toe several times a second.

"I hate this," Terico whispered, short of breath. "It's not enough. It's not nearly enough."

"You must rest," Rilv said. "If you are ill-prepared to face Delkol, he will kill you, take the Elpis fragments, and then have the powers of a god. He would be very difficult to deal with then, and thousands of people would die."

"I understand," Terico said. "I have to find Delkol... I have to find him now." "I have scouts searching for his present location," Rilv said. "I will let you know as soon as he has been spotted. In the meantime, you must get ready to fight."
Terico sat still for a minute, going over everything Rilv had said. If Terico could get a hold of the rest of the Elpis, he would have the power to save Suran.

He just needed to find Delkol.

•

Rilv left when Terico assured her he would rest in his bed. He had to be helped into the bed because his body had gone numb, but afterward Terico lay there, thinking only of Suran.

Once Rilv was gone and Terico had recovered from his numbness, he got out of bed and used the Elpis fragments to find where Delkol was hiding. Terico had expected Delkol to use the golden Nexi stone to find Terico and fly to him right away, but it seemed Delkol was hoping to invade the city for the select purpose of obtaining the full Elpis.

Terico activated the energy and searched for Delkol the same way he had after flying out of Suran and Lanek's airship. The process was just as painful and difficult as before, but Terico forced himself to keep at it.

Seconds turned to minutes, and though Terico was able to access the golden Nexi energy, he couldn't visualize any clear image of where Delkol was.
Is he hiding himself with the Elpis somehow? Terico wondered. He fought back the pain and continued to search. His head rang with a dozen headaches, and it soon became too much for Terico to handle. He dropped his Elpis fragments and gripped his head tight.

This can't be happening, he thought. *Why is the Elpis failing me now? Right when I need it most...*
Time passed slowly, and Terico could do little to make the pain of the Elpis go away. It lingered on, much stronger than it ever had before. He was using its power too much, and too soon. He felt as if a part of him had melted away from the inside, never to be fully healed again.

I'm dying, he thought. *If I keep using the Elpis like this...*

His own life was of little concern at the moment. He sat on his bed and stared down toward Suran, wishing above all else that he'd find a way to save her. All his efforts thus far availed him nothing, though. He hadn't even come close to saving her.

It's not right, Terico thought. *It's not right for you to die.*
Her breathing only slowed down, however. Terico tried willing himself to recover from his Elpis use, but there was nothing he could do. The pain and exhaustion only remained, and even as day turned to night, Terico still felt overwhelmed by his repeated access of the Elpis's energies.

The room turned dark, and Terico found himself kneeling by Suran's bed once more. She hadn't spoken at all since she responded to Terico's marriage proposal. He gripped her hand once more, and felt as if he was dipping his hand into icy water.

No. Not yet. Please hold out a little longer, Suran...
He stood up and felt for a pulse in her wrist, then in her neck. There was no heartbeat. He placed an ear over her heart and listened for ten seconds, but there was no response.

Wide-eyed and breathless, Terico immediately took his Elpis pieces and held them over Suran's heart. He accessed the Elpis energy and exerted every ounce of strength he had to bring healing energy to Suran's heart. It was too hard to control. In seconds the power of the Elpis brought unbearable pain to every nerve in Terico's body. He threw aside the Elpis pieces and gripped the side of Suran's bed, struggling to keep standing. Breathing heavily, Terico stared down at Suran's unmoving form through rushing tears.

"Please... wake up, Suran," Terico whispered. "Please wake up." She simply lay there, placid and soundless.

There was still no heartbeat, and her body only remained frigid and still. Suran had stopped breathing, and there was no response when Terico tried to shake her awake.

He knelt down and lay his head against Suran's, falling into a cycle of continuous weeping.

Suran was dead, and once again Terico's power availed him nothing. The night grew darker with each passing hour, and the complete exhaustion and torment of his body slowly forced him into a deep sleep. He soaked Suran's pillow with his tears, and flooded his dreams with visions of what may have been.

•

11

A WAR OF VENGEANCE

The next day came and passed, leaving Terico to rest and recover from his repeated use of the Elpis fragments. As he had expected, Rilv was displeased he had used the Elpis before he was ready, as it would make it impossible for him to fully recover in time to face Delkol at full strength. Terico could not get himself to care for Rilv's words, as she had made it clear she did not care whether Suran lived or not. In fact, Rilv was probably hoping Suran would die quickly, before Terico could try using the Elpis to save her.
Rilv went on about how Terico had jeopardized the entire kingdom, and how he had placed Suran's life before the lives of the thousands who lived in Setar. Terico felt he would have made the same choice again if put under the same circumstances. A part of him would have even sacrificed the city if it could bring Suran back, as cruel as this sounded.

He held on to one last possibility for bringing Suran back, though. The full Elpis was said to give one godlike powers. In time, Terico felt there was a chance he could bring Suran back to life.

Upon learning of her death, Rilv and the doctor prepared to take Suran away to prepare for burial. Terico demanded they leave her in bed, however. If Delkol was going to strike soon, Terico intended to obtain the Elpis from him and try healing Suran with its full power. Rilv complied with the demand, perhaps just hoping to keep Terico on her side. They both understood Terico was necessary for defeating Delkol.

Perhaps it was the one thing Terico and Rilv could see eye-to-eye on. Delkol had to die, both as retribution for what he had done, and for the safety of the Fiefs Kingdom.

In a way, it was the only thing Terico had left. His home was gone.

His parents were gone. Suran was gone. And though Turan was still alive, for all intents and purposes he was gone too. All that was left was the hope in a revenge that could ease Terico's misery. Even if it helped just a little, it would be worth it to kill Delkol.

And yet, Terico found himself questioning if even that would please him.

What *would* killing Delkol do for him? It wouldn't really change anything.

Everyone would still be dead.

No, the Elpis, Terico thought, staring blankly at the ceiling. *There's still the Elpis. If I have all four pieces, I can do whatever I wish. I can save Suran. I can save everyone. Nobody will be able to stop me. I can destroy the Brotherhood. I can destroy the whole Fiefs Kingdom. There won't be any more war then. Nobody else would have to suffer again.*

Rilv eventually returned in the afternoon, looking utterly exhausted herself. Terico realized she pretty much had the safety of the kingdom on her shoulders, but he couldn't get himself to pity her.

"A messenger of the Fiefs army has brought this for you." Rilv handed Terico a thin scroll, forcing him to sit up and read it.

"The Kingdom of Fiefs will fall by tomorrow evening. I offer you, Terico, the same choice I offered your father. Give up the Elpis fragments, or I will repeat what I did in Edellerston—only on a much grander scale. You should understand well how serious I am when I say I am willing to kill every man, woman, and child in this land.

I do not seek to destroy this city. My only wish is to claim my rightful place as king of Fiefs. Unless you wish to have the blood of Setar's entire populace on your hands, I suggest delivering the two Elpis fragments you have by noon tomorrow."

Delkol's letter meant little to Terico. Obviously Terico wasn't going to give up his pieces of the Elpis. And it was a blatant lie that Delkol did not wish to destroy the city. Terico doubted there was anything the man enjoyed more than the bloodshed of innocent life.

"His armies will invade tomorrow then," Terico said.

"Yes," Rilv said. "Do you wish to respond to this message?"

Terico handed the scroll back. "There's no need. Just prepare the armies. I will try to defeat Delkol as soon as I can."

"Our armies are assembled," Rilv said. "Reinforcements may arrive tomorrow, if we are fortunate—but we can not rely on this possibility." "I will kill Delkol," Terico said.

It is all I have left to live for.
"Rest as much as you can in the meantime," Rilv said. "Do not use the Elpis until you fight Delkol." She tore apart the message Delkol sent and left the room.

Terico agreed and lay back down. His thoughts drifted from one thing to the next, and nothing in his head seemed to make sense anymore. It may have been in part due to his repeated use of the Elpis, but Terico felt he mainly just couldn't grasp the series of events his life had spiraled into the last few days. One minute Suran was alive again, and the next minute she was dead again. How was it that life could play out so cruelly? The fact that it was Terico's fault Suran died only made the pain worse, as well as the fact it was Terico's best friend who killed her.

Every happy moment of Terico's past felt as if it had shattered. Long gone were the days Terico would sit in class with Turan and Suran, and enjoy chatting together and planning their small adventures. Though it was only a few weeks ago that he had been doing just that, it felt like an entirely different lifetime.

Some time in the afternoon, Areo, Borely, and Kitoh came to visit to see how Terico was doing. The three had been spending most their time training with some of the special forces within the Fiefs royal army, preparing for the upcoming battle with the Brotherhood and Shire armies. They each expressed condolences for Terico's loss, and recounted how they were all thankful for Suran and everything she had done for them during their brief time with her. Terico didn't want to dwell on the subject, especially with Suran's body still present in the room.

"I hope the three of you will be able to find your way once this is all over," Terico said. He knew that none of them had really wished to get so caught up in all this. "And I hope you'll all get through this battle unscathed."

"I'll be okay," Kitoh said. "I've been given this." He held up a Nexi stone that shined a very dark yellow—perhaps an orangeish yellow.

"What is it?" Terico asked.

"It was a gift from Vursa to Setar a long time ago," Kitoh said. "There are eigni who are capable of creating new kinds of Nexi stones, and this is one of the most powerful ones ever created. If the user is strong enough, a magnificent creature can be summoned."

"That's good," Terico said. "We'll need all the help we can get to hold off the Shire armies. I'm sure you'll be able to wield that Nexi stone well."

Kitoh didn't respond, but he looked less afraid than he had while on the airship. Terico hoped the boy would be able to fulfill the wishes of his parents and return to his city with the respect he'd deserve. It was probably going to be a rough life for the child, but Terico felt confident Kitoh would be able to handle the trials ahead—and likely with a reserve Terico could never be capable of.

"Don't worry, we'll watch over him," Borely said.

"You need to watch yourself," Areo said. "Remember all those times I had to save your life on that Brotherhood airship?"

Borely's face tightened and glowered, though he kept from looking back at Areo. "It's hard to forget. You've only reminded me of it a hundred times now."
"I won't be there to save you every time you get in trouble," Areo said.

"I'll be fine!" Borely yelled. "You just watch whose neck it is you sink your teeth into out there. I'll be ready to punch through your heart the moment you turn against us."

"Is this another joke of yours?" Areo asked. "There's no way you would land a punch on me in a fight, of course."

Terico looked to Kitoh and sighed. "I'm glad they're getting along so well."

"I think it *has* improved a little..." Kitoh said.

Terico didn't care to tell the two to work together any more than he already had before. They wouldn't have to be together on the battlefield, so this was probably the last time they'd be together. Unless, of course, Borely was still trying to get Areo to pay for his ship. Terico doubted things would end well for Borely if the sailor continued to push that agenda.

Eventually the three left to return to their training and preparations for battle. Terico was left alone once more, and there was nothing to do but lie in bed and ponder everything he had gone through since that fateful day. The day Edellerston was attacked had flung Terico on an adventure he never could have imagined undertaking. It was all drawing to a close now, and he knew his life would change forever over the next twenty-four hours.

His primary objective was obvious. Kill Delkol. And in the process of obtaining his revenge, Terico would also gain the remaining two Elpis fragments. With their leader dead and the full Elpis in Terico's hands, the Shire armies would have no choice but to retreat.

And then what?

I could destroy all those armies. Obliterate the Brotherhood forever.
With the full Elpis, this would be a simple matter, Terico believed. There would be no more pain from utilizing the Elpis, and Terico would be free to access any and all Nexi powers whenever he pleased.

There's only a few other things I would use it for, though, Terico thought. *Bring Suran back to life. Heal Turan, assuming he hasn't died in the battle. And bring back my parents, and all of Edellerston, if it isn't too late.*
Terico thought those killed in the attack on Edellerston may have been dead too long for Terico to bring back to life. Their spirits had left several weeks ago now, and there were likely limitations to what even the Elpis could do.

There was no telling what Terico would be able to do, however. He had to obtain the second half of the Elpis in order to find out.

As night fell, he drifted to sleep, plotting all the ways he would use his Elpis fragments in order to kill Delkol. Once Delkol was finished off for good, Terico's new life could finally begin.

•

Sleep came to Terico unwillingly. After all, how could a reasonable person sleep when the one he loved lay dead in the very same room? And yet he slept, the constant barrage of painful thoughts breaking his mind and dulling his senses.

Kill Delkol, and all will be right again, Terico thought over and over. The night passed without interruption, as Rilv had instructed the nurses to make sure Terico got all the rest he could. He received food in the morning, which helped him get his strength back. Though he still had a horrendous headache, Terico felt the pain in his body had dissipated for the most part. He was sore and numb, but he felt he'd be able to fight by the time he'd face Delkol.

He pushed himself out of bed and stood up, his weak legs nearly collapsing beneath him. Holding on to his bed and Suran's, Terico spent a few minutes just trying to get feeling back to his legs. Maintaining this position was difficult though, as Terico's arms were weak and dull as well.

Terico fell to his knees and took slow, deep breaths. Though most of the pain from the Elpis had faded away, it was more difficult to move than Terico had expected. On top of this, his vision turned blurry, and slowly darkened over the next several minutes. Terico shut his eyes, hoping his eyesight wouldn't give him any trouble when it came time to fight.

Perhaps an hour passed before Rilv arrived with a couple royal guards. Terico forced himself to stand, but wasn't able to hide his discomfort in the act of doing so.

"You still haven't recovered," Rilv said.

"I'll be fine," Terico said. "The Elpis will strengthen me."

Rilv simply tightened her gaze on Terico a bit in response.

"You worry about the Shire armies and the Brotherhood," Terico said. "I will kill Delkol as fast as I possibly can." He knew he couldn't promise a quick victory, so he didn't bother pretending. There was no doubt in Terico's mind that Delkol had a plan in mind for him, and it wasn't unlikely that Delkol had discovered new and powerful uses with the Elpis. The fight would be difficult, but Terico felt confident he would find a way to defeat Delkol. Once on the battlefield, it all boiled down to split-second decisions.

Delkol may be the more experienced fighter, but Terico knew he could pull through with superior ingenuity and dexterity. He also felt he would be better-prepared to handle the pain of the Elpis, having experienced so much of it over the past twenty-four hours.

One of the guards with Rilv placed a set of clothes and several pieces of armor on Terico's bed. The other guard added some more armor, and held out a sword for Terico to use. Terico took it and looked it over. It was about the same size as the longsword he had back in Edellerston, though there was a stark difference in quality and detail. Just looking at it, Terico could tell this blade was much sharper, and the fine metals embedded in the hilt easily made this sword many times more valuable than all of Terico's previous swords put together.

"Is this the sword of the king then?" Terico asked.

"No," Rilv said. "You have not been officially instated as king yet. But I don't intend to send you out there poorly armed. This is a sword of the royal Fiefs line. Our armies will recognize you as a leader, and will be looking up to you for strength in this battle."

Terico nodded, understanding that the situation regarding the royal succession was likely a matter of great discussion amongst the ranks at the moment.
Rilv and the guards left Terico to change, asking him to join them outside the castle once he was ready.

The uniform was black with purple and gold embellishments, while the armor gleamed a brilliant white and yellow. Once he got his uniform on, Terico tied each of the metal guards to his body, covering his torso, arms, legs, and sides. The sword slid into its metal sheath with the clean, precise sound of a perfect fit.

He walked slowly toward the door, a deep, stinging pain starting to develop all throughout his body. It was difficult to push himself this soon, after using the Elpis as many times as he had.

I need the full Elpis, Terico thought. *I'll... probably die if I don't get it*. And if not by Elpis poisoning, then by Delkol's own hand.

It took some time for Terico to find the strength to walk out the door. He nearly jumped back when he opened it, finding Lanek standing directly in front of him. Lanek glared at Terico—the elf looked like a standing corpse.

"I have one question," he said, his voice low and torn apart.

Terico nodded. He wasn't sure what Lanek would do now that Suran had died. Rilv said that Lanek had mourned for Suran while Terico was asleep, and that she had kept watch to make sure Lanek didn't do anything to Terico—apparently she had learned from Lanek how Suran had been entrusted to Terico's care when the Brotherhood boarded the airship.

"Who killed my little sister?" Lanek asked, supreme loathing oozing with every word.

Terico had never seen Lanek with such a horrific expression. The elf's hair was uncharacteristically tattered and unkempt, his eyes bloodshot and ringed with fatigue.

"A member of the Brotherhood," Terico said, afraid to reveal that Lynx's true identity was Turan.

"I need details," Lanek said. "Describe him."

"He's young," Terico said. A part of him didn't want to say more, but another part felt compelled to. "About my height. Blond hair. Goes by the name *Lynx*. Wears the uniform and mask that all the Brotherhood wear."

"Short and blond," Lanek said. "Is there anything else?"

Obviously the easiest way to identify Lynx was with the large smile painted on his mask, but Terico didn't want Lanek to kill Turan. Even with Turan having killed Suran, Terico didn't want Turan to suffer if he could help it.

Lanek gripped Terico's shoulders. "There has to be something more. Tell me how I will find this boy." "That's all," Terico said.

"Rilv does not know I'm here," Lanek said, gripping Terico a little tighter. "I need more to go off of. Think! There must be more."

Terico remembered very clearly Lanek's threat to kill him if anything were to happen to Suran.

And thinking about it, there was no reason to hold any details back

from Lanek. If Turan did die, Terico would be able to use the full Elpis to revive him.

"There's a smile painted on his mask," Terico said. "He has an insane personality." There was also a chance Turan would seek Lanek out anyways, considering Turan's goal was to kill everyone Terico knew.

"A smile," Lanek said. He let go of Terico and turned away, saying nothing more. The elf's thoughts were wholly focused on revenge.

How many more people will die today? Terico wondered. He placed a hand on the wall to keep his balance. *How many more people will seek revenge before this is over? This is hell.*

•

Rilv led Terico through the city, which for the most part was deserted. The general populace had relocated behind the walls of the castle, leaving only soldiers and powerful Nexi users on the streets. Everyone was grim, tired, anxious. Setar was prepared for a battle to the death, but Terico's feelings felt distant. Though the war was fresh for this city, Terico felt he had been fighting it for weeks now.

Everything had been taken from him. Was there anything left for him to fight for?

He had to keep reminding himself. Revenge against Delkol. The power of the full Elpis. A redemption of everything he had lost.

There was no certainty in any of this, though. Would killing Delkol fill any of the emptiness inside of Terico? And would the Elpis really give Terico the power of a god? Every time Terico used the Elpis, it had given him a great deal of agony. And even with the power the Elpis contained, Terico hadn't been able to save those he loved. The Elpis didn't save Jujor. The Elpis didn't save Suran.

And it certainly wasn't saving Terico.

What if even the full Elpis availed him nothing?

Perhaps that was why it was broken apart and hidden away. Perhaps there really was no way for the Elpis to be used for good. Perhaps it was a power that only granted misery to its users.

Terico stared at all the vacant stands, all the boarded-up houses. Such an empty, foreboding city. Terico just wanted to leave it all.

Once near the tall, stone city walls, Rilv and her guards led Terico through the masses of soldiers. Many of the soldiers were carrying large Nexi stones up the stairways to the catapults positioned atop the walls.

As soon as Delkol's army began its attack, there would be many defensive measures put into place to slow them down.

Some soldiers stopped to stare at Terico a few seconds. Perhaps there were rumors of him floating around already. Terico didn't care if everyone

started looking to him to be a leader or a king. The troops had their generals to guide them—Terico was just the one who could use the Elpis. There was only one person for Terico to fight, and once that was done, perhaps the battle would end as well.

Rilv led Terico past the front lines of the assembling armies and toward a stairway up the city wall.

"Our reinforcements have not arrived yet," Rilv said, "so the battle will be quite difficult at first. The longer we can delay, the better."

"I doubt Delkol will wait any longer than noon," Terico said. "I will fight him as soon as I find him."

"He will not make it easy for you to reach him," Rilv said. "He knows you have two fragments of the Elpis, same as him. If he can weaken you in any way before he faces you, he will."

And in all honesty, Terico already was in a much weaker state than he should have been. Walking this long had tired him out, and brought back the pain in all the cuts and bruises covering his body. His headache had grown a bit stronger again as well.

"I will kill him," Terico said, following Rilv up a stairway. It was all he could say. He knew that the chances of him succeeding were slim, but it was the only thing he had left to hold on to. He had to kill Delkol. What else was there left for Terico?

Once atop the city wall, Terico gazed out at the distant Shire armies, all in a grand formation that stretched out as far as Terico could see from east to west. The hills in the horizon were covered with soldiers in black armor. There were also large numbers of Brotherhood members in white—Terico imagined Delkol was amongst one of those groups of soldiers.

"They have strength in numbers," Rilv said. "They were assembled quickly, however, so they have no large machinery, save for a single airship. Our airships have been repaired enough to handle that, and to aid in the city's general defense afterward. Delkol is a significant element of the Shire army's power, however. He is a charismatic figure who has promised a great deal for his troops. The fact Delkol has killed our king gives them great confidence."

"If I kill him quickly, they'll lose the will to fight," Terico said.

"It would be best if you do so before the armies breach the walls," Rilv said. "We have suffered greatly in the Brotherhood's recent attack. The fact is we are greatly outnumbered, and it will only be a matter of time before the entries are broken down. The Brotherhood amongst the Shire army's ranks are greatly skilled with Nexi, and will likely have the means to sneak in quickly."

"I understand," Terico said. He had enough to worry about without all this pressure Rilv was piling atop of him.

The sooner I kill Delkol, the fewer lives that will be lost.
How many people will die with each passing minute it takes me to seek out Delkol and kill him?
The amount of blood that will be on my hands... Perhaps there will never be a limit to it.

•

The sun rose high above the battlefield. Terico watched the Shire army, waiting for the moment Delkol would order his soldiers forward. A small figure rose in the sky, and Terico kept his eyes on its approach. It was Delkol, flying in his transformed state. The power of the Elpis fragments had turned his armor black, his skin light gray, and his scar and eyes a sickly white. He stopped in mid-air a good thirty or so meters in front of where Terico stood.

"Hold your fire," Rilv told the nearest soldiers running the Nexi catapults.

"So he comes to me," Terico whispered, gripping his Elpis pieces. "Terico, the boy who would never be king," Delkol cried out in a booming voice. He somehow projected his voice with the Elpis. "You may have some royal blood in you, but otherwise there is no good reason for you to rule this land."

Terico didn't care about becoming king of Fiefs. All he wanted was to see this man dead.

Delkol went on without waiting for a response. "My offer still stands. Give me your half of the Elpis and allow me to take my rightful place as ruler of this kingdom. In return, nobody will have to die today. Do you wish to have the blood of an entire city on your hands, boy? I imagine you are tired of death."

"Not quite!" Terico yelled. He activated his half of the Elpis and shot himself into the air, straight for Delkol.

Already flying back the moment Terico began to transform, Delkol

blasted himself down toward his gathered armies. At the same time, a creature swooped down for Terico from above, forcing him to stop pursuing Delkol.

It was a death bird—the giant creature Delkol rode on when escaping the castle with the Elpis piece he stole from there. It reached for Terico with long, ragged talons made of bone, gleaming white and red. Terico forced himself back a couple meters to avoid the skeletal bird's attacks. The death bird swooped back up to Terico, far faster than he expected. Fighting back the pain enveloping his body, Terico created a burst of frozen air to materialize in front of him. He flew backward, letting the death bird fly into the light blue Nexi energy. Terico floated to the side, watching for the beast to plummet, its wings too frozen to fly with.

The creature rushed straight through the frozen air. Though most of its body was covered with patches of ice, it continued flapping its skeletal wings—and still headed for Terico. It was a creature of bone and bloody muscles—the fact it could fly in the first place should have been impossible.
The ice simply cracked and broke apart as the death bird flapped its wings.

Terico charged toward it, unsheathing his sword and filling the blade with orange Nexi energy in the process. The death bird slowed down and pushed itself backward, just outside the range of Terico's blade. Terico swung again, but the death bird flapped its wings inward farther, slamming a giant bone against him.

Silently, the creature dove toward Terico, who careened backward, rushing toward the ground. The pain of the attack doubled under the influence of the Elpis, and Terico had trouble regaining control of his flight. He managed to keep himself from colliding with the ground, but the death bird was already upon him. At the last moment he raised his sword and released a burst of water at the swooping beast. The water blasted the death bird back a few meters, but it quickly recovered.

Terico forced himself to fly backward before the death bird could slam its giant skeletal beak into his body. Though wielding the power of the Elpis, getting torn in half would still be instantly fatal.

I'm wasting my energy on this bird! Terico thought. *Delkol's letting it weaken me while he hides amongst his armies.*
Terico considered just ignoring the bird and flying toward the Shire troops, but he knew the soldiers would attack him—and he had no intention of fighting off an entire army before getting to Delkol. Terico also considered heading back toward the city so the archers atop the wall could help him.

This would only endanger the lives of the city's first defense, however.
Terico also wasn't certain if arrows would have any effect on this creature.

The death bird flapped its wings faster, gaining several extra meters on Terico with each stroke. Forcing himself to fly faster would strain his mind even more than he already had. He activated the brown Nexi energy and released it toward the death bird. The creature forced itself upward, and the majority of the sticky material missed it completely. The death bird dove for Terico, its open beak revealing dozens of thick, misshapen fangs.

An ear-splitting shriek broke through the air just above Terico. A massive red and yellow bird collided into the death bird, sinking its talons and beak into the fleshy bits of muscle holding its skeletal body together. This second bird was engulfed in flames, and as it brought the death bird plummeting toward the ground the creature's prey caught on fire as well.

It was a giant phoenix. It took a few seconds for Terico to figure out where it came from—it had to have been summoned by the special Nexi stone Kitoh was given. One of the most powerful stones the eigni had ever created, Terico remembered.

The two birds crashed into the ground. The phoenix tore into the muscle tissue of the writhing death bird, ripping apart the deadly creature's bones. The death bird pecked its beak into the phoenix and tried clawing at it, but the phoenix was quick to snap the death bird's neck. With a few wrenches of its beak, the phoenix ripped the death bird's head off entirely, though the creature still continued to fight back. The phoenix proceeded to disconnect the wings from what was left of the burning muscles of the bloody beast, keeping it from moving further.

Terico looked down to the Shire armies, which marched at a brisk pace toward the city walls. Delkol was among them somewhere, but Terico couldn't spot him. The majority of his soldiers were dressed in black, and Delkol had surely stopped using the Elpis, considering how his transformed state would make him easier to notice. He was also conserving energy, while Terico would waste away if he didn't find Delkol quickly. The Shire armies reached the phoenix, which flew away from the burning remains of the death bird. A number of archers tried shooting down the phoenix, but the giant bird managed to avoid them. The legions of soldiers continued toward the city walls, where catapults began to fire giant Nexi stones toward the approaching masses. The city defenses began with large green Nexi, which blew apart into dozens of thick vines upon landing. Some soldiers were taken down by the stones themselves, but many more were tied up by the swarming vines. A number of soldiers fought off the vines with their swords, while others used fire Nexi to burn them down.

The Fiefs armies continued by launching brown and red Nexi into the crowds of charging Shire troops. Many Shire soldiers became stuck in the swamps that burst out from the brown Nexi while tens of others were blown apart by the fiery red stones.

Terico continued to search for Delkol, careful to keep out of range of the archers' arrows. Though it was agonizing, Terico forced himself to access the golden Nexi energy in order to locate Delkol's position. Terico screamed from the pain, his body trembling in mid-air high above the hundreds of enemy soldiers passing below him. There were so many people all in one location, it was difficult to search through them, even with the Elpis guiding his vision.

Shutting his eyes, Terico caught sight of several groups of Shire soldiers— some armed with lances, some with swords, and others with longbows. They were closing in on the castle walls now. Members of the Brotherhood led the way to three of the city entryways, blasting away at the massive doors with red, orange, and tan Nexi stones. Fiefs soldiers fought them back with Nexi stones thrown down from above, but for every Shire soldier that was killed, several more rushed in to take his place. The Brotherhood members also managed to avoid most of the attacks, using their skills with the Nexi to create effective defenses.

His head pounded twice as fast as his heartbeat, but Terico forced himself to keep using the Elpis to locate Delkol. The sooner he found Delkol, the better chance he had of attacking Delkol before the Elpis wore him out.

The golden Nexi energy guided Terico's vision to an area far from the city walls, where many Brotherhood fighters were congregated amidst the Shire armies. Terico's sight focused in on a caped figure standing amongst some of the masked fighters in white. It was Delkol, unsheathing his sword.

Delkol activated his Elpis fragments, transforming back into his demonic form and rising a couple meters off the ground. Terico's vision pulled back a ways, revealing the phoenix swooping down toward Delkol. A number of archers tried shooting the bird down, but the phoenix was too fast for their arrows. Delkol held his sword back and charged it with orange, white, and purple Nexi energy. His blade shifted between the three colors, vibrating violently and releasing sparks of blinding light.

With an extra burst of speed, the phoenix rushed down for Delkol. Just before the creature could tear Delkol in half with its fiery talons, Delkol shot off a bolt of lightning through the nearest wing, causing the phoenix to turn slightly. The next moment, Delkol was suddenly flying straight into the phoenix's body, slamming his blade through the bird's chest. The screeching beast blew apart into bloody, fiery chunks all around Delkol, who continued to push his vibrating blade through the phoenix's body.

Once through the other side, Delkol turned around and enveloped himself with water to douse the flames of the phoenix that caught on to his body. The phoenix turned its long neck and attempted to jab its sharp beak into Delkol's torso. Delkol flew to the side of the bird's attack and proceeded to lob its head off in one swoop. The giant bird collapsed in a smoldering heap, the passing Shire troops raising their swords and cheering for their victorious leader. Delkol floated above the corpse of the beast and stared directly at Terico, who had to be at least a hundred meters away.

Delkol closed his eyes and smiled. His control of the Elpis was extraordinary, to say the least. In half a minute he took down the summon of one of the world's most powerful Nexi stones, and he didn't look the slightest bit troubled by it.

There was no doubt about it—with the full Elpis this man would easily vanquish everything that stood in his way, just as he easily killed everyone in the Edellerston cathedral.

Terico opened his eyes and cut off access to the golden Nexi energy. He had Delkol's location. It was now only a matter of killing him.

The Elpis energies surged within Terico's body, and with the proper focus Terico forced the power to send him flying toward Delkol. The masses of Shire soldiers turned into a blur beneath him, while Terico's mind broke into pieces, the building torment of the Elpis reaching a horrific climax.

He unsheathed his sword and dove for Delkol, prepared to kill him by any means possible.

•

A flood of Shire soldiers stormed into the city. Borely readied himself for the moment he could jump into the fray.

Hold them off until Terico gets the full Elpis, Borely thought. *And then...* He still wasn't quite sure what he would do next. Trying to persuade the hundred-year-old vampire woman to pay him back for his boat had turned fruitless. She kept saying she had payed him back by saving his life on the Brotherhood airship, but Borely argued that he wouldn't have been on the airship in the first place if he hadn't lost his boat.

No use expecting her to cooperate, Borely decided. *She is a vampire, after all...*
He forced himself to forget about Areo. Now was the time to focus on the approaching Shire soldiers. Borely wondered how many he could defeat by the time the battle ended. Beating down some enemies would help him blow off some steam, Borely decided.

The front lines of the Shire troops were taken down by the repeated volleys of Fiefs archers. A number of Brotherhood members leaped over the corpses and activated tan Nexi stones, forming a barrier from the next series of arrows fired.

Fiefs swordsmen rushed in to hack away at the barrier, followed by lancers who took down the Shire soldiers slipping in from the sides. Several red Nexi were thrown over the wall of dirt, sending tens of Fiefs soldiers bursting into flame.

The Shire and Fiefs armies converged upon one another, and the area around Borely turned into a battleground littered with the dead and dying. The air filled with the clanging of metal, the whooshing of arrows, and the sounds of glowing Nexi stones. One Fiefs soldier ahead of Borely was knocked back by a jet of water, while a Fiefs soldier to Borely's right ran a lance through the side of a Shire soldier wielding an axe.

Borely found an opening and powered the orange Nexi stones embedded in his fists' metal knuckles. He knocked a Shire swordsman in the side, sending him flying into the back of another. Hearing the growth of Nexi vines, Borely turned and shot away the approaching plant appendages with the blue Nexi in his metal headband. A Fiefs archer shot the enemy, allowing Borely to turn and block the attack of a large Shire swordsman. Borely nudged the blade to the side and landed a Nexipowered punch on the man's face, knocking him out cold.

With a few seconds open to breathe, Borely looked to where Kitoh was positioned atop the city wall. The eigni boy didn't have his special Nexi raised in the air anymore, implying he had stopped controlling the phoenix he summoned. Borely wondered if Kitoh lost control of it, or if the phoenix had somehow been killed. Neither situation sounded likely, but there was no way for Borely to find out from here. He resumed fighting the nearby Shire soldiers, careful to watch for their weapons and Nexi elements.

An especially tall Shire lancer shot off a stream of swamp substance from a brown Nexi embedded in his spear, but Borely managed to deflect it with the water of his dark blue Nexi. With an extra push of energy, Borely directed the water into the man's stomach, flinging him back a few meters.

All at once, a dozen or so Brotherhood members charged into the area, assisting their fellow Shire soldiers against the Fiefs troops. A particularly fast Brotherhood fighter with long, thick blades attached to his arms sprinted through, slashing apart every Fiefs soldier he passed. Borely positioned himself and timed his punch for this masked man.

"Eat this!" Borely powered his punch with an extra boost of energy, but instead of connecting with the man's head, Borely got him in the shoulder. There was an earsplitting snap of broken bones, but the Brotherhood fighter didn't react in the slightest. Instead he swung a blade for Borely's head, completely taking Borely by surprise. Borely turned his head and activated his dark blue Nexi at the last moment, pushing the man's bladed arm back.

The man stumbled back a bit, and a nearby Fiefs swordsman blasted him with a fire Nexi. The Brotherhood fighter charged for the swordsman, completely disregarding the flames enveloping his body. The Fiefs soldier was stabbed with both blades, and in seconds the masked man was leaping back toward Borely.

"This is just wrong!" Borely yelled. This man was *on fire*, but was *still* fighting with the tenacity of a ravenous wolf.

Borely shot a jet of water at the man, who dodged and slashed a blade toward Borely's chest. At the same time, a nearby Shire lancer jabbed his weapon at Borely from the side, but Borely dodged him while stepping back from the Brotherhood fighter. In one quick movement Borely grabbed the lance from the Shire soldier and slammed the end of it into the Brotherhood man's neck.

The Shire soldier immediately lifted a tan Nexi stone and flung a large rock at Borely—one bigger than his head. Borely turned and landed a punch on the stone, shattering it with the force of his orange Nexi. Before the soldier could attack again, Borely ran at him and knocked him out with a punch in the face.

"Lynx!" a boy screamed, probably about ten meters east of Borely. The voice sounded familiar, and Borely caught a glimpse of an elf with long turquoise hair rushing toward the area where Borely was fighting. It was Lanek, one of the elves who ran the airship that took him to this city.

A figure stood up directly in front of Borely. It was the Brotherhood fighter he had stabbed through the neck with a lance. The man ripped the weapon out of his throat and jabbed it toward Borely.

"You've got to be kidding me!" Borely yelled. He bashed aside the lance, knocking it out of the masked man's grasp. Not only was this masked man still on fire, but he was fighting with a shattered shoulder *and* a hole through his neck. And not even crying out in pain!

Borely repeatedly blocked the man's swinging bladed arms, waiting for a good opening to beat him down. The man was fast though, and didn't seem to grow tired at all from his rampage.

The Brotherhood fighter swung both his blades inward, straight for Borely's neck. Borely grabbed both blades with his metal gloves. Before the enemy could push away, Borely fired his dark blue Nexi, shooting the man directly in the face. The man's head tore off entirely, the neck already cut up from the lance earlier.

Borely turned and found Lanek releasing a blast of purple Nexi energy, knocking away a couple Shire swordsmen in his path. The elf rushed toward a Brotherhood member—one wearing a mask with a smile painted across the bottom of it.

The Brotherhood member released a stream of brown Nexi substance. Still charging, Lanek used his purple Nexi to push away the swamp material. Borely had to dodge a large glob of it, while the Brotherhood fighter used an earth Nexi to block the majority of the swamp substance.

"Die!" Lanek screamed, quite louder than Borely imagined him capable of. As he blasted aside a Shire soldier with Nexi energy, Lanek unsheathed a long, thin rapier. He connected his purple Nexi stone atop the small circular handle, charging the blade with loose energy.

Just as Lanek was upon him, the masked fighter called Lynx brought up his sword to block the attack. Lynx's sword shattered into several pieces, one of them flinging back into his right arm. Like the man Borely fought, Lynx didn't cry out in pain or even seem to notice the injury.

Some of the Brotherhood fighters are experimented on, Borely remembered. Perhaps some were capable of fighting at full strength, even when suffering life-threatening wounds.

Before Lanek could jab his rapier into Lynx's chest, Lynx slipped back and fired another jet of swamp material. Lanek avoided the attack, but the opening gave time for Lynx to grab a sword from a fallen Shire soldier. Lynx charged it with orange Nexi energy and rushed toward Lanek.

Borely turned at the sound of screaming coming behind him. A Fiefs soldier was yelling for everyone to fall back, and it took a few seconds for Borely to find the source of the screaming. He stepped back upon sighting several Fiefs soldiers in the distance flying several meters into the air. At least a dozen vines were zipping through lines of soldiers, picking out those from Fiefs and tossing them in random directions.

It was Augurc, assisted by a number of Brotherhood members and the endless masses of Shire soldiers continuing to push their way through the gates. While Fiefs soldiers fought against the Shire armies, Augurc would control all the vines running out his arms, picking up several Fiefs soldiers at any given moment. Borely watched from a distance as Augurc picked up swords and lances from the ground and began impaling the Fiefs soldiers he held entangled in his vines. Once they were impaled, Augurc swung them around the battlefield. The blades sticking out of the soldiers' bodies slammed into the heads of other Fiefs soldiers, preoccupied with the Shire soldiers they were already fighting.

Several Shire soldiers gathered together and simultaneously activated fire Nexi toward Augurc, hoping to catch his vines on fire and guide the flames to his body. Augurc raised his right hand and instantly formed a cloud of frozen air around him, and even managed to harden it into solid ice. The massive wave of fire melted away at the ice, but there was just enough of it to defend himself. As soon as the fires dissipated, Augurc sent all his vines for these Shire soldiers. With the assistance of a couple Brotherhood members, they were all killed in seconds.

Fiefs numbers were dwindling fast, and though Borely was managing to hold his own against the Shire soldiers that came against him, he knew he wouldn't last long against more of the Brotherhood fighters. And having seen Augurc's power on the Brotherhood airship, Borely was reluctant to go against him.

I didn't come here to fight a war, Borely thought. *I just need to survive. Just get out of here...* As soon as he thought it, he felt a twinge of guilt. People were dying at the hands of the two Shire brothers. Borely couldn't just abandon this city and let the Shire armies destroy everything.

And besides, wasn't this the sort of adventure he lived for? He took a deep breath and ran forward, grinning.

•

A lance flew just to the left of Areo's head—she had heard the weapon thrown at her and knew to not move her head at the last moment. As soon as the lance leaped at the lancer a couple meters away. Upon slitting the man's throat, Areo turned and found a Brotherhood member shooting a large rock at her. Areo quickly took her tan Nexi and fired a similarly-sized rock at it. Once the two stones collided and deflected out of her path, Areo sprinted for the masked fighter.

She sunk her claws into the man's chest, but he responded by lifting his tan Nexi and activating it again. Areo shoved him aside, causing his torrent of hardened earth to pass just to Areo's right. She slipped behind the fighter and stabbed him in the back. He immediately slammed his elbow hard against Areo's face, not even crying out in pain from his injuries. Areo ignored the bruise forming around her black eye and tore her claws out either side of the man. Though she knew she had cut apart his lungs and heart, Areo took a couple steps back just in case the man would get back up again. To her relief, the Brotherhood fighter stayed dead this time.

Seeing she had a couple moments to spare, Areo sunk her teeth into the man's neck. Once she had taken a few gulps of his blood, Areo let the corpse drop back to the ground. Filled with a renewed vigor, Areo hurried toward one of the stairways leading up to the wall, taking down a couple Shire soldiers along the way.

Kitoh was still where Areo had left him, guarded by the archers who continued to fire upon the Shire armies below. Areo had asked Kitoh to wait a bit before turning into a dragon, worrying that Delkol would seek out Kitoh just as he had the phoenix Kitoh summoned. There were now tens of Shire soldiers fighting their way up the thin staircases. Most were taken down by the Fiefs troops stationed on the wall, but the continual pressure of the ever-growing number of Shire soldiers was wearing them out.

Areo rushed up the stairway, clawing away at any Shire soldiers she came across. Once atop the wall, she found Kitoh helping man a catapult with ice Nexi. She turned at the sound of vines. Tens of vines worked their way up the wall, grasping onto nooks. Areo looked down to find several Shire soldiers sliding upward, forcing the taut vines into their green Nexi stones. Before they could bring themselves up to the top of the wall, Areo tore apart each of the vines with her claws. Most of the soldiers managed to reactivate their Nexi's vines to grab onto footholds, keeping them from falling all the way to the ground.

A few dozen meters away, Areo saw at least twenty other soldiers in black working their way up the wall. There was nobody there to stop them from climbing onto the wall—the Fiefs soldiers there were killed in arrow fire. Areo looked the other way and found even more Shire soldiers using vine Nexi to ascend the wall. A number of Fiefs guards used red Nexi to burn down the vines, but several more vines would appear every time they managed to burn one down the entire way.

It was only a matter of time before the walls were overrun with Shire soldiers. Areo needed to get Kitoh out before they were overwhelmed. She ran to the boy and informed him of the situation.

"I can join the battle," Kitoh said. "Terico is fighting Delkol, and I'm needed now."

Areo looked down at the swarms of Shire soldiers pouring through the broken gates. With her heightened vision as a vampire, she was able to spot a number of individuals very quickly. Lanek was fighting a member of the Brotherhood, and Borely was rushing toward a number of Shire soldiers. Just past them was Augurc Shire, the man Areo and Borely had to escape from back on the Brotherhood airship. Augurc was flinging soldiers around with the vines coming from his arms, taking out dozens more with each passing minute.

"We need to get down there," Areo said, pointing toward Augurc. Kitoh nodded and took out his transformative Nexi stone. It was all he needed at this point, he had explained.

Areo held a hand atop of Kitoh's fist. She looked sternly into the eigni boy's eyes. "Are you sure you wish to do this?"

"My people expect me to," Kitoh said. "This is what my parents want me to do."

"Are you sure *you* wish to do this?"

Kitoh looked up into Areo's eyes a few moments before nodding again.

"Let's go, then."

After scoping out the area a bit, Kitoh leaped off the wall, jumping toward the battlefield within the city. Areo jumped after him, and as Kitoh fell he transformed into a large blue dragon. Areo landed atop his back just as Kitoh spread out his wings, causing himself to lift from the ground just in time. He glided straight down the cobble-stoned street, letting his long, batlike wings bash against Shire soldiers. Kitoh had enough control of his dragon form to keep from hurting any of the Fiefs soldiers in his path, to Areo's relief.

"Take me to Augurc," Areo said. She kept her eyes on Borely, who was fighting off a couple soldiers at once. He was being way too reckless, far too rash.
Not that this came as a surprise to Areo, of course. But did she have to keep saving his life like this? She considered just leaving him to fend for himself—after all, they weren't in this together anymore. But then she remembered that evening spent on his ship. His boorish attempt to win her over through a fish dinner and sentimental conversation.

He's an idiot, Areo thought, *but he doesn't deserve to die.* She leaped off of Kitoh and slammed her claws through the neck of a Brotherhood fighter about to fire a red Nexi at Borely.

"Thanks for dropping by," Borely said before turning to punch a swordsman away.

"I just happened to be in the area," Areo muttered. She tore her claws out either side of the Brotherhood man's neck, nearly beheading him. Areo glanced past Augurc, watching Kitoh land atop a couple Shire archers. The dragon was quick to bash away the remaining archers with his long, bony arms, keeping them from firing their arrows at him.

There were still a couple more Shire soldiers accompanying Augurc, who stared toward Areo and Borely with the same emotionless face he maintained back on the airship. He dropped the dead, impaled Fiefs soldiers his vines carried, then turned away to face Kitoh. Augurc's vines each ripped out a sword or lance from one of his dropped corpses, effectively arming himself with at least a dozen weapons. Kitoh meanwhile charged through a group of Shire soldiers, batting them away with his wings and stomping on those that fell over.

One soldier ran to Borely while the other charged for Areo. Borely was quick to blast away his enemy's sword with a brief jet of water. As the man fumbled for a Nexi stone, Borely slammed a hard punch in his face. Areo faced her opponent, who wielded a couple hand axes. He charged both of them with orange Nexi energy and leaped toward Areo. Blocking with her claws would be futile, and so would forming a barrier of earth. Knowing that her enemy would know this, Areo used her tan Nexi to create a wall of earth in front of her. As the soldier hacked straight through the hardened earth, Areo dashed around the back of the wall and slid her elongated claws into the man's neck. He fell to the ground, gagging.

Areo considered getting more blood, but Kitoh was already turning to face Augurc, who walked toward the massive dragon with an air of indifference. Kitoh breathed a torrent of fire directly at Augurc. The man placed his right hand over his face just before the giant waves of flames engulfed his entire body, as well as the bloody corpses of soldiers piled about the vicinity.

The fire flowed all around Augurc, covering him entirely. Areo hoped this was the end of him, but waited to see his melted or charred remains lying on the ground.

After a few long seconds of this, the fire passed and the smoke cleared away. Augurc stood right where he had been, covered in water and bits of ice sliding down his body. He had continually frozen himself as the dragon's flames enveloped him.

Borely charged after Augurc from behind. Augurc heard Borely's stomping and turned around, utterly disinterested. Augurc raised his hand and charged his light blue Nexi stone. Areo ran to Borely and pulled him back before he could be engulfed in the massive burst of frozen air Augurc released.

"Watch it!" Borely yelled.

"Don't just charge in there," Areo said, pushing Borely back. "He'll freeze you to death if you get too close. Unless you think you can punch away freezing air." She took a few steps to the side to separate herself from Borely.
Augurc was surrounded on three sides by Areo, Borely, and Kitoh. He pointed some of his vine-controlled weapons toward Borely, some toward Areo, and the rest toward Kitoh.

"You two again," Augurc said. "And the dragon."

Areo wondered if he would say anything more, but Augurc's tightlipped face only tightened further. Was he... *upset?*

To Areo's surprise, Augurc turned to Kitoh and sprinted toward the dragon. It took a moment for everyone to react to this decision, including Kitoh.

The dragon lurched forward and snapped his jaws at Augurc, faster than Areo expected. Yet despite Kitoh's speed, Augurc managed to step aside of the dragon's fangs. At the same time, Augurc caused a vine to shove a lance into Kitoh's left eye. The dragon roared, but Augurc remained unfazed. He leaped forward and slammed his right hand against Kitoh's long neck, releasing a burst of frozen air against the dragon. Kitoh roared louder and stumbled to his side, half his neck frozen.

Meanwhile Areo and Borely both ran toward Augurc from behind, but somehow the man was able to fight them both off with the many weapons held by his vines. Even while fighting a dragon, Augurc was able to take on both Areo and Borely without needing to see them. Areo dodged one sword and batted away a second one, then sliced apart the vine holding a lance. The vine instantly grew a bit longer to grab the lance before it hit the ground. Augurc continued to attack Areo with multiple weapons, keeping her from reaching him.

Areo leaped back from the vines and various weaponry, then activated her tan Nexi stone. She caused a large stalagmite to burst out of the ground beside Augurc. He leaped aside just before he could get impaled. Borely meanwhile avoided Augurc's attacks and fired a jet of water.
Incredulously, Augurc also managed to avoid this as well.

Augurc turned toward Areo and caused several more vines to jab their weapons at her. The man's control over the vines was uncanny—they were not only fast, but incredibly precise. Areo dodged a sword shot for her leg, then a lance jabbing toward her head. Immediately she had to step aside of a sword swinging for her side, then step over a second sword and duck beneath a third one. She relied more on her hearing and sense of the vines' motion rather than on her sight, and managed to keep up with Augurc's repeated attacks.

Areo heard Borely fall, and she realized he was about to get impaled with a lance. She turned and clawed past a couple vines holding swords. Borely managed to jet away the lance aimed for him at the last moment, still having enough energy to activate his dark blue Nexi. Several vines zipped behind Areo all at once.

Simultaneously they shot for her, and Areo realized there was no way to avoid them all. She positioned herself to take the attacks as best she could. One sword cut through the side of her left arm while a lance pushed through the right side of her hip. The other two swords barely missed her head and chest. Screaming, she immediately turned and clawed away the vines holding the sword and lance that hit her.

Without even a moment's pause, the two cut vines flew against her, shoving her backward.

Straight into the path of another sword. The vine shoved the blade through Areo's back and out her stomach. Before she could even react, a knifewielding vine lurched down for her head. Areo tried to leap back, but was held in place by the sword in her waist.

In one swift motion, the knife slit across Areo's throat.

•

Terico and Delkol exchanged blows, managing to block one another's attacks with their swords. They each charged their blades with orange energy, then white energy, then finally purple energy, knocking each other back with every attack.

After one such impact, Terico flew back a ways and forced more sparking white Nexi energy into his blade. His vision turned a blinding white for a few seconds, but he could still see where Delkol was and what he was doing—Delkol's very presence was abundantly clear in Terico's mind, just from the sheer amount of Elpis energy emanating from him. Terico shot off a bolt of lightning at Delkol, who created a barrier of earth out of thin air in front of him. The floating wall of dirt exploded into bits, which Delkol then launched at Terico, each of them sharpening into small spikes. Terico released a shockwave of purple energy around him, blowing away each of the sharp stones before they could reach him. Delkol was immediately upon Terico, swinging his blade with the added force of orange Nexi energy. Terico's insides still shook from the purple Nexi energy he had accessed, but he managed to activate a burst of red Nexi at Delkol. The detonation of fire pushed Terico back, but he wasn't able to maintain a strong connection with the fire, which Delkol easily swatted away with a release of light blue Nexi.

Before Terico could attack, Delkol released a series of vines from his sword. Glowing silver feathers ran up the vines, causing them to fly for Terico more quickly. Terico caused a layer of brown Nexi substance to surround him. The silver Nexi-powered vines shot straight through the floating swamp material, but the vines were slowed down, making it possible for Terico to keep track of all of them. The instant the vines poked through the other side of the swamp substance, Terico set the vines on fire with red Nexi energy. He fought through his burning headache and caused the flames to rush down the vines, straight back to Delkol.

Terico blasted apart the swamp substance with purple Nexi energy, then shot himself toward his enemy. Delkol caused his vines to fall off his sword before Terico's flames could reach him. Terico shot off a blast of light blue Nexi from his sword, but Delkol managed to cover himself with protective yellow energy in time. Delkol shot up to Terico and swung his blade for
Terico's head. With orange Nexi powering his sword, Terico blocked Delkol's attack.

Delkol's blade also glowed orange, but Terico realized there was gray energy flowing through it as well. He felt his heart skip a beat. His eyes widened at the sight. The reminder of all he had lost.

"One of my brother's subjects informed me of your most recent loss,"
Delkol said, unable to hide his glee. "Poisonous Nexi energy... There is no Nexi greater than this. Save for the full Elpis, there is no force on the entire planet that can stop the cold grip of death!"

Terico shoved Delkol's blade back, but Delkol immediately caused a blast of purple energy to knock Terico to the side. Silver feathers sprouted from the end of Delkol's blade, growing several meters in four razor sharp arcs. Terico avoided the feathers, but flew straight into a second blast of Delkol's loose purple energy. Terico rebounded toward Delkol, barely avoiding the gray and silver blade.

Vines suddenly emerged from the sword and encircled Terico's body. Orange energy filled the vines, causing them to tighten before Terico could slice away at them. Terico tried accessing the purple Nexi energy to free himself, but the agony of the Elpis was overwhelming him.

Delkol swung Terico down straight for the ground, flinging him into the hard earth from at least twenty meters in the air. Terico slowed his fall with the loose purple energy he finally managed to access, but the impact still nearly knocked him unconscious. Accessing the Elpis's energy filled Terico's entire body with unthinkable agony. His muscles felt like they were tearing into little bits when he tried to move. Even screaming from the pain became too difficult to do, his voice fading away and his throat filling with icy, stinging blood.

Delkol floated a couple meters above, an ecstatic grin spread across his transformed face.

"Did you think you were my equal, simply because you have two pieces of the Elpis, just as I do? You never stood a chance against me, Terico. You are young and naïve, while I am an experienced swordsman and master of Nexi. I have killed at least a hundred times as many people as you have.

"Did you think your determination would be enough for you to defeat me? My determination far exceeds yours! You may have the burning of revenge in your heart—at least a couple weeks' worth. But I have hundreds of years' worth of the Shire line's lust for revenge built up in my heart. I am ready to explode! I am ready to overpower everyone that opposes me with the pain and misery of over half a millennium!"

•

12

THE FATE OF DESTROYERS AND SAVIORS

"Areo!" Borely screamed. He punched away a vine-guided lance and avoided the swing of a sword.

With Areo stabbed through the stomach, she was unable to avoid the attacks Augurc followed up with. A vine brought down a long knife and slashed it at Areo's throat.

"No!" Borely yelled. He punched aside two more swords and sprinted to Areo before Augurc could stab her even further.

With all the concentration Borely could muster, he activated his dark blue Nexi and shot off a thin jet of water. Slight motions with his head directed the water to slice through the vines near Areo, including the one attached to the sword lodged through her back. Before Areo could fall to the ground,
Borely grabbed her and continued to run away. He glanced back and found Augurc sending several weapon-wielding vines toward him. Borely considered shooting another jet of water at them, but didn't feel he'd have the energy to fire one and still be able to keep fighting much longer.

Several massive water jets fired through the vines and weapons approaching Borely. He stumbled forward from the sudden bursts of water, but managed to keep hold of Areo. Once he regained his footing, he turned and found a group of Fiefs soldiers charging into the area—accompanied by a troop of eigni in red and teal uniforms. Borely guessed they had come to assist the city at Rilv's request. The eigni repeatedly fired large bursts of water toward Augurc, who was forced to call for reinforcements. A troop of Shire soldiers fighting atop the city walls headed down a number of staircases, rushing toward Augurc's location.

Borely carried Areo to a spot past a group of Fiefs soldiers who worked together to hold back a couple Brotherhood fighters. This was the safest area Borely could find, but he knew it probably wouldn't stay that way much longer. He looked down at Areo and found her wounds just as terrible as he expected. There was no way Borely was going to be able to heal her, even if he did have the means to perform the first aid or operations her body required.

"Blood," Areo whispered.

She needed blood. Of course—vampires could regenerate if they drank enough blood, Borely remembered. He looked around for any nearby corpses, but found he had brought Areo past the region of greatest bloodshed. Borely would have to work his way past the nearby skirmishes in order to take Areo to a corpse for some blood. There wasn't enough time.

Can't believe I'm doing this, Borely thought. He lowered his head down to Areo's mouth, then brought her head up a bit so she could bite into his neck.

"Borely..." Areo breathed out.

"Hurry up," Borely said. "You need blood to live. I have some. Just don't turn me into a vampire. I'll kill you if you go too far."

Areo immediately sunk her fangs into Borely's neck. As Areo sucked blood from Borely's body, he felt his skin turn a little cold. His insides felt numb, but there was a scratching feeling in his bones. Perhaps it was the altered flow of blood in his body. For at least a minute, Areo continued to devour Borely's blood.

"A...Areo..." Borely struggled to say. His eyes rolled back for a moment, but he forced himself to keep conscious. "Stop..."

Areo took a few more gulps of Borely's blood before lifting her fangs from his neck. She stepped aside of Borely, who lay on the ground, all the strength in his body drained away. Gritting her teeth, Areo wrenched the sword out of her stomach. She screamed and fell to the ground, blood pouring down her waist.

Fangs clamped down into Borely's neck once again. He pushed back instinctively, memories of his brother flooding through his semiconscious mind. Areo held Borely down and sucked more blood from his neck. Apparently the first round of blood sucking was just to heal her neck, and this time she needed to heal her stomach now that the sword was pulled out.

Borely felt all the energy in his body fade away, and any effort he made to resist Areo was hopeless. Long, weary seconds passed, and Borely slowly found himself unable to even move. His limbs hung lifeless, and he felt his heartbeat slow down, growing quieter and quieter.

She's killing me to save herself, Borely thought. *I wish... I wish...*
"I wish... I could have lived... a little longer," Borely whispered. He felt Areo's teeth release from Borely's neck. "Quit being so dramatic. You'll be fine."

Borely opened his eyes and sat up. He blinked a couple times, regaining his vision. His breathing returned to normal, and though he was greatly weakened, he didn't feel he was in any danger of dying. He looked over at Areo and saw that her neck and waist were free of the wounds Augurc had inflicted on her.

"Thank you," she said. "I'm afraid you won't be able to fight anymore right now, but I'll make sure you get through this alive—no matter what." "Just hurry and kill Augurc," Borely said.

And hope Terico kills Delkol, he added in his head.
Areo nodded and turned back to the battlefield. Borely watched her join with some of the eigni assisting the Fiefs soldiers against Augurc, and realized a couple of the reinforcements were Kitoh's parents. This group of eigni must have come from Vursa. Augurc used a number of free vines from his arms to push himself away from the jets of water the eigni shot at him, and still had the power to control other vines to kill off every soldier that drew near to him.

Borely realized he still had some energy held up in his metal gloves. If he could find the strength to land a good punch, he could use his orange Nexi stones at least a couple more times. He pushed himself to his feet and followed a couple Fiefs soldiers who finished off a Brotherhood member. Borely quickly found himself back in the fray, where soldiers on both sides of the war utilized weapons and Nexi abilities of every kind. In the center of it all was Augurc, taking down several Fiefs soldiers with every swing of his blade-wielding vines.

"Master!" Areo exclaimed. "Brother!"

Borely looked to where Areo was looking, and found five vampires leaping down from the roof of a nearby building. Each of them wore hooded black robes, though Borely imagined they all had pink Nexi stones to enable them to be in the sunlight at all. Apparently Areo knew two of these vampires.

"How are you all here?" Areo asked.

"Little Sister!" one vampire exclaimed. "Setar called for aid, so we borrowed some Rite Nexi and hurried over."

"Now's not the time—Augurc takes priority," one of the vampires said. He was a man who looked worn-out with centuries of age, despite having the appearance of someone in his late twenties. "Jenba, Areo— come with me." Areo and one of the other vampires followed, this one a man with thin eyes, and perhaps in his thirties. The three rushed toward Augurc, their claws all extended.

The remaining vampires assisted the eigni and Fiefs soldiers, who were beginning to get overwhelmed by the ever-increasing masses of Shire soldiers.

Borely fought off a Shire swordsman that leaped in front of his path. It was difficult to keep up with him, as Borely relied solely on what little strength his body held. His head turned dizzy from all the effort of blocking the man's attacks, and it was difficult to find a good opening to counter with. He didn't want to use what little power he had left for his Nexi stones—it was vital to save them for Augurc.

The swordsman swung for Borely again, and this time Borely simply blocked the blade with the metal palm of his left hand, then delivered a punch to the face with his right fist. Once the man was knocked out, Borely continued toward Augurc.

Areo and the two other vampires slashed away at Augurc's vines, which failed to retrieve their fallen weapons as the three continued to cut through the growing vines. Augurc continued to grow more and more vines, now just hoping to grab at least one of the three vampires. They were all fast, but Areo was especially quick, energized by the blood Borely offered her.

As he held them back with his vines, Augurc bent down to the corpse of a Fiefs soldier and lifted him off the ground. Augurc pushed his right hand into a deep wound in the man's body.

"Get back!" Borely screamed, recognizing what Augurc was about to do. Areo was too busy with the vines to notice, and the other two vampires wouldn't know the full extent of Augurc's abilities.

A web of interconnecting ice shards exploded from the corpse's body, expanding even faster than it had back on the Brotherhood airship. Areo rushed out of the way, just barely fast enough to avoid the long, thin icicles growing toward her. One of the other vampires was quickly stabbed in the leg by an icicle, and about to get impaled a half-dozen more times. The vampire who led the two rushed back to him and pulled him away before they could get caught in the web of ice.

From a safe distance, Borely circled the ever-growing ice formation. He was careful to avoid all the fighting Shire and Fiefs soldiers, and rushed toward Augurc from the side. From atop a nearby building, Borely caught sight of a Brotherhood member—a masked woman with long purple hair. She raised a bow and arrow and aimed it toward the vampire carrying his injured comrade. With the vampire nearly surrounded by the growing mass of ice, there wouldn't be any way to dodge the arrow.

Borely fired a jet of water at the woman, forcing her to leap aside. She released her arrow in the process, but it flew into the web of ice harmlessly. Borely nearly fell to the ground, his energy almost depleted. The Brotherhood member raised her bow again, quickly arming it with another arrow. Borely realized she was aiming for Areo this time. Areo was still escaping from the growing web of ice, which had expanded to where many Fiefs and Shire soldiers were fighting. Most turned and fled from the attack, while others were impaled, ally and foe alike. It was an ability too powerful for even Augurc to manage perfectly.

Before the Brotherhood member could fire at Areo, Kitoh appeared from behind the building, his neck apparently healed from Augurc's ice Nexi attack. The woman turned, but Kitoh bashed her off the building with his wing before she could fire at him. Kitoh flew from the building toward Augurc, who launched all his vines toward the dragon. Before his wings could get entangled in the vines, Kitoh diverted himself toward the many Shire soldiers continuing to force their way into the city. He released a giant blast of fire at the soldiers, breaking up their ranks and giving an opening for more Fiefs soldiers to attack.

Borely turned back to Augurc, who still appeared unfazed despite the great deal of Nexi energy he had surely expended. The web of ice was expanding more slowly, and the icicles were not growing as far as they had before. Areo turned toward Augurc from the side, slicing her way through the web of ice shards. At the same time, Borely continued toward Augurc from the other side. To reach Augurc, he would have to break through some of the tangled ice shards. He activated the orange Nexi in his left fist and plowed his way through, keeping it powered only the slightest bit. There was just enough energy for him to punch through the ice with one long, continuous punch.

Augurc was still bringing his vines back from his attempt to entangle Kitoh. He looked from Borely to Areo, then back to Borely—perhaps trying to decide who to attack. In an instant, a large, thick icicle emerged from Augurc's right palm. Borely was just a few steps away.

Without warning, Augurc turned back to Areo and thrust his spear of ice at her. Areo was faster than Augurc anticipated. She was already past his attack, and clawed up and down Augurc's chest with two swift swipes. Augurc stumbled back—straight to Borely's other fist. Borely used the energy of his right fist's orange Nexi to power the attack, landing a solid punch into the side of Augurc's head. Augurc took the hit and stumbled to his left, turning toward Borely in the process.

It didn't knock Augurc out, incredulously. The large man just took a punch powered by an orange Nexi straight to the head. To Borely's astonishment, Augurc held his ground and looked back at Borely, his eyes utterly void of emotion. Before Borely could even react, Augurc thrust his ice spear into Borely's chest.

What... was all that came to Borely's mind. He was too weak to move, too exhausted to scream. The frozen weapon remained in his body, the pain unbearable—and yet Borely could do nothing.

"Borely!" Areo screamed. She jabbed her claws toward Augurc's face. Augurc turned in time to release his hand from the icicle that grew from his palm. He stepped back and ran, clutching the deep, bleeding wounds across his torso.

Borely fell to his knees, but Areo knelt down to keep him from collapsing. She quickly pulled the icicle out of Borely's chest, and this time he screamed from the pain. It simply took his senses a few seconds to realize just what had happened.

He was dying.

The icicle had punctured a lung, and perhaps cut into his heart as well. It was difficult to tell—all Borely could feel was the unbearable pain of the deep wound, burning all the way through to his bleeding back. Areo looked over Borely's wound, frowning deeply.

"It's a fatal wound... but I can still save you," Areo said, her voice trembling. It wasn't like her to get nervous.

It took a few seconds for Borely to realize what Areo meant. "No. Don't do it."

"This will be extremely painful," Areo said. "And it will take a lot of effort to adjust..."

"No! Don't do it!"

Areo bit into Borely's neck once more. She sunk her fangs in and injected her blood into Borely's body.

Unbearable pain flooded through Borely's entire body, as if all his blood had turned into acid. For perhaps an entire minute, Areo continued to transfer more of her blood to Borely's body.

He was changing. His very being was transforming from the inside. Borely screamed, visions of his past flooding his mind.

In his mind, he was a child again. A child who lost everything all at once. His parents. His home. His way of life. His very innocence. He was a child who had to kill his own brother.

An insane, bloodthirsty vampire.

Borely's vision slowly grew darker. He could see Areo lifting her head from Borely's neck, but he could feel nothing but the agony of his transforming body.

Areo looked down at Borely, blood dripping down the side of her mouth. For a moment Borely thought she was crying, but the moment passed quickly. Vines wrapped tight around Areo's body all at once. She was lifted into the air, then pulled away violently, unable to move any of her limbs.

Borely's vision went out entirely, and his limp body fell flat against the bloody stone street. He could still hear the rage of the battlefield around him.

"Save for my brother, you are the one person who has ever scarred my body," Augurc said. "You will make a valuable test subject, vampire." Borely wanted to curse Augurc. He wanted to curse Areo. He wanted to curse himself.

But before he lost consciousness, a singular thought formed in the center of his mind.

Living will be worse than dying.

•

Terico stared up at Delkol, unable to move as Delkol's demonic figure transformed further. Thick black horns emerged from Delkol's whitened hair—a large one curved upward from the left side of his head, while a smaller one curved downward from the right side. What looked like giant teeth emerged from his shoulder guards, while his arm guards unraveled, his light gray skin forming long, jagged spikes. His armor emanated a darkness that clashed with the swirling white patterns glowing within, and a tattered silver shroud emerged from his back. In a way the strands were shaped like feathers, but the wind circling around Delkol showed they flowed more like hair.

Delkol gazed down at Terico, his eyes entirely white. "My control of the Elpis is greater than yours. Victory against me was impossible from the very start." He pointed his sword toward Terico's face and filled his blade with sparking white Nexi energy. The light blinded Terico, forcing him to shut his eyes. It was too difficult to move on his own—he needed to use the Elpis to get him to move.

His whirling mind accessed the tan Nexi energy within the Elpis. Delkol released a bolt of lightning just as Terico caused the earth beneath him to erupt. Terico flew in the air, and the lightning passed into the mass of earth he lay on. His sword lifted forward, Terico crashed into Delkol, who barely managed to avoid Terico's blade.

They both fell to the ground, Terico's hand grasping Delkol's face. Terico remembered one of the Nexi stones his mother used when fighting Delkol. The clear Nexi, used for transferring abilities from one person to the other. If it was impossible for Terico to reach Delkol's level of Elpis control on his own, Terico could simply *take* some of that power. He accessed the clear Nexi energy within him and forced as much of Delkol's power to flow into him as he could. For several seconds Terico found his mind clearing, gaining a better understanding of the Elpis. His vision improved, his limbs strengthened, and the many forms of agony flowing through his body lightened a little bit.

I can still fight, Terico thought. *And I can still kill you, Delkol. I know how you fight, and I know what you want. I will kill you!*

Screaming from the pain of the transfer, Delkol swung his sword at Terico's side. Terico caused a thin wall of silver feathers to materialize between him and Delkol's blade, blocking the attack. Delkol gritted his teeth, his face contorted with rage. His body glowed the gray light of the poison Nexi, and Terico immediately let go of Delkol's face. Terico flew back a few meters, a reinvigorated force building up within his very soul. He felt his body transforming in a way similar to Delkol. His hair lengthened, extending nearly a half-meter backward. Two thin horns curved upward atop his head, and swirling black flames breathed in and out of existence amidst his hair. His armor glowed black, and filled with white spirals that pulsated with a shaky, metallic echo. Terico's arm guards turned to ice, forming sharp, jagged protrusions down their entire length.

Delkol pushed himself off the ground and floated to the same height as Terico. At first Terico thought he was going to say something, but Delkol simply stared at Terico with empty, ominous white eyes.

A massive section of earth blew out of the ground, at least fifty meters long. Delkol slammed his sword down into it, then released a shockwave of purple Nexi energy to break the earth into giant chunks. Terico flew back from the exploding earth, avoiding the hardened dirt and stones that collided and broke apart around him. Delkol pointed his sword at Terico, exerting the tan Nexi power to send hundreds of rocks toward Terico.

Terico enveloped himself in yellow Nexi energy, protecting himself from the stones that flew into him. The chunks of earth battered him back and forth, and once he spotted an opening he sent himself flying toward Delkol, sword raised for the kill.

A sphere of fire encircled Delkol, then blew out in all directions. Terico caused water to surround him, then launched a series of vines from his sword once he passed the wall of flames. Delkol caused the air between him and Terico to freeze, forcing Terico's vines to turn to ice. Terico immediately accessed the light blue Nexi energy, and used the frozen vines to cause icicles to extend toward Delkol. Before the ice could reach him,
Delkol charged his sword with orange energy and beat apart everything Terico sent at him.

Delkol's blade swirled with dark blue and gray energy. Terico cut through his vines and flew down toward Delkol, waiting for his attack. Delkol fired a giant stream of pallid gray water, which Terico barely managed to avoid. From the water emerged vines covered in thin silver feathers, reaching out for Terico. At the same time, Delkol caused another massive portion of the earth to burst up from the ground, and even used red Nexi energy to melt the rock—effectively creating a stream of molten lava under his command.

Terico covered himself with yellow Nexi energy and created a series of barriers made of earth, swamp, and silver feathers. He deflected the majority of the vines, hacking away at those that slipped past his defenses. Delkol redirected his jet of poisonous water, which Terico was simply unable to avoid, as the stream of lava reached for him from every other direction. Terico flew through the water, using the silver feathers to deflect the majority of the poisonous energy. The water quickly wore down the glowing yellow barrier protecting him, so Terico forced his mind to access the purple Nexi energy. He created a shockwave around him to blast away the water, then flew as fast as he could, escaping Delkol's barrage of poison before it could weaken Terico.

But before Terico could fly to Delkol's location, several more bursts of lava erupted from the ground, all flying toward Terico far faster than he could keep up with. He encircled himself with several layers of ice. As soon as the lava impacted the barriers, Terico rocketed out of the sphere of steam that ensued, avoiding the chunks of molten rock that followed.

If he kept having to defend against constant attacks from all sides, Terico knew he'd wear himself out quickly, even with the power of the two Elpis fragments. The pain within his body was steadily growing more and more torturous, but he kept from screaming. He had grown so used to the pain, that it seemed to simply be a part of who he was—it was almost as normal a function as breathing.

Accept the pain, Terico thought. *It was pain that brought me to this point. This is my driving force... This is what I have become. I am agony.*

He flew toward Delkol, charging his sword with red and green energy. At the same time, Delkol launched himself toward Terico, filling his sword with light and dark blue energy. Their blades clashed, unleashing the elements against one another. They each covered themselves with protective energy, then turned the yellow glow into a blinding white light. With every swing of their blades, they whittled down each other's strength and power, little by little.

Delkol screamed, causing his cloak to expand and create hundreds of silver feathers. Terico floated back a few meters, watching as the feathers began vibrating, their hue turning to a violent gold. Terico immediately accessed the power he felt most heavily amongst the Elpis energies flowing within him.

Black flames enveloped his entire body.

Delkol's golden feathers launched for Terico, too fast to even see. The blurs of golden light exploded around Terico, the feathers melting the instant they came into contact with Terico's black flames.

Accessing this power drained Terico considerably, and it suddenly became difficult just to keep himself flying in the air, and keeping his sword lifted up and steady. As soon as Delkol's golden feathers were expended, Terico cut off access to the black flames, which resumed to flickering sporadically in his hair.

Sweat dripped down Delkol's face, and Terico could tell he was breathing heavily. There was no way Delkol was going to relent, however.

Delkol swung his sword repeatedly, flinging a series of icicles, rocks, and jets of water at Terico. They were blind attacks driven by rage, but it was difficult to keep avoiding the projectiles. Terico was hesitant to use the yellow Nexi energy any more than he already had, knowing that every move he made from this point on would be vital for his success. It wouldn't be much longer before the pain of the Elpis overpowered Terico's determination to kill Delkol—there was only so much the body could withstand, and Terico had accessed the fragmented Elpis far too much over the past few days.

While flying back and forth between Delkol's attacks, Terico focused his mind on the Elpis energies within him, searching for the teal Nexi energy. As soon as he felt access to it, Terico stared down at Delkol and focused as hard as he could on the words he wished to communicate to him.

You are a disgrace to the Shire family line.
From the very beginning, you were a failure, Delkol.
We are ashamed you had ever been born.
With descendants as hopeless as this, there is no chance for regaining our rightful place as rulers of the Fiefs Kingdom.

Terico projected these words into Delkol's thoughts, filling Delkol's mind with the vague, shadowy voices of his beloved family line.

"No!" Delkol screamed. He stopped firing projectiles at Terico and gripped his head with his free hand. "I'm the one who learned of the Elpis! I've given my entire life to reclaiming the throne! I won't stop! I won't stop now!" As he shrieked, a whirlwind of silver feathers circled around him, keeping Terico from attacking.

The fact Delkol was able to maintain such power even while screaming at the voices in his head was unsettling. It meant Delkol's control over the Elpis was still much greater than Terico's. Strength and determination wasn't going to be enough for Terico—not when he was in this much pain, and with so little energy left to spare.

"I'm not a failure!" Delkol yelled amidst the flurry of silver feathers. "Every day of my life, I've worked toward this point! You will accept me! You will all accept me! You will be overwhelmed with pride when you see me, Father!"

As Delkol screamed, Terico shot himself down to Delkol and exerted all his strength to covering his body with yellow Nexi energy. Upon reaching the spinning barrier of feathers, Terico released a burst of purple energy, pushing away enough feathers to create a brief opening. Terico flew in, but the speed at which the feathers flew still caused some of them to fly into him. Most deflected off his yellow barrier, but a few sliced through his armor and scraped his skin. The beating of the Elpis energy within him filled the gashes with stinging pain, but Terico instead focused on his sword, filling it with orange and white Nexi energy—just as his father had when fighting Delkol.

Delkol heard Terico breach through the barrier of silver feathers, and turned just as Terico swung his sword at him. Delkol shot backward, his remaining swarms of feathers following to either side of him. Still swinging, Terico released the white energy from his blade, and sent it flying with the added strength of the orange energy. The orange-glowing bolt of lightning shot straight through Delkol's torso, leaving a gaping, bleeding hole the size of a fist.

"No!" Delkol screamed, falling toward the ground. Terico flew after him, intent to keep attacking him.

Delkol released several vines from his sword, forcing Terico to slow down to hack away at them. At the same time, Delkol's wound began to heal—he was flooding his body with the healing energy of the Elpis.

He's weakening, Terico thought. I have him!
Terico forced a giant arm of dirt to emerge from the ground beneath Delkol. Before the hand could smash him, Delkol flew to the side and sent himself upward once more. His wound was almost entirely healed, and even his armor was beginning to piece back together somehow.

Delkol flew higher, and Terico pursued, following Delkol toward the city. Still flying backward, and his sword pointed toward Terico, Delkol bellowed an order at the top of his lungs.

"By the royal blood flowing within me, I command you all to rise and destroy my enemy!"

All at once, hundreds of white glowing lights appeared from the ground below. Terico looked down to find figures of people—ghostly apparitions— flying straight toward him.

The spirits of the Shire soldiers slain in the battle below.

Terico found Delkol glowing with indigo light—the energy of the soul catcher Nexi. Delkol was able to control the souls of those under his command.
Hundreds upon hundreds of souls flew up to Terico, their ethereal weapons raised and gleaming. They chanted Delkol's name, their voices distorted and distant, despite how quickly they drew near. Fighting Delkol's fallen army would be suicide, Terico knew—he would quickly run out of energy to fend them off. The only option was to kill Delkol.

Immediately.

Terico blasted himself to Delkol, who raised his sword with an expression of pure satisfaction. The soldier spirits were quickly gaining on Terico, encircling him from all sides. Terico ignored them and forced himself to fly faster.

At the same time, Terico and Delkol both filled their blades with orange Nexi energy. Terico slammed his blade against Delkol's, and they both flew downward. Delkol held strong, but Terico forced himself to continue pushing down on Delkol, flying toward the earth as fast as he could.

Delkol grinned. His shroud spread to either side of him, the sharp, hairlike feathers separating and turning golden. Even while guiding hundreds of spirits toward Terico, he still had the strength to activate his shroud of razor-sharp blades. Delkol launched the feathers at Terico, a dozen of them zipping clean through Terico's armor and body in an instant.

Screaming, Terico pushed himself back, away from Delkol, and straight to the swarms of spirits behind him.

With orange Nexi energy built up in his arms, Terico threw his two Elpis stones away. Terico launched one stone dozens of meters to his right, the other he sent flying far to his left. Terico's transformed state held, his mind still connected with the two Elpis fragments.

"The Elpis!" Delkol screamed.

At the same time, Terico collided straight into the spirit masses, all of which thrust their weapons at him. In an instant, Terico's entire body was punctured with ethereal swords, lances, arrows, axes, and knives. The weapons afflicted his spirit with deadly wounds, so it was his soul that was tearing apart and dying. The pain was still there, however. The allencompassing agony was akin to an explosion from every pore of his body, but Terico accepted it.

He was about to have his revenge.

Delkol blasted toward the Elpis stone tumbling away to his right, his eyes wide and his outstretched hand trembling. As the spirits continued to stab at Terico's soul, Terico kept his eyes fixed on Delkol, able to see him through the vaguely transparent spirits with his heightened vision.

Just as Delkol's hand and face neared the glowing fragment, Terico activated the red Nexi energy inherent to the Elpis. The fragment released a massive detonation—a fiery blast that exploded directly into Delkol's arm and face. The flames melted Delkol's arm away and disfigured his bleeding face and torn-open neck. At the same time, the massive shockwave sent Delkol flying backward—straight toward the other Elpis fragment.

Terico activated the green Nexi energy within the stone, causing vines to wrap around Delkol's body and bind him tight. With what was left of his energy, Terico shot out of the multitude of spirits, directing his flight toward Delkol. Though skewered with at least twenty glowing, transparent weapons, Terico pushed himself toward Delkol, filling the blade of his sword with all the silver and gray energy he could muster.

Gray feathers flew within Terico's blade, and Terico suddenly felt an overwhelming sense of exhaustion—as if he had never slept in his entire life. His spirit was dying, and as he stared down at Delkol—the man's bound form steadily drawing closer—Terico wondered if it had all been

worth it. Terico slammed his blade into Delkol's chest, and immediately silver feathers began tearing Delkol apart from the inside. Delkol screamed, blood flying from his mouth and neck. The poisonous energy within Terico's sword flooded into Delkol's body, and Terico continued to fly downward.

As Terico and Delkol neared the ground, Terico found his energy entirely wasted. He let go of the sword and let his connection with the Elpis fragments slowly dissolve. Terico fell back, separating from Delkol, who continued to plunge toward the earth.

For a moment, Terico felt like he was floating in the air. The wind rushed all around him, and the sky was a vast, infinite blue. Delkol's army of spirits had faded away, leaving nothing but an empty sky. An endless expanse. The very embodiment of limitless possibilities.

He reached up toward the sky, wishing for something to hold on to. Anything to keep him from falling.

There was nothing.

Terico crashed against the hard earth, landing flat on his back. His body filled with

a jolt of pain, but by this point Terico had grown entirely numb to it all.
The weapons that had impaled him faded away, leaving behind a shattered, dying spirit.

He lay still, perfectly still. His transformed state was slowly dissipating, his connection with the Elpis tenuous, fleeting.

He was too tired to feel anything.

It's over, he thought, and he closed his eyes.

•

With the only hand he had left, Delkol gripped the sword sticking out of his chest. The blade dug into his palm, and thick blood slowly dripped down his forearm. He couldn't feel anything. Just the overwhelming beat of his heart, pounding pain into every fiber of his being. It might not have even been his heart, actually. When he concentrated on it enough, he realized his heart was beating very slowly, weakly.

Delkol stared up at the sky, barely able to see anything. He wanted to scream, but it hurt to even breathe. It was too difficult to look to either side of him, and everything was a bright, painful blur anyways. He doubted he would see anything but bloody corpses, but if there was a chance the other two Elpis pieces were nearby...

He slipped his weary hand into his pocket, pulling out his two Elpis fragments. There was just enough strength inside Delkol to maintain a connection with them. He gripped them tight and tried to heal himself— any part of himself.

It was a useless effort. Over the course of his fight with Terico, he had drained himself of energy. Perhaps if he hadn't summoned the army of spirits, he would have enough strength to pull this sword out, at the very least.

But he had wanted to be sure. He wanted to ensure Terico's death, no matter the cost. He couldn't hold back—not even the slightest bit. He had to give his all.

Perhaps he went too far. Perhaps he had become *too* determined.

No, Delkol thought. *No. No. No! I never wavered! I gave my all, each and every day!*

He felt the last of his energy fade away, his connection with the Elpis finally severed. His body reverted back to its normal state, a painful transformation that did nothing to heal Delkol's wounds. The poison of the gray Nexi sunk into every organ of his body, the agony accentuated by his use of the fragmented Elpis.

If I had all the pieces... I'd live.
They were so close. In mere walking distance!

He struggled to sit up, but he couldn't even move. The poison weakened him, and the wounds Terico inflicted on him were killing him on their own.

No! Delkol tried to scream.

This world was robbing him of the one thing he ever aspired toward.

I'm so close... So close!
He could see his father looking down at him, deep concern etched in his eyes.

One day you will regain the land of our forebears, Father said. *This continent needs a strong ruler again. One who can bring peace and stability to the world. One who has not only the royal blood of the great ones, but the will and might to instill both fear in his enemies and reverence in his subjects.*

The Fiefs line has become corrupted over the centuries, Delkol. The Shires are a part of that royal line, but in our separation we have maintained our integrity. One day you will claim the throne of the Fiefs Kingdom, and the land will become one again.

A strong kingdom... with an inspiring king.
Delkol's eyes burned in the light of the sun. He set down his Elpis fragments, and with a weak, shaking hand, he forced what was left of his eyelids shut. He let his hand linger, feeling the cross-shaped scar across his right eye.

Brother... Delkol thought. *You have the strength to finish what I've started. It was you who gave me this scar. With that strength... scar this entire land. Then once this kingdom has been humbled, take what is rightfully ours.*

•

Slowly Terico felt life fading away from him. The pain lingered on—in fact, it seemed to intensify—but he could tell he was passing away. He still had a faint connection to his two lost Elpis fragments, deep in the recesses of his icy, pounding mind. His body was still in its transformed, demonic state... There was still time.

It was difficult, but Terico fought through the pain of the Elpis, struggling to access the healing energy once more. The remaining Elpis pieces were close... There was still hope for him, and for everyone he had lost. It was impossible to scream, and barely even possible to move, but Terico could still feel the Elpis's power. He shut his eyes as hard as he could, concentrating on its healing energy. His body seared with pain, but inside— deep inside—he could feel something. It wasn't cold, wasn't hot. Just the sense of things melding back together. As if the healing energy was filling in the punctured holes in his soul, keeping it alive.

Terico's body and armor transformed back to normal, and he lay on the earth. Motionless. Barely breathing. Knowing his time was short. He had exhausted every ounce of his energy, and now his connection with the Elpis was thoroughly dissolved. His spirit was intact, but it was too late to save his body. He had used the fragmented Elpis far too much, and now he paid the price of its poisoning effect.

Perhaps if he had gained the full Elpis, everything would have been different. Any attempt to move was hopeless at this point, and it took all of Terico's effort just to think of anything besides the pain.

Delkol is dead, Terico thought, and for that he could smile—if only in his mind. Delkol would never again kill an innocent victim. The world was a better place without him, and the blood spilled in Edellerston was at last atoned for. Delkol received his just punishment, and Terico was glad to be the one to deliver it.

He knew though that deep down, nothing had really changed. It was good that Delkol died, but that didn't bring back Terico's parents. It didn't bring back his friends. It didn't bring back Suran.

Could the full Elpis have done that? Terico already had his doubts, but now it felt even more certain that some things simply couldn't be changed. And what if his loved ones were happier where they were now? Even if bringing them back to life was actually possible, would it have been the right thing to do?

Suddenly all of Terico's wishes felt strange, complicated. What had he been working for all this time? What did he ever hope to accomplish in his life? It was all over, and Terico wasn't even certain if the path he walked was the right one.

What would become of him now?

Was his revenge worth it? Was killing Delkol worth dying for?

Terico felt the life fade away from his body, and through his closed eyelids he could make out a white silhouette. Slowly, ever slowly, the pain inside of him dissolved, and the pounding in his head dissipated. The agony he had become faded away, bit by bit.

And as the pain disappeared, Terico found his vision improving. The white silhouette turned blurry and gained its color.

Through tear-filled eyes, Terico looked up at Suran. She smiled at him, the same smile she always gave. Back when they were in Edellerston.

Suran bent down and took Terico by the hand. Terico sat up and let Suran lift him up. She helped him to his feet, and it took a few seconds for Terico to grasp where he was.

An entirely different world. A field free of corpses, free of blood, free of agony.

His heart had stopped beating entirely, and Terico realized he wasn't even breathing anymore. He was a spirit, and this was Suran's spirit holding his hand. Suran pointed ahead, and Terico found other spirits appearing a couple meters away. Jujor and Febraz were there, and so were all the people Terico knew in Edellerston. Suran's parents, as well as Terico's classmates, his associates, and his neighbors.

And at the very front stood Terico's father and mother.

Terico turned back to Suran and squeezed her hand. Her smile turned into a silent giggle, and Terico found himself smiling as well. In a way, he had gotten precisely what he hoped for.

•

Lanek dodged the burst of swamp material Lynx fired at him, then jabbed his rapier toward the masked boy's arm. Lynx took a few steps back, taking a couple heavy breaths. Lanek also felt weary, but was determined to kill this boy—even if it was the last thing he did.

"Fall back, Lynx!" a deep voice ordered. "Gather all the Brotherhood you can."

Lanek looked past Lynx to find a large man with a bandana and vest, and a series of green Nexi embedded in his arms. This was Augurc Shire, Lanek realized. There were a number of vines sticking out of his arms, and wrapped amongst them was a young, unconscious woman. The vampire who came with Terico... Areo, Lanek recalled.

Lynx muttered something unintelligible beneath his mask and the chaos of the battlefield. Lanek rushed for Lynx, not willing to let him get away. In one swift movement, Lynx turned around and sprinted off, quite a bit faster than Lanek could hope to keep up with. At the same moment, Lynx tossed back a red Nexi stone, letting it arc right back to Lanek.

Immediately Lanek swung his rapier against the stone, hitting it in mid-air. The stone flew off to the side and exploded a couple meters away. The blast knocked Lanek to the ground, but he had hit it far enough to keep the flames from reaching him.

Lanek pushed himself back to his feet and ran in the direction Lynx dashed off to. All around him, Shire and Fiefs soldiers fought to the death. Amongst them he saw eigni, vampires, a dragon, and even Brotherhood members, but the boy in the smiling mask was gone.

A couple Shire soldiers got in his way, and Lanek dealt with them as fast as possible. But once he was running again, Lanek could find no sign of where Lynx disappeared to.

Members of the Brotherhood started to retreat, slipping back outside the city walls. Many of the Shire soldiers followed, and in turn the Fiefs soldiers pursued, not about to let their enemies escape so easily. A number of eigni used their dark blue Nexi stones to create a giant sea serpent made of water, which they caused to fly amongst the fleeing Fiefs troops alongside Kitoh, still in his dragon state. The tide was turning on the battle, but Lanek hadn't found the revenge he was looking for.

I'm sorry, Suran, he thought. *Perhaps it was pointless in the first place, but I needed something... I needed some way to rectify this...*
Perhaps there was no way to make things right. Suran was lost, and the world

would never be right again.

Lanek ran with some Fiefs soldiers, following them outside the city gates. He soon found himself standing amidst a sea of corpses. Many still had arrows sticking out their backs or torsos, while others rested as burnt, smoking remains—the victims of fire Nexi. Others still lay strangled in vines, while others rested with the deep, bloody wounds of the sword.

Walking to a small open area, Lanek couldn't help but wonder how it all came to this. The power struggles this world had to endure... How much blood was spent this day, Lanek could never imagine.

Amidst the fields of decay Lanek found a boy with dark blue hair, lying lifelessly, about a dozen gashes spread across his armor and deep into his body.

It was Terico, Lanek realized. Lanek bent down and checked his pulse, but there was nothing. There was no heartbeat and no sign of breathing.
Lanek searched the area and found Delkol's fallen body as well, lying perhaps ten, fifteen meters away. He was clearly dead.

So Terico was successful, Lanek thought, *but died in the process.* A number of emotions passed through Lanek's heart, but he felt too numb and hollow to let them linger for long.

He checked both Delkol and Terico's bodies for the Elpis fragments, but didn't find them in their hands or in any of their pockets. Lanek searched the area and eventually came across two of the pieces, hidden amidst the field of corpses far away from one another.

Lanek continued searching until his eyes grew sore, but there simply was no sign of the other two fragments. They were gone.

•

The days passed, and once the battlefield was cleansed everyday life in Setar resumed just as it always had. Lanek mused that most of the populace was entirely unaffected by this brief war, but he decided that was for the better.

It was a bright, hot day, and Lanek busied himself with fixing his airship. Its crash left it a complete disaster, but he didn't want to just give up on it.
This wasn't just his airship—but his parents' airship, and Suran's airship.

Though he didn't particularly enjoy it, this was a time for him to get his hands dirty.

Once evening fell, Lanek stopped his work to take a rest and look up at the stars for a while. It was something he would do with Suran from time to time. She told him that it was something she would do with Terico, as well.

Perhaps they could have been happy together, Lanek thought. He had always been reluctant to let anyone grow close to his beloved sister, but over the past few days he found himself realizing that Terico probably would have taken good care of her. Perhaps if Delkol had never set his sights on Edellerston, things would have worked out nicely for Suran and Terico. Just imagining how life could have been for them... it filled Lanek's heart with misery.

The sound of approaching footsteps broke Lanek's train of thought. He stood up and found himself face to face with Rilv, the head royal servant who dragged him and Suran into this unfortunate venture in the first place.

"Good evening," she said. "I have answers for your questions."

"I'm surprised you came to me personally," Lanek said, folding his arms.

"It is the least I could do, after you retrieved half the Elpis," Rilv said. She glanced to the right a moment. "I could also use the fresh air."

Lanek had asked to be informed of anything Rilv learned concerning the missing two pieces of the Elpis, as well as anything regarding the location of Terico's associates.

"The two pieces of the Elpis you found are still hidden in the castle, where only I can access them," Rilv said. "They are being kept under constant watch, as you can imagine."

"But the other two pieces?" Lanek said.

"It is likely that Augurc has them," Rilv said. "Once it became clear that Delkol was killed, Augurc hurried to the location his brother had fallen to and retreated with the two Elpis fragments. He was in a hurry to leave— otherwise he probably would have searched for the other two pieces."

"They weren't by Terico," Lanek said, "and I believe Augurc had little energy left at that point. Terico's associates all fought him, and he probably wouldn't have been able to fight any longer."

"He is probably experimenting on the Elpis as we speak," Rilv said.

"We will have to retrieve the fragments from him as soon as we ascertain his current location."

"Does he want the same things his brother wanted?" Lanek asked.

"Possibly," Rilv said. "Augurc's greatest concern has been with his experiments, with creating the perfect army. Now that his brother is out of the picture, there is no telling how Augurc will choose to use that army."

Lanek sighed. "And what of Terico's associates? Kitoh, Areo, and Borely?"

"Kitoh has returned to Vursa with his parents," Rilv said. "He lost an eye and suffered a few other bad wounds, but he will live. There is still no word on Areo—she is likely still being held captive by the Brotherhood. What Augurc intends to do with her, I can not imagine. As for Borely, it seems he has left with the vampires who came from Istal. What business he has with them, I do not know."

Lanek let all this information sift through his mind a bit before he nodded. "Sounds like everyone is worse off."

"Misfortune always accompanies a battle," Rilv said. "In the end, Delkol was defeated, and the city suffered no civilian casualties. War has been averted, potentially saving thousands of lives. This is about the best one could hope for."

"I suppose," Lanek said.

Perhaps in the end, in the great scheme of things, things had worked out quite favorably. But how could he go on with his life like this? Every day felt hollow... empty.

It was going to be a struggle to get up each day. To keep working on this airship. To go to sleep every night.

It was always going to be a struggle, Lanek realized.

•

Lanek stared up at the full moon, unable to sleep. After gazing at it for some time, he tinkered some more with a few airship parts. He didn't get much of anything done. It was just to fill the time. He couldn't sleep, and there was nothing that could satisfy him anymore. Minutes passed. Hours passed. It was all the same to Lanek now.

He sat down on the ground and focused on the cool, soft breeze. He stared out at the fields, which not so long ago had been covered in blood, craters, weapons, and corpses. Beneath the soft glow of the moon, everything looked pristine once more.

There were footsteps. Light, gentle footsteps, barely discernible beneath the soothing wind.

Lanek squinted toward a faint glow in the distance, and his eyes slowly adjusted to the small, white lights. Two figures. A boy and a girl.

Terico and Suran.

They walked through the field, hand in hand. Lanek smiled, and his heart suddenly felt a little lighter. And yet at the same time... a little less empty.

Lanek blinked, and they were gone. How long the spirits of Terico and Suran lingered, Lanek couldn't be certain. But he continued to gaze out across the field all through the night, thankful that these treasured souls had at last found peace.

•

The End.

Haders

The Cycle of Hatred and Despair Continues...

Five years have passed since the tumultuous finale of ELPIS, and though a catastrophic war has been averted between the Fiefs and Shire Kingdoms, the safety of the world is threatened by the Elpis-enhanced experiments of Augurc and his Brotherhood.

A plan is formed to locate powerful Nexi stones known as Haders, crafted centuries ago for the purpose of combating the Elpis. Two unlikely teams are formed, both of which find conflict every step of the way in their search for the Haders.

One team includes Borely, who finds himself struggling to come to terms with what he has become—a bloodthirsty vampire—the very thing he has long despised. His greatest goal is to find Areo, the one who saved his life and brought him to this state. But will the Haders enable Borely to rescue Areo from the clutches of the Brotherhood, or will he have to rely on another power in order to save her?

Meanwhile the airship-pilot elf Lanek finds himself enlisted for the other Hader-searching team, and realizes that deep down he is still suffering over the loss of his precious sister. Will finding the Haders and bringing down the Brotherhood be enough to avenge her, and finally bring peace to Lanek's aimless spirit?

Find out more at
www.facebook.com/Hellfunpublishing

<u>Work by Aaron McGowan:</u>

The Elpis Novel Series:
Book #1: Elpis [ISBN: 978-0-9945522-2-8]
Book#2: Haders [ISBN: 978-0-9945522-3-5]

Aslash D Series:
AslashD: Descension (Part One) [ISBN: 978-0-9945522-4-2]

Elpis Comic Book Series:
Elpis (Comic) #1 Father [ISBN: 978-0-9945522-4-2]